BLOOD MOON

Also by the author
in the Inspector Challis Series

The Dragon Man
Kittyhawk Down
Snapshot
Chain of Evidence

BLOOD MOON

GARRY DISHER

SOHO

First published in Australia in 2009
by Text Publishing Company Pty, Ltd.

First published in the United States in 2009 by

Soho Press, Inc.
853 Broadway
New York, NY 10003

Library of Congress Cataloging-in-Publication Data
Disher, Garry.
Blood moon / Garry Disher.
p. cm.
ISBN 978-1-56947-563-8
1. Challis, Hal (Fictitious character)—Fiction. 2. Destry, Ellen
(Fictitious character)—Fiction. 3. Police—Australia—Melbourne Region
(Vic.)—Fiction. 4. Melbourne Region (Vic.)—Fiction. 5.
Australia—Fiction. I. Title.
PR9619.3.D56B56 2009
823'.914—dc22
2008040713

Paperback ISBN: 978-1-56947-631-4

10 9 8 7 6 5 4 3 2 1

for Lee Goldberg

1

On a Tuesday morning in mid-November, late spring, the air outside the bedroom window warm and pollinated, Adrian Wishart watched his wife urinate. He happened to be sitting on the end of the bed, dressed, comb tracks in his hair, tying his shoelaces. She was in the ensuite bathroom, perched naked on the loo, wearing the long-distance stare that took her so far away from him. She didn't know she was being observed. She tore off several metres of toilet paper, patted herself dry, and as the water flushed it all away he came to the doorway and said constrictedly, 'We're not made of money.'

Ludmilla started and gave him a hunted look. 'Sorry.'

Folding in on herself, scarcely moving, she opened the glass door to the shower stall. He rotated his wrist, tapped his watch face. 'I'm timing you.'

Little things, but they cost money. No one needed a long shower. No woman needed that much toilet paper. No need to leave a light on when you go into another room. Why shop for groceries three or four times a week when once would do?

Adrian Wishart watched his wife turn her shoulders under the lancing water. It darkened her red hair and streamed down her body—a body a little heavier-looking in the thighs and waist, he thought. She was doing her daydreaming thing again, so he rapped on the glass to wake her up. At once she began to work shampoo into her hair.

Wishart slipped out of the ensuite, out of the bedroom, and made his way to the hallstand where she always stowed her handbag. Purse, mobile phone, tampons, one toffee—so much for her diet—diary and a parking receipt that he checked out pretty thoroughly: a parking station in central Melbourne, maybe from when she'd attended that planning appeals tribunal yesterday. He unlocked her phone, scrolled through calls made, stored text messages, names in her address book. Nothing caught his eye. He was running out of time or he'd have fired up her laptop and checked her e-mails, too. Then again, she had a computer at work, and who knew what e-mails she was getting there.

Her little silver Golf sat in the carport, behind his Citroën. The odometer read 46,268, meaning that yesterday she'd driven almost 150 kilometres. He closed his eyes, working it out. The round trip between home and her office in Waterloo was only seven kilometres. That meant one thing: instead of driving a shire car up to the appeals tribunal in the city yesterday, she'd driven *her* car.

Their house was on a low hill above the coastal town of Waterloo. He stared unseeingly across the town to Western Port Bay and fumed: They were not made of money.

He checked his watch: she'd been in the shower for four minutes. He ran.

Ludmilla was towelling herself, skin beaten pink by the water, slight but unmistakeable rolls of flesh dimpling here and there as she flexed and twisted. She was letting herself go. He scooped the scales out from under the bed, carried them through to the bathroom and snapped his fingers: 'On you get.'

She swallowed, draped her towel over the heating rail, and stepped onto the scales. Just over 60 kilos. Two weeks ago she'd been 59.

Wishart burned inside, slow, deep and consuming. Presently his voice came, a low, dangerous rasp: 'You've put on weight again. I don't like it.'

She was like a rabbit in a spotlight, still, silent and waiting for the bullet.

'Have you been having business lunches?'

She shook her head mutely.

'You're getting fat.'

She found her voice: 'It's just the time of the month.'

He said, 'At lunchtime on Friday I called you repeatedly. No answer.'

'Ade, for goodness' sake, I was in Penzance Beach, meeting with the residents' association.'

He scowled at her. The Penzance Beach residents' association was a bunch of do-gooding retirees intent on preserving an old house. 'Your car, or a work car?'

'Work car.'

'Good.'

They breakfasted together; they did everything together, at his insistence. She drove to work and he walked through to the studio and arranged and rearranged his architectural pens, rulers and drafting paper.

2

Meanwhile in an old farmhouse along a dirt road a few kilometres inland of Waterloo, Hal Challis was saying, 'Uh oh.'

'What?'

'A flaw.'

The detective inspector was propped up on one elbow, playing with his sergeant's hair, which was spread over the pillow mostly, apart from the stray tendrils pasted to her damp neck, temples and breasts.

'I find that most unlikely,' she told him.

Ellen Destry was on her back, her slender limbs splayed, contentedly. Challis continued to fiddle at her hair with his free hand but his gaze was restless, taking in her eyes, lips and lolling breasts. She looked drowsy, but not quite complete. She hadn't finished with him yet, and that was fine by him. He freed his hand from the tangles and ran the palm along her flank, across and over her stomach, down to where she stirred, moist against his fingers.

'What flaw?' she said unsteadily.

'Split ends.'

'Not in this hair, buster,' she said, punching him.

He rolled onto his back, pulling her with him, and as he took one of her nipples between his lips the phone rang. She said 'Leave it' fiercely, but of course he couldn't, and Ellen knew that. Because he was pinned beneath her, it was she who snatched up the receiver. 'Destry,' she said, in her clipped, sergeant's voice.

Challis lay still, watching and listening. 'He's right here,' she said, rolling off and handing him the phone.

'Challis,' he said.

It was the duty sergeant, reporting a serious assault outside the Villanova Gardens on Trevally Street in Waterloo. 'That apartment block opposite the yacht club, sir.'

'I know it.'

'Victim's in a coma,' the duty sergeant went on. 'Name of Lachlan Roe.'

'Mugging? Aggravated burglary?'

'Don't know, sir. Uniforms took the initial call. The nextdoor neighbour stepped outside to fetch her newspaper and saw Mr Roe lying on his front lawn in a pool of blood.'

'Anyone from CIU there?'

'Sutton and Murphy.'

Scobie Sutton and Pam Murphy were detective constables on Challis's team. 'Crime scene officers? Ambulance?'

'The techs are on their way; the ambulance has been and gone.'

Challis, wondering why he'd been called, rolled his eyes at Ellen, who grinned and waggled her breasts. When he reached out a hand she ducked away, rose from the bed and padded naked to the window. He watched appreciatively. 'Cute ass,' he drawled, covering the receiver with his hand.

She did a little shimmy and opened the curtains. The morning sun lit her, and the dust motes eddied, and the world outside the window was vibrant: the chlorophyll, the spring flowers, the parrots chasing and bobbing.

Challis returned to the phone. 'So it's all under control.'

There was a pause. Finally the duty sergeant said, 'It could get delicate.' That meant one thing to Challis: the victim was well known or had connections, and the result would be a headache to the investigating officers. 'In what way?'

'The victim's the chaplain at Landseer.'

The Landseer School, a boarding and day school on the other side of the Peninsula. Not quite as old as Geelong Grammar, Scotch College or PLC but just as costly and prestigious. Some wealthy and powerful people sent their kids there, and Challis could picture the media attention. He glanced at his bedside clock: 6:53. 'On my way,' he said.

He replaced the handset and glanced again at Ellen, who remained framed in the window. Struck by the particular configuration of her waist and spine he crossed to her, pressed himself against her bare backside.

She wriggled. 'Do we have time?'

'Certainly not.'

In the shower afterwards, Challis outlined what he knew of the assault. 'The Landseer School?' said Ellen in dismay.

'Exactly,' Challis said. He watched the water stream over her breasts, fascinated.

'Keep your mind on the job, pal.'

'Fine,' he said, 'I'll attend at the assault.' He stepped out and started towelling himself, watching as Ellen wrapped one towel around her head and another around her body.

She gave him a complicated look. 'And you want me in the office?'

He nodded. 'If you could follow up on that sexual assault from Saturday night…'

This was delicate territory, there was the faintest tension between them. He was her boss, they were living together and it was too soon to know what the fallout would be. But it would come, sooner or later. It was there in their minds as they dressed, Challis in a suit today, guessing he would need to make an impression on the media or his boss later. He knotted his tie, watching Ellen pull on tailored pants, low-heeled shoes and a charcoal jacket over a vivid white T-shirt, the dark colours an attractive contrast with the shirt and her pale skin and straw-coloured hair. It was a familiar outfit to Challis, sensible work wear for a detective who might sit at a desk one minute and be obliged to trudge through grass to view a corpse the next, but she still managed to look spruce and intemperate. Her clever, expressive face caught him watching. 'What?'

'I'll never tire of looking at you.'

She went a little pink. 'Ditto.'

They breakfasted at a rickety camping table on the back verandah, where the sun reached them through a tangled vine heavy with vigorous new growth. Realising that he'd forgotten the jam, Challis returned to the kitchen. He was pretty sure that one jar of quince remained from the batch he'd made back in April, but when he checked the pantry, he saw that the spices, condiments and tubs of rice and pasta were on the middle shelves, where he'd traditionally stocked jam, honey and Vegemite. These had been moved to a bottom shelf.

3

Challis and Destry left in separate cars, knowing the job would scatter them as the day progressed. Ellen's new Corolla was bright blue but streaked with dust and mud like all of the locals' cars. Challis followed in his unreliable Triumph. It had held its secrets firmly for years, but now they were all coming out: rust patches at the bottoms of the doors and in the footwells, oil leaks, corrosion, a broken speedo cable, a slipping clutch, a whining differential. And the shockers were shot: he hit a pothole in his driveway and felt the jarring through the steering wheel.

He glanced across at his house as he left the driveway. It was a pretty building, in the Californian-bungalow style, dating from the Second World War. It sat naturally in the landscape on three acres of grass, fruit trees and vague scrub, the only neighbours an orchardist and a vigneron. He liked the seclusion; seclusion was his natural state. But did it bother Ellen? Until her separation and divorce from Alan Destry she'd lived at Penzance Beach, in a small suburban house right next door to similar houses, amid people who mowed their lawns, cooked on backyard barbecues, knocked on the door to ask for a cup of sugar, sometimes played music too loudly.

Perhaps he should be asking: *would* the seclusion bother her, over time? They'd only been together for three weeks. He'd asked her to house-sit while he took leave to be with his dying father, and within a couple of hours of his return they were lovers. It had surprised them both—kind of. She'd muttered something about finding her own place, but only half-heartedly, and he urged her to stay.

He tried to sort out his reasons now. Of course, attraction played the greatest part, desire, affection, even though he hadn't spelt out any of this to her. They were not good at endearments. There were no 'I love you's yet. It seemed they both thought endearments and declarations were currency too easily squandered.

And he couldn't discount the fact that he'd returned to the Peninsula from his father's funeral feeling vulnerable and a little unhinged. He wasn't sleeping, the job promised continued human misery and droning days. The death of his father was raw in him. Back when his mother had died he'd thought about her every few minutes at first, then every few weeks, and every few months, fading into occasional happy memories, but then when his father began to die the grief was rekindled. Double grief. Now, when least expected and often when least wanted, he'd hear his parents' voices, see their faces and remember the past with frightening clarity.

Challis had never been a man to need a crutch, but Ellen Destry was a balm to him, in addition to everything else.

On the other hand, they worked closely together. Too closely, on problems too complicated, for love to work as well? Never mind that some police bureaucrat was bound to wave a regulation in their faces sooner or later. Challis reached the end of the dirt road and pulled over. He'd replaced the old cassette player with a CD unit and was in the mood for Chris Smither. 'Drive You Home Again' blaring, he turned onto the sealed road toward Waterloo. Soon he was passing an aspirant French chalet and a Tuscanesque villa, new houses that didn't sit naturally in the landscape but had claimed the high ground from the ever-shrinking farmland. It sometimes seemed that he'd blink and a new mansion would have gone up overnight.

The towns of the Peninsula were also changing, their original dimensions swelled by new housing estates which attracted young families shackled to debt on house-and-land packages they couldn't afford. The social divide between them and the cashed-up retirees and sea-change professionals was growing; the schools, hospitals, welfare agencies and police were overburdened.

He came to the intersection with Coolart Road and stopped for an approaching school bus. The mock colonial paling fence on his right contained a herd—mob? fleece?—of alpacas. Ten years ago there hadn't been any alpacas on the Peninsula. Now they were everywhere, looking like toys, made-up creatures. Then the bus was past, 'The Landseer School' scrolled across its big rump. Challis sighed: one of the most exclusive schools in the country, fees close to twenty thousand a year, a place he'd normally have nothing to do with—and now he'd have to send in one of his officers to see if it was linked to the assault on its chaplain.

Following the road past vines and more alpacas he came to the garden centres, plumbing suppliers and timber yards on the outskirts of Waterloo. One of the biggest towns on the Peninsula, Waterloo had been down-at-heel at one time but was undergoing a renaissance: a K-Mart, new housing, a delicatessen that offered imported delicacies, the old fleapit second-hand shops bulldozed to make way for small arcades with smoky glass. It was all bringing some pride back into the place.

He skirted the southern flank of the town, coming to Trevally Street, a long street that ran parallel to the shoreline, residential on one side, parkland, the municipal swimming pool, skateboard ramps, coin barbecues, walking paths and a yacht club on the other. Apart from a crammed collection of brightly coloured nylon tents on a vacant lot beside the tennis courts, it was all familiar to Challis.

Those tents. The first had appeared on Friday afternoon, dozens more on the weekend, erected by eighteen- and nineteen-year-olds who'd come to Waterloo intent on celebrating the end of their Year 12 exams. Schoolies Week. The main schoolie playground continued to be Queensland's Gold Coast, followed in popularity by the Victorian towns of Lorne and Sorrento, but cost, distance, overcrowding and parental nervousness had led some kids to seek out low-rent alternatives, like Waterloo. Last year a hundred of them had discovered the town, which had reeled a little. This year many more were expected and the locals were better prepared. The motels and boarding houses were offering special rates, vacant land had been opened up for camping, and there was a greater police and volunteer presence to cope with the drunkenness, overdoses, assaults and tears.

It hadn't been enough to stop Saturday's sexual assault, however. The victim, an eighteen-year-old from one of the girls' schools in the city, hadn't known her attacker, hadn't seen him, in the dunes late at night, hadn't been able to identify him in any way. All they had was a spill of semen on her T-shirt and shorts. What was the betting there'd be no DNA match to anyone in the system?

Challis slowed the car, spotting Scobie Sutton's Volvo station wagon parked outside the Villanova Gardens apartments. The Volvo was twenty years old but still pristine, a car that had never broken the speed limit—which didn't mean that it was ever driven well, for Scobie Sutton was a well-known lousy driver. There was also a police car and a black Astra soft-top.

The Villanova Gardens was named after an Italian sailor who'd jumped ship a hundred years earlier, when Waterloo was a huddle of fishermen's makeshift tents and cabins. Challis parked, got out and glanced both ways along the street, spotting Pam Murphy and a uniformed constable knocking on doors. Few street lights in this part of town, he noticed. He eyed the apartments. They were double-storeyed, in a row of ten, each with a small, incorporated garage, hedges for privacy, and an upper-level balcony that he guessed gave a view across the yacht basin and Western Port Bay to the distant smoke stacks of the refinery on the other side. Uninspiring, but you could honestly call it a view.

He approached number 6, fishing ID out of his suit coat and

showing it to Andy Cree, the constable who'd been stationed to keep a log of all those authorised to enter or leave the building. Cree was a new recruit to the station, young, athletic, engaging, always wearing the easy air of a kidder. Challis preferred that to shyness, ineptitude or flunkeyism, but Cree was in a lazy mood today, in no hurry as he logged the details. Keeping it light but firm, Challis said, 'I've got all day, Andy.'

Cree flushed. 'Yes, sir.'

'Who's here? Who's been and gone?'

Cree checked the log. 'Ambulance guys have taken the victim to hospital. Constable Murphy's doing a doorknock along the street with Constable Tankard. The crime scene technicians aren't here yet. DC Sutton from CIU, and the victim's brother, name of—'

Challis said, 'The brother? What's he doing here? This is a crime scene.'

Cree's face flickered, then cleared. 'He said he wanted to take toiletries and pyjamas to the hospital. Constable Sutton gave the okay, sir.'

Challis made to go in, then paused. 'Where was the victim found?'

There was a low hedge running beside the footpath. Cree pointed over it to the small patch of lawn between the street and the front door. 'Lying right there, sir.'

There were also hedges on either side of the yard. Given the hedges, the sparse street lighting and the darkness of night, it was possible to see why Roe hadn't been spotted by his neighbours or passers-by until daybreak.

'And there's blood on that rock,' Cree said, pointing to a hefty stone lying on the concrete pathway leading to the door. It was painted white and had been removed from the border around a bed of roses. Nodding his thanks, Challis walked up the short, narrow path to the open front door and into a hallway that led to a cramped living and dining area with a kitchen through an archway, and beyond that a door that probably led to the laundry and a bathroom. Minimalist but expensive fittings and furniture, he noticed quickly, before glancing up the plain staircase to the upper level, where the bedrooms would be. And where voices were raised.

Challis pulled hard on the banister to propel himself up the stairs. He tracked the voices to a small office at the rear, where Scobie Sutton stood by helplessly as a man dressed in jeans and a polo shirt wrapped a power cable around a laptop computer that had been on the desk under a window. Sutton looked up. 'Sorry, boss…'

The detective had the bony narrowness and angularity of an undertaker, an impression reinforced by his dark suit and glum air. He gestured feebly as if to grab the laptop. Meanwhile the other man dodged him and turned to Challis. 'Who the hell are you?'

Challis told him coldly.

'Well, my name is Dirk Roe and for your information my brother was almost beaten to death last night. Or this morning.'

Challis glanced at Roe's hands: they were well kept and unmarked. He shifted his gaze to the man's face, which wore the sour look of someone who'd once been admired and was waiting for it to happen again. Roe was no more than twenty-five, with a round, faintly stupid schoolboy face, reinforced by spiky hair, black jeans, a pale yellow polo shirt and running shoes, which were two fat slabs of vividly-coloured rubber. There was a soul patch above his pudgy chin, rings in both ears.

Challis stepped into the room, saying, 'I can sympathise, Mr Roe, but I must ask you to leave. This is a crime scene, and our crime scene officers haven't processed it yet.'

'But Lachie was bashed *out*side, on his front lawn.'

'His attacker might have been inside the house before the assault.'

'My brother doesn't know people like that.'

'People like what?'

'Violent people. Criminals,' Dirk Roe said. He tucked the laptop under his arm and made to edge past Challis.

'Sir,' Challis said, 'I must ask you to leave the laptop behind.'

A flicker of something passed across the young man's face. 'But Lachie might need it. He could be in hospital for days.'

Challis shook his head. 'Impossible, I'm afraid. The computer could hold information that would help identify your brother's attacker.' He paused. 'Did you meddle with it in any way?'

Dirk Roe wouldn't meet his gaze. 'Me? No. Why?'

'Either way, the computer stays.'

'I don't think you know who I am,' Roe said.

Challis was immediately weary of this game. 'So, who are you?'

Roe drew himself up. 'I manage Ollie Hindmarsh's electoral office—and you know what *he* thinks of the police.'

Ollie Hindmarsh was Leader of the Opposition in the state parliament and his electoral office was a short distance away, around the corner in High Street. Hindmarsh was a law-and-order tyrant and his way of attacking the Government was to accuse the police force of corruption, cronyism and being run by union thugs. Most cops loathed the man.

Challis smiled emptily. 'You manage his electoral office?'

'Yep.'

'Meaning you answer the phone and lick envelopes.'

'Listen here, you. I—'

'Sir, I must ask you to wait outside. Scobie?'

Sutton had been wearing an expression of faint alarm, as if aware of undercurrents that he couldn't identify. A man with a decent narrowness of range, he went to church regularly, was loyal to his wife, and had almost no insights into human nature. He wasn't a bad cop. He was dogged. But he wasn't quite a good cop, either. He shuffled forward apologetically and, after a tussle, removed the computer from under Roe's arm and took him by the elbow. 'Sorry, Dirk.'

Challis frowned. Did the two men know each other? He filed it away and they all walked downstairs, reaching the living area just as the forensics officers appeared in their disposable overalls and overshoes. 'Great,' said one, 'a contaminated crime scene.'

'Yeah, yeah,' said Challis. 'Your main area of focus is the lawn outside the front door.'

'And the bloodied stone on the pathway. What about inside?'

'Dust for prints, check for blood and fibres, the usual.'

Dirk Roe swayed and stumbled a little, as though finally registering the fact that violence had been used against his brother. Scobie escorted him outside, saying, 'Don't stay here Dirk, head across to the hospital. Are you okay to drive?'

'I think so.'

Why hadn't Roe gone straight to the hospital? Challis wondered. He joined Sutton on the footpath and together they watched Roe drive away in the black Astra. Challis said, 'Scobie, you and Pam finish up here. I'll check on the victim. Briefing at noon.'

'Boss.'

Challis paused. Andy Cree had abandoned his station to chat with Pam Murphy, half a block away. He was a head taller than Pam, languid and suave, and Challis heard her break into laughter. Then she spotted him, flashed him an embarrassed smile, and turned to continue her doorknocking. Cree wandered back, saying, 'Sorry, sir.'

'Constable.'

Challis turned to Sutton. 'Check if there's any CCTV coverage from local businesses.'

'Boss,' Sutton said.

4

Ellen Destry had reached the Waterloo police station, which was on the roundabout at the head of High Street, with a Caltex service station, a McDonald's and Waterloo Stockfeed on the other three corners. The building itself was a low-slung tan brick and glass structure set amongst some bark-shedding gum trees with access from a little side street. It was a major regional station, serving Peninsula East, and employed uniformed police, CIU detectives, crime-scene officers, probationary constables and several civilians: clerks and canteen staff, and the collators, who gathered, analysed and cross-referenced all intelligence relating to solved and unsolved crimes and the movements and associations of known criminals on the Peninsula.

She parked outside the station and entered through the foyer, where a middle-aged woman was watching the duty sergeant witness a statutory declaration. She tapped in her code, entered the network of offices and corridors behind the reception desk and checked her pigeonhole: a circular for the end-of-year Police Ball, a reminder that she owed $12 tea money, and a copy of the November *Police Life* magazine. Hal had been on the front cover once, years ago, after he'd played a role in the arrest of the Old Peninsula Highway killer. He hadn't liked the attention. He liked to slip through life unnoticed.

The cells, interview rooms, admin offices and canteen were on the ground floor. Ellen took the stairs to the upper level, which housed CIU, a couple of briefing rooms, a small gym and a tearoom. The Crime Investigation Unit was small, with four detectives rostered on nights, four on days. It never worked out quite like that, of course. There was always someone away sick, attending a training course or giving evidence in court. When extra hands were needed they were seconded from other CIU teams, mainly from Mornington and Rosebud.

Sitting at her corner desk in the controlled chaos of the open-plan CIU room, Ellen routinely checked her e-mails—and began to realise that she felt faintly miffed about being asked to do desk work today. It was great having Hal back, but she'd headed a major inquiry while he was away, and she'd acquitted herself well. She wanted to be out and about, not stuck behind a desk.

Still, there was never anything minor about a sexual assault. Seeing no e-mails from the forensic science centre, she phoned, identifying herself and the case number. 'Sexual assault,' she prompted, 'in Waterloo last Saturday night.'

She heard the tapping of a keyboard on the end of the line, and eventually the forensic technician said, 'Semen on the victim's clothes, right? We're backed up here, Sergeant Destry. DNA takes time.'

Ellen sighed. 'Just checking,' she said, and hung up.

She stared at the ceiling battens, not seeing them. There was nothing unusual about a sexual assault on a Saturday night; nothing unusual about that anywhere in the world. But the victim in this case had been a schoolie, she'd been assaulted during Schoolies Week, and her attacker might have been a fellow schoolie.

Or a 'toolie'. one of the locals who preyed on the school leavers. Older men, mostly, some with records for theft, dealing drugs and sexual assault. They were sly and predatory, and seemed to hate the schoolies for everything they lacked: education, job prospects, money, youth, good health, a clean record.

Had toolies been active at last year's Schoolies Week? Waterloo hadn't been the least bit prepared for the event. The police had had to deal with three drug overdoses, two claims of drink spiking, the theft of tents, sleeping bags and backpacks, and a vicious mugging that placed a kid in hospital minus his runners, iPod, mobile phone and wallet. They'd made several arrests, for serious assault, drunk and disorderly, drug use and obstructing police, and Ellen had also heard rumours that some local girls had been sexually assaulted.

Meanwhile the local residents had been up in arms over the noise, the brawling, the drag races and burnouts on the foreshore, and the stoned, drunk, drug-addled or distressed and weeping kids wandering the streets and through the shops and passing out in pools of blood, piss or vomit on front lawns. The street cleaners worked overtime, raking up condoms, beer cans, unpaired shoes, knickers, makeshift bongs and paper scraps from the beach and parkland areas.

What made it worse, in many ways, was the behaviour of the rich kids. They arrived in costly cars and were indifferent to the money they splashed around. They expected it to get them out of trouble. Accustomed to expensive overseas holidays, they were viciously bored and disappointed in humble little Waterloo, and took it out on the locals and the poorer kids.

It was a conundrum for the town's worthies. On the one hand, they deplored the bad behaviour; on the other, they estimated that the schoolies would inject up to $200,000 into the local economy, and no one wanted to deny these kids a holiday by the sea. So the mayor and the councillors had worked out a strategy. The community would provide camping areas, counselling and general information. The police would liaise and mingle with the schoolies, but also strike hard against public drunkenness and hooliganism, levelling $100 on-the-spot fines for drinking or possessing alcohol in an open container in a public place, lighting campfires on the foreshore, and sleeping in a car rather than a designated campsite tent or a room in a hotel, a motel, a boarding house or a bed-and-breakfast establishment.

Ellen had selected Pam Murphy to be the main liaison officer for the police, figuring the young detective would be more sympathetic and understanding than Scobie Sutton. But Ellen also kept a watching brief, and so now she logged on to the Schoolies Week website. She hadn't known it existed before Murph told her. Maybe the kids didn't know about it, either, or maybe it was poorly designed, or inadequate. She should find out.

The site, mounted by the state government via the Education Department, was out of date, concentrating on the traditional schoolies hotspots of Lorne, Portsea and Sorrento. We're not big enough yet, Ellen thought.

She checked the 'useful phone numbers' list. The obvious ones were there—state-wide numbers for the police, fire brigade, ambulance, twenty-four-hour drug and alcohol advice, poisons information, sexual assault and suicide hotlines—but no local numbers. What if the schoolies camped at Waterloo wanted a youth worker or a clean needle? Even a bus or a taxi?

She scrolled down. All reasonable advice: check home regularly, look out for each other, keep your room locked, secure your valuables, carry ID at all times, together with enough money—separate from your wallet—to pay for phone calls and transport. If in trouble, seek help from the police and official volunteers.

She read on. Never swim under the influence of alcohol or drugs. Drink plenty of water. Eat at least one solid meal a day. Space your drinking. Be alert for drink spiking and dodgy strangers. Don't get into a car with a stranger or an inebriated driver. Don't let your friends go off with strangers, get hassled by others or sober up alone. At Portsea two years ago a kid had drowned in his own vomit.

Next, accommodation. Last year some kids had trashed a motel room and been thrown out of a bed-and-breakfast joint near the boardwalk. It occurred to Ellen that maybe kids were being ripped off by landlords. The website advised them to check the fine print on their accommodation contracts—would she have thought to do that, when she was eighteen?—and get a receipt for the bond money. She scanned through: complaints procedures, Accommodation Code of Practice, blah, blah, blah.

Ellen rubbed her eyes. She hated computer work. As she continued to follow the links she had to admit that the information was useful and solid—but did the kids read it? She thought of further local information that was sorely lacking. Like where to swim safely, for example. How Western Port Bay emptied treacherously when the tide went out, so that you could find yourself stranded on a mud bank and drown when it came racing in again. The black spots in the mobile phone coverage. The fact that it can be cold at night, and that November can be rainy. The fact that many shops and restaurants in the little burg of Waterloo closed early.

Also, where the town of Lorne offered its schoolies a free clinic, a free shuttle bus and plenty of youth workers wearing distinctive orange T-shirts, Waterloo offered a handful of untrained volunteers from the local church communities operating from a safe haven called the Chillout Zone, in the grounds of the Uniting Church behind High Street. Ellen had called in last night and found herself helping Pam Murphy to dispense drinks and snacks to wasted, lonely, bored and befuddled kids, or those who were simply broke.

And Scobie Sutton's wife, Beth, had been lurking there. According to Murph, Beth Sutton had been at the Chillout Zone since Friday, handing God-bothering leaflets to the schoolies and murmuring to them in an intense monotone.

Ellen looked up from the monitor and into the distance. The volunteers. Pam Murphy had introduced her to last night's bunch—she'd vetted them all, she said—but Pam couldn't be everywhere at once, and wouldn't it be easy for some pervert to pass himself off as an official volunteer or youth worker?

'Nothing about this job gets any easier,' Ellen muttered. She looked at her watch. The others should be returning from the Trevally Street assault soon.

5

Caz Moon was on Trevally Street. She was walking to work, HangTen, the surf shop up on High Street, where she was the manager. For now, anyway. Caz was no cute surfie chick—suntanned, blonde, mini-skirt, chewing gum snapping in her jaws. Caz couldn't be bothered with any of that. Her jeans and T-shirt were cheap, her hair and makeup vaguely Goth. She was saving her money. She was slim, quick and clever, twenty-one years old, and very soon she would leave Waterloo far behind, leave her peers to their pregnancies and joblessness.

Caz Moon hadn't reached the crime scene yet, although she could see the police car, the uniforms and the tape in the distance. She was still down on the stretch of Trevally devoted to seedy boarding houses, run-down motels and faded holiday apartments, all of them facing patchy parkland between the coin barbecues and the boardwalk that ran out into the mangrove swamp. The parkland was Tent City this week, flimsy green and blue nylon structures flapping in the breeze. No one stirring, though. The little dears were still sleeping it off.

It was in front of the Sea Breeze Holiday Apartments that Caz spotted a red Subaru Impreza with a spoiler, racks and customised mag wheels. She swayed, feeling unmoored suddenly. Unwelcome sensations flooded through her, momentarily flattening her capacity to think. A year ago, it had been. Schoolies Week last year. She remembered the sounds of his breathing and her undies ripping, his faintly rotten cocaine and amphetamine skin, the sand packed in hard ripples beneath her spine, the bile in her mouth and the knowing stars high above.

Josh, his name was, one long, rollercoaster night, Josh sweet at first, then the flashes of paranoia, his eyes looking wildly through her, then the sweetness again. She knew more, now, about the mood swings associated with ice. And maybe he carried a whole pharmacy around in his pocket, for the next thing she remembered was feeling dazed, her limbs sluggish, Josh on top of her in the darkest hours of the night.

And here he was, back in town again in his little red car.

Caz Moon closed her eyes and willed it all away, willing raw anger in its place. She breathed in and out. She smiled. She set off again in her unreadable way, down along Trevally Street toward the Villanova Gardens apartments.

A detective watched her and she watched the detective, a young woman with a clipboard, who suddenly veered away from knocking fruitlessly on nearby doors to head Caz off, her face with that cool, blank, unimpressed look they all have.

'Hi,' the cop said. 'My name's Detective Constable Pam Murphy.' She paused, cocked her head. 'I've seen you around town. You work in the surf shop, right?'

'Manager,' Caz said. She took the initiative and shot out her hand. 'Karen Moon. Caz.'

'Hi,' the cop said, shaking her hand. 'Listen, we're investigating a serious incident in Trevally Street last night. Mind if I ask you some questions?'

Caz glanced past the cop to a beefy uniformed guy doorknocking on the other side of the street, and beyond him to one of the apartments, where a slinky guy stood guard, looking bored. 'Fire away.'

The questions began: 'Do you live nearby?' 'Do you regularly use

Trevally Street?' 'Did you pass along here late yesterday evening or in the early hours of the morning?' And so on. It didn't take long. Caz soon established that she hadn't seen or heard anything.

All true. But she did lie. The lie was in not informing the young detective with the taut body and probing eyes that she'd been raped last November. At night, on one of the beaches. And that she knew where to find the guy who'd committed it.

Caz Moon was maintaining a very specific, retributive rage about that.

Ludmilla Wishart also saw the police car, the crime-scene tape and the doorknocking officers. She saw them from the side window of her Golf as she passed along Trevally Street on her way to the planning office. Normally she might have been like any other gawking citizen and stored her impressions to share with her workmates around the tearoom table, but felt too low for that. Felt too *fat*.

Was she fat? Her best friend, Carmen, would say, 'If anything, Mill, you're too skinny.' Sometimes, when Ludmilla was feeling strong, she believed Carmen; the rest of the time she believed Adrian. Why did it matter to him so much? She wanted to look good for him as one does with a lover or husband, but looking good for Adrian was exhausting. The effort and the anxiety wore her out. She relied on little acts of resistance to keep going. Her friendship with Carmen, for example, in which she could be herself, crack jokes, let her guard down. Adrian was wary of Carmen. He probably knew Carmen loathed him. As Ludmilla stopped at a roundabout she thought about hiding or breaking the bathroom scales. But Adrian would only go out and buy another set.

The bad feelings rising in her, she drove on again, finally turning into a side street half a kilometre away from the crime scene and slowing for the entrance to Planning East. The hectic pace of residential and commercial development on the Peninsula had placed an enormous strain on the shire's planners in recent years, and now separate and independent planning departments handled applications in the western, eastern and southern zones. Several planners worked at Planning East, Ludmilla was the infringements officer, and their boss was Athol Groot. The only parking spot available was next to his Mercedes, an old white classic, and Ludmilla parked very carefully, very precisely, knowing what he was like.

Thinking about her boss reminded her of Adrian, and she sat for a few minutes, her heart hammering. It often happened: Adrian would find fault, and her heart would get the wobbles. The only solution was to stumble into her office, *Ludmilla Wishart, Planning Infringements* on the door, and stretch out on the floor, one hand over her heart, monitoring its erratic progress.

She wanted above everything else to be a cool, collected person. She thought she'd glimpsed that quality, very briefly, in the young woman detective on Trevally Street. What would it take? Leaving Adrian, according to Carmen.

'What are you doing?'

It was Mr Groot, squat and heavy in her doorway, wearing the kind of expression that said he didn't care one way or the other if she were ill, so long as he didn't have to do anything about it.

John Tankard and Pam Murphy finished doorknocking Trevally Street and wandered back to the Villanova apartments, comparing notes. 'I found one witness who backs up Lachlan Roe's neighbour,' Tank said. 'He heard two men shouting just after midnight and saw a guy wearing a hoodie running along Trevally Street toward the library. Didn't get a look at his face.'

Pam snorted. 'A guy in a hoodie.'

'Bet you'd like a dollar for every time you've heard *that*,' Tank said.

He bumped shoulders with her. Until a few weeks ago, Murph had been his partner. Now she was in plain clothes, a CIU hotshot, and he was stuck with that prick Andrew Cree. When their shoulders touched, she moved apart from him. Just slightly, almost nothing to it, but Tank knew it was a rebuff.

Meanwhile Cree, God's gift to women and policing, was watching their approach.

'How's it going, Andy?' called Murph in a voice that made Tank's antenna go up.

'Too much excitement in this job,' Cree said.

Pam laughed.

Bitch, thought Tank. He knew that he was out of shape and hopeless with women. Here's Cree, fit, assured, an Arts graduate, for fuck's sake, and not ... direct. Saying things between the lines.

He comforted himself with the thought that he knew something Pam didn't—the great Andrew Cree was afraid of the dark. True. Before their daybreak callout to Trevally Street this morning, Tank and Cree had been patrolling outside the town limits, on duty since 4 a.m. The darkness had been all around them, their headlights picking out the ghostly shapes of dead gum trees and the coal eyes of foxes on the prowl. Nothing unusual but Tank had begun to wonder why Cree was all hunched over the steering wheel, his shoulders up around his ears. Then, suddenly, he got it: the guy was scared. Young Andrew had grown up in some endless tract of Melbourne, where the night was never truly dark and no snakes or spiders lurked. Not like the back roads of the Peninsula. No streetlights out here, old buddy, old pal, old chum. Out here the darkness closes in tight around you. Ghosts and gremlins roam.

'Okay, guys,' Pam was saying now, 'we're finished here. Thanks for your help. Grab yourselves some morning tea and then return to what you were doing.'

'Don't know if I can stand the thrill of it,' Cree responded, throwing her plenty of eye and mouth work as if to say he could stand the thrill of *her*.

Prick.

6

After leaving the Villanova apartments, Challis drove to the hospital. A forensic science officer, carrying several brown paper sample bags, was trudging purposefully across the carpark as though holding strong emotions in check. She stopped when she saw Challis. 'A nasty beating, sir.'

Challis nodded. 'More than one person involved?'

'Hard to say. Nothing much under the victim's fingernails. Lots of blood on his hands, face and clothing—probably all his, but we'll check.' She rattled the paper sample bags at him. 'The good news is I found what looks like mucus on the elbow of his jacket. We'll check the DNA against his DNA.'

Challis thanked her, went in and tracked down the doctor who'd treated Roe. A Russian, Challis guessed. About fifty, exhausted-looking and very thin, with a bony, hooked nose. 'He is lucky he is found before it is too late, I think,' the doctor said, escorting Challis down a corridor, the white walls and green linoleum streaked here and there, the black spoor of rubber soles and tyres. 'The coma continues. Impossible to say when he will regain consciousness.'

Lachlan Roe had sustained cracked ribs, a broken nose, a broken ring finger on his right hand—possibly sustained when he tried to ward off his attacker—and severe swelling of the brain. 'In my opinion this man was punched quite viciously and then kicked when he was on the ground. Is possible his brain has sustained some damage.'

They entered a small ward, where the doctor pulled back a curtain, revealing the chaplain of the Landseer School lying beneath a window overlooking the rear of the Waterloo Fitness Centre. Roe breathed shallowly out of a badly bruised and swollen face. Broad white bandaging was wound tightly around his head and Challis glimpsed a bandage striped across his chest.

Dirk Roe, plumply miserable, sat in a chair pulled close to his brother's bed, muttering into the telephone on the bedside table. Glancing around sulkily when Challis and the doctor entered, his face immediately cleared. 'Speak of the devil,' he said into the phone. 'The cop in charge just walked in...Yes, sir...I'll put him on.' He thrust the phone at Challis, the gesture somehow dismissive and contemptuous. 'My boss wants a word.'

Oh, hell, thought Challis. He took the phone, said his name crisply.

Ollie Hindmarsh's reply filled his ear, the voice deep-chested, hectoring and familiar from numerous television and radio interviews. 'You know who I am?'

'Yes.'

'This is a nasty business,' the politician said, 'very nasty.'

Challis said nothing.

'Made an arrest?'

'Not yet.'

'Any suspects?'

'Too soon to say.'

Hindmarsh grunted. After a pause he said, 'At least you have rank. I don't want this fobbed off onto a sergeant or a constable.'

Challis said nothing.

'Did you hear me? I want you to stay on top of this, Inspector.'

'It will be treated seriously; as seriously as we treat all violent crime,' Challis said, feeling like a public relations flak.

'Hardly reassuring,' barked Hindmarsh. 'Mr Roe has done enormous good in the local community and I want his attacker brought to justice.'

I'm not Channel 9, thought Challis. I'm not the *Herald-Sun*. He said, 'If that will be all…?'

'Who's your superintendent?'

Oh, Christ, Challis thought, and told him.

'McQuarrie? Played golf with him once. Based in Frankston?'

'Yes.'

There was no good-bye, just a click in Challis's ear. He gave the handset to Dirk Roe, who smirked. To wipe it off his face, Challis said, 'I will need to question you later in the day.' He gave Roe his card. 'Meanwhile if you think of anything pertinent, or if your brother wakes up, give me a call.'

'Whatever.'

Challis shook his head and left the hospital. Back in CIU he found Ellen Destry at her computer. He told her about the phone call. 'He's going to sic McQuarrie on to me.'

'What a jerk.'

'At least we've got nothing else on of any great seriousness, so all stops out.'

She mock saluted him. 'Right you are, boss.'

'I'll bust you back to uniform if you're not careful.'

'I look good in a uniform,' she said.

Challis walked away shaking his head. In his office he stared at his in-tray for a while, at the paperwork that swamped his days and gave him a permanent, low-level sense of anxiety and aggravation. The memos and reports induced dreaminess, and soon he was staring out of his window at the sky—blue, even and featureless. He got up and stood at the glass, staring down at the carpark beneath his office. It was nothing to look at—cramped, potholed, fringed with peeling gum trees—but more interesting than the sky, with the cops and civilian employees always clocking on and off. Among the vehicles were big four-wheel-drives, humble family sedans, a snappy little European cabriolet, and a couple of boy-racer V8s, all glossy paintwork and testosterone. Not for the first time, he reflected on the police station as a microcosm of the wider community.

Then he saw Scobie Sutton arrive. Sutton circled the area before parking inexpertly beside a rubbish skip that had been rusting away in the far corner since renovation work two years earlier. He was followed by Pam Murphy, who parked her little Hyundai briskly and strode past Sutton in her take-no-prisoners way, Sutton trudging like a wind-whipped scarecrow across the yard.

Challis grinned, left his office and walked down the corridor to the tearoom, where he spooned coffee grounds into the espresso machine. This was the morning ritual in CIU: he made the coffee, the others took turns to provide pastries from the bakery in High Street—unless it was Scobie's turn, in which case he brought scones, cupcakes or muffins baked by his wife. Challis preferred the pastries.

When the coffee was ready he loaded the coffee pot, four mugs and a jug of microwaved milk onto a tray and carried them to the briefing room, where the others were already waiting, Ellen arranging almond croissants on a plate in the centre. She knew what he liked.

Challis always stood during briefing sessions. It allowed him to move between whiteboards with a pointer during complex cases, or otherwise simply prop up a wall while everyone tossed around ideas. This morning there was only one matter of any urgency, the attack on Lachlan Roe.

'I've just been to the hospital,' he said. 'Roe is still unconscious. It was a pretty frenzied attack, we could be looking at brain damage. And it didn't help that he was lying in the open all night.'

Ellen licked icing sugar from her fingers. 'Forensics?'

'Plenty of blood, mostly from Roe presumably. A possible mucus smear on his elbow that might be from his attacker. We won't know until the DNA results come in. There might also be some fibre evidence from his clothing.'

He turned to the others. 'Scobie? Pam? Any witnesses?'

Sutton stirred in his seat. He looked tense. 'No CCTV, sorry.'

'Murph?'

Pam Murphy was new to CIU, persuaded to make the switch from uniformed work by Ellen Destry, who'd noticed her aptitude for detection. She was thirty, with the taut, neatly put together look of an athlete, her hair short and layered. Like Ellen, she was dressed unremarkably. She swallowed some coffee and checked her notebook.

'We managed to question most of the neighbours before they left for work. The woman who found the victim said she heard shouting last night, around midnight. She didn't do anything about it because she assumed it was the schoolies from the tents across the road. They've been partying hard every night since Friday. Another witness saw a young man in a hoodie running away from the area late last night. Didn't see his face. We still need to follow up on a couple of shift workers who'd already left this morning.'

'No one saw anything earlier in the evening? Someone hanging around, an unfamiliar car on the street?'

Scobie threw his hands up. 'It's Schoolies Week. The joint's full of strangers and strange cars.'

Challis uncoiled from the wall, nodding philosophically. 'If the attack was random,' he said, pulling out a chair and helping himself to a croissant, 'and there's no DNA evidence, no witnesses, we're stuck. But Lachlan Roe might have pissed someone off, so let's look closer at him. Standard victimology: where he works, who his associates are, finances, hobbies, interests, last known movements, the usual drill. In particular, the brother and the school.'

He paused, looking hard at Sutton. 'Scobie, this morning you gave Dirk Roe permission to collect personal items for the victim?'

Scobie wouldn't look at him. 'Correct.'

'How did Dirk know that his brother had been attacked?'

Scobie coughed, shifted about in his seat. 'I phoned him.'

'You know these men?'

'Yes.'

'How?'

Sutton looked hunted and tried to find a place for his hands. 'My wife...through the church.'

'You thought you'd do the right thing,' said Challis flatly.

'Yes.'

'Scobie, the brother could be our assailant.'

Sutton swallowed. 'I doubt it. They were close.'

'Perhaps you should recuse yourself,' Challis said.

In fact, that was the last thing he wanted, if only because he couldn't afford to lose the manpower. But he needed to know that Scobie Sutton wouldn't try second-guessing any aspect of the investigation.

'I'm fine, boss. Honest.'

'Even so, I don't want you talking to Dirk—or his brother, if and when he regains consciousness. Finish the doorknock, okay?'

'Boss.'

'Ellen, if you could check out the school angle?'

'Will do.'

Challis turned again to Pam Murphy. 'Murph, you'll continue to liaise with the schoolies.'

She'd been sitting quietly, taking everything in. 'Sir.'

'But keep your ear close to the ground. Maybe they saw something last night. Maybe Lachlan had made himself unpopular, told them to keep the noise down; maybe he made unwelcome advances and they beat him up for it.'

'Boss.'

'Meanwhile, there's bound to be some media attention in the next few hours. Some influential people send their kids to Landseer, and the victim's brother works in Ollie Hindmarsh's electoral office on High Street.'

He allowed that to sink in. 'Any questions?'

Headshakes and murmurs.

'Okay, see you late afternoon for a further briefing.'

They gathered their folders, coffee mugs and plates and began to file out, but Pam Murphy said, 'Sir, there is one thing,' squirming in her seat, looking embarrassed.

'What?'

'The eclipse.'

'The what?'

'Wednesday's eclipse.'

She squirmed again in the face of his amused scrutiny, but soon Challis began to glimpse where she was going with her reference to the eclipse. At present the moon was almost full, sitting high over the land at night, agitating the crazy people. Like all police officers, he knew about a full moon. But Wednesday night promised extra craziness, for the earth was due to pass directly between the sun and the moon, and the latter, according to the Bureau of Meteorology, would glow eerily red for some time.

He began to nod. 'You think it'll set off the schoolies?'

With relief she said, 'They're saying it's going to be the ultimate high.'

'Uh huh.'

Ellen was amused. 'Unless it's a cloudy night.'

Pam turned to her seriously and said, 'In which case they'll be disappointed, Sarge, and looking for other diversions.'

Ellen rubbed her hands together briskly. 'Fair enough. I'll speak to the duty sergeant for you. Some extra uniforms should do the trick.'

'Thanks, Sarge.'

7

The desk phone rang as soon as Challis was alone, a reporter from the *Herald-Sun* in Melbourne. Then he was obliged to go downstairs and speak to a reporter from the local rag. Finally McQuarrie rang, the superintendent sounding apologetic for once. 'Just had Ollie Hindmarsh bending my ear.'

'Bent mine too, sir.'

'Getting anywhere?'

'Too soon to say.'

'We need to cover ourselves.'

That was typical of the man. 'With respect, sir, I intend to investigate this *without* one eye on the media or our esteemed local member of parliament.'

After a long pause, McQuarrie said, 'Fair enough. Just keep me posted.'

The only cure for the aggravation was more coffee. Challis brewed a fresh pot, shut his door, switched off his mobile and told the front desk to say he was out of the office until noon.

He started by examining Lachlan Roe's laptop. He expected it to be password protected, which meant long delays until the department's IT experts got around to examining the machine, but within moments he was in. Either the chaplain's got nothing to hide, he thought, or he'd been confident that no one would ever be poking around in his files.

Challis went straight to Roe's e-mail, finding only a dozen innocuous messages in the in-box. He checked the folder of deleted e-mails: nothing. Had the brother emptied it? Finally he scrolled through the e-mails *sent* by Roe, and hit paydirt. Hating to read anything on-screen, he printed out the offending item. The subject line was 'Someone finally spoke up' and the message read:

Proud To Be A White Australian

Someone finally said it.

How many are actually paying attention to this?

There are Aboriginals, Torres Strait Islanders, Kiwi Australians, Lebonese Australians, Asian Australians, Arab Australians, Boat People from all over the place, etc. And then there are just Australians.

You pass me on the street and sneer in my Direction.

You Call me "Australian Dog", "White boy", "Cracker", "Honkey", "Whitey", "Caveman". And that's OK. But when I call you, Black Fellarr, Kike, Towel head, Sand nigger, Sheep Shager Camel Jockey, Gook or Chink, You call Me a racist.

You say that whites commit a lot of violence against you, so why are the Housing Estates the most dangerous places to Live?

Question: Why didn't the Aboriginals explore the world like my European Forebears did? Answer they were waiting 60 thousand years for the water around Australia to go down before they set off.

You have the United Arab's union, College Fund. You have Invasion Day. You Have Yom Hashoah, You have Ma'uled Al-Nabi. If we had White Entertainment Television, We'd be racists.

If we had White Pride Day.. You would call usRacists.

If we had White History Month, Racists.

If we had any organization for whites to advance OUR lifes. We'd be racists.

If we had a College fund that only gave white Students scholarships…..You know we'd be racists.

"White colleges". That would be racist.

Your allowed to march for Your rights. If We march for Race and rights we are called racists.

You are proud to be black, brown or bringle, your not afraid to announce it. But when we announce our White Pride . You call us racists.

You rob us, break into our homes, even shoot. But, when a white police officer shoots a Muslim gang member or beats up a Lebonese Drug-dealer and Rapist when running away and a threat to Society, You call him a racist.

I am proud.

But, you call me a racist.

Why is it that only Whites can be racist?

There is nothing improper about this message.

Lets see which of you are proud enough to circulate it.

Challis had seen plenty of these things over the years. He was more interested in tracking the e-mail. According to the printout, it had been forwarded to Lachlan by his brother, Dirk, who had asked him to forward it to others. Challis put it together: Dirk hears that Lachlan has been assaulted and races around to the Villanova apartments to get rid of compromising material before the police can mount a thorough search. He has just enough time to delete the white-pride e-mail from the in-box of Lachlan's laptop, and again from the list of deleted items, but Lachlan had forwarded the offending e-mail to various people and Dirk hadn't had time to remove it from the 'sent items' box.

Challis pored over the message again, tracking its history.

Originating from *smilingeyes* with a hotmail address, it had been forwarded to four people: *aquapac*, *homefries* and *reddog*, who had netspace, optusnet and hotmail accounts respectively…

…and *sutton.s@police.vic.gov.au*.

Challis breathed in and out. It didn't mean that Scobie was a racist, or welcomed getting racist messages: he might simply have given his e-mail address to the wrong person. Challis continued to scan the printout. Red Dog, bless him, or her, had forwarded the e-mail to about thirty people. What had those thirty—the Lang Family, kathk67, wayneheidi, Elissa Devereaux at the defence department, and dirkroe, amongst others—done with it? Deleted it in disgust? Read it and nodded sagely? Relished the hate and passed it on? Clearly Dirk Roe had forwarded it to Lachlan, and Lachlan to people in his address book. Following a cyber trail like this would be a nightmare. Challis was hoping that finding Roe's attacker would prove to be simpler than that.

Meanwhile, what else had Dirk deleted from Lachlan's computer? Challis returned to the desktop screen and clicked on Recycle Bin. It was empty. He entered Internet Explorer and clicked on 'Favorites', finding Microsoft, the Commonwealth Bank, eBay and numerous expected sites, but also links to 'useful counselling sites' and 'Dirk's Blog'. Challis clicked on the former: it took him to a movie site called 'LolitaClips'. He clicked on the latter and found himself at a blog called 'The Roe Report' and the strange, ugly world of Dirk Roe.

Roe had plenty to say on many topics, none of it enlightened. For example, there was his take on education. While in favour of the Prime Minister's desire for more Australian History to be taught at school, Dirk believed that 60,000 years of Aboriginal History could be squeezed into one lesson. 'As is well known,' he wrote, 'your typical aboriginal historical site is a mound of rubbish. Let's be honest here, aboriginals and success hardly go hand in hand. This fact, although racist to some, is a fact nevertheless, and must be faced.'

Something had to be done about the employment of Indian

doctors, too, Dirk argued. He was very clear about that. What was less clear was why. Challis tried to unpick the incoherent thoughts: Roe seemed to be saying that Indian doctors were physically repellent or poorly trained or Islamic terrorists, or all three.

He read on. A lot of it was innocuous and undirected doodling by Dirk: football tipping, speculations about the sex lives of Labor parliamentarians, praise for his boss, Ollie Hindmarsh, a belief that the United Nations was corrupt, and his personal list of the best fifty albums released since 1 January 2001 (no jazz, no classical). Challis was mildly disappointed to see that Mark Knopfler and Emmylou Harris's *All the Roadrunning* wasn't listed.

Dirk also invited his readers to post their replies. These were archived, and Challis scrolled through for a while. He found some echoes with the White Pride e-mail, reinforcing his sense of how extensive, subterranean and interconnected racism was. Scratch your neighbour's back, he thought, and uncover a bigot.

Like the Macclesfield Cricket Club member who had posted his thoughts to The Roe Report on being obliged to play cricket against a Jewish team. 'Being of German origin, I have to apologise that these Yids are in existence at all. My grandfathers did their best during the war but must have missed a few.'

To which Dirk Roe responded: 'Pity: now they control all the world's banking and trade.'

With a follow up from Lachlan Roe: 'And they undermine the Christian faith.'

Feeling grubby and sour, Challis shut down the computer. He propped his feet on the edge of his desk and stared out at the sky above Waterloo. Some scraps of cloud had moved in. Nothing much surprised him any more. He wasn't even astonished that Dirk Roe had been so stupid as to put his name to the blog, there were other cases of young Liberal Party wannabes posting their views on the Web. They'd soon been outed by the press and party officials, but Challis knew there must be others who were cannier, more guarded.

37

Meanwhile, how was he going to play this? It was his firm belief that most violent crimes were straightforward: you looked for the simple answer first. Yes, you gathered evidence, but mainly you asked who hated the victim, and why. Concentrate on the victim, then trace, interview and eliminate all witnesses, friends, enemies and acquaintances, and hope you end up with an individual who cannot be eliminated.

But if Lachlan Roe's assailant was somehow linked to the White Pride e-mail, or Dirk Roe's blog, the list of people to be investigated was huge. And what approach would work? A knock on the door, an invitation to come into the station for a chat? Or quiet infiltration, to tease out the embittered, the jaded, the jealous, the crazy, the wronged and the aggrieved?

Challis marked Scobie Sutton's e-mail address with a green highlighter, then picked up the phone. 'Scobie? I need to see you. Now, please.'

8

Ellen Destry drove to the Landseer School in the car pool's new Camry, not wanting to spend another minute in one of its tired, uncomfortable, plasticky, poorly engineered and odiferous Falcons. She glided across the Peninsula, passing boutique vineyards, shrinking orchards, riding stables and paddocks that had been pegged out for new housing or landscaped to death with stone walls, ponds, terraced gardens and the vast mansions of local plumbers and Melbourne embezzlers.

All that money, she thought angrily, and no taste at all. As a copper, of course, you had to approach things with an open mind. But that didn't alter the fact that some people were bad and evil, others ugly, stupid and tasteless, full stop.

Finally the road went up and over a line of hills, offering a sweeping view of Port Phillip Bay before delivering her to the Nepean Highway and then to a stretch of vines between the highway and the bay. Two stone pillars announced The Landseer School, and inside the fenced vines was a further sign, Landseer School Viticulture Program. Ellen followed a well-kept dirt road between arching pines, coming to a mock castle and a scattering of other school buildings in a setting of manicured lawns and garden beds.

She glanced at her watch: 10.30 a.m. A couple of gardeners were about, but no kids, not even on the playing fields, which were vividly green, contrasting with the brilliant white of the goalposts, hurdles, line markers and fence rails. There was money here, too. And maybe even some intellect.

Ellen parked between a black BMW and a white Land Rover and climbed the worn stone steps of the main building, where she crossed a tiled verandah and pushed through heavy wooden doors to the reception desk. At one time the area would have been open and cavernous, but was now divided and subdivided into corridors and offices with low ceilings. There was still plenty of old wood panelling about, however, and the air smelt pleasantly of furniture polish. One wall was dense with photographs: the school in 1913, the first Landseer Pinot Noir bottling in 1985, the Year 12 Debating Championship team in 1962. A couple of past headmasters.

Then a woman with a professional smile spoke from behind a waist-high counter. 'May I help you?'

Two minutes later, Ellen had signed the visitors' book, clipped a name tag to her lapel, and was being escorted through a wing of the building to a massive oak door, a discreet sign on it reading 'Headmaster'. Not 'Principal'. What happens if they employ a woman? Ellen wondered. Perhaps the Landseer School wouldn't dream of employing a woman to head it. Her suspicions were oddly confirmed when the headmaster greeted her in an English accent slightly plummier than Prince Charles's. And here she'd been thinking that the cultural cringe was dead.

'A terrible business,' Thomas Ashby said. 'Unconscionable. We're deeply shocked.'

Ellen regarded him carefully. It was possible that he meant it. Ashby was lanky, dark-haired, expensively suited, faintly indifferent and impatient but too well-mannered to display it. It was possible that he didn't welcome the publicity, hated women or found police attention grubby—or tick all of the above.

'I'll need to examine Mr Roe's office,' she said.

He inclined his head gravely. 'And so you shall.'

I bet he's had someone go through it with a nit comb, thought Ellen. 'But first some background on his job here.'

'His *job*? His job was school chaplain.'

'I'm aware of that, but—'

'This involved mentoring, crisis counselling and guidance in values and spiritual matters. And some religious instruction, but only in the context of, say, an English or History lesson. We are non-denominational here at Landseer.'

'I see.'

'Do you?'

'Did he have any enemies in the school community? Staff or students?'

'Of course not.'

'Didn't rub anyone up the wrong way with the "values" he imparted?'

Ashby glanced at his watch. 'I have another appointment. My deputy will show you around.' He lifted the phone on his desk and pressed a button. 'Kindly ask Mrs Moorhouse to come to my office.' He replaced the phone, got to his feet, buttoned his suit coat and came around the side of his desk, one hand out in the unmistakeable intention of guiding Ellen out by the elbow or the small of her back. She dodged him neatly, entered the corridor and heard the costly click of his door sealing him in with the leather, the book spines, the gleaming walnut and the glorious sea views.

Ellen hovered: was she to wait for the deputy principal, or return to the reception desk? There was the snap of shoe leather and a small, round, short-haired woman appeared. Another irritated person of importance, thought Ellen, taking one look at the deputy head's grim mouth and air of purpose. She decided to take charge.

'Mrs Moorhouse? Sergeant Destry from the Crime Investigation Unit. I'm here investigating a serious assault. The victim is your chaplain. I need full access to his office and files, and I may wish to interview staff and students who had anything to do with him in the past few days.'

The woman came to a halt, heaved a sigh, gestured loosely with one hand. 'Yes, I am aware this is serious business. We've already had Ollie Hindmarsh on the line this morning.'

Ellen went very still. This smacked of interference. Of information being controlled, delayed or withheld. 'What did he say?'

Moorhouse regarded Ellen for a moment. Then, as if satisfied, she said, 'What he said was doublespeak. He's a politician, after all. What he *meant* was he didn't want any shit to stick to him or to the school.'

Ellen grinned. It was possible that Moorhouse was the real driving force behind Landseer but destined to remain unacknowledged and never promoted to the top job. 'It's not my intention to ride roughshod over anyone.'

The deputy head said elliptically, 'Riding roughshod might be the best thing. Follow me.'

They passed through endless dim corridors, Moorhouse asking, 'What happened, can you tell me?'

Ellen outlined the circumstances, concluding, 'But Mr Roe's still in a coma. It was a pretty vicious assault.'

'Oh dear,' Moorhouse said without feeling. 'Any brain damage? Not that you could tell, necessarily.'

Ellen snorted. 'I take it you didn't like the man.'

Moorhouse powered on through the corridors, leading Ellen past anonymous offices and up and down bewildering short hallways and staircases. 'Oh, put it down to sour grapes. I have a psychology degree and specialist training as a counsellor, in addition to my teaching credentials. I've counselled kids for years. Why do we need a chaplain?'

Ellen said lightly, 'So you bashed Mr Roe over the head out of professional jealousy.'

Moorhouse snorted, 'I wish.'

She stopped at a flimsy door, a sign on the wall reading: *School Chaplain*. 'Mind you,' she said, 'I did shove him away in a forgotten corner.'

She unlocked the door and stood aside. 'Take your time. I'll be in my office next to the reception desk.'

'Wait.' Ellen touched the woman's upper arm fleetingly. 'Can you give me a few more minutes?'

'Of course.'

There were two chairs in the dismal office. Moorhouse took the straight-back chair, Ellen the squeaky swivel chair behind the desk. Opening her notebook, Ellen said, 'Tell me about Mr Roe.'

The deputy head stared at the wall, appearing to weigh up her words, so that Ellen was afraid the earlier frankness would be replaced by spin, but then Moorhouse said, 'First, I don't hold with the government supporting a chaplaincy scheme, not when there are experienced counsellors available. I believe in the strict separation of church and state.'

'This is a *private* school,' Ellen pointed out.

'No matter. I believe in a secular education. It protects kids from dogma and superstition. It prioritises rational inquiry, which usually flies out the window when the God-botherers get involved.'

'Mmm,' said Ellen, 'but what does this have to do with Lachlan Roe?'

'Oh look,' Moorhouse grimaced apologetically, holding up a finger, 'it's possible that many chaplains are able to forget their religious ties and training and give helpful, neutral advice. But not Roe.'

'He preached? Gave bad advice?'

'Both.'

'How on earth would a man like that be appointed school chaplain?'

'It's hardly a system where quality control matters,' said Moorhouse sourly. 'Lachlan's brother works for Ollie Hindmarsh, and Ollie Hindmarsh's children went to Landseer, and Ollie Hindmarsh championed the chaplaincy scheme, and Ollie Hindmarsh is on the school council.'

'Ah.'

'No talent required.'

'What do the kids think of Mr Roe?'

'They're not stupid: they think he's a joke.'

Ellen had been searching the chaplain's desk as they talked, finding stationery items, a lump of chewing gum and an empty bottle of vodka. And a diary.

'But some of them do make appointments to see him,' she said, spinning the diary around, her forefinger stabbing the name Zara Selkirk. 'This kid. Yesterday afternoon.'

Moorhouse peered at the entry. Something in her face shut down. 'Oh.'

'I'll need to speak to her,' Ellen said.

'I don't believe she's in today,' Moorhouse said.

9

Ludmilla Wishart finished a morning's work in her office at Planning East, then drove to Penzance Beach, a secluded holiday town several kilometres around the coast from Waterloo. She was relieved to be out and about, away from both the hovering of her boss and her husband's suspicions. Adrian had phoned her several times, saying, 'Just checking in, darling' and 'What shall we have for dinner?' and 'Keep your receipts if you use the Golf today.' He needed to know where she was and what she was doing. He'll phone again, she thought, and someone in the office will tell him I'm out, and he'll stew on it. Her heart fluttered. She didn't know how much longer she could go on like this. But you don't just walk out on a marriage, do you?

Ludmilla parked her Golf outside a beach shack on Bluff Road and knocked on the screen door. A hazy shape appeared. 'Mill! Good or bad news?'

'Good news, Carl.'

She stepped back to let him out. Carl Vernon was in his sixties, whiskery, gnarled and appealingly untidy in shorts, sandals and black-rimmed glasses. 'The Trust came through for us?'

Ludmilla showed him a fax. It said that the property known as 'Somerland', on Bluff Road in Penzance Beach, had been classified by the National Trust as a building of historical importance. He gave her an exuberant hug. 'Mill, that's fantastic.'

The grey-haired man and the young woman stood side-by-side and gazed across to the exclusive seaward side of Bluff Road, which ran along the top of a cliff overlooking the township and the sea. Somerland was a small fisherman's cottage dating from the early years of the twentieth century. In profile it had a nineteenth-century style sawtooth roofline, with a verandah, a crooked chimney and a paling fence. Nestled amid ti-trees and pines, it was the best-situated house in Penzance Beach, with glorious views of the curving sand, the breakwaters fingering the little bay, the yachts puddling about in the stretch of water between the town and Phillip Island.

Carl himself enjoyed only a small slice of that view, over Somerland's low roof and between one wall and a clump of ti-trees, for he lived on the wrong side of Bluff Road, the humble fibro shack side. But that didn't matter. What mattered was that he and his neighbours lived increasingly in the shadows of the vast, prideful glass and concrete structures to the left and right of Somerland, places that were written up in *Architectural Digest* but didn't pretend to be homes. Carl and his neighbours didn't want another monstrosity to go up, and they especially didn't want the old fisherman's cottage to be pulled down.

And Somerland had certainly been under threat. There were two plastic-sleeved notices tacked to stakes at the driveway entrance: a demolition permit dating from May, and a more recent application to build a mansion that would out-monster all of the others. All moot now: using her influence and knowledge, together with the help and drive of Penzance Beach locals like Carl Vernon, Ludmilla had succeeded in convincing the National Trust to classify the old house.

'The next step is an emergency application for heritage protection from the planning minister,' she told Vernon. 'I've already set that in motion.'

They gazed at Somerland. It dreamed under the silent pines as if it had taken root there, merging naturally with the soil, the trees and the sky. It might have gone unrecognised and been demolished if Carl

Vernon hadn't decided to keep mentally active in his retirement years by writing a history of Penzance Beach. According to his research, Somerland had been built by the town's founder and remained in the descendants' hands until last year, when the elderly owner died.

Carl gave Ludmilla another hug. Insects snapped in the trees and the perfumed air. Somewhere a radio played in a back yard. A child dressed in a faded yellow skirt and pink T-shirt came banging out of the house next door, grabbed a tricycle and buzzed around on it. 'Hi, Mr Vernon!' she called.

Vernon waved. 'Hi, Holly.'

Holly disappeared around the side of the house to the back yard. 'I thought only leathery old retirees lived up here,' Ludmilla murmured.

Vernon noted the hint of teasing, mostly because it was so rare. 'I represent that remark!'

She smiled gloriously, just as a small red car crept into view on Bluff Road. A Citroën diesel, a costly, pert little thing. Ludmilla Wishart groaned and swayed. Alarmed, Vernon placed his arm around her. 'Mill?'

She recovered. 'It's nothing.'

His arm was still supporting her. She shrugged it off and put some distance between them while the Citroën seemed to speed up a little, as though it knew where it was going now. It swept into the kerb, tyres scratching up dust, and a man got out. He was about thirty, wearing a white cotton shirt over dark blue cargo pants and deck shoes. His face as he came storming up to Carl's verandah was in a rictus of fury, waves of strong emotion rolling off him, barely contained.

'Ludmilla,' he said, and Carl thought how apt was the phrase 'through gritted teeth'.

'Please, Adrian,' Ludmilla said.

The guy turned to Carl, switched on a big smile and shot out his hand. 'And you are?'

Vernon hadn't been a teacher for nothing. 'No, the question is: And *you* are?'

'Mr Vernon,' Ludmilla said tonelessly, 'this is my husband, Adrian. Darling, Mr Vernon is behind the campaign to save that old fisherman's cottage I was telling you about.'

She pointed. Adrian Wishart glanced across at Somerland without interest and back again, sizing up Vernon. 'Is that a fact.'

'I just came to let Mr Vernon know that it's been classified by the National Trust.'

'You drove all the way here to tell him?' Wishart said, still with that huge smile, using a reasonable voice. 'Could have phoned.'

Ludmilla went white and small. 'I mustn't keep you any longer, Mr Vernon.'

Vernon watched husband and wife leave his front yard, one flinching, the other as stiff and twisted as steel cable. He heard Ludmilla say, 'Please, Ade, you mustn't follow me, not when I'm working.'

'You think I followed you, darling? Certainly not. I have a client to see in the next street.'

Well, no one believed *that*, under the blue canopy of the sky.

10

'It's nothing to do with me,' Scobie Sutton said.

'Nothing to do with you? Scobie, that's your e-mail address—your *official police* e-mail address,' Challis said, stabbing the printout with his forefinger.

'Nothing to do with me.'

Sutton was like a sulky adolescent on the other side of Challis's desk, his bony limbs lost in the folds of his dark jacket and trousers. He wouldn't meet Challis's eye.

'You were the recipient of a racist e-mail. What if the press gets hold of this? What if Ethical Standards takes a long, hard look at you?'

'Nothing to do with me.'

Challis had also printed out the many pages of Dirk Roe's blog. He arranged them side by side where Sutton could read them. 'Your little pal is also responsible for *this* crap.'

'Boss,' pleaded Sutton, finally looking up, 'I don't sympathise with this stuff, honestly I don't.'

'Then how did the guy get your e-mail address?'

Sutton's gaze slid away. 'Beth,' he said desolately.

'Your wife? I'd have thought she'd be the last—'

'She's been unhappy,' said Sutton in a rush. He paused, searching for the words, flinching a little as a couple of officers passed by in the corridor, laughing about something. 'It hasn't been easy for her,' he continued. 'When she lost her job it really threw her. She's been out of work for ages and…She's depressed, boss.'

Challis folded his arms, grim in face and posture, inviting Sutton to get on with it.

Sutton complied hastily. '*Very* depressed. Thinks the world is a bad place and getting worse, only no one is listening to her. She feels very alone. You can imagine how that makes *me* feel.'

He waited for acknowledgment but Challis merely stared. He swallowed. 'She won't talk to me about it. Won't talk to our minister, either, or friends or family. In fact, she stopped going to our church and she doesn't have anything to do with any of the old crowd.'

Challis regarded him carefully. Sutton was a decent man, a churchgoer of the family-values kind. In Challis's experience, people like that were hesitant to extend their decency in certain directions. Towards gays, for example, or Muslims. Still, some sympathy was due. 'I take it that Beth found someone who would listen?' Challis said.

Sutton's face lit up. 'Exactly!'

'Dirk Roe?' Challis said doubtfully. He gestured over the array of printouts. 'The guy's a moron.'

'Not Dirk—Lachlan, the one who was attacked. He can be quite compelling.'

'I don't understand. He's a school chaplain.'

Sutton squirmed. 'He's a bit more than that.'

'I'm listening.'

'Well, Dirk and Lachlan were brought up in one of those big fundamentalist churches, the kind where you smile and clap hands for Jesus.'

Challis knew the kind. One of the smaller outfits—only 40,000 of them worldwide, and half of that number in Australia—liked to bankroll the election campaigns of conservative politicians and attack left leaning or green candidates. They were against voting, reading novels, wearing short pants, attending football matches, letting their kids go to university. Opposed to contraception, mobile phones and computers. Sad crackpots, he thought, but surprisingly powerful. Challis recalled dimly that Ollie Hindmarsh was one politician who gave an ear to those nuts. Sutton continued: 'Dirk drifted, but Lachlan grew even more devout and narrow and a couple of years ago he broke away to form his own congregation. The First Ascensionists, they're called.'

'And Beth has joined them?'

'Yes,' said Sutton with a strangled wail.

'How big are they?'

'Not very.'

'What do they believe in?'

Sutton shook his head in distress and bewilderment. 'They're very strict about a whole range of things, as you'd expect. They believe that you can avoid sin by avoiding non-believers, and that's why Beth avoids *me*. Also Lachlan has convinced everyone he's the direct spiritual descendant of Saint Paul and the only route to salvation. "I am the vessel," that's what he told me. He says that God will lift true Christians out of the world in a rapture. The rest will suffer a period of intense tribulation, then Christ will return to Jerusalem and rule for a thousand years before a final apocalyptic battle with evil.'

Challis felt his eyes glaze over. People believed this bullshit, it mattered to them. It mattered enough for cynical politicians to get close to people who spouted it.

'So you've talked to this bozo.'

Sutton tensed in his chair and said, 'I tried to talk to him about Beth.'

Challis went cold. 'Where were you last night, Scobie?'

Sutton jumped. 'At home with Roslyn.'

His twelve-year-old daughter. 'Where was your wife?'

'At the Chillout Zone, handing pamphlets to schoolies.'

Challis guessed that these alibis could be verified pretty easily. Meanwhile he was starting to wonder how many other Scobie Suttons were out there, men and women who had the inclination to harm Lachlan Roe for taking away their loved ones. 'Scobie, I'll ask again, did you assault him?'

Sutton was so appalled that Challis believed it. 'Me? How could you say that? How could you even think it?'

'All right, settle down. But you did try to talk to him about your wife. When was that?'

'A few weeks ago.'

'So Roe's a preacher, but how the hell did he become school chaplain at a place like Landseer?'

Sutton shrugged. 'The Ascensionists are pretty low profile. And respectable—doctors, teachers, local business people...'

'How does Dirk fit into all this?'

'He's less fanatical than Lachlan, but they *are* brothers,' Sutton said.

That wasn't what Challis meant. 'Maybe it suits these people for Lachlan to be based at that school, and Dirk in Ollie Hindmarsh's electoral office.'

Scobie Sutton looked all at sea. His take on the situation was small, personal and domestic, and here was his boss floating a conspiracy theory. 'Don't know, boss,' he muttered.

Challis jack-knifed forward. 'All right. So what are they doing with your e-mail address?'

'It's Beth. She's trying to get me to come across to the Ascensionists, and so now I keep getting all these awful e-mails.'

Challis shook his head slowly. 'Mate, you're in a pickle.'

Scobie Sutton began to weep. 'I'm at my wits' end.'

'What I don't understand is why you called Dirk to the scene this morning.'

Scobie was mildly astonished. 'But his brother was hurt. Naturally he'd want to help him.'

Challis breathed in and out. God save him from good people. 'Scobie, I hope you can see that I can't have you working this case.

Your judgment is shot, and you're a potential suspect.'

'Boss, please.'

'We've plenty of other cases that need attention.'

'Yeah, right, a serious spate of ride-on mower theft.'

'Constable,' Challis barked.

'Sir. But sir, can't I continue the doorknock, work on the periphery?'

'No. I can't rely on you to be neutral and alert. And cancel that e-mail address, get yourself another one.'

'Boss,' said Sutton miserably.

'What happens to the congregation if Lachlan dies?'

Scobie blinked and said 'Don't know,' but his gaze also flickered, indicating that he'd thought about it. Challis read his mind. Scobie hoped that Lachlan would die so that the Ascensionists would fall apart and he'd get his wife back. He felt guilty about that desire—but not too guilty.

'I mean it, Scobie. You stay out of this.'

'Boss.'

By now it was noon. Challis called Ellen Destry at the Landseer School and told her about finding the White Pride e-mail and Dirk Roe's blog. 'Couple of sweethearts, the Roe brothers,' he said.

'That concurs with what I'm finding here,' Ellen replied. 'I'm still interviewing but the feedback's pretty consistent: Lachlan Roe was loathed by pretty much everyone. The kids who *did* go to see him said he didn't give guidance or advice, just made them get down on their knees and pray for forgiveness—when he wasn't making sexual innuendoes, that is. The staff are convinced he was hired to please Ollie Hindmarsh. Do you think Hindmarsh knows what the guy was like?'

'I guess we'll find out soon enough. Briefing in the pub at six o'clock?'

'Count me in.'

Challis mused for a while on the notion of blogs, Dirk Roe's in particular. What had happened to privacy? Dignity, restraint—none of that had meaning to the cyberspace generation. Anyone could run a blog, every half-baked, boring or vicious thought, feeling or grievance out there for all to see. Maybe you don't feel the normal human restraints of self-consciousness and embarrassment sitting alone at a keyboard in a dark corner. Maybe it all seems instantaneous, ephemeral. But their words could come back to bite them and anyone associated with them.

Like Ollie Hindmarsh, thought Challis with a grin.

He checked with the hospital, learned that Dirk was still at his brother's bedside, and headed there in his rattly Triumph.

'No change?'

'None,' said Dirk, sounding like a man oddly pleased to find himself at centre stage for a while.

Challis decided to wipe the smug look from the young man's face. 'This material,' he said, 'originating from you, was found on your brother's computer.'

One by one he dropped the printouts into Roe's lap. Roe grew panicky, first recoiling as if he'd been soiled, then scrunching the pages together.

'Go ahead,' Challis said, 'I've made copies.'

'Please.'

'Please what?'

'I can explain.'

Dirk was young, soft-looking, still unformed. As if he had no character traits, only impulses. 'So, explain,' said Challis.

'It doesn't mean anything. It's only a joke.'

'Not everyone would think so.'

'I shut down the blog this morning, honest.'

'How long has it been running?'

'Only a month.'

'Long enough to offend people.'

Roe tried to muster principles and dignity in the antiseptic air. 'Look, I was expressing a few home truths, that's all—nothing wrong with that.'

'Did you receive any threats in return?'

'No.'

'Angry posts to your blog, phone calls, letters, knocks on the door?'

'Nothing like that.'

'How involved was Lachlan?'

They both looked at the blanched, wasted face of the brother. 'Not very.'

'I saw at least one post from him on your blog.'

Dirk shrugged his soft, round shoulders. 'Now and then, when he had something important to add.'

'Important,' said Challis, his face, voice and eyes as flat and hard as stones. 'This e-mail—'

'I didn't write it! It was sent to me!'

'But you forwarded it to dozens of others.'

Roe slumped. His face under the gelled spikes was pink and rounded, like a boy's. Sweat beaded his upper lip and forehead. 'Leave me alone. I didn't do anything.'

'Where were you last night?'

'Kaos, in Frankston, ask anybody.'

Kaos was a club where twenty-somethings like Dirk Roe ruined their livers and eardrums. It also had excellent camera surveillance of the dance floors, bars and inner and outer doors. 'What time did you get home?'

Dirk shifted. 'I went home with someone, stayed the night.'

'I'll need name, address and phone number.'

'Whatever.'

'Your parents. They were strict, weren't they?' said Challis, guessing.

Dirk's jaw dropped. 'How did you know?'

'Strict, devout, everything regimented…'

Roe shifted in his seat. 'I don't see what…'

'Did your father beat you and your brother?'

Challis saw from Roe's face that it was true. 'What about your mother?'

'They were strict, so what?'

'What did you and your brother fall out over?'

'Fall out? Who told you that? Over what?'

Challis shrugged. 'His new church. The fact that he had a following. The fact that he's older and more successful.'

'I'm successful.'

Challis always looked for the chinks and opened them up. 'You're a jumped-up office manager.'

'Yeah—for the Leader of the Opposition, who gave you a hard time on the phone this morning.'

'Who would sack you in a heartbeat if he knew about your blog.'

At least, Challis hoped that were true. There were men and women in Hindmarsh's party who would probably like to adopt it as the official party position.

'Please, I closed it down.'

Challis shook his head wearily. 'You didn't think, did you?' he said as he left the room and returned to the station.

11

Tankard's and Cree's first call-out after the Lachlan Roe assault scene was a suspicious car in Somerville. 'The Hoon Hotline called it in,' said the dispatcher.

'Wow,' said Cree. 'A car parked across some old biddy's driveway, driver and passenger asleep inside. I mean, can I stand the excitement?'

'They could be casing the joint,' Tank said, replacing the handset and settling back in the passenger seat of the divisional van.

'What's this Hoon Hotline anyway?'

Tank decided not to let Cree get to him. 'The guys in Traffic Management set it up. We had hoons running riot every night. Speeding, drag racing, burnouts, generally terrorising everyone. Now all the locals have to do is call the hotline. We show up and lay down the law, on-the-spot fines, driving charges. Confiscate the car sometimes,' he said. 'It works.'

The Somerville address was a cul-de-sac. They found a red Holden SS Crewman parked across the driveway of number 7, the tattooed and shaven-headed driver and passenger asleep or stoned. Tank called in the plate number, listened, and beamed at Cree. The vehicle was stolen.

The cameras, mobile phones and laptops inside it proved to be stolen, too. You have to laugh sometimes, thought Tank as he made the arrests. In his experience, most criminals were like the guys in the red Crewman: complete morons. They thought they could lose the police helicopter if they drove faster. They'd cruise around with a broken taillight, and a dead body or a kilo of heroin in the boot. They'd assume the police surrounding their house at 5 a.m. would go away if they ignored the doorbell. They didn't seem to understand that there were good reasons why the family next door owned a plasma TV and they didn't; or that actions had consequences.

'I wonder how their minds work sometimes,' he said, as he and Cree returned to Waterloo and booked the hungover duo.

Cree gave him a cryptic look and smile. 'Exactly.'

Stopping for coffee in the canteen they saw Pam Murphy in the distance, sitting with other female officers. Cree said over the steam from his cup, 'You ever noticed how this joint's crawling with women?'

'Not really.'

'How to get ahead in the Victoria Police,' Cree said, watching him. 'Grow a pair of tits.'

Suspecting a trap, Tankard ignored the remark. He knew he could be a bit of a dinosaur, but the women he worked with—his old partner Murph, bosses like Ellen Destry—they'd earned some respect over the years.

Maybe all Cree saw was the dinosaur? Tank sighed. The day stretched miserably ahead. At least I'm not scared of the dark, he thought.

They were scarcely out of the station, Cree driving again, when the dispatcher directed them to a disturbance at the Benton Square shopping centre on the other side of the Peninsula.

'Yeah, that makes sense,' Cree said, 'sending Waterloo cops to fight crime in Mornington. The Mornington boys are sent to Waterloo, I suppose.'

Tank continued to ignore him, but the guy had a point. Police resources hadn't kept pace with change on the Peninsula. The population levels had soared, but not police staffing levels or budgets. The result was abysmal response times, with some minor crimes like burglaries attended to days late or not at all, and no money to buy, maintain or upgrade equipment. You couldn't even go to the supply room and expect to find a ballpoint pen or a set of batteries for a crime scene camera. The twelve detectives stationed at Rosebud and Mornington had the use of only two unmarked cars between them, complicated by the fact that each shift employed four or five detectives, each working his or her own caseload, or needing to attend court. No wonder follow-up visits, surveillance and evidence-gathering suffered. Tank, eyes closed, let the mild spring sunshine warm him through the glass.

But Cree never shut up for long. 'Mickey Mouse policing.'

Tank opened his eyes. In profile, Cree's features were perfectly proportioned, probably heart-stopping to the women. 'Not like the big city, right?'

'You said it.'

Tank slumped gloomily against his door, missing Pam Murphy. But it was early days. Maybe Cree's larrikin grin would grow on him. Maybe the guy would pull his finger out. Not that Tank himself was the kind of copper to go above and beyond the call of duty, but at ten minutes to knockoff yesterday afternoon Cree had refused to book a guy for public drunkenness, saying the paperwork would eat into their leisure time. Tank didn't want to get into the habit of letting his new partner take shortcuts like that.

He directed Cree off the Peninsula freeway and east toward Mount Martha, through farmland that was being gobbled up by housing estates, all of the new houses breathing over each other, robbing the air, breeding domestic misery and truancy. Like the kids who terrorised shoppers at Benton Square. This wasn't the first time Tank had encountered them. They roamed in packs and liked to surround drivers attempting to enter or leave the carpark. Anyone who remonstrated was punched and abused or had their headlights smashed.

Tank wound his window down as Cree steered into the shopping centre. He could hear shouting. 'There,' he said, pointing.

A clump of people, some of them shaking fists and pushing and shoving each other near a car that had stalled at an awkward angle, one wheel up on the kerb outside the plate glass window of a bakery. An elderly man sat on the kerb nearby, holding his head in his hands.

Cree braked sharply and piled out, pushing through, sending bystanders reeling. Tank followed; he was a big man, overweight, and getting in and out of the divisional van always slowed him down. He elbowed his way to where two men held a teenage boy to the ground, one on his legs, the other on his shoulders.

'Okay,' Cree shouted, 'what gives?'

His right hand was on the holster of his .38 revolver. His mobile phone was in his left. Jesus, Tank thought, and nudged him aside.

'Thank you, gentlemen, we'll take it from here.'

'The little bastard almost caused an accident,' said one of the men. 'We made a citizens' arrest.'

'Yeah,' said the other man.

The people milling about them shouted, 'Doing your job for you,' amongst other things.

Then a woman came barrelling through, screaming, 'I'll have the lot of you up for assaulting my boy.'

Tank closed his eyes. The paperwork when all of this was sorted would take hours. With any luck, no one would press charges. With any luck, the boy would get a fright, start attending school again, become a model citizen.

And so the morning progressed. Next up was a broken shop window back in Waterloo. Apparently a nineteen-year-old had been ejected from the Waterloo Arms the previous night and taken it out on the neighbouring hairdressing salon. 'Go figure,' Tank murmured. The hairdresser was less sanguine. 'This is the third time in eighteen months, four grand each time to replace the glass, who's going to insure me now? Why the hell can't you patrol High Street regularly? Why can't you install CCTV?'

Good point, Tank thought, scribbling in his notebook while Cree chatted up a young redhead who was cutting an old woman's hair.

After that, a burglary in Penzance Beach, no signs of forced entry. 'It has me baffled,' the homeowner said. She was old, trembly, distressed.

It didn't baffle Tank for long. He took one look at the dog—a huge, ancient Labrador, and another at the big dog flap on the back door and informed Cree that the man they wanted was Ricky DaSilva.

'How do you know?'

'You'll see.'

Ricky DaSilva was tiny, no bigger than a child. They found him in the pub with the old woman's purse in his pocket. But was Cree impressed with Tank's deductive powers? All Cree said was, '*It has me quite baffled.*'

Instinct told Tank to bite his tongue. He knew that envy was making him exaggerate Andy Cree's faults. Envy, jealousy, *sexual* jealousy…

After lunch they were called to a domestic in the Seaview housing estate. They found a woman with a black eye and a bruised torso, revealed when she lifted the edge of her T-shirt. 'Me ex-husband done this,' she said. 'Coupla days ago. I want the bastard charged.'

There was a code of practice for these kinds of assaults. First they took the woman back to the station, where a doctor examined her. The next stage was a photographic record of her injuries, ideally in the presence of a senior female officer, but Destry and Murph were out, and no one else was available—same old story, the general and chronic shortage of staff at Waterloo. So they roped in a young female constable from Traffic and took the battered woman into the victim suite, where Cree set up a camera. 'We need to photograph your injuries,' Tank explained.

The woman gulped, nodded, and removed her T-shirt, revealing pillowy breasts inside a grimy bra and a pattern of old and new bruises. 'Not your usual look?' joked Cree, snapping away with the camera.

The young cop giggled. Cree grinned at her. The woman blushed and looked away. Oh, fuck, thought Tank, grabbing the camera. 'Andy, maybe you could take a coffee break, start the paperwork or something?'

'Whatever.'

When Cree had left the room, Tank took the young Traffic constable out into the corridor. 'She's a *victim*, okay? She's vulnerable. It's taken her a lot of courage to report this.'

Those words had been said to him, once upon a time. The constable looked at the floor. 'Sorry, Tank.'

'Enough said.'

They went back in and finished the job. Afterwards he told Cree: 'Look, pal, if you and I are going to spend time together, you might want to rethink your attitude.'

'What attitude?'

'Exactly,' Tank said.

Four o'clock in the afternoon. Pam Murphy had spotted Tank with that cute new guy but was too busy to chinwag with them. First she made her way down High Street to the foreshore, where the schoolies were already partying. A number of cars were parked facing the mangroves and the yacht basin, tailgates up, revealing mattresses and sleeping bags, surfboards and eskies full of beer and bourbon-and-cola cans. A few dome tents had been pitched nearby. Otherwise the scene was full of kids, most of them standing around blearily, holding bottles and cans, others standing on the roofs of their cars, dancing to the music that blared from competing sound systems. They were all having a bad hair day, and the guys hadn't shaved for some time. Guys and girls, they wore shorts, boardies, singlets or T-shirts, often over bathing suits. Most were in bare feet, grimy feet. These weren't the swimming, surfing or bike-riding schoolies, but, by the same token, they weren't overdosing, harassing the locals or fighting, either. Plenty of energy, though: the girls were on the lookout for a hot guy, the guys for a hot girl. Looking for love. Like everyone.

All kinds of regulations were being broken but Pam turned a blind eye. She wandered among the kids, introducing herself, handing out ID bracelets, informing them about the Chillout Zone, telling them to eat, drink plenty of water; advising them to stay in their own groups and look out for each other.

Then she wandered back up High Street. Many of the shoppers and shopkeepers knew her and nodded hello. There were schoolies here, too, in clumps and pairs strolling, window-shopping. Some of them knew her; some she'd helped. One group, clacking through the T-shirt racks outside HangTen went into a mock panic. 'Cool it, guys, ditch that ecstasy, hide the vodka, it's … *Schoolie Patrol*!'

'Very droll,' Pam said.

She lingered to chat with the kids. High Street was mild and docile under the springtime sun. Then a car pulled into the kerb, glossy red, a hot little Subaru—the kind of toy your well-heeled schoolie might drive, she thought enviously. She'd been known to buy the wrong kind of car and pay too much for it. She saw a young guy get out from behind the wheel, his girlfriend from the passenger seat, and saunter into HangTen as if they owned it.

A minute later, they came out, the guy looking royally pissed off.

Caz Moon, working one of the cash registers in HangTen, saw the red Subaru pull into the kerb. For just a moment then, everything clenched tightly inside her, but by the time Josh strolled in, holding the hand of a female version of himself, she had recovered.

Before she'd quite known she was going to do it, Caz called across the shop, 'Hello, Josh. Raped anyone yet?'

He was good-looking in that blond, vacant, mouth breathing,

never-had-to-think, -feel, -question-or-want-for-anything private school way. Right now he was staring about vaguely. Perhaps he was stoned, perhaps he hadn't heard her. 'Josh?' she said again, lifting her voice above the racks of brightly coloured scraps of cotton. 'Raped anyone so far this season?'

She rang up a sale, gave a kid her change. HangTen was pretty cool for Waterloo; had the right labels. The local kids liked to hang out there, occasionally buy a Billabong T-shirt or some Rip Curl board shorts. Not her scene, however.

She continued to stare at Josh. Finally he woke up. He looked at Caz, a dangerous flush settling over him. There were two other sales assistants, a handful of customers, and all were watching, waiting.

'How about it, Josh?' said Caz.

He didn't rise to it. Instead, he said, 'Fuck you,' and dragged the girlfriend out. She wore painted-on jeans and heels she couldn't manage. She wailed 'Joshua!' and he told her to shut up.

Caz smiled at her customers, shrugged, said 'Schoolies,' as if that answered everything.

When that young copper came in, wanting to know if there was anything wrong, Caz put on a brilliant smile and said, 'Not a thing.'

12

Late in the afternoon Challis's desk phone rang, the duty sergeant. 'Sir, Superintendent McQuarrie's here.'

Challis had been expecting this, or at least a summons to regional headquarters. 'Send him up.'

'He wants you to come down, sir.'

It was petty and needless, meaning that the super was summoning him and not the other way around. Challis trundled down the stairs, but backtracked before he reached the bottom, re-entering his office and grabbing the White Pride e-mail and the photocopied pages of the Roe Report.

As expected, the superintendent was in the ground floor conference room, a dim, quiet enclave that resembled a boardroom done up on the cheap. What was not expected was that McQuarrie hadn't come alone. He was standing with Ollie Hindmarsh.

'Inspector,' said McQuarrie, a small, tidy individual who always wore the look of a man who'd been adored, but only by his mother and long ago. He shook Challis's hand, then gestured at the politician. 'I'm sure you know Mr Hindmarsh.'

Challis nodded, reaching his hand to the Leader of the Opposition, who turned the shake into a brief contest of strength and said, 'In the interests of my electorate, including the school community and Mr

Roe's many friends, I thought it important to see at first hand how the investigation's going.'

Challis nodded gravely, intimating that he didn't believe a word of it. 'I understand.'

'Lachlan Roe is a very fine fellow. I don't want this swept under the rug.'

Challis regarded Hindmarsh carefully, wondering how to play it. The man was clearly attaching great importance to the case, coming all the way down to Waterloo when Parliament was in session. That was one thing. The other was that he'd apparently said 'jump' to McQuarrie and McQuarrie had jumped—maybe because Hindmarsh was notoriously critical of the police and the superintendent wanted to make a good impression. Would there come a point at which McQuarrie placed his officers ahead of pleasing a shithead like Hindmarsh?

'We're in the process of following several leads,' Challis said flatly.

'What does that mean, "in the process?" The processes of the Victoria Police don't withstand much scrutiny, in my opinion.'

Challis had sympathy with some of Hindmarsh's publicly expressed criticism of the police. Surely when you chose to be a police officer you were making a profoundly simple vow to yourself and the world to be one of the good guys? Challis knew all the arguments—that most police officers were honest and hardworking, but a handful were bound to burn out, err or act dishonestly because they were only human, the work was nasty enough to turn anyone's mind, and like all large organisations the force was open to nepotism and inefficiency—but he thought there was a limit to how far you could push that line. He was capable of turning a blind eye, even of tweaking legalities a little, so long as justice was served and no one got hurt, but he was beginning to believe that only a kind of cultural rottenness in the police force explained the growing instances of bullying, cronyism, sexism, racial thuggery, homophobia and resistance to change. Not to mention plain old criminal activity. Sure, Ollie Hindmarsh liked to use these instances to political advantage, but they were real, not beat-ups.

Not that Challis would ever say any of this. Wishing McQuarrie were not so gutless, he gazed steadily at Hindmarsh, fixing on the man's fierce, hooked face.

It was the face of an outraged but boozy prophet. Hindmarsh, big and barrelly, fifty years old and a womanising ex-league footballer and Army veteran, was an anachronism in a world of sleek lawyers and publicists. He'd been known to fiddle his expense account, assault reporters and photographers, and harass the young women who worked for him. A union basher, a hawk in military matters and suspicious of immigrants, he was the kind of stern father figure that most Australians—despite their veneer of cheery individualism and non-compliance—yearned for.

And there were plenty of men like Hindmarsh around. Challis met them from time to time, and had a pretty fair understanding of what formed them. They were often born into money, but not necessarily love and intimacy. They'd be sent to exclusive boys-only boarding schools which filled that void with a competitive and repressive masculinity, and where the few women they ever saw had teaching, nursing or servant roles. No wonder they went on to become aggressive and autocratic CEOs and politicians, driven to succeed but also aloof, insecure and blinkered.

Challis himself had had two encounters with Hindmarsh. He was sitting in a Qantas jet one Monday morning, about to fly to Sydney to extradite a woman wanted for murder, when Ollie boarded. He'd delayed taking his seat at the head of the plane and remained standing for several long minutes, so that everyone saw and recognised him. And during a charity dinner in the Waterloo town hall a month later, Challis had gone looking for the men's room in a warren of corridors and found Ollie screaming into the face of a waiter: 'Do you know who I am? I've half a mind to grab you and run you against a wall, you scumbag. You're an absolute joke.' Hindmarsh was red-faced, his veins popping, spittle flying. It seemed reasonable to assume that hotel staff, airport clerks and chauffeurs around the country had received the same treatment over the years.

The guy was also Mr Everywhere. Challis kept finding Ollie's publicity leaflets in his letterbox, two or three photographs of the man on every fold—turning a sod for another housing estate, singing to a roomful of pensioners, cutting a ribbon, introducing a chaplain to a school community.

'Perhaps we should sit, Mr Hindmarsh,' Challis said now, taking charge.

That threw both men for a moment, but Challis sat and they followed. Hindmarsh made an effort. 'Look, we're reasonable men here and—'

Challis cut him off. He dealt out the photocopied e-mail and blog pages one by one across the heavy table. 'This,' he said, 'is a provocative and racist e-mail forwarded to Lachlan Roe by his brother, Dirk. Lachlan then forwarded it to others.'

He glanced at Hindmarsh and McQuarrie. He had their attention. 'And these pages'—he stabbed them with a forefinger—'are taken from a blog called the Roe Report. It is viciously racist, to the extent that it breaches racial vilification statutes. Criminal charges may be laid. The material appears to have been written and posted by Dirk Roe, with contributions from Lachlan Roe. Dirk Roe is the manager of your electoral office, Mr Hindmarsh, am I correct?' Challis didn't give the man a chance to answer. 'And Lachlan Roe was appointed chaplain of Landseer with your support? One of my best detectives has spent the morning at the school. She assures me that Roe is deeply disliked there, by staff and students. I have also learned that Lachlan Roe heads a…fringe religious sect.'

Hindmarsh patted his thinning hair as though to reassure himself that some remained. He coughed. 'I happen to believe in the fundamental decency of his platform. The fact remains—'

Finally, McQuarrie stirred. 'The fact remains, Mr Hindmarsh, that you employed one racist and assisted another,' he said, his voice starting with a squeak but gaining in strength. 'One would like to see how *that* plays out in the media.'

'You little shit,' growled Hindmarsh. 'I've a good mind—'

Challis had never seen McQuarrie so firm and dignified. 'My officers and I are not vindictive. We don't play games. We don't play politics. It hardly needs to be said that Dirk Roe's blog is public property. There's a very good chance that members of the media already know about it.'

Hindmarsh opened and closed his mouth. 'Fucking Dirk, fucking stupid little…'

McQuarrie tipped back his chin. He didn't like the language. 'Will that be all?'

Hindmarsh nodded. He looked lost.

When the man was gone Challis said, 'Thanks, sir.'

But the honeymoon, if that's what it had been, was short-lived. The superintendent gestured dismissively, as if he'd forgotten Hindmarsh already, and said, 'Certain things have come to my attention.'

Ellen, thought Challis.

'Oh?'

'Are you…How do I put this…Are you and Sergeant Destry…?'

'In a relationship sir, yes.'

McQuarrie blinked. Some of the irritation faded. 'Hal…'

Challis waited.

'You *work* together, man.'

'Sir.'

'In the same unit, the same police station.'

'Sir.'

'Surely you see the pitfalls…'

'Yes, sir.'

'For a very good reason, there are regulations…'

'Sir.'

'Hell of a mess,' McQuarrie looked away, then back at Challis. 'You could be accused of undue influence. Of bias and favouritism. What do your colleagues think? Or the constables who have to answer to you both? And what happens if events in your "relationship" spill over into your day-to-day police work? It's not on, inspector.'

Challis had thought of all these things and more, but said nothing. There was something in McQuarrie's manner, if not his words, to indicate that the man wasn't being his usual autocratic, blowhard self. He was beginning to sense that McQuarrie wanted to find a palatable solution rather than punish or reprimand. It can't be that he's a *romantic*, Challis thought. No. Maybe he's developed a streak of humanity though—or vulnerability.

The super had a lot to thank Ellen Destry for, at any rate. When Challis had been away last month, she had uncovered a paedophile ring with links to the senior sergeant at this very police station, a man whom McQuarrie had entrusted to be his eyes and ears. That man was dead now, but only after murdering another policeman at Waterloo. It was evident at the time that McQuarrie hadn't believed Ellen was up to the job.

And he owes *me* a debt, thought Challis. I tracked down his daughter-in-law's killer.

He wants to do the right thing by us.

'For God's sake, Hal, is it serious? I mean, do you intend to marry?'

Challis wanted to laugh. 'Too soon to say, sir.'

McQuarrie shook his head and the late afternoon sunlight angled in, picking out dust motes in the air and streaks on the window glass. 'I've been giving it some thought, Hal.'

'Sir, I have, too, but it's all so recent and—'

'In the old days, one of you would have been posted to Outer Woop-Woop. It would have been nipped in the bud.'

Challis waited.

Suddenly the superintendent sprang to his feet. 'Leave it with me,' he said, and left the building.

13

It had been a long, dull Tuesday for Ellen Destry. By 4 p.m. she'd
finished questioning staff and students at Landseer and was driving
to the Mount Eliza home of Zara Selkirk, the Year 11 girl who'd been
Lachlan Roe's only appointment the previous day. Winding roads took
her to a couple of acres at the highest point of the town, to a house
and terraced grounds on a slope that faced south along a curve of Port
Phillip Bay. Here the hills folded in and out, giving an impression of
privacy to the people who could afford the land and the views.

Ellen parked and pressed the doorbell of a vast loft house, the roof
pitched at sixty degrees, two huge dormers above her head.

'Yeah?'

A girl, no more than fourteen years old; wearing the Toorak
uniform, not Landseer. Ellen introduced herself and said, 'Are you
Zara?'

'No.'

'But Zara lives here? Zara Selkirk?'

The girl shrugged.

'May I speak to her?'

After a second, or a year, the girl replied, 'She's not here.'

The little interrogation continued like that. Eventually Ellen
understood that the girl was Chelsea Hooper, Zara's stepsister.

Chelsea hated Zara, hated her stepmother. There were at least three reasons for that: one, the stepmother was an evil witch; two, the stepmother liked to fly to the snowfields of Europe and the States with Chelsea's father and leave the kids to flounder; three, the stepmother had taken Zara, but not Chelsea, to see Delta Goodrem perform in the city last night.

'We have an apartment in Southbank,' Chelsea explained.

Hating the rich, Ellen said, 'So Zara and her mother stayed in your city apartment last night rather than drive back here to Mount Eliza?'

Chelsea gave the question a great deal of thought. 'Yep.'

'When will they be back?'

Chelsea shrugged.

Ellen turned to go. Behind her the girl said, 'Is this about the chaplain?'

Ellen faced her again, tingling. 'You knew that Zara had an appointment to see him yesterday?'

'Yep.'

Ellen tried to tread delicately around this. 'Did Zara confide in you about why she wanted to see him?'

'*Wanted?* That's a laugh. She *had* to see him. It was part of her punishment.'

'Punishment.'

'Like that was going to work,' said Chelsea scornfully.

On the other side of the Peninsula, Josh Brownlee was drunk. He'd started drinking after that encounter in the surf shop, and hadn't stopped, except to do some ice. That little slag, shouting about rape so everyone could hear.

Who the fuck was she? Bitch.

As soon as he'd left the shop he'd ditched the chick he was with, dumped her back at her motel. A whiner. Too clingy. The type you screw once and then can't get rid of. Fuck that. Josh drove straight around to the beer garden of the Fiddlers Creek pub and got steadily wasted.

The afternoon had passed hazily by and now it was almost five o'clock. Why the fuck had he come back to Waterloo, this shit hole? Last year was different, a lot of shit happening, the Year 12 exams plus family shit, a lot to forget. Getting wasted with his mates had made sense. They couldn't afford the Gold Coast, but Luke's dad had a holiday house near Waterloo, which was better than nothing. Now it was like a year later, his mates had moved on and he was no longer a schoolie. In fact, he kept getting sideways glances from this year's schoolies. What are you doing here, loser? Did you have to repeat Year 12 at another school?

And this morning he gets called a rapist in public.

Josh thought back to last year, pissed the whole time, dope, ice and GHB. The sex. There'd been chicks from Grover Hall, St Helen's, Mount Eliza Girls' Grammar…that skank Virginia, any excuse to show her tits, the 'virgin' part of her name long redundant. Who else? That chick. Tori Walker. Walker the Stalker, from Banbury College, fuck her and she'd fall in love with you.

It hadn't taken Josh and the guys long to realise that it was better to hook up with the local slags, state school desperadoes from Waterloo and Two Bays secondary, hoping to snare themselves a rich private-school guy. Josh and his mates would do those dogs behind some secluded sand dune, bury their knickers in the sand, piss off out of there while they were too drunk or high to notice. Who were they going to complain to? They'd never seen you before, didn't know who you were or what school you went to.

It wasn't like that this year.

Josh kept drinking, becoming steadily blacker inside.

John Tankard, off duty now, was also sitting in the Fiddlers Creek beer garden. He gazed around at the patrons, wondering if he'd spot anyone he'd put away, and saw Josh Brownlee getting drunker and drunker. Schoolie prat, he thought idly. He turned to scowl at Andy Cree. It was Cree's turn to walk across to the veranda bar and bring back a round, but the guy was still glued to his mobile phone, checking messages, sending messages, his bony thumbs flying over the keypad. Furthermore, he was drinking chardonnay.

Wanker.

Just then Cree's senses registered the full malign force of John Tankard's scrutiny. He crooked an eyebrow. 'Got a problem?'

'Got a thirst,' Tank said.

Cree gave him the once-over and the message was plain: *You drink too much and it's made you fat*. But then he said, 'Check this out,' and passed Tank his mobile phone.

'Still got a thirst,' Tank said.

'Keep your panties on,' Cree said, getting to his feet and weaving away between the metal tables.

Tank turned his attention to the guy's phone, peering at the little screen: Christ, a digital image of a schoolie passed out on the lawn in front of the shire offices. Tank poked inexpertly at the keys, wondering what other photos Cree had taken, and came to a Holden he'd last seen wrapped around a tree two weeks ago. Then Cree was back with their drinks, saying in a mock, true-Aussie voice, 'Here you go, buddy, wrap your tonsils around this.'

'Fuck you.'

'Not on a first date, John.'

Tank knew it would be a mistake to respond. If it came to a battle of words, Cree would win.

Scobie Sutton went home knowing that he'd better talk to his wife about the wickedness of Dirk and Lachlan Roe. Beth was his special love, and she was his heartache. He knew the pain, bewilderment and sense of injustice that drove her, but didn't know how to make her feel better.

Beth felt things too keenly, that was the problem. She'd worked with the shire's disadvantaged families and kids for many years, and when she came home in the evenings would relate some of the awful things she'd seen or heard about, her voice low, tragic, desolate, insinuating itself into Scobie's head. Poor Ros: 'Mum!' she'd say, 'talk about something happy!'

And then a budget-conscious finance manager had sacked Beth, which really pulled the rug out from under her feet. Scobie suspected that she was deeply depressed—tinged with mania. Since last Friday she'd been fired up about saving the schoolies from sex and drugs, and had been seen at the Chillout Zone, distributing leaflets. Not from the Uniting Church—the Suttons' church—but the damn First Ascensionists.

Scobie was losing her, and he couldn't bear it.

Tossing his keys into a bowl on the little hallway table, he walked through to the kitchen and knew at once that the house was empty, the air was so stale and unlived in. He swallowed and searched the place anyway, sitting room, dining room, three bedrooms, carport and weedy front and back gardens, seeing, with new eyes, the neglect, the dust, the unwashed dishes, the unmade beds. He wanted his wife back.

Her desk was a card table in the spare bedroom. It was a loveless room, with a single bed, bare walls and a cheap white wardrobe. Beth's crackpot leaflets were stacked neatly with other literature on the coverlet of the bed and on the floor. The family's computer took up most of the desk. Beside it was a manila folder containing a stack of e-mails that Beth had printed out, and there at the very top Scobie saw the one that Challis had practically shaken in his face that morning. There were annotations in the margins, green ink, in Beth's big, childlike hand: *My darling husband, some important information for you to think about.*

Feeling an overflowing pool of sadness, Scobie knuckled his eyes. But crying didn't solve anything. He washed the dishes, made the beds, compiled a shopping list. Soon it was 5.30 p.m. Normally Roslyn was home from school by four, but she'd joined the choir and they were rehearsing for tomorrow night's school concert. She wouldn't be home before six. That gave him time to shop and have it out with his wife.

But would Beth even listen? That was the question.

Scobie drove to the supermarket, quietly fracturing inside. Last night when he'd kissed his daughter goodnight she'd clung to him, hadn't wanted to let go.

'I have bad dreams,' she said.

He'd nuzzled the crown of her head. 'What about?'

'Someone's going to let a bomb off on my bus.'

'Oh, sweetheart.'

He rocked her for a while, her flannel pyjamas faintly stale, reminding him that if he didn't do the laundry these days, it didn't get done.

'Dad?'

'Yes?'

'What if you get shot?'

'I won't get shot,' he said firmly. 'This isn't America. Hardly anyone owns a gun here.'

'But what if you do?'

He guessed what was going through her head. She was afraid of being alone if he died. Scobie felt a little resentful then. Hated his wife a little despite her pain and helplessness.

'Dad?'

'Yes, sweetheart?'

'You'll come to the concert?'

'Wouldn't miss it,' he said, knowing that if this year's concert was anything like last year's, some eleven-year-old guitarist was bound to play 'Smoke on the Water', a great song ruined forever.

'Will Mum?'

'She won't want to miss it either,' Scobie had told his daughter, wondering if that were a lie.

He relived this and other conversations as he wheeled a shopping trolley up and down the aisles of the supermarket. In particular, he relived the special hell of shopping for Roslyn's concert dress last Saturday, a task that should have fallen to Beth. What did he know about shopping for girls' clothes? He was none the wiser now, knowing only that his daughter belonged to a class of female for whom there were no suitable clothes. At twelve years old, with tiny, tiny breasts, she was too old for the kids' section of every store they entered. Too young surely for the truly appalling teen wear: micro skirts and tops that were mere scraps, the flimsy fabric barely extending from bellybutton to nipple. Eventually they bought a plain but pretty skirt and top in Myer and went home.

And another headache to look forward to: How was he supposed to help Roslyn with her first period?

He wheeled his shopping to the car, raised the tailgate, stowed it away. Then a kid was there, about Roslyn's age but years older in all other respects. A nuggetty kid from one of the estates. Full of nerve. 'Finished, mister?'

'You want to return my trolley and claim my hard-earned money from the coin slot,' said Scobie evenly.

The kid pantomimed guilt and embarrassment. 'You got me,' he said, slapping his hand against his forehead.

Scobie offered a smile he only half felt. 'Go on, then, take the blessed thing.'

The kid raced away with the trolley, shouting, 'Suckerrr!'

That's about right, Scobie thought. He drove home with his shopping and then he went in search of his wife.

By late afternoon the schoolies had drifted back from the surf beaches, the bike paths and walking tracks. They'd scrubbed themselves in the shower, pulled on clean outfits—jeans, T-shirts, mini-skirts, cargo pants—and were roaming through the town, looking young, healthy and almost appealing. Pam Murphy found them buying beer, trying on sunglasses, flipping through racks of CDs. They seemed to be taller than she remembered her generation being; fitter, blonder. They formed and reformed in clusters and their sounds were grunts, bursts of laughter, the liquid snap of chewing gum, the scuffling of bare feet and the heel slaps of their sandals. They seemed nice. They didn't seem very bright. They glanced at her photograph of Lachlan Roe and said they'd never seen him before.

Pam ranged widely through the streets, takeaway joints and pubs. She handed out identity bracelets, gave a teary kid a $20 bus fare, helped an old woman hose vomit away from the footpath in front of her house. Just as she got to the Fiddlers Creek carpark, John Tankard was leaving. He didn't see her. She went in, looking for schoolies, and found Andy Cree in the beer garden. He gave her a huge smile, face creasing, the kind that says 'only you', and although she didn't believe it for a minute, it was nice to be on the receiving end. 'Pull up a pew,' he said.

'I can't really stay long.'

But she sat, and he turned all of his attention to her, full wattage, so she lingered and sipped a lemon, lime and bitters for a while. 'White wine?' she said, raising an eyebrow at his glass.

'I'm trying the local wines one by one.'

It hadn't occurred to her before that anyone would want to do that. I've lived in the area for too long, she thought. I take it for granted. She gave another mental tick to Cree, along with those for his looks, body, ratbaggery, willingness to have a proper conversation and ability to make her laugh. 'Should keep you going for a while,' she said. 'What did Tank have? One of the local pinot noirs?'

It was Cree's turn to laugh, and she walked out of there with a date to look forward to.

She glanced at her watch. Time for Inspector Challis's end-of-day briefing. First she called in at the Chillout Zone, to tell the volunteers she'd be back that evening, and found Scobie Sutton in a corner with his wife. Beth Sutton seemed distressed, hands scraping down her cheeks, crying, 'No, it's not true.'

14

Challis got in the drinks and then Ellen told them the story of Zara Selkirk and the chaplain of Landseer.

'Punishment?' said Pam Murphy.

'Yes.'

Challis set down his glass. 'The stepsister told you this?'

'Yes.'

'But you haven't confirmed it with this Zara kid yet.'

'Hal,' Ellen said, 'she wasn't home.'

They were in the little side bar of a pub called the Two Bays, down from the yacht club and next to a maritime museum that consisted of a couple of anchors and a fishing net. The Two Bays was the main watering hole of the Waterloo police because it was favoured by yachting types and not the kinds of men, women and adolescents they'd arrested over the years—which didn't mean that the yachting types were not criminals, just that they were less likely to have a criminal record and break a beer bottle or billiard cue over the head of a police officer who'd wandered in for a quiet drink.

Challis was drinking Cascade lager, Ellen gin-and-tonic, Murph lemon squash. He'd stop at one drink. The others would, too. They'd all had experience of long drinking sessions when they were young, in which everyone was expected to buy a round of drinks and the fallout might be a breath test or an accident on the way home and the loss of a career. Or the breakdown of a marriage. Or poor job performance and a spreading waistline. Challis thought back to an early posting, a rural station where he was a sergeant and had lost his wife's regard to one of his colleagues. They'd all been heavy drinkers. It got incestuous. Eventually his wife and the colleague had lured him to a lonely back road to kill him. He'd been an impediment to their love or their lust and it was as if killing him was their only solution. If it hadn't been a drinking culture, would they have taken more civilised measures? The pair of them had been jailed. The guy was still behind bars. Challis's wife had taken her own life there.

He shook off the memory and said, too sharply, 'When will you question her?'

A flicker of emotion in Ellen's face. 'Tomorrow,' she said, after a pause.

Oh, hell, thought Challis. 'Sorry,' he said, drawing his palms down his cheeks. 'I had McQuarrie *and* Hindmarsh on my back this afternoon.'

'Hindmarsh?' asked Ellen, appalled.

'Sooner you than me, boss,' Murphy said.

Ellen gazed at him sympathetically. Behind her a large tinted window looked on to a little inlet and wharf where the fishing boats tied up. She said, 'Did you tell him about the e-mail and the blog?'

'You betcha.'

'Did it shut him up?'

'Yep.'

Pam Murphy was following the conversation with bewilderment. Challis showed her the printouts, watched her read them. 'Could be motive lurking here, boss.'

'Don't I know it. But let's go back to the Landseer connection first. Ells, could you go through it again?'

Ellen took a deep breath. 'A Year 11 kid called Zara Selkirk was Lachlan Roe's only appointment yesterday. When I learned that she wasn't at school today I went around to her house. Her stepsister, Chelsea, answered the door. She was alone: father in London on business, Zara and stepmother in town.' Ellen paused and looked at her colleagues with a bright, empty grin. 'Apparently Chelsea is often alone. We're talking about serious wealth and non-serious parenting here.'

Challis nodded. In his twenty years of police work he'd seen that the very wealthy were just as likely to overlook their kids as the very poor. At least the poor had reasons. He'd noticed something arid in the neglectful rich, even as they believed they had a creative side because they attended opera openings, a spiritual side because they were fond of their children, and an emotional side because they were always infuriated by someone or something. 'You'll need to confirm that Zara and her mother were up in the city last night.'

Ellen looked at him levelly and said, 'Of course.'

Challis winced again. 'Go on.'

'It's a long shot, but they might have wanted harm to come to the chaplain. Apparently Zara and two of her friends developed a hatred for the school librarian, Merle Richardson, and thought they'd try a little cyber bullying. They set up a fake Facebook site for Mrs Richardson in which she outlines her sexual fantasies and supplies a phone number and e-mail address. The poor woman had a breakdown.'

'The kids were found out?' Pam asked.

Ellen nodded. 'But not reported to police. They weren't even expelled or suspended.'

Challis wasn't surprised. The school wouldn't have wanted the publicity—and nor would the victim—and although cyber bullying was rife in schools and other institutions, the regulations and legal actions and penalties lagged far behind.

'Apparently young Zara is pretty bright,' Ellen continued, 'and did a couple of Year 12 exams this year. When it seemed that the school *might* take action against her, the mother charged down to the school and threatened to sue if Zara's exam performance suffered.'

'And they backed down,' Pam said.

'In a heartbeat. To hell with the reputation and mental and physical health of a member of staff—a wealthy parent always comes first. Bastards.'

They all felt the disgust, but Challis had to move on. 'How does the chaplain fit into all this?'

'It was decided that Zara would apologise to Mrs Richardson and he'd be the mediator.'

'All three were present?'

Ellen shook her head. 'Mrs Richardson took legal advice and didn't attend.'

'Good for her,' Challis said. He paused. 'But that raises the question: did *she* harm Roe? I can't see any of these people having a strong enough motive.'

'True,' Ellen said, draining her gin-and-tonic. 'The headmaster would make a better target.'

Challis nodded. 'See if he'll talk to you. Murph, your turn.'

'Nothing to report, boss. I've been showing Roe's photo to the schoolies, but no one recognises him. I'll keep doing it tonight.' Then she gazed at Challis and said pointedly, 'Has Scobie come up with anything?'

Challis gave her a wry look. She was wondering why Sutton wasn't at the briefing. 'I've taken him off the case.'

He outlined his reasons, backed up by the printouts of the e-mail and Dirk Roe's blog, which lay on the table between them.

'Let's see,' said Ellen.

She pored over the material. He liked the way her brow knotted when she concentrated, liked the shapeliness of her hands. His gaze swung to Pam Murphy's hands: stubbier, more squared off. He said, 'I questioned Dirk at the hospital this afternoon. He said he'd removed the blog from the Web.'

Ellen shook her head wearily. 'What is it about blogs? Why do people do it?'

Pam said, 'You old timers, you don't understand.'

'I understand they add to the meanness in the world,' Ellen said. 'They give inadequate people like Dirk Roe a chance to indulge their worst and weakest instincts. A thought pops into their heads and they think it's valid simply because they had it. Furthermore, blogs are free and don't require face-to-face contact with a fellow human being.'

Finding Pam staring at her, head on one side, Ellen went on hotly, 'If you knew what those Landseer girls did to that poor woman...'

Pam nodded. 'Fair enough, Sarge.'

Ellen cocked her head at Challis. 'Could Dirk have hurt his brother?'

'Not directly. His alibi checks out.'

'Paid someone to do it?'

'Anything's possible,' Challis said.

He told them about his afternoon, digging into the backgrounds of Lachlan and Dirk Roe. 'Raised in a fundamentalist church, a strict upbringing, spare the rod and spoil the child, plenty of guilt and repression, a familiar story.'

'Maybe,' said Ellen, 'but how did this one play out in particular?'

Challis told them about a conversation he'd had with an aunt. 'She was a member of the same church, married to the younger brother of Lachlan and Dirk's father. After she'd had a couple of kids she started to question things—and was kicked out. They won't even let her see her kids.' He held up his hands as if to forestall objections. 'True, she has an axe to grind, but one of the things that bothered her was the behaviour of Lachlan and Dirk, especially when they played with her children, who were younger. It was unhealthy, she said. Wrestling games, fondling and touching. She called them strange and repressed.'

They all absorbed that. Pam began to sift through the printouts of the Roe Report. 'Look at all these user-names: how are we going to track them all? Do we have to track them all, boss?'

'If necessary.'

'I thought CIU would be more glamorous, somehow.'

'What do you call this?' said Challis expansively.

'I call it pressure from above,' Pam said. 'Sir.'

Challis gave a mock glower. 'One good thing about pressure: I asked Hindmarsh to pressure the lab for a quick DNA result on that mucus on Lachlan Roe's sleeve.'

15

'I treasure this,' Ellen Destry said later, in the gentle twilight.

They'd driven home from the pub and now they were on foot, halfway up the hill behind the house.

'Walking with me?'

'Walking.' She snuggled against Challis briefly. 'And walking with you.'

If she didn't walk every day she felt sluggish, muscle-locked, unfit. She quite liked these evening walks, loved walking with Hal, but unspoken was the fact that she missed her dawn walks on Penzance Beach. Now her dawns were spent having sex or making love or whatever you wanted to call it. Which was fine—enjoy it while it lasts.

She pumped her arms and lengthened her stride. This wasn't the beach, it wasn't dawn, but had its compensations. It was a pretty corner of the world, a patchwork of vines, orchards and grazing paddocks stitched together with gravel roads lined with fences and trees. The birds were busy feeding their young. The air smelt fresh: one of the farmers had been slashing the spring grasses.

Then she recoiled. 'What's that awful smell?'

Sharp, basic, sinus-burning. She tracked it to a tangle of bracken between the side of the road and a cattle ramp. 'Shells?' she asked, peering into the gloom, one hand over her nose and mouth.

'Abalone,' said Challis, joining her.

The pile was half a metre high, grey and ghostly in the half-light, each ribbed and unlovely shell the size of a saucer. 'Some guy dumps them along here every year,' Challis said. 'One day I'll nab him.'

'A poacher?'

'Probably.'

'Huh,' Ellen said, storing away another piece of useless information. 'This doesn't happen in Penzance Beach.'

He squeezed her and laughed. 'It's pretty wild out here on the frontier.'

They looked up. A helicopter was slicing across a corner of the darkening sky. It was some distance away but the sound was unmistakeably that of a police Dauphin, more turbo whine than eggbeater chop. They glanced at each other. There were a couple of notorious black spots on the Peninsula, blind intersections where motorists had lost their lives. The locals liked to speculate what the cut-off point was before VicRoads improved safety by installing a roundabout or chopping down a few trees: ten lives? Twenty?

'Hal?'

'Yes, oh gorgeous one.'

She took his hand in hers. 'What are you going to do about your plane?'

He was restoring a vintage aeroplane. Correction: he *had* been, but now it sat gathering dust in a hangar on a little local airfield. Ellen was oddly bothered by that. She had no interest in the plane but the idea of Challis with an interest apart from police work—apart from *her*, for that matter—was important. She thought back to life with her husband. Alan had several obsessions—the fact that she'd been promoted to sergeant, the electricity bill, their daughter's boyfriends—but he'd had no *interests*. Had that been her fault? Was it her fault that Hal Challis no longer fiddled with his old wreck of an aeroplane?

'I honestly don't know,' he said.

She squeezed then released his hand.

'I wish I had more time,' he said.

'Do I take up your spare time?'

'I like spending it with you.'

She bit her lip. 'Hal, I can't be everything to you, or for you.'

'Of course not. I know that.'

'And you can't be everything to me.'

'Is this going somewhere?'

They walked in the deepening shadows, down the final slope toward his house. Their house. Ellen's head was whirling with a whole stack of issues, apparently unrelated but joined in complex ways.

'Hal, do you sometimes find it hard working together with me?'

'Yes.'

He said it promptly. That was good. 'In what way?' she asked.

'I keep wanting to touch you. There you are, sitting at your computer, and I want to rip your clothes off.'

She did and didn't want to hear that. She moved half a pace away from him and folded her arms.

But he wasn't thick, or stubborn, and said at once, 'I hate having to give orders to you, so I try to make it sound like a suggestion. I'm always conscious of not sounding critical, or questioning your judgment, but sometimes I find myself needing to do that. But if I do, will you take it the wrong way? And what do Scobie and Pam think? Do they feel I give you preferential treatment? But you are a sergeant.'

It came out in a heartfelt rush. Ellen linked arms with him again. 'Something needs to change. But not yet.'

She sensed that he wanted to say more about working with her, but the moment passed. Instead he said, 'Do you like living with me?'

'Yes,' she said firmly, not feeling a hundred per cent firm.

Hal said nothing but they continued companionably to the driveway entrance and up to the house. They'd bought a stir-fry mix from the butcher: all they had to do was toss it in a spitting wok and cook some rice. They would eat in tonight. They would eat together. They'd had a walk. This was a good evening and, in their line of work, good evenings were rare.

At their house outside Waterloo, Ludmilla Wishart was playing the piano. She played frequently, and expertly, and Adrian hated it. Her eyes, mind and body when she played were not there with him but far away, possibly in a better place—according to her—and he hated that.

He stopped her slender fingers on the keys and said, 'I'm hungry.'

She gasped and came back to earth. Hurried to the kitchen to make things better.

Scobie Sutton went home miserably from the Chillout Zone. Rather than accompany him, Beth had climbed onto her bicycle, saying she'd sit with Lachlan Roe until he regained consciousness. 'He needs me.'

'Beth, it could be days, weeks.'

'He needs me.'

'So do *we*, love. And he has his brother.'

'That so-and-so!'

He'd tried his hardest but she wouldn't listen. Scobie felt aggrieved, stuck between two uncomfortable forces: his boss and his wife. Neither one wanted or needed him, it seemed, yet they both held sway over him. He was betting that Challis would never remove Ellen Destry from a case. The benefits of sleeping with the boss. I'm still useful, aren't I? he demanded. I could be tracking down witnesses, tracing, interviewing, eliminating. Instead of which you want me investigating the theft of a ride-on mower.

He boiled inside. When he got home at six-thirty there was Roslyn, a small, wan figure in the dark kitchen, her school atlas open at the mess that was the Indonesian islands. With a scrape of her chair she was on her feet and hugging him fiercely, weeping so copiously that her tears soaked his shirt. 'Sweetheart,' he said, overwhelmed.

She hugged him tighter, released him, returned to her homework. He tried to help her as he cooked chops for dinner, but the Roe brothers had taken root in his mind and he wanted to harm them in some way. He examined that notion, surprised that he didn't feel any guilt.

Caz Moon knew where the anger had come from today, the courage, but she'd been a little in awe of herself even so. She hadn't always been angry and brave. For months after the rape she'd been, in her own words, a mumbling mess, contained on the outside, contained enough to manage the surf shop, but distraught on the inside. She couldn't believe some of the feelings she'd had: defilement, yeah, but guilt, too, for letting it happen. As if she'd had a choice!

To make it worse, her memories had been hazy at first, no clarity or definition, so she wasn't sure what had happened. But slowly she pieced it together and even more slowly she'd picked herself up off the ground.

And now, as the evening light eased toward full darkness, Caz Moon couldn't believe her luck. Here was Josh Brownlee again, queuing to get into Retro, the club behind the RSL hall, hitting on the youngest sister of someone she'd gone to school with, what was her name, Hayley, Hayley with a bare midriff, heavily kohled eyes, nipples like pebbles in the cool air, a skirt less than a whisker past her groin, chewing gum and enjoying Josh's pickup bullshit.

'Josh! Joshy!' cried Caz. 'Raped anyone yet? He's a rapist,' she informed Hayley, Hayley's mates and everyone else in earshot.

Josh lunged at her, she dodged away laughing, and that cop lady was there again, saying, 'Everything okay here?'

'Fine!' said Caz in her sparkling voice.

The cop glanced at Josh, then at Caz and murmured, 'Do you want to report a crime?'

'Me? No!'

'Caz,' said the cop flatly. 'I just heard you accuse that boy of rape.'

'Me? I was just kidding.'

The cop stared at her, not in the least bit satisfied. Finally she shoved a photo under Caz's nose. 'Have you seen this man?'

'Not me,' Caz said, striding off in her conquering-the-world way.

When Pam looked, the boy had disappeared.

16

That was Tuesday. Wednesday was Ludmilla Wishart's thirtieth birthday and the first caller was her friend, Carmen Gandolfo, who sang Happy Birthday down the line as Ludmilla was about to eat her muesli. Ludmilla blinked back a couple of tears: Carmen was good for her, large in body and spirit, a real tonic. Plus it mattered that even though she knew what Adrian was like, Carmen had called her at home, not work.

They exchanged a few pleasantries, Carmen apparently slurping coffee or tea. 'I'll call in at your office later with a little something.'

'Size doesn't matter,' Ludmilla said, 'so long as it's expensive.'

'On my salary?' demanded Carmen. Another slurp. 'So, what have you got planned for tonight?'

Ludmilla said in a guilty rush, 'Adrian's taking me out to dinner.'

'Darl,' Carmen drawled, putting a lot of doubt and disapproval into the word.

With a whine that she hated, Ludmilla replied, 'I can't leave him, you know that. I'm scared he'll hurt himself if I do.'

'Utter bullshit.'

'Please, Carmen.'

'Get him into a MENS program. I can set it up for you.'

Carmen worked as a counsellor with the shire's community health service. MENS—Men Exploring Non-violent Solutions—was a behaviour-change workshop for violent or abusive husbands or partners. Ludmilla knew there was a snowball's chance in hell of Adrian entering such a program. He wasn't some uneducated labourer but an urbane, highly educated professional; and he'd hardly ever hit her.

'Please,' she said miserably.

Last time they'd had this conversation Carmen had said, 'It's your funeral—and I mean that literally,' but this was a birthday call, so Carmen steered the conversation onto cheerier matters. Ludmilla was soon laughing and buoyant, but glancing at the kitchen clock anxiously and keeping an ear open for Adrian, who was in the bathroom down the hall, scraping his electric razor over his lean chin. She didn't have much time. She thanked Carmen for the call and was rinsing her cereal bowl at the sink when the phone rang again. Her mother said, 'How's the birthday girl?'

'Hello, Mum.'

They chatted for a couple of minutes, then Ludmilla's mother said, 'Is that gorgeous husband of yours taking you somewhere nice tonight?'

Ludmilla had tried confiding in her mother several times in the past few years, but she simply failed to listen. She adored her son-in-law. Adrian could do no wrong. Bolstered by her conversation with Carmen, Ludmilla said the worst thing she'd ever said about her husband: 'Mum, Mr Adorable punched me in the stomach last night.'

'Oh, don't be silly.'

'I'm thinking seriously of leaving him.'

'You've always been a complainer, Ludmilla. A marriage requires work. You need to try harder.'

Ludmilla realised with a start of fear that Adrian's razor had fallen silent. She murmured urgently, 'I'd better go.'

And there was Adrian, standing in the doorway, both hands behind his back. He cocked his head: 'Your mother?'

How much had he heard? 'Yes,' Ludmilla said. She added reassuringly, 'It was a quick call.'

To her relief, he nodded. Ludmilla couldn't win sometimes. If she made a call, he'd see it as money they'd never see again. If someone called her—especially if they spoke at length—he'd feel that she'd removed herself from him. Often he'd time her, glaring pointedly at the Longines watch she'd bought him. He'd time her, calculate the distances she'd driven, count the money she'd spent on groceries.

His grins used to melt her. He grinned now, saying 'Ta da!' and bringing his hands out from behind his back.

He flourished a birthday cake at her. Chocolate, three candles for the thirty years, a scalloped edge and other fancy bits, 'Happy Birthday' scrolled across it in white icing.

Then Ludmilla frowned, looked more closely at the icing. '*Hippy* Birthday,' it said.

Her face crumpled. 'Adrian!'

'Just a joke…'

'I'm not fat.'

'Ludmilla, it's just a joke.'

'I'm not fat,' she wailed, touching her hips.

He was deadly quiet and serious now. 'We have to face it, darling, your thighs are bigger.'

She collapsed into her chair at the kitchen table. 'I can't go on like this.'

Adrian was bright and shiny from the bathroom, groomed to within an inch of his life. He stood behind her chair, dug his fingers into her neck and murmured, 'The only way you'll leave me is in a coffin.'

She gasped, jerked away from him.

'Mill,' he said reasonably, 'I could snap your neck, you know I could. Listen,' he said, moving around now and crouching beside her, one hand stroking her between the shoulders, the other on her knee, 'I apologise, I went too far.' Suddenly hot tears spurted from his eyes. 'I

93

didn't mean to hurt you. You mean the world to me. It's all the pressure, the disappointments, am I good at what I do, why aren't I getting any recognition…'

'Oh, Ade,' she said, crying too now.

'I shouldn't take it out on you, I know I shouldn't.'

Ludmilla knew that Adrian was chronically depressed. Although he'd had plenty of freelance drafting and design commissions since their marriage, for which he earned reasonable money, the jobs had been small—married friends getting him to mock up preliminary drawings for a house extension, for example—or otherwise disappointing, like the shire commissioning him to design a public toilet block for the Waterloo foreshore only to reject it, calling it too outlandish. The larger commissions, the offers of a partnership with a prestige firm, had been elusive. Meanwhile there were certain types of people, the legions of the vulgar, whom Adrian Wishart could not possibly work with, and standards he would not compromise. Ludmilla felt for him sometimes. It was hard for truly creative people.

'I know,' she sniffled, squeezing his hand.

He hugged her affectionately, sprang to his feet and briskly went about getting himself some breakfast. She envied the way he could recover from setbacks. Then the news came on, the police still investigating the assault on the Landseer School chaplain, a car bomb in Baghdad, some footballer arrested for drunk driving—'Your honour, consider the terrible pressure my client is under,' Adrian chortled, making her smile.

Then he patted his lips. 'Forgot to say, I'm playing squash tonight.'

He said it every year. And every year she said, 'You are not, mister. You're taking me out to dinner.'

Mock astonished, he jabbed his chest. '*Moi?*'

'Yes, you,' Ludmilla said. Inside, she didn't know whether to laugh or cry.

'Completely slipped my mind.'

'It did not.'

It was almost like love. They ate their breakfast in a warm glow and when Ludmilla next got up to clear a plate away, she heard the whiplash snap of his fingers. She turned: he was holding up his coffee mug for a refill.

She fetched the pot. Just as she was pouring, the phone rang. Ludmilla didn't know who, apart from Carmen and her mother, would be ringing at this hour. She glanced anxiously at Adrian; he glanced pointedly at his watch.

She swallowed and picked up the handset. 'Hello?'

It was Carl Vernon in Penzance Beach, sounding deeply distressed about the old fisherman's cottage on Bluff Road.

17

Elsewhere in Penzance Beach that Wednesday morning, Pam Murphy was jogging. Like Carl Vernon, she lived on the bluff above the beach, but hers was a rented fibro-cement shack and it was several blocks back from any view of the sea, along a rutted dirt track at the edge of farmland. She didn't know Vernon, and was only dimly aware of the push to save the fisherman's cottage on the cliff top opposite his house. Still, she loved living in Penzance Beach, loved living so close to the water, which was only minutes away on foot.

Her route this morning took her first along the top of the bluff, the flat blue sea and Phillip Island showing between the dark pines on one side of her, a range of fences, yards and holiday houses on the other—silent weekenders, expensively curtained and gloomy at this hour on a weekday morning.

Then she came to a concrete cliff top bench, signs that warned of unstable edges, and a flight of wooden steps to the sand below. She pistoned down, then back up, then down again, until her legs burned and her heart hammered. She was running a marathon soon, and liked to push herself hard like this. Her body and mind crackling with alertness and energy, she began to lope along the beach, weaving in and out of the kelp drifts and exposed reefs at the edge of the water, where the sand was wet and hard. She passed old people walking dogs, a power-walker, seagulls, sharks' eggs, the carcass of a seal. No dolphins keeping pace with her today, only a tanker far out on the water, heading for the refinery near Waterloo.

So a morning like most others, but Pam always noticed the tiny differences between one day and the next. The two breakwaters along her route were almost covered in sand this morning, for example, and yesterday there'd been no kelp. Had the wind risen last night, the waters raced? If so, she'd slept right through it. And with the blood beating strongly through her, body zingingly alive, she thought about Andy Cree.

She came to the little stile on the low plank wall at the bottom of the cliff, stepped over it and was lost in the ti-trees, their trunks and roots like dark hanks of rope. Dodging to avoid the traps in her path, all sounds shielded from her, Pam powered up the crooked track to the cliff top. Finally she burst through the bushes and onto the road.

And stopped in her tracks. She struggled to take it all in. There was a gap in the vista, but what? Then she realised: the old fisherman's cottage had been flattened. Heavy bulldozers were growling and scraping among the pines. People were milling about, shouting angrily, some of them in tears. Eight security guards, beefy, beer-fed thugs dressed in black, maintained a line of defence between the protesters and the demolition crew. The latter, wearing hard hats, jeans, work boots and gloves, were wielding mallets and loading dump bins in concert with the bulldozers.

It was implacable, unstoppable. It was noisy, dusty and shocking to witness. Pam felt tears spring to her eyes and she crossed the road to join the protesters.

One man detached himself from the group. He was bony, grey-haired but fit looking, and Pam recognised him as someone she saw walking along the beach from time to time. He clearly knew her, for he said, in a clear, booming voice, 'You're a police officer, right?'

Pam nodded. 'What's happening?' she said, even though she knew it was a dumb question.

She'd always liked the old house. She passed it every morning when she burst through from the beach below. She thought of it as part of the old Penzance Beach, a pretty house amid the million-dollar architectural wet dreams on either side of it, which were constructed of smoky glass, corrugated iron and tropical rainforest timbers and referred to as 'our beach shack' by the Melbourne stockbrokers and cocaine lawyers who owned them.

'Can't you stop it?' the man said, clutching her wrist.

She removed it gently. 'A bit late for that, Mr…'

'Carl Vernon,' he said. 'Please, do something.'

Pam weighed her options. The demolition was well advanced and well organised. She was one lonely copper. She didn't know the facts.

'Perhaps they have permission,' she said lamely.

'Permission! The house was unique! It was classified by the National Trust yesterday!'

That was enough to go on with. Pam strode toward the site, Vernon beside her, saying, 'They have no right. There was an emergency application for heritage protection lodged with the planning minister.'

They reached the security cordon. 'Wait here, please,' Pam said, and she made to step between two of the guards, men built like concrete slabs, no necks, shaven skulls. In its sweet, blind way, the state government had allowed the security industry to regulate itself, with the result that many security guards had criminal records and a penchant for methamphetamine-fuelled rage. Knowing that, Pam wasn't intimidated by these jokers. 'I'm a police officer,' she said levelly, looking each man in the eye. 'If you lay one finger on me, I'll fuck you up for good.'

They blinked. She passed through to another thickset man, who wore the hard, unimpressed face of work-site bosses the world over. One foot propped on a pile of fence palings, he was watching a bulldozer tip rubble into a skip. Pam was astonished to see a mattress complete with a woollen underlay go tumbling in, followed by a refrigerator and a microwave. Then another 'dozer roared in: a splintered wardrobe, a dusty rug, shards of glass, corrugated roofing iron, a woollen overcoat.

The foreman gave her a quizzical look and spat unhurriedly at her feet. 'How did you get in here?'

'I'm a police officer.'

Watching her wordlessly, he fished a sheet of paper from his shirt pocket. It was warm from his body, almost moist. She scanned it: a demolition permit.

'But as I understand it,' she said, returning the document, 'the house was classified by the National Trust yesterday.'

'But not *protected*,' the foreman said. 'Besides, the Trust is weak as piss. A hobby for the idle rich.'

He looked as though he were about to give an explosive lecture on the subject but thought better of it. 'Look, a call came in last night, flatten the place first thing this morning. I checked out the legal situation, me and my boys are in the clear.'

Pam was disgusted. 'You couldn't even empty the rooms first?' she asked, shouting above the sounds of the bulldozers as a scoop of planks and a leather armchair were tipped into the skip.

The foreman snarled, 'Because of those loonies—' he pointed to the protesters '—it had to be done this way. People like that, nothing better to do…' he finished, shaking his head.

'What's going up in its place?'

'Fucked if I know,' the man said, looking pointedly at the houses on either side, monstrosities that blocked the sun.

'Who's developing it? Who called you?'

'That's confidential information.'

Dispirited by the waste, greed and contempt, Pam crossed the road to where Vernon had rejoined the protesters. 'There's nothing I can do. Sorry.'

'Arrest them,' a woman said, tears in her eyes.

'They have a valid demolition permit.'

'That's not the point. We were under the impression that the Ebelings valued the house.'

'The Ebelings?'

'Hugh Ebeling and his wife.'

Pam had never heard of them. 'I'm very sorry, I'm as heartsick as you are, but it's a civil, not a police matter. I suggest you take it up with the shire.'

That made the teary woman angry. 'The shire? Don't you think it's significant that the house was heritage listed yesterday, and demolished by the Ebelings today, just before an emergency protection order could be granted? They were tipped off by someone on the inside.'

'Are you reporting a crime?'

The woman looked flustered. Carl Vernon took charge, thanking Pam and speaking calming words to the men and women who milled about helplessly. He said, as Pam began her slow jog toward home, 'If we can prove anything, will you look into it?'

Pam waved, her way of saying yes. She was tired, hungry, needed a coffee. She jogged past the site; already the guards were piling into two black Range Rovers with tinted windows, the demolition workers beginning to load the bulldozers onto semitrailers.

Thirty minutes later, Pam returned, driving past on her way to work, hair damp, coffee and porridge sitting comfortably in her belly. The site was empty. She braked cautiously: no it wasn't. Some of the locals were fishing around in the rubbish skips, retrieving electrical goods, furniture, clothing and books.

Good luck to them. She tried to figure out what kind of person would authorise and abet the bulldozing of that pretty little house and saw only a terrible barrenness.

She drove away slowly. She saw Carl Vernon outside a nearby cottage, beside a silver Golf, talking to a young woman with red hair. At the bottom of the hill she braked suddenly for a red Citroën. She tracked it as it passed, seeing it slip into the shadows beneath a plane tree near the crest and remain there.

Pam Murphy shrugged, accelerated and headed to the police station in Waterloo, where she parked in a corner of the yard, away from the bird-shit gums. She entered by the rear doors, using her swipe card, collected a sheaf of circulars and memos from her pigeonhole, and climbed the stairs to CIU. She had things to do.

She was bemused to find that she'd beaten the others to work: usually she was late. Thinking she should mark the occasion by brewing the coffee, Pam wandered into the tearoom and stared doubtfully at the coffee machine that Challis had installed. The boss loved his coffee. Never drank instant. Made terrific coffee, too, and had shown her how to load the machine, but now all of that information had vanished into thin air.

Challis saved her from making a fool of herself. He came easily up the stairs, looking fresh and benign, as though he'd had a good shag this morning. Perhaps he had: living with Sergeant Destry seemed to be doing him good. He would never be called Laughing Boy by the troops—his face saw to that, with its narrow planes, dark cast and air of permanent scepticism—but he was lighter on his feet these days, burned more slowly, as if a great weight had been removed from his shoulders.

They stood about for a while, waiting for the coffee to brew. She told him about the bulldozed house, about the man named Hugh Ebeling and his contemptuous act, but Challis was distracted. 'Ebeling,' he murmured. 'Don't know anything about the guy.'

There was a way of finding out, though. All Pam needed was for Challis and the others to leave the building for an hour or two.

18

While Challis and Murphy drank their coffee that Wednesday morning, Ellen Destry was standing in the grounds of the Landseer School with the deputy head, watching as buses, BMWs and Range Rovers pulled in, unloaded and pulled out again. She saw one Chinese face and one Indian, but the school community was pretty much a monoculture. The Landseer School for Blonde Children, she thought.

'That's Zara,' Moorhouse said, pointing suddenly.

Tall, fair, faintly voluptuous, gloriously self-absorbed. Ellen began to move, saying from the corner of her mouth, 'I'll need you to sit in while I interview her.'

'I'd have insisted anyway,' Moorhouse said.

Ellen nodded. It was playing out as she wanted it to play out. It would look bad if she questioned Zara Selkirk without an appropriate adult present. Moorhouse had status but was not, it seemed, in thrall to the money, power and prestige that surrounded the school; and the school was a better environment for Ellen's purposes than Zara's home, where she might find herself obstructed by a parent or a lawyer.

Besides, she wanted to ambush the kid.

Five minutes later, they were in Moorhouse's office, an environment of papery smells and disordered bookshelves and files, Zara Selkirk saying, 'I was sick yesterday. I brought a note from my mother.'

'Cut the crap,' Ellen said. 'You wagged school. You went up to the city after school on Monday afternoon, attended a concert that evening, and spent the night in your family's Southbank apartment. A day's shopping with your mother yesterday, and back home last night.'

Zara Selkirk sulked. 'What's it to you?'

'I'm not a truant officer. I'm investigating the assault on the school chaplain.'

'You can't pin that on me. I wasn't even here.'

'But you were at school on Monday. Yours was the only appointment in his diary.'

'So?'

'So tell me about it.'

'Not fair.'

'Zara,' said the deputy head, 'the sooner you answer the sergeant's questions the sooner you can return to class.'

There was a moment when the girl seemed almost to weigh these options. Her face cleared and she said, 'Because of some stuff that wasn't even my idea I had to like you know, apologise to some old … the library lady. Like she's not even a teacher or anything.'

Ellen said distinctly, 'Zara, you and your friends set up a fake Facebook page that caused immense distress to an innocent middle-aged woman who's not in a position to defend herself.'

'Well it was a joke. She should learn to take jokes.'

'Why did you meet with Mr Roe on Monday?'

'He was like the go-between.'

'He was the mediator between you and Mrs Richardson?'

Zara Selkirk said, 'Yeah,' as though everything was obvious and why didn't Ellen get it.

'But she didn't attend?'

'Bitch went to a lawyer.'

'Zara,' warned Moorhouse.

The girl's face grew drowsy with satisfaction. 'Well she is.'

Ellen stepped in. 'What did you and Mr Roe talk about?'

With a twist of her mouth, Zara Selkirk said, 'Pervert. He said I should write to her but mainly he was interested in my tits.'

Ellen, remembering what Hal had discovered about the Roe brothers' upbringing, visualised the scene. Lachlan Roe, forty years old, the Landseer chaplain but an unloved or unlovely man, waits in his poky office for the only appointment of the day. The Year 12s are no longer around, they're off enjoying Schoolies Week—not that they'd ever sought his advice or counselling anyway. It's a long morning. All of his mornings are long. Maybe he wanders the corridors, looking for lost souls, a staff member perhaps, but no one wants him. He returns to his office and logs on to a pornography site or his brother's blog or reads and sends e-mails.

Then soon after lunch there's a knock on his door. 'Come,' he calls, in his smooth, disarming way.

The sixteen-year-old who slips into his room has the breasts of a woman and the face of a child. The chaplain notices these things in that order. She's wearing aspects of the Landseer girls' uniform, a white blouse over a long charcoal skirt, so he can't assess her legs, but her wrists and hands are soft and plump. He takes in her hair, which is the kind of blonde that is almost white, her expressive lips and her body language, which both entices and expresses contempt for him. She doesn't want to be in the same room with him.

'How did he seem to you?' said Ellen now.

'Who?'

Ellen closed and opened her eyes and said carefully, 'What kind of mood was Mr Roe in?'

'A dirty-old-man mood.'

Lachlan Roe is slender, of medium height, and believes he has an air of boyish charm. He's the same age as the child's father but he's not uncool, like most fathers. He's youthful looking in his black silk T-shirt and grey linen jacket with the cuffs turned back.

The jacket that later collected another person's mucus.

He lets Zara wait on his strip of carpet for a long moment, then loads his face and body with soulful gentleness and murmurs, 'Hello, Zara, please take a seat.'

She's a gawkily lovely teenager, and an old ugliness stirs inside him. There in his sterile office the drowsy mid-November sun streams in, banding the threadbare carpet, the girl's lap and one forearm, her fine hairs fairly glowing, so that he swallows and coughs nervously.

Ellen could see it all. 'Was there any *specific* thing Mr Roe did or said that made you feel uncomfortable?'

'You think I attacked him. I told you, I was at a concert.'

'I know that. I'm trying to get a feeling for the kind of man Mr Roe was…is.'

Zara considered this, looking for traps. 'If you think I paid someone to attack him, well I didn't. And my dad didn't do it, 'cause he's away.'

'Zara, what did Mr Roe do and say?'

'He goes, do my parents know why I'm here? I go, yes, they said I had to apologise to old Merle. He goes, "Well, Zara, they are your parents, one does have a duty to one's parents." Moron.'

'Zara,' said Moorhouse.

'Well, it's not fair. He said I had all these unworldly people around me and I was like, defiled by them.'

'Defiled? What did he mean by that?'

'I told him it wasn't my idea, the Facebook thing, it was Amber and Megan. He said purity comes from separating yourself from defiling influences and was I a lesbian. Pervert.'

Ellen thought she was probably right. 'What else?'

'He got this mad look on his face. He said he could see my future. Drugs, sex, backpacking in Europe and stuff.'

'Backpacking in Europe?'

'He was barking mad. He said I would meet some guy with caramel skin and liquid eyes who would ask me to deliver a package.'

'What package?'

'How should I know? I'm supposed to listen to this guy?'

'What else? Did he touch you?'

Zara shuddered. 'No way. Just told me as chaplain he understood the teenage mindset. I said, Yeah, but do you have any like, formal qualifications?'

Ellen and Moorhouse exchanged a smile. 'What did he say?'

'He said, forget further study, university is too narrowing, forget travel, I'll meet drug couriers and terrorists. He said it's my duty to get married and have children and honour my parents. "You young people come to me with your tight clothes and your soul-damaging mobile phones, wanting Godless freedoms,"' Zara said mincingly, hooking her fingers in quotation marks around the chaplain's words.

'What then?'

With an apologetic glance at Moorhouse, Zara Selkirk said, 'I cleared out, sorry.'

'He didn't raise the issue of your apology to Mrs Richardson?'

'He said, "I am the elect," like he was God or Jesus or something. I was a bit scared, actually. He was so weird.'

'Did you tell anyone about the session?'

Zara looked away. 'No.'

'No one?'

'Like, who would believe me?' Zara said.

19

The morning passed. Pam Murphy followed up on a handful of residents' complaints that probably stemmed from schoolies' exuberance—used condoms on the front lawn of a house opposite the foreshore tents, a parked car sideswiped in the same area, the shoplifting of Bolle sunglasses from HangTen—but mostly she was waiting for CIU to empty.

Finally Challis left to interview Dirk Roe's office colleagues and the members of Lachlan Roe's congregation, and Scobie Sutton headed out to track down a ride-on mower. The poor guy looked wretched.

Still, there was always a lot of traffic on the first floor, uniforms coming and going with paperwork that demanded attention, the station's new sergeant and senior sergeant keeping an eye on things, the IT geek returning with Lachlan Roe's laptop, someone from the canteen taking lunch orders… Pam ordered a tuna salad, and she thanked the sergeant for letting her have Tank and Cree as backup that night, during the eclipse, but mostly she kept her head down and waited.

When it was quiet, she logged on to the Law Enforcement Database. Strict protocols were in place for using LED, and she was breaking most of them, but the image of this morning's wilful destruction wouldn't leave her alone and soon she had Hugh Ebeling's details on the screen. The man who'd torn down Somerland just so he could dominate the ridge and the sky above Penzance Beach was forty-two years old, a property developer, married to Mia, aged forty. Mia was a senior executive with LottoLink, a Swiss company that had recently acquired licences to sell scratch cards and install poker machines in Victorian pubs and clubs. So, not short of a dollar. No children.

They lived in Brighton—pronounced 'Brahton', Pam believed, by the nipped, tucked and Botoxed men and women who lived there. Presumably Penzance Beach would be their weekend residence. Two houses overlooking the water, lucky devils.

They owned a Range Rover, a Maserati and BMW. Hugh had lost two points for speeding, Mia nine. Various parking infringements. No criminal record for either person but Hugh had been sued by a consortium of clients for building on a flood plain in northern New South Wales, and Mia was a discharged bankrupt.

But casual dishonesty and steering close to the wind were probably not unusual in the nouveau riche circles the Ebelings moved in. Pam continued her search, and by way of links to the *Age* and *Brighton Argus* newspapers and a residents' action group, discovered that numerous well-established trees on the roadway between the Ebelings' Brighton house and the waters of the bay had been chopped down or poisoned. The Ebelings had expressed outrage at the destruction, but it was widely believed that they'd ordered it, wanting a sea view from their top windows.

Finally, Mia's cousin was Justice Stephen Marlowe of the state's planning appeals tribunal. You might as well give up, Pam thought, throwing down her pen in disgust. You're never going to beat the bastards.

Scobie Sutton drove to a dealer in second-hand farm machinery in Cranbourne and found the stolen ride-on mower. He knew the dealer was vaguely bent, but he was too deeply fatigued and discouraged to pursue that angle. Instead, he said, 'Can you give me a name?'

'I can give you a numberplate.'

Which belonged to a van owned by Laurie Jarrett on the Seaview Park estate in Waterloo. Jarrett was well known to the police.

After that he drove to the hospital and there was his wife, at the bedside of Lachlan Roe. 'Sweetheart, come home please, we need you.'

'He hasn't moved. He hasn't said anything.'

They looked at Roe's pinched, bruised face, the bandages swaddling his head. 'Sweetheart, let the nurses do their job.'

'I've been talking to him non-stop,' Beth wailed. 'Not a flicker.'

'Come home. You're tired. You need to sleep. It's Ros's concert tonight. Please, Beth.'

'Full moon tonight,' said Beth in her new, wild-eyed way.

'Ros's concert tonight,' said Scobie firmly, feeling that his heart would break.

She came eventually, as though drugged with something you could never measure or trace.

After viewing the bulldozed remains of Somerland with Carl Vernon, Ludmilla Wishart returned to Planning East and made a flurry of phone calls. Yes, the minister had received the emergency application to protect Somerland, but hadn't intended to act on it until Friday, after he'd had further advice and consultation. His minder said that the minister wished to convey his deepest regrets, but the demolition had, on the face of it, proceeded lawfully, thank you, goodbye.

Then the calls began. A journalist from the local paper. Distressed Penzance Beach residents. And anonymous callers, abusive callers, placing her in the pockets of wealthy developers. 'I'm not!' she insisted, but these were not people who were interested in debating the point.

In fact, she was pretty sure who had tipped off the Ebelings. She'd gathered plenty of evidence over the past weeks and months, but when and how she should use it, she didn't quite know.

She also fielded calls and e-mails from Adrian. Nothing unusual about that. Sometimes he contacted her several times a day; had done so for the past three years, ever since they got married. This morning the calls came every thirty minutes, always beginning, 'It's me: where are you?'

And she'd say, 'In my office.'

Given that he always seemed to know when she hadn't been in her office, she found this question puzzling. The morning progressed. At one point she stood in a corner of the window and peered out. The planning office sat with Centrelink, the Neighbourhood House and a childcare centre opposite a small park, and there was her husband, at a park bench with his laptop. The fact that he was sending her e-mails meant that he was piggybacking on someone's wireless network. Her heart began its arrhythmic palpitations and soon she was on her back gulping for air, one hand over her chest until the scary beat evened out, until she was a normal person.

When she looked again, he was gone.

Then Carmen arrived to take her to lunch, Carmen's glossy black hair, red skirt and green top brightening the drab grey world of the planning office. 'For you, madam,' she said with a curtsy, presenting Ludmilla with a small parcel wrapped in royal blue paper decorated with gold stars and moons, a parcel almost too beautiful to tear open.

'A tennis racquet?'

Carmen's big, clever, expressive face fell. 'Aww, you guessed.'

It was an MP3 player, sleek and black. 'I've loaded it with some albums I think you'll like,' Carmen said. 'Plus it plays FM radio, video clips and voice recordings—I thought you could use it to record your field notes.' She snatched it from Ludmilla. 'Here, let me show you.'

Ludmilla was intrigued. 'I need never leave home.'

A little cloud passed over Carmen's face. 'Oh, you'd better leave home, Mill.'

They went out, Mr Groot coming to his office door and looking pointedly at his watch.

Josh Brownlee rose at lunchtime that Wednesday, feeling wrecked. He wanted some kind of release. He wanted to hurt someone. He stumbled from his motel room opposite the yacht club and made for High Street, passing the Chillout Zone at the Uniting Church, the Zone pretty quiet, no schoolies, only a handful of volunteers wearing the hallowed look of people who work uncomplainingly, sunnily, with Young People.

He wandered up to McDonald's, where he ate a hamburger, followed by an ecstasy tab washed down with a can of Red Bull, and overheard a slag from Grover Hall say she was taking the ferry across to Phillip Island. So he hung back and followed her, nothing particular in mind, except that she really filled out her T-shirt. But when he reached the dock a dozen other schoolies greeted her, all with that healthy glow, wearing shorts, hats and daypacks, many of them wheeling bicycles. God he despised them, even as he felt a tiny, nasty, carnal bite to see all those bare legs.

20

Challis bought a ham and salad roll for lunch and ate it in his office. He'd spent all morning driving from house to house, office to office, trying to get a fix on Lachlan Roe and the First Ascensionists. He heard the same story, over and over again: 'Lachlan is a lovely, lovely man...Can't think who would want to hurt him like that...I hope you find the monster who did it...'

Dirk? No one had much time for Dirk. But Dirk was young and foolish rather than evil. Looked up to his brother.

No one could back up the aunt's claim that the boys were twisted.

It was a relief to hear the phone ring and have Superintendent McQuarrie summon him to regional headquarters in Frankston. 'As soon as you can, inspector.'

'Sir.'

The old, peremptory McQuarrie. Challis finished eating and clattered down the stairs and out to the carpark. Maybe it's going to be Outer Woop-Woop for Ellen or me after all, he thought, as he steered onto Frankston-Flinders Road.

Twenty minutes later he was threading around a series of shopping-centre carparks, looking for somewhere to leave his car. Frankston, a suburb on the outermost southeastern edge of the sprawl that was Melbourne, was the kind of place that says there is no such thing as too much commerce. He found a slot in the baking sun, trotted across a busy street to the complex that housed the police and the magistrates' courts and took the lift to the top floor.

Superintendent McQuarrie answered, 'Come,' to Challis's knock. Challis found him sitting behind a vast desk, looking small and tidy—in full dress uniform today, for some reason, loads of braid, chrome and brass hanging from his chest and shoulders, as if to diminish the size of the desk and inflate his own. An open laptop sat before him; beside him was a portable screen, the Victoria Police logo shimmering there in hazy focus.

'Inspector.'

'Sir,' countered Challis.

'I know you're a busy man. I won't waste more of your time than is necessary.'

So not the sack; a demotion or a transfer? wondered Challis.

'In order to achieve benchmark aims and improve forward efficiency, I'm proposing three new initiatives for the Peninsula.'

Challis gazed at the super, wanting to say: You summoned me all the way up here to listen to some gobbledegook? Besides, he was pretty certain that the initiatives had come from Force Command, not McQuarrie.

McQuarrie began to peck at the keys of his laptop as if it might bite him. 'First, a specialist sex crimes unit.'

Well, Challis would welcome that, they all would, but the image that swam into view on the screen showed a crime scene, detectives with clipboards and shirtsleeves standing around watching forensic experts in disposable oversuits and overshoes searching on and around a body on a stretch of waste ground.

'Wrong slide,' said McQuarrie crossly. 'All right, let's leave the sex crimes unit for now. Another proposal is for a self-contained IRU, or initial response unit, which will attend crime scenes and carry out all the tasks currently undertaken by several disparate individuals. It will consist of thirteen officers: a sergeant, eleven senior constables and one constable. It will be solely responsible for securing the scene, recording it via photos and video, and collecting evidence such as fingerprints, DNA and fibres. This evidence will then be passed on to the relevant divisions for analysis—the fingerprint division and the Forensic Science Centre, for example. Once the information has been recorded and analysed, it will be handed on to CIU for further investigation.'

Challis had mixed feelings. What if the evidence got lost? What could be done about the inevitable delays when there were three stages in the process? Would an officer in such a unit feel 'loyal' to the evidence he or she had collected, and want to follow through? Then again, it would free a CIU head like himself to manage targeted operations more simply, and also free up uniformed police, who often got bogged down at crime scenes and spent hours standing around.

But he didn't say any of this. He wanted to see what else McQuarrie had in mind.

'Any questions?'

'The idea has merit, sir.'

McQuarrie narrowed his gaze at Challis, expecting a trap. When it didn't come, he said, 'Right, let's see the next slide.'

It was a breakdown of the proposed unit, with boxes and arrows. McQuarrie skipped over it. Another image appeared: a roomful of desks, computers and analysts.

'Right, Project Nimbus. As you know, this has been trialled successfully in other regions. Briefly, tactical intelligence officers will be employed to target particular crimes, monitor the movements of known criminals and their associates, including those recently released from prison, and identify geographical hotspots on the Peninsula.'

Challis said, 'An extension of the work currently done by the collators, sir?'

McQuarrie frowned. 'If you like. But the collators are still only useful *after* the event. Our aim is to become increasingly strategic and proactive.'

He began to count on his fingers. 'Imagine being able to identify crime and traffic hotspots and place officers there *before* there's trouble. Or being able to anticipate the intentions of a loose confederacy of individuals. Or knowing *when* certain types of offences are likely to occur.'

This would have helped Ellen and Murph with Schoolies Week, Challis thought.

'We need to make informed decisions based on evidence,' McQuarrie said. 'What we have now is a culture in which information is *not* shared between stations and districts, where a vital piece of intelligence is locked inside a computer somewhere, and young or lazy officers fail to complete or write reports, or do follow-ups.'

Challis quite liked the idea. What kinds of data would he log into such a system? Environmental factors, certainly. For example, drought. With drought came the theft of water and livestock, and increased social distress leading to domestic violence, suicide and threats to public officials. He went into a kind of musing daydream, staring past McQuarrie's head at the sky outside the window, the wispy cloud and scrappy birds flying past. Economic factors like recession, he thought; there's always an associated increase in property crimes. And ethnic clustering. One of the Frankston inspectors had told him what a headache it was, educating young Sudanese men: they reacted aggressively to being arrested or questioned by female officers, for example, and believed that a learner's permit was a full driving licence and one car registration payment covered them forever.

And Challis thought about the recent spate of car break-ins around the little three-screen Waterloo cinema: was he correct in thinking they occurred mostly on Tuesday nights, when the cinema offered half-price tickets and the adjacent carparks and streets were full?

But would Ellen want to head such a task?—assuming that's where McQuarrie was going with this meeting. Challis couldn't see it. She'd want to be more hands-on in any new prospect being mooted for her.

'Finally,' McQuarrie said, irritably searching for the correct slide, 'we come to sex crimes.'

21

At 4 o'clock that afternoon, John Tankard arrived at the Waterloo cop shop, feeling pretty rested. After leaving Cree in the Fiddlers Creek yesterday he'd driven out to Berwick, where his parents and little sister lived. He'd downed a couple of coldies with the old man—who'd been a copper in London before bringing his young family out to Australia, and was now groundskeeper of a golf course—and 'helped' Natalie with her Bog People homework project, Nat grabbing the mouse and keyboard from him because he was so slow and clumsy, and so fascinated. Then he got stuck into his mother's shepherd's pie—she hadn't wanted to migrate, and still clung to the things that brought comfort and reminders of home—and was tucked up in his own bed by eleven o'clock. He'd slept in this morning, knowing he wasn't on duty until this afternoon.

He was nursing a coffee in the canteen when Pam Murphy—looking good in jeans and a close-fitting white T-shirt—was in his face, saying, 'Where's Andy?'

'Dunno.'

'Well, has he come in yet? Tonight could get messy and I need to brief you guys.'

Tank wanted to say, Don't take it out on me, I'm not the one who's late. He drank his coffee.

'Could you find him for me?'

Feeling maligned, Tank went looking. 'Seen Andy Cree?' he said, in the canteen, the carpark, the sergeants' common room, the front desk, the gym. No sign of Cree. All he found was some guys watching porn in a forgotten storeroom in a back corner of the police complex.

'You fucking morons,' he said.

A guy from the Traffic Management unit, three probationers, and the guy who washed dishes in the canteen. They were huddled around a DVD/VCR combo, watching five guys jacking off onto a kneeling woman. They all turned half lidded eyes on him, sleepily aroused.

'Turn that crap off. Get back to work,' Tank said, feeling like someone's father or teacher.

'Come on, Tank,' drawled the guy from Traffic, 'pull up a pew and pull on your pecker.'

They all sniggered, arranged around the screen on milk crates. The air was thick with cigarette smoke and something thick and undefinable, as if some ugliness were exuding from their pores. John Tankard, who for years had been the bad boy of Waterloo, found himself snarling like one of his old sergeants. 'All of you, back to work.'

The kitchen guy and the probationers scuttled away, edging around Tank, who filled the doorway and watched expressionlessly as the guy from Traffic made slow work of turning off the machine and boxing up the DVD. Tank guessed they'd been watching stuff that had been seized on a raid. 'Seen Andy Cree around?'

'Not me.'

Tank, feeling even more like the wise old man of policing, sighed and went back upstairs to report to Murph. He tracked her down to the CIU briefing room, where photographs of Lachlan Roe, Dirk Roe, the Landseer School, a teenage girl and a man he realised was Ollie Hindmarsh, the local member of parliament, were arranged on whiteboards. And there was Cree, standing with her at the far end of the briefing table, near a stack of folders and leaflets. Before he could stop himself, Tank retorted, 'Jesus, Andy, I've been looking everywhere for you.'

Cree gave him a mild look of inquiry. 'Well, here I am, John.'

Tank managed to keep his trap shut. But what really pissed him off then was Murph saying briskly, 'Gentlemen,' as she got down to business. The word and its delivery didn't feel right. The old Pam, who until a few months ago had been his patrol partner, would never have sounded like this, as if she'd had a senior-officer transplant. Plus she was barely noticing him, and in his dim way he realised that her body was taut, humming, and it certainly wasn't him doing that to her. Fucking Cree. Tank jerked out a chair and plonked himself down and folded his arms, making it clear he didn't have all day.

No one noticed. 'This is Lachlan Roe, our assault victim,' Murph said, handing them each a photograph. 'Tonight, as we keep an eye on the schoolies, I'd like you to show it to everyone you meet.'

Cree got there quickly, the prick. 'CIU thinks Roe was hanging around the schoolies? What, selling drugs? Buying? Looking for pussy?'

She smiled at him. 'Just a possibility. Your main task tonight is to keep an eye on the kids. It's the eclipse, and they're all hyped up about it. Maybe the sight of a red moon will bliss them out and we can all go home to bed early; maybe it will stir them up.'

Her gaze lingered. Cree gazed back. To break up the love-fest, Tank said, 'So how do we play it?'

She turned to him reluctantly and said, 'Mingle, John. Let yourselves be seen. Talk to the kids, let them know you've got their backs if they get into strife. Warn off the toolies, step in if an argument looks like brewing, confiscate car keys from kids who are too drunk or high to drive. And turn a blind eye to minor infringements. Don't make unnecessary paperwork for yourselves. Let the kids have their fun, so long as no one gets hurt—schoolie or local.'

She swung around to Cree again, as if seeking his okay. 'Any questions?'

'How do you mean, mingle?' Tank demanded. 'We're coppers. We look like coppers. We're old, to them.'

With a quick glance at the ceiling and down again, Murph said, 'That's the whole point. We're not there to spy, we're there to give help and comfort. Be a presence. Get chatting. Give advice. If anyone needs food or water or money, provide it.'

'We get reimbursed?'

Pam merely smiled. Tank said in disgust, 'Terrific.'

'I'm talking about ten bucks for a bus fare, Tank, not your annual salary.'

She was glancing at Cree. Tank felt very lonely in the world. 'Whatever.'

By late that same afternoon, Ellen Destry had finished at the Landseer School. She'd re-questioned the library staff and anyone who'd taught Zara Selkirk, learning only that the girl and her two Facebook friends were no better or worse than other spoilt-brat bullies who'd passed through the school. Ellen heard stories of binge drinking, drug taking and sexual romps, and the careless, unreflective and vulgar culture that allowed it to happen. Moorhouse said, 'I'm a generation older than many of these parents. It's as if they don't know how to be parents, how to apply discipline. Of course, they're also too rich and too busy. Needless to say, we've placed filters on the school's computers, banning access to sites like Facebook.'

Good luck, thought Ellen. The kids have home computers. They can access software that will get through any filter a school or a parent cares to install.

Next she drove to a small brick house beside the railway line in Baxter, where the spring weeds were rampant and Merle Richardson spoke in a defeated whisper: 'I just want to forget about it and get on with my life.'

Ellen said gently, 'How did you feel when the school offered an apology, to be mediated by the chaplain?'

Richardson screwed a damp handkerchief between her knuckly fingers. 'Too little, too late.'

'Did you resent the chaplain's role? Could he have been more supportive of you?'

'I know what you're implying. I want nothing to do with an apology. My brother urged me to get legal advice, and the lawyer told me that accepting an apology would compromise my chances of getting a financial settlement from the school.'

'Did you tell the school that you were seeking legal advice?'

'My lawyer did.'

'Did you cancel the meeting with the chaplain?'

'My lawyer did.'

'Did the chaplain try to change your mind?'

'I've had nothing to do with the school or anyone in it since the abuse happened.'

Ellen nodded, wondering if she could charge Zara Selkirk and her friends with stalking, misuse of a telecommunications device, and manufacturing pornography. 'Okay, thank you,' she said, hoping that Merle Richardson got millions in compensation.

She was trudging toward her car, head down, when she saw that she was missing a wheel trim. She cursed, blaming the rough dirt roads near Hal's house—her house. Two weeks earlier, she'd lost another wheel trim, finding it again on one of her walks. Could she keep losing and finding wheel trims?

By now it was early evening. Before starting the engine she called Challis. It went to voicemail. 'It's only me,' she said. 'Heading for home. See you when I see you.'

It was often like this: they wanted to see each other, eat with each other, spend the evening together, but always the job's obligations intervened, the overdue reports, pending phone calls, last-minute interruptions.

As Ellen drove away she could feel Merle Richardson behind a curtain, watching, waiting, feeling unsafe. Distracted by feelings of impotence, she at first didn't realise that she'd made a wrong turning, one that took her up into the southern edge of Frankston. She drove past little houses, parks and shops, past kids on bikes and commuters returning from the station or the city, and wondered how it would be to live like that again, amid neighbours. Quite a few of the houses were for sale. Could she afford to buy one? Did she want to live here?

More to the point, did she want to live alone? Would that hurt Hal? Could she hurt him?

She corrected her direction at the next roundabout. The traffic was streaming out of Frankston and boxed her in. She was deeply fatigued, and on the outskirts of Somerville saw a broken-backed magpie in the waning light, its bewildered mate hopping out of the path of her car with what seemed to Ellen to be a look of reproach and appeal.

Challis had ended up spending the entire afternoon with McQuarrie. He returned to Waterloo feeling fired up, wanting to talk to Ellen. But she wasn't in CIU, and, instead of driving straight home, he made the mistake of checking his e-mails and message slips. Soon evening settled and he was returning phone calls from the media and handling a stack of paperwork. His IN tray, like the top of his desk in general, was overflowing with material from numerous cases, including the Roe assault: forensic reports, investigation and crime-scene worksheets; witness lists and statements; field notes; sketches, photographs and cased videos; interview transcriptions; and ongoing investigative narratives, which were updated from time to time as needed. No murder book just now, thank God.

But then he came across an internal alert notifying him that one of his officers had accessed the Law Enforcement Database that morning. It was a touchy issue: when the system was first set up, bored coppers had used it to look into the private lives of TV stars and celebrity footballers, and before long the abuse had grown more serious. One officer had been demoted for accumulating information on his estranged wife's new lover, a handful of others admonished for searching the files of a parliamentary candidate who'd campaigned on the issue of police corruption, and one detective sacked for leaking LED material on one drug dealer to a rival dealer.

Challis didn't know why Pam Murphy had logged on, only that an audit had triggered automatically when she logged out. He didn't doubt that she'd searched the database as part of her official duties, but she hadn't advised him first and now he was obliged to follow it up.

He leaned back, lacing his fingers behind his head. He was a very private man. He hated for anyone to know anything about him, but they did know things, and there was little he could do to control the flow of information. At the same time, his daily work demanded that he uncover people's secrets. The issue of privacy ceased to exist, in many investigations. Achieving justice, and maintaining public safety, demanded that he dig up, expose and use the things that people wanted to hide. It was another illustration of the great divide: us and them, the police and the general mass of people. That's why access to the LED database had to be tightly controlled. A lesser man than Challis might want to use it to learn if his new lover had secret debts, for example, or if his lover's daughter was involved in the drug scene.

Meanwhile, who was Hugh Ebeling, and why had Pam Murphy been looking into his affairs?

The phone rang again and the front desk said, 'Sorry, Inspector, but we've got a missing person and there's no one else available.'

Challis groaned. Mis per cases were a headache. A spouse, partner or child might have very good reasons for disappearing, and police attention might make things worse for them. Many returned of their own accord, or at least made contact, but some feared they'd be harmed if they did. Of course, others were missing because they'd been murdered and their bodies disposed of. 'Details?'

'Best if you came down and talked to the gentleman concerned.'

The time was eight o'clock.

22

Challis clattered down the stairs and joined the duty sergeant at the front desk. Night had settled; there was deep darkness beyond the light outside the main entrance. 'This is Mr Wishart, sir.'

Wishart thrust his hand over the desk, knocking the sign-in book askew. 'Adrian Wishart,' he said. His grip was firm but so moist that Challis cringed.

He made a rapid scan of Wishart. Age, mid-thirties. Medium height. Artfully tousled hair, unmarked hands, and casual but costly looking jacket and trousers, so he probably worked indoors for good money. Clean-shaven: in fact, freshly shaven, his lean, ascetic features almost gleaming. Some kind of cologne drifted faintly in the disturbed air, disturbed because Wishart was trembling, suppressing powerful emotions, or giving that appearance. Challis read the body language and decided that Wishart was inventing it, behaving as he imagined a husband should behave. Still, Challis wasn't about to read too much into that. He'd been wrong before, people behaved oddly in the presence of the police, and Wishart's concern might not be loving but material: she'd run off with all of his money, for example.

'Your wife is missing?'

'Yes,' said Wishart in a rush. 'Ludmilla. Today's her birthday and we're supposed to go out for dinner.' He glanced at his watch. 'She normally gets home at half-past five.'

Challis checked his own watch. Just after eight o'clock. 'Perhaps she went straight to the restaurant?'

'No. I was expecting to find her at home, we'd have a drink, get changed, go out.'

Challis looked past him into the darkness. The light was odd out there. The eclipse. He turned to Wishart and said, 'What time did you get home?'

'About six.'

'Where do you work?'

Wishart frowned. 'At home.'

Challis frowned. 'I thought you said you came home about six.'

Wishart's expression cleared. 'What I mean is, I work from home but I'd been up to visit my uncle in Cheltenham. He had a present for Mill.'

'Is "Mill" short for Ludmilla?'

'Yes. Anyway, she turned thirty and he had a present for her. We've been close, you know—since my parents died.'

'His name?'

'Terry.'

'Terry Wishart? I'll need his contact details.'

The man looked perplexed. 'Okay.'

'What do you do?'

'Architect.'

'Your wife?'

'She's the infringements officer at Planning East.'

Challis frowned, placing the office mentally. 'Next to Centrelink?'

'Yes. She's not there, her car's not there, and she's not answering her phone.'

'Why didn't you wait at home for her and call us instead of coming in?'

'I did wait. I waited for ages, then thought to check the carpark,

126

and was passing the police station and thought—'

'It's all right,' said Challis smoothly. 'Have you rung her work colleagues? Her friends, family?'

'Her mother's in Sydney. She wouldn't go there. I rang her friend Carmen. She said she saw Mill at lunchtime, said Mill was going to be out and about for work all afternoon. I'm worried.'

Challis said carefully, 'I have to ask you this: have you argued with Ludmilla recently? Is there anything in your relationship that might lead her to pack a bag and leave?'

'Absolutely not.'

'Have you checked her belongings?'

'Yes. First thing I did. Nothing's missing.'

'The first thing you did? So there was a reason why she might have packed a bag and left?'

'No! I mean, after it became clear she was late, I made several phone calls, and it was Carmen who said I should check to see if she'd done that, packed a bag and left.'

'Has she done this kind of thing before?'

'Never! It's not like her.'

How many times have I heard that? thought Challis. It was another of mankind's great lies, like a poor man can get into the White House. In his experience, most people were blind to their loved ones' inclinations and potential. On the other hand, it paid the police to listen, just in case. He said, 'Another hard question: do you have any reason to believe there could be someone else in her life? Phone calls she takes in another room, alterations to her habits, new clothes, returning late from work…'

Wishart looked wretched. 'I don't know. I doubt it very much. It's not like her. She was so busy at work. She never stays away overnight. If she has a conference interstate or overseas, I go with her.'

'You said she could be out in the field. Doing what?'

'Inspecting, issuing warnings, following up on things. She said something about an old house that had been illegally demolished.

127

People are always clearing vegetation without a permit. Stuff like that.'

'She could be inspecting a property some distance away. She forgot the time, or she has a flat tyre or engine trouble. You called her?'

'Went to voicemail.'

'The Peninsula is full of black spots where there's no mobile reception.'

Wishart's bony white fists beat the desk gently while the duty sergeant looked on. 'I know that. I've thought of that.'

'Then perhaps you should go home,' said Challis, 'and sit by the phone.'

'But I did the right thing, didn't I, reporting it?'

'Yes,' said Challis firmly, knowing all he could do at this stage was put in a few calls to hospitals and other police districts. It was far too soon for anything official.

'What if she's been in an accident? What if she's unconscious?' Tears spurted. 'What if she's dead?'

'The best you can do this late in the day,' said Challis, 'is go home. I'll start making some enquiries. Go home and call someone to be with you, a friend or family member. This uncle, for example. I'm sure you'll hear something soon.'

'That's all? For God's sake.' Wishart moped out.

'She's done a runner,' the sergeant said.

'You could be right.'

Challis went out to examine the moon. He'd missed most of the eclipse. All he saw was a reddish smudge amongst the stars and the hard edges of the trees around him.

23

Scobie Sutton, his wife Beth and his daughter Roslyn joined the other hundred or so adults and kids in filing out of the school hall at eight o'clock and on to the basketball courts. 'Just for ten or fifteen minutes,' the school principal said. 'It's not every day the moon turns red.'

They stood there, looking up. Wispy cloud above, atmospheric streaks, and there was a partial moon above them, blurred, a kind of wine colour. Some enterprising types tried to photograph the effect, the kids began to run around and there was an air of giddiness. Roslyn had already played her piano solo and sung 'Zulu Warrior' with her little choir, and 'Smoke on the Water' had been mangled—twice—so Scobie was feeling pretty good, his wife's oddness temporarily forgotten. Until he looked down at her and saw that she was bunching the neck of her blouse in one hand and muttering some kind of incantation, as though encouraged in further madness by the moon.

Ellen Destry looked at the moon shadows from Hal's kitchen window. It was eight-thirty and she was warm and pink from her bath, wrapped up in pyjamas and thick socks. Then a peacock sounded its unearthly cry from the farm on the other side of the hill and the light painting the yard was sufficiently altered to draw her out onto the lawn. She craned her neck, but couldn't see what the fuss was about, and went back inside to zap a lean beef casserole in the microwave.

She was pouring herself a glass of Elan red when the kitchen phone rang.

'Destry,' she said.

'It's only me.'

'I left a message—'

'I got it. I could be late: a woman's missing.'

Ellen closed her eyes. 'Young? I mean, a schoolie?' She'd have to take charge if it was a schoolie.

'No.'

Ellen said, 'Do you want me to come in?' She did and didn't want to.

'No, I'll be fine. Don't wait up.'

But she would, and they both knew it. She replaced the handset, removed the casserole and ate it with the wine in front of the TV, some crap on one of the commercial channels. It was during an ad, her attention wandering, that she began to take stock of the sitting room. She switched off the TV and stood on the worn rug between the armchairs and wondered what, exactly, bothered her about it.

The dimensions were pleasing. The room was long, broad, with a high ceiling and a large window looking out onto a few shrubs and a paling fence. Bookshelves took up the end wall, with one shelf for CDs. Then, conscious that she was living a cliché, she began to note the things she itched to change. More colour, for a start: paint the walls, brighter cushions, a new rug. Vases of flowers every day. New curtains. A few—

The phone rang again.

'Destry.'

A woman chirruped, 'Is that Mrs Challis?'

Ellen went very still, very tight. 'No, it is not.'

'Can I speak to her, please?'

'What makes you think there's a Mrs Challis?'

'Er, this is Mr Challis's number.'

'So if a woman answers she must be Mrs Challis?'

There was a long pause, freighted with doubt and confusion. Ellen said sweetly, 'Now, as you know, we're almost ten years into the twenty-first century: have you ever heard of a man and a woman with different last names living together, by any faint chance?'

The woman sounded unsure. 'Ye-es.'

'All right, how about this: have you ever heard of a woman *marrying* a man and keeping her own last name? Think carefully, now.'

The voice came in a rush, almost in tears, so that Ellen felt mean. 'This is a courtesy call from Telstra, asking clients if they're satisfied with their current plans. If I could speak to the man or the lady of the house…'

Ellen slammed the phone down. Night was settling around the house and the light was very queer. She finished her glass of red and poured another.

Pam Murphy stood on a patch of cropped lawn between the coin barbecues and the foreshore trees, watching the moon turn red in silent stages as the earth glided between it and the sun. She'd been expecting a blood red, but it was no red that she could name. It was a chocolaty red, a rusty red, a bruised red with touches of old blood, rendered mistily by thin, vapoury clouds high in the atmosphere. Like everyone around her, she stood transfixed. All human activity except the need to congregate and worship was suspended for an hour or so. If she'd been expecting the schoolies to hallucinate, turn strange, self-destructive or violent, she was mistaken. The red moon mellowed them. They swayed to inner choruses and seemed inclined to kiss and hug each other.

As she gazed, a little dreamy, hard, slim arms slid around her. A pair of dry lips tugged briefly on her ear lobe. The sensation was there and gone before she'd quite registered it, leaving a tingle somewhere inside her.

She whirled around. 'That could be considered harassment, constable.'

'Sorry, got caught up in the moment,' Andy Cree said.

He gave her a look. She'd seen the same look on the boys who'd snatched a kiss and a feel at high school socials and she'd seen it on young offenders, those who had good looks, nerve and invincibility on their side. She was fighting down a grin, trying to stop her body responding to the force-field of his, when she noticed John Tankard standing nearby, looking daggers at them. She sighed. They had a job to do. 'Focus, constable,' she said, stepping back.

Andy snapped a salute at her. 'Aye, aye, ma'am.'

'You know the drill: mingle.'

She watched Cree fade into the queer half-light, past the skateboard ramps and the barbecues toward the strip of half-a-dozen motels and bed-and-breakfast joints. Meanwhile Tank had wandered off toward the tents, where some of the kids were clustered around a campfire with blankets and guitars. They flickered in and out of the firelight and snatches of Dylan and Baez drifted toward her. Dylan and Baez. Even *I'm* too young for Dylan and Baez, she thought.

Otherwise there seemed to be no purposeful movement anywhere, only a sense of dreaminess. Waterloo was spread beneath the gentle moon and so far there hadn't been a single pub brawl, drag race or outbreak of tears.

Pam took High Street first, going up as far as Blockbuster Video and the Thai restaurant, and back down to the foreshore reserve. She saw schoolies congregating outside the pubs and noodle and pizza outlets, but she also saw plenty of locals and their kids. Everyone was blissed out and so she developed a sense of waiting for things to go wrong. Midnight would come and the booze and drugs would run out and the buzz wear off, and disappointments and grievances would set in. She shouldn't be alone then. The three of them would need to roam as a unit and watch each other's backs.

Time drifted and Pam drifted. She wanted to feel alert but the night air was mild, subtly perfumed—the gardens in bloom; the ozone tang of the sea; even the dope the kids were smoking—and full of benign fellow-feeling.

Half hoping that she'd encounter Andy Cree, she drifted to where it was darkest, the rocks and the occasional scoops of sandy beach between the parkland and the mangroves. She picked her way left, toward the refinery, and then right, toward the next town, Penzance Beach, but not intending to walk anywhere near as far as that. Here and there she found lovers embracing, solitary dreamers, small huddles of murmuring schoolies, and all around her there was the suck and surge of the black water, the scrape of fabric against skin and soft moans, sighs and caught breaths. None of it was her business.

Then she clambered over a breakwater, attracted by sounds of distress. In the shredded moonlight she saw the oily mud and spindly lines of a mangrove pocket, and a kid floundering there, sunk to his shins. She saw him retch violently, waver upright, wipe his chin, pitch over at the waist again. He was almost naked, wearing only red scraps over his groin, as though his underpants had become skewed as he struggled against the mud and his impulse to retch.

Pam climbed down the slick rocks and reached the spongy mud. The moon above her was no longer red but a high, misty white orb that slipped in and out of scrappy clouds. Tricky light, but Pam saw, as she got closer, that the boy *was* naked. It wasn't cotton fabric on and around his groin but something like paint or lipstick, applied in thick, bold stripes.

'The bitch poisoned me,' Josh Brownlee said wretchedly.

24

Thursday morning.

The two friends had been walking between Shoreham and Flinders at seven-thirty when they found the body. Not that they stumbled upon it: rather, they stumbled upon some cows. They'd never seen cows on the beach before. Joggers, yes, dogs, dead seals, daily fitness walkers like themselves, but never cows, even though farmland abutted the beach.

Two women aged in their forties, one with short brown hair, the other with shoulder-length dirty blonde hair. Short Brown Hair indicated the cliff looming above their heads and said, 'We climbed to the top and found a hole in the fence.'

Challis followed her pointing finger. Trees and bushes clung thickly to the sloping face of the cliff and along the ridge. He'd left Ellen up there with the crime scene officers and taken the women back down to the beach, so that he could sort it all out. 'You saw the cows and went to investigate.'

'Wouldn't you? There's a big house up there. We thought we should tell someone.'

Challis smiled a kind of apology. He really didn't want anyone to be stroppy with him right now. 'I need to write a simple narrative of events,' he said. 'You climbed to the top, and then what happened?'

'We went to the house,' said the blonde one. Both women were approaching middle age but were lithe and fit, comfortable with their bodies, the beach and their daily walk together.

'There was no one home,' the other woman said.

Challis nodded. He'd already knocked. A huge new house, Swiss chalet style with sheds and a barn, set a couple of hundred metres back from the cliff where the land began to rise again, allowing commanding views along the beach in both directions and far out to sea. Views achieved at a cost, Challis thought: he'd counted five huge ash circles and dozens of tree stumps.

'And that's when you saw the car.'

'Yes.'

Challis pictured the setting on the headland above him. Apart from bashing your way up through the bushes on the cliff face, or climbing fences on neighbouring farmland, your only access to the chalet was via a newly gravelled farm road that wound across paddocks from Frankston-Flinders Road, a kilometre away. You'd pass the driveway entrance on your way to Flinders and wonder what lucky sods lived along it. There were mystery driveways and private roads all over the Peninsula and they all led to money. This driveway stopped at a double gate in a post-and-rail fence one hundred metres uphill and behind the house and sheds.

'The car was…' prompted Challis.

'Stopped at the gate with the driver's door open. We didn't touch it.'

'Go on.'

'At first we didn't know if it belonged to the house or to someone visiting,' said the short-haired one, 'but we needed to tell someone about the cows.'

'So you approached the car…'

The friends, until then enlivened by their adventure, seemed to flinch. 'And that's when we saw Ludmilla lying on the ground,' said the blonde.

Challis was astonished. 'You recognised her?'

'When I got closer,' the blonde said.

He'd already called in the numberplate. The car, a silver Golf, was registered to one Ludmilla Wishart—not that he'd made the mistake of assuming victim and registered owner were one and the same person, a fuck-up he'd made many years ago, back when he was a probationary constable. But he'd taken one look at the body and recognised her from the photographs left by Adrian Wishart last night.

'I need to know if either of you touched the body.'

'I did,' said the woman with short hair. 'I'm a midwife. I couldn't feel a pulse.'

'Did either of you stand or crouch near her?'

'Yes.'

Challis nodded. The ground around the body was hard, but the women might have shed hair, lint or threads. One of them had vomited some distance from the car and the body. The other contaminants? The weather, the killer, the various experts attending at the scene.

'You called it in by mobile phone?'

'Yes. The ambulance got here first, the police soon afterwards.'

A couple of uniforms from Waterloo, who had called CIU, getting Scobie Sutton. 'How well did you know Mrs Wishart?'

'I recognised her, but I don't...didn't know her except professionally. She struck me as strict about regulations, but also fair. Not a planning Nazi—not with me, anyway.'

Challis tried to put that with what he'd seen up on the headland thirty minutes earlier. Ludmilla Wishart was lying on her side at the rear of the car, blood pooled beneath the spread of auburn hair, upper body in the dirt, feet in the roadside grasses. The driver's door was open.

She'd been felled with one powerful blow to the back of the head, according to Dr Berg, the pathologist on duty today. Rigor was fully established, Dr Berg said, meaning she'd been dead for twelve hours or more.

'No one else came along while you waited?'

'It's not a through road.'

Challis nodded. 'Thanks for your time.'

He took their details and watched them walk back toward Shoreham, shoulders touching, deep in conversation. If the owners of the chalet were away and no one used the access road, the body could have remained undiscovered for days. He turned and made for the shallowest incline on the cliff face, where a rudimentary path switchbacked between bracken, ti-trees, mossy logs and blackberry canes. Two minutes later he was at the top again, scratched, burred and out of breath. With one hand on a rotting post for a fulcrum, he vaulted the fence. It was a poor excuse for a fence, broken wires snaking through tangles of grass, the top barbed strand almost rusted through, the posts leaning or fallen away to friable remnants.

He trudged along a newer fence line that ran perpendicular to the cliff top and past the chalet. The grass was damp and cow pats sat like broad plates of evil black mould wherever he put his feet. But at least he'd thought to bring rubber boots with him.

And there was Ellen, by the victim's car. Since yesterday evening he'd almost told her several times that McQuarrie wanted her to head a new unit, but the super had sworn him to secrecy for the time being. He wanted Challis to think about *which* unit, given her abilities and inclinations. 'Take your time and get back to me,' he'd said.

Feeling burdened suddenly, Challis waved as he climbed the slope. She waved back. 'Having fun?' she called.

He joined her, replying, 'My daily exercise. Any joy?'

'Not yet.'

Together they gazed past the silver Golf to where Scobie Sutton and the two uniforms were performing a grid-pattern search for the murder weapon. 'The doc thinks a tyre iron.'

'From the victim's car?'

Ellen shook her head. 'Hasn't been disturbed.'

At that moment a tow truck appeared. Scobie put up his hand to stop it. The driver nodded, switched off, settled with a newspaper. He might be there an hour before the scene was released so that he could load the car and cart it to the forensic science centre in the city.

Meanwhile the pathologist was still examining the body and the crime scene officers were searching the immediate area around it, stepping from one metal plate to another and often ducking with paper sacks and tweezering up some tiny fragment of possible evidentiary value. Others were examining the dirt for tyre impressions, and one was poking around inside the car.

'Are we thinking the husband?' asked Ellen.

'He's first on the list. But she was the shire's planning infringements officer, so she probably made enemies.'

Ellen nodded. Scobie was approaching, holding an evidence bag carefully. 'Found some dry mud.'

'This is the countryside, Scobie,' Ellen said.

He flushed. 'It's not soil from this area. This is dark clay, the mud is reddish.'

They peered into the evidence bag. A faint odour of the grassy earth wafted from the neck. Not an ordinary clump but smooth and regular on two sides. 'Well spotted, Scobie,' Challis said. 'From the inside of a wheel arch?'

'Looks like it.'

'Get it to forensics along with everything else, ask them to work out the make and model of car, if possible, and where on the Peninsula the mud comes from.'

'Will do.'

'And when you get back to CIU, start checking the victim's last known movements since lunchtime yesterday. Check if she used her credit card anywhere, phone calls, the usual.'

'Boss,' said Sutton. He looked more alive than he'd done for days, Challis thought.

'We also need to know who owns this property and why Mrs Wishart was here.'

'Can't Pam do that?'

'Pam's working an assault from last night.'

'Fair enough,' Scobie said. He looked inquiringly at Challis and Ellen. 'The husband?'

'First port of call.'

The technician searching inside the car called, 'Found a laptop, inspector—under the passenger seat.'

Challis called his thanks and sat in the CIU Falcon with Ellen, trying to think his way into the desires, hurts and fears of the killer. He always did it, always did it immediately, even at the risk of jumping to early conclusions. Of course they'd look at the husband first. Statistics told them to look at a family member ahead of anyone else. Also, Challis knew to search for the simple answer first. It would involve the five key factors of victim, motive, weapon, evidence and culprit. So far, all he had for sure was a victim and by implication a culprit.

25

When the forensics officers had finished with the scene, Challis and Destry left, Ellen driving, Challis working his mobile phone, arranging for the loan of a couple of detectives from Mornington. That completed, he folded his arms in the passenger seat and mused for a while. 'The victim's car,' he said.

'What about it?'

'There was no mud inside the wheel arches.'

'Or the road corrugations shook it loose.'

Challis shaded his eyes, for they were heading into the rising sun. 'The mud Scobie found wasn't from her car. The shape was wrong.'

'Or it came from a car that was on that road legitimately.'

'Yeah, yeah, rain on my parade.'

'Just doing my job,' Ellen said. It was what they did, floated scenarios and sank the weak ones.

Challis placed his hand on her thigh. That was wrong on all kinds of professional levels but McQuarrie had offered a way out yesterday and besides, he wanted to feel the coiled strength in her, the heat and promise.

'Don't,' she said, adding, 'boss.'

He folded his arms. 'Approximate time of death, according to Freya Berg, was sometime late yesterday afternoon or evening. The husband came into the station at around eight.'

'It was cool by late afternoon, early evening,' Ellen said, 'but she hadn't put her cardigan on, it was still on the back seat. She was wearing just a T-shirt. That points to an earlier rather than a later time of death.'

'Unless she was someone who never felt the cold; or she'd been sitting in the car, waiting for someone.'

Ellen turned down the corners of her mouth, thinking about it. 'Either way, we need to know the husband's movements for the whole afternoon.' She paused. 'Does it seem personal to you, Hal? She was bashed by someone she knew rather than a passing fruitcake?'

Challis thought about it. 'There was real anger there. Same with Lachlan Roe.'

'God, they're not connected?'

'I didn't mean that, only that we might not be looking at a stranger in either case.'

They crested small hills and slowed for the township of Balnarring, stuck behind a Landseer School bus, which pulled into the shopping centre and stopped to collect a handful of kids. Ellen accelerated away, past the garage, the fire station and dwindling houses until they were in a region of rampant spring grasses, kit homes, boutique wineries and alpaca herds. There was a sign outside one house, 'Giant Garage Sale Saturday'. A low, moist field was dotted with ibis and herons. A bouquet of flowers lay wilting at the base of a tree, a death tree, scarred where a car had collided with it.

Challis daydreamed. He'd miss working with Ellen. He wouldn't miss being her boss, though. She should head the new sex crimes unit, he thought suddenly. With the population explosion and increased social distress on the Peninsula, *reported* rapes and sexual assaults were on the increase, meaning that the true figures were much higher. The only drawback was that Ellen would be expected to operate out of Mornington. 'I can't have you both in the same station, Hal, surely you see that,' the super had said.

But Mornington was only twenty minutes away.

Soon Ellen was steering past more houses and over a school crossing, and the smudge in the distance was Waterloo. On the outskirts she turned left and up a winding rise to where big new homes sat on large lots and the sounds of the weekends were ride-on mowers, trail bikes, clopping hooves and barbecues. Professional people like the Wisharts lived on this estate, alongside prosperous shopkeepers and expert tradespeople. They had huge mortgages, distant bay views across Waterloo on the flatland below and all the space they needed for their kids and their gardens.

A prosperous enclave, but still a million dollars away from the clifftop property where Ludmilla Wishart had died. What had she been doing there? Who lived there? City people, guessed Challis, remembering the long grass and dusty windows. They visit the place only occasionally and therefore don't *need* a vast chalet but merely want one.

'Where to?' asked Ellen.

She'd come to a couple of branching roads named for ex-prime ministers. 'Menzies,' said Challis. 'Lot 5.'

She steered with a twist of the wrist. Challis liked watching her, even as he was thinking about the murder and how he'd inform Adrian Wishart that his wife was dead. 'Where was her handbag?' he said suddenly.

'Exactly.'

'Opportunistic? A mugging? But it's not a through road. The handbag was taken to make it look like a robbery? They missed the laptop under the seat.'

'Scobie's checking out her credit card, so that might tell us something. Especially if it's been used to buy a surfboard or something.'

Ellen eased the CIU Falcon gently over the kerb and into the driveway of a corrugated iron house. Challis decided that he liked the house. It was partly the iconic appeal of the corrugated iron, which could be found on every roof and woolshed in rural Australia, and partly the design of this particular house, which was saved from looking like an outback shed by dormer windows set in a steeply pitched roof, a balcony and broad verandas. And he was feeling anticipatory: he wanted to take a closer look at Wishart, know that he was the killer, and wrap this up by teatime, but, at the same time, he was dreading being the bearer of bad news.

A red Citroën was parked in a carport hung with vines. 'Won't be a moment,' he said, and as Ellen marked time with her seatbelt, keys, mobile phone, jacket and notebook, he trotted to the Citroën and crouched at each wheel arch. There was dust, no mud, and the recess was a different configuration from the one that had shaped the mud found at the murder scene.

He rejoined Ellen and they walked along a patterned concrete path to the front door, which opened before they reached it. Adrian Wishart, unshaven, red-eyed, hair awry, in tracksuit pants and a T-shirt.

'You've found her.'

Ellen said gently, 'May we come in, Mr Wishart?'

'You've found her.'

'Let's go inside,' Ellen said, Challis admiring the ease and effectiveness of her ways. It was a combination of her voice, level gaze and decisiveness. It worked on bullies, drunks, the grieving, the hostile and the disturbed.

The door opened onto a short hallway, rooms on either side, one of them a working studio with drafting tables, pens, rulers, angle-poise lights and coiled blueprints. At the end of the hallway was a vast room with thick beams, a fireplace, wall-to-ceiling bookcases, island benches and discrete sitting, dining and TV watching areas. Four huge sofas, shaggy rugs on wooden floors. Framed architectural drawings shared wall space with avant-garde photographs, watercolour paintings and a couple of Central Australia dot paintings.

'I don't know what I'm supposed to do,' said Wishart peevishly. 'Do I offer you tea or coffee?'

Ellen took his elbow and led him through an archway to a kitchen alcove. Here there was a plain wooden table with a scuffed surface, a table for the morning cereal, newspaper and coffee, a table for visitors who might drop in. Challis followed, recognising that Ellen's instincts had been right again: the sitting areas were too vast and open, the kitchen was intimate. She sat Wishart on a chair at the table, took the adjacent chair and said, 'I'm very sorry, Mr Wishart, but a body has—'

A wail broke from Wishart. 'No, please, please don't say it.'

'We have reason to believe it's your wife,' said Ellen gently.

'I should see her. I should be with her,' Wishart said, pushing back his chair.

Ellen stopped him. 'Soon enough, Mr Wishart. Meanwhile, is there anyone we can call on your behalf? Family member? Friend?'

The wind went out of Wishart's sails and he slumped at the table. Then he sprang up again. 'Tea? Coffee?'

'I'll do that,' Challis said. He'd watch and listen now as Ellen went to work.

'How did she die?' asked Wishart.

Ellen told him.

Challis watched Wishart swallow and ask, 'Where?'

Ellen told him, adding, 'Do you know why she was there?'

Wishart had almost no energy. The question seemed to defeat him. 'No idea.' Then he rallied a little. 'Sorry, where did you say?'

Ellen told him again. 'Do you know why she was there?'

'Her job—she's the planning infringements officer,' Wishart said. 'If it's the place I'm thinking of, it belongs to Jamie Furneaux. He's some cousin of the Premier. Anyway, he cut down a heap of trees and burned them. Someone called the fire brigade, and he tried to shut them up with a big donation, but it was too late, someone dobbed him in.'

'He didn't have permission to remove the trees?'

'No.'

'She was there to serve him with an infringement notice?'

Wishart shook his head. 'To check that he'd carried out reclamation work, you know, planted new trees.'

'The job made her unpopular?'

'Hell, yes.'

Adrian Wishart's indignation seemed to swell into fury, and he rose from his seat, stabbing his finger at Challis, who was beside the bubbling kettle. 'I told you something was wrong last night. If you'd done something about it instead of, of…'

Ellen said firmly, 'Please, Mr Wishart. We believe that Ludmilla was already dead when you contacted the station.'

He sat, all at sea. His neat, narrow head shaking in big, doubting sweeps he said, 'Are you sure she didn't fall and hit her head?'

'We don't believe so.'

He looked up. 'Will I have to identify her?'

'We'll take you there and bring you home again.'

'Now?'

'The sooner the better.'

'But your tea, your coffee.'

'After that,' said Ellen gently.

Challis poured the tea. He disliked tea, but the only alternative was instant coffee. He delivered the mugs of tea to the table with a bowl of sugar and a bottle of milk, and sat to one side, trying to be unobtrusive but sensing that the husband was powerfully aware of him.

'Is there anyone we can contact, Mr Wishart?' said Ellen.

'I'll be okay.'

'What about your wife's family? Would you like us to inform them?'

'There's only her mother, and she lives in Sydney.'

'Friends. Her friends, or friends you have in common?'

Here Wishart pitched about in his seat briefly. Eventually he said, 'There's Carmen. She and Mill are very close. Were very close,' he added with a little gasp.

Ellen scribbled the woman's address and phone number onto a page of her notebook. Wishart watched her moving hand alertly, Challis watched Wishart. Wishart said, 'Speak to her workmates if you want the names of anyone who had a grudge against her.'

'We will,' Ellen said.

'Her workmates,' Wishart repeated, 'not her boss.'

Ellen cocked her head at him. 'Why not?'

Wishart waved a hand about vaguely as if he regretted the clarification. 'Nothing in particular. Apparently he doesn't spend much time in the office, and when he is there he likes to look over everyone's shoulder.'

'Your wife didn't like him?'

Wishart tried to find the right words. 'He could be demanding,' he said finally.

'Demanding,' said Ellen.

'Yes.'

She took an exploratory sip of tea, and said casually, 'Perhaps you could tell us about what kind of day you had yesterday, Mr Wishart.'

'What kind of day? It was all right. Went to visit my uncle Terry.' Tears spilled as he said, 'Then Mill didn't come home and I got worried.'

'You work from home, I believe?'

Wishart's gaze was jumping between Ellen and Challis. 'Yes.'

'You're a draftsman?'

Challis had told her the man was an architect. The insult was deliberate. 'Certainly not,' Wishart said. 'I'm an architect.'

'You were working on a project yesterday?'

Wishart said airily, 'Oh, there's always a project.'

'Did you go out, perhaps to confer with a client?'

'I know what you're doing. You think I killed her, my own wife.'

'We don't think that, Mr Wishart. The sooner we eliminate you from our inquiries, the sooner we can start looking for the real killer. It's standard procedure to check with those closest to the victim first.'

Wishart began weeping angrily. 'This is awful. Mill and I...we're not the kind of people to come to the attention of the police.'

'May I ask why you went to see your uncle?'

'He had a present for Mill. It was her birthday yesterday, her thirtieth.'

'He couldn't give it to her himself?'

'He has a shop to run, up in the city. He can't get away, whereas I'm more flexible.'

Ellen added the uncle's details to her notebook. 'What time did you see him?'

'All afternoon. I haven't seen him for a few weeks. I got home about six, expecting to see Mill, waited for a while, then made phone calls and went looking for her before reporting her missing.'

So it wasn't a sure-fire alibi. Then again, Challis mistrusted those.

Wishart swallowed visibly. 'Was Mill...was my wife...'

Ellen said, 'She wasn't interfered with.'

'Her face?'

'Untouched.'

Wishart flopped in relief. They were all silent for a while, Challis and Destry watching Wishart closely. Eventually Challis said, 'I'm afraid we'll need to search the house, Mr Wishart, paying particular attention to your wife's papers and computer.'

He looked up at them. 'But...'

'Standard procedure,' said Ellen smoothly.

It wasn't until they were guiding him out to the car that he said, 'There's something I need to tell you.'

Challis felt that old tingle, expecting a confession, but Wishart said, 'When I reported her missing last night I told you she wasn't having an affair. But I think she was.'

26

Pam Murphy was in Waterloo, the hospital carpark, waiting for Josh Brownlee. When he emerged she fell into step with him and said, 'So, Josh, want to tell me about it?'

Josh blinked against the morning light. He was wearing jeans, T-shirt and sandals, clothing that Pam had bundled together from his motel room last night, after delivering him to the hospital. She'd searched the beach and foreshore but hadn't found what he'd been wearing when he was ambushed.

And how had he been ambushed? *'Josh!'* she snapped, to get his attention, 'I saved your life last night. Now, tell me what happened.'

He'd showered but hadn't shaved and the whiskers stood out like prickles. His eyes were red and his dazed air said that he still had drugs in his system. But what drugs, and had he taken them willingly? Last night she'd waited while the Casualty nurse took blood and urine samples and this morning she'd sent them to the lab for analysis. She suspected they'd find one of the date-rape drugs, like GHB, meaning he wouldn't remember anything.

She'd also asked the lab to fast-track Brownlee's DNA analysis. When the manager demurred, she lied and said it was related to the Lachlan Roe case, remembering that Inspector Challis had asked Ollie Hindmarsh to put pressure on the lab as a favour to him.

'Mr Hindmarsh is keen for a result,' she said.

'That prick,' said the lab guy.

'You got it,' said Pam.

She was hoping, *betting*, that Josh's DNA would match the DNA found on the young woman who'd been sexually assaulted on Saturday night.

'My car's over here, Josh,' she said now.

He followed her dumbly along the root-erupted bitumen paths. The air was heavily scented with eucalyptus from the young gum trees that surrounded the potholed carpark. 'Hop in,' she said, 'and I'll take you to your motel.'

Ensuring that he was strapped in, she started the car. 'We haven't been able to find the clothes you were wearing last night. Pity: they might have given us some evidence about what happened to you.'

His mouth hung open. That was pretty normal, Pam reflected. She'd been in close contact with eighteen-year-olds all week and they were all mouth-breathers. It made them look dumb. Many of them *were* dumb. She shook off this train of thought and said, 'Who did you meet with last night, can you remember?'

His face twisted comically in concentration.

'Friends?' Pam prompted. 'A girlfriend, maybe?'

'I think so,' he croaked.

'Well, who? You said, when I found you, "The bitch poisoned me." Who were you talking about, Josh?'

'Don't remember.'

'Were you on anything, Josh? Ice? Ecstasy? It's all right, I'm not from the Drug Squad.'

'Nothing. Beer. Couple of vodkas.'

'So it's just a hangover you're feeling?'

'Yeah.'

'Josh, someone took you to a lonely spot in the mangroves, stole your clothes and painted your balls with lipstick.'

He twisted in his seat, a twist that reached all the way through him.

Not revealing her general glee, Pam said in a businesslike voice, 'You don't remember any of that?'

'No.'

'Sounds like revenge to me, Josh.'

'No.'

'Someone had it in for you.'

'No.'

The voice and manner were sulky, Josh leaning against his door, wanting to get away from her.

'Maybe—indulge me here, Josh—maybe you had an encounter with someone at Schoolies Week last year, or this year, and it got a bit out of hand, mistaken signals, she said no and you thought she was really saying yes.'

'Didn't happen.'

'And she wanted to get back at you.'

'No.'

'Or it didn't happen to her but to her friend.'

'Don't know what you're talking about.'

'Or maybe she was drugged unconscious, which makes it academic whether she said yes or no or gave mixed signals.'

'Why don't you leave me alone?'

Pam reached the roundabout by the post office and turned left, down to the bay and the holiday flats, motels and bed-and-breakfasts. 'It would take a pretty special person to take that kind of revenge,' she mused. 'I can see her in my mind's eye: clever, patient, determined, very, very brave.' She turned her head. 'How brave are you, Josh? Not very, I'd say.'

'I want to go home.'

'There's nothing stopping you, Josh. And heaven knows, I wouldn't want to hang around here much longer, not when there's a vengeful female on the loose.'

'Not,' said Josh, not knowing what it was he wanted to say.

'Someone like Caz Moon. You remember Caz, don't you? Works

in HangTen?'

Josh went rigid in the passenger seat, pointing agitatedly through the windscreen ahead. 'That's my motel.'

The Sea Breeze Holiday Apartments, dating from the 1960s, cheap, forlorn and barely viable at most times of the year. 'I know Josh, I collected a change of clothes for you last night.'

He looked about in a hunted way that kept her smiling on the inside. 'I found your stash, by the way. But like I said, I'm not Drug Squad.'

'Leave me alone. I haven't done anything.'

'Why did you come here, Josh?'

'Schoolies Week. I'm allowed.'

'But you left school *last year*. Had such a good time you had to repeat it?'

'Leave me alone.'

'Partying, drinking, drugs, sex, you had to come back for some of that good shit.'

There was a nasty flash in his eyes and his knuckles went white. Pam flinched: if he had an ice habit, he could be violent and unpredictable. 'Steady, Josh.'

'I'm reporting you.'

She decided to push a little more, tensing her body in case he struck out. 'The sex, Josh. Cool dude like you, you always get lucky, right? You wouldn't need to use a date-rape drug, would you?'

That nastiness came back, but then he piled out of the car and ran toward his room, a corner room on the ground floor. Pam watched him pat his pockets, saw him remember that his wallet and keys were missing, and change direction, scuffing slowly toward the manager's office. He'd sort it out, Pam reflected. Mum and Dad would be there for him, just as they always were for kids like him. Her phone pinged. A text from Andy Cree.

27

Late Thursday morning, and Ellen Destry was sitting across from Carmen Gandolfo in the Mornington office of Community Health, which was a converted 1940s house on a street of similar houses, some of which were residential but most were clinics now—dental, medical and physiotherapy. Gandolfo's window overlooked a black wattle that leaned dangerously over the fence dividing it from the next property. Did Gandolfo know what a shallow root system wattles had? Should she say something? But now wasn't the time…

'Murdered?' Gandolfo was saying. She looked damp and wretched, sniffing, mopping her eyes.

'I'm terribly sorry,' Ellen said. 'I understand that you were close to Mrs Wishart.'

'We're best friends!'

'I'm sorry.'

Fresh weeping. 'You want to know who killed her? Look no further than her husband.'

'He was violent? Abusive?'

'Controlling. Incredibly controlling.'

And so are a lot of people, thought Ellen. She gazed at the other woman for a moment. Carmen Gandolfo was large but compact, with vast, cushiony breasts and auburn hair in a sunburst around her big head. A wry face, under the grief.

'I know this is difficult for you, but I do need to ask you some questions,' Ellen said.

Gandolfo said damply, 'Fire away.'

'Let's start with your meeting with Mrs Wishart yesterday.'

Gandolfo opened her mouth to reply, then froze. 'You think *I* killed her?'

'Of course not,' said Ellen smoothly, keeping an open mind. 'But you did have lunch with her, and she didn't return to the office.'

'She had appointments all afternoon! So did I!'

'You had lunch together…'

Gandolfo told Ellen where they'd lunched, what they'd ordered, what they'd talked about. 'It was a special lunch. Her thirtieth birthday. I gave her an MP3 player.'

Ellen made a note: where had that got to? 'And then?'

'Then I came straight here for my two o'clock appointment. I was booked solid all afternoon and didn't leave until six.'

'Then you went home?'

'No. I had two clients to see, elderly women in a retirement village. I didn't get home until about eight o'clock. My husband had dinner ready.'

'Thank you. Now, tell me about Mr Wishart.'

Ellen watched Gandolfo pull herself together and grow reflective, as if conscious that she should be fair and accurate, that Ellen wouldn't want hyperbole. 'I've known Ludmilla for about five years. We met at a shire Christmas function. She was going out with Adrian at the time; she'd met him when she was one of the planners, and he'd consulted with her about a building he'd designed. They married about three years ago. Mill and I became really good friends.' She paused. 'It was limited, though. Adrian could be very difficult. I had to see her alone, and almost never at her house.'

'Tell me more about him. About the marriage.'

'He's an architect,' said Gandolfo, and stopped. Ellen waited.

'He's the kind of man who's always disappointed. He's always being let down by someone or something. It's never *his* fault: or rather, nothing's ever good enough for his exacting standards. He could be very successful if he was willing to compromise, but naturally his clients or business partners end up disappointing him.'

'Did his wife disappoint him?'

'Constantly, I'd say, but not in ways that would disappoint a normal person, and not because she wanted to annoy him.'

'Did he punish her for it?'

'Yes.'

'How? Did he hit her?'

Gandolfo said slowly, 'Mill was holding herself very stiffly one day, about two months ago. She was in obvious pain, holding her stomach. She said it was her period, but she didn't get bad periods. I think he'd hit her.'

'Was she ever hospitalised, to your knowledge? An accident in the garden, a fall off a chair…'

'No. Look, it was mainly psychological stress that he put her through.'

'Such as?'

The desk phone rang. Gandolfo watched it apprehensively until it cut out. 'Like I said, he was incredibly controlling. He chose what clothes she wore, what hairstyle. He kept a close eye on her spending—even though she probably earned more than he did. He had an awful temper. He'd yell at her, get very angry about small things, then beg forgiveness and act like he loved her to bits, so she was always on tenterhooks.'

Ellen had heard it all before. 'You witnessed this?'

Gandolfo moved about in her chair. 'Kind of. I mean, I saw it in him, and Ludmilla would let slip some of the things he said and did to her.'

So, nothing hard and fast, thought Ellen. 'What else?'

'She supported him emotionally. He was always going on about his breakthrough, which to my mind was never going to happen. He had fussy standards, like that little car. It had to be a Citroën, it had to be European, it couldn't be something cheap and reliable like a Toyota. He turned the best room in their house into a studio and filled it with top of the range drafting and drawing equipment. All that took money, so she was always steering clients his way via her job, drawings, blueprints, proposals things like that. They needed the money, but he considered the work beneath him.'

Ellen saw a small man, a fearful man. 'Beneath him?'

'He gave that indication, but I think he was afraid he'd fail. And because he denigrated the work he did, he lacked a sense of purpose and control, it seems to me. Therefore he made sure he controlled Mill. He became really obsessed with what she was up to. Of course, she wasn't up to anything, but he'd ring her six or seven times a day, send her texts and e-mails all day long, drop into the office on the stupidest pretext or hang around on the street outside. He needed to know where she was at all times. It was as if he thought she had a secret life.'

'Maybe she did.'

'No! She was so loyal it broke my heart.'

'What did she do about the phone calls and visits?'

'What could she do? She tried to talk to him about it but his line was, "You're my wife, I'm allowed to call you" or "I just happened to be passing, sweetheart."' Gandolfo paused. 'Mill told me it was uncanny the way he always seemed to know if she'd been out making field visits during the day.'

'He followed her?'

'Probably.'

Ellen tried a different tack. 'So they had money troubles?'

'I didn't say that. Adrian's work had slackened off recently, but they didn't have debts, I don't think. Where are you going with this?'

Ellen was going in several directions. If the Wisharts had been struggling, was Ludmilla Wishart taking backhanders to finance her husband's lifestyle? Had she delivered an ultimatum to him: *It's time you got regular work*? Had he killed her because she'd left him everything in her will? Was he expecting a huge life insurance payout? Ellen didn't ask any of these questions, merely stared and waited.

Carmen Gandolfo cocked her head eventually. Behind the rawness appeared a look of calculation. 'Adrian already owned the land their house is on before he met Mill. He designed the house, but I think most of her money went into paying for it. Mill told me once that everything was in their joint names, the property, her car, their bank accounts. He made sure of that.'

They watched each other for a while. 'Did she ever talk about leaving him?'

'*I* talked about it,' Gandolfo said. 'She'd listen, agree with everything I said, then tell me that he'd fall apart if she left him, and she couldn't do that to him.'

Ellen had heard that before, too. 'She must have revealed things about her marriage if you were urging her to leave him.'

Gandolfo twisted her mouth pensively. 'Well, to some degree. She had more spark when Adrian wasn't around, she was prepared to have a bit of a laugh about him. She'd tell me things that appalled me, yet she took them for granted. He'd time her phone calls, for God's sake. He'd time her on the loo, tell her she was using too much toilet paper. He was a bully, a control freak, and in my experience as a counsellor those men are dangerous.'

And in my experience as a cop, Ellen thought. 'Did Mrs Wishart say exactly where she was going after you had lunch together?'

Gandolfo blinked at the direction change. 'Only that she had to make some field visits.'

'What was entailed in these field visits?'

Gandolfo spoke slowly, as though stating the obvious. 'There are strict regulations about what you can and can't do on your own land. You know. You can't put up a five-star hotel or clear native vegetation or demolish an existing structure without a permit. Milla's job was to follow up infringements and pursue action, which might be a fine and orders to repair the damage.'

'A job that would have made some people angry.'

'I know what you're getting at. You think someone like that killed her.'

'I have to look at all scenarios. Did she ever say that she was threatened or abused by anyone?'

'Not really. There was a lot of public scrutiny, and it's not as if anyone was ruined financially or went to jail.'

'People have been killed for less.'

Gandolfo winced. 'She did mutter something about planning deliberations being leaked to the wrong people.'

'By an insider? A shire employee?'

'I guess so.'

'Did she give a name?'

'No, but I got the feeling she didn't trust her boss. She was pretty upset yesterday, something about a property developer who bulldozed an old house before a heritage protection order could be placed on it. That's all I know.'

Ellen nodded. All of this could be verified easily. But Carmen Gandolfo wasn't finished:

'I think it was Adrian who killed her, I really do,' she said fervently, her upper arms quivering.

Ellen waited.

Gandolfo deflated. 'Did she suffer?'

'It was a vicious blow, but very sudden and immediately fatal.'

There was a long pause. 'Poor Mill,' said Gandolfo miserably. 'When things got too much for her she'd have panic attacks, cardiac arrhythmia.'

'By too much do you mean dealing with people who blamed her because they'd been caught out and had to pay for it?'

'No, I mean dealing with a jealous, obsessive stalker of a husband. Look, this man comes across as warm and charming. I'm sure he sounded genuinely grief-stricken when you talked to him this morning. It's all an act.'

Wishart *had* seemed genuine. Perhaps it wasn't an act, thought Ellen. Perhaps he'd killed his wife but was mentally unstable and able to rationalise it: 'Someone else killed her' or 'Yes, I killed her, but she provoked me so it wasn't my fault.'

'He's cunning,' Gandolfo said.

Ellen got to her feet, nodding slowly. 'I promise I'll bear that in mind.'

28

'That's awful!' Athol Groot, head of planning for the shire, put a plump hand over his chest and slumped into his chair. 'I mean, I saw her yesterday morning, staff meeting, and she seemed fine.'

Challis didn't state the obvious, that of course Ludmilla Wishart had been fine back then. The guy was shocked, that's all, trying to assimilate the information. 'What time was the meeting?'

'Ten o'clock.'

'She was here all morning?'

'Yes. I think she went to lunch with a friend and had various outside appointments after that.'

Groot's office continued the theme of the foyer: grey tufted carpeting, frosted glass, gleaming pale wood that might have been supplied by Ikea, and fluorescent lighting at saturation point. Everything was new and probably intended to be cheerful and comfortable but it irked Challis.

'What can you tell me about her job?'

Groot was about fifty, jowly and in poor shape, with sparse hair, an unhealthy flush and too many kilos straining the fabric of his trousers, shirt and jacket. He had tried to compensate with a youthful tie and narrow black-rimmed spectacles, but only succeeded in conveying incongruity, not youthfulness. He looked desolately at the floor and murmured, 'She was our infringements person.'

Challis nodded encouragingly.

Groot looked up, mustering himself. 'Here in Planning East we process applications, give advice and feedback about what can and cannot be allowed, and examine projects on completion—anything from that backyard granny flat you build for your elderly mother to a huge new shopping centre. We're bound by federal, state and local regulations, and they change over time and from district to district.' He paused, said challengingly, 'Where do you live?'

Challis told him.

'Zoned rural,' Groot said, nodding wisely. He counted on his fingers: 'No further subdivision permitted. If you erect a new house you'll need permission to go higher than eight metres. The roof must be a muted colour, nothing glary. You're not allowed to cut down any of the notable trees. I could go on.'

Please don't, Challis thought. 'And Mrs Wishart's job?'

'Naturally there are individuals who ignore the regulations.'

'Mrs Wishart investigated these instances?'

'Yes. I did too, when she was overloaded.'

'We'll need access to her files, diary and computers.'

'Some of the information contained therein is confidential.'

Challis hoped he'd never have to read any of the man's reports. Besides, he was pretty sure that planning applications were on the public record, so that objections could be lodged. He said nothing but presented Groot with a warrant. Groot read it, his hands trembling a little. 'This seems to be in order.'

'Let's get started. Then we can be out of your hair.'

They stepped into the foyer, where the two Mornington detectives on loan to Challis were waiting. Their names were Schlunke and Johns, but everyone on the Peninsula knew them as Smith and Jones. Challis nodded, and all four men continued along a corridor to an office opposite a photocopying room, where a young woman was standing numbly, watching sheets of paper spill into the collating trays of one of the machines. Her eyes and nose were raw from weeping.

'Mrs Wishart was popular?'

'Very,' Groot said, unlocking the office and stepping in quickly ahead of the detectives, the set of his body tense, as though the killer awaited them or Ludmilla Wishart had left incriminating files open on her desk.

The Mornington officers began to unplug the computer and box up the files. Challis went straight to the desk diary. He motioned to Groot. 'Can you explain these entries?'

The chief planner stooped to peer at the page, breathing audibly. 'Staff meeting in the morning,' he murmured, 'lunch with CG—her friend—then three appointments: Tyabb 3 p.m., Penzance Beach 4 p.m., Shoreham 5 p.m.' He straightened his back with a thoughtful frown. 'Let's see…Tyabb was an unauthorised bed-and-breakfast. The people concerned had built a second dwelling on their property, but instead of demolishing their original dwelling they'd restored it and rented it out to holidaymakers. They said they didn't know they needed permission and a permit, but that's no defence.'

'Penzance?'

'Ludmilla had been helping a residents' action committee,' Groot said shortly.

'To do what?'

'Get a heritage protection order on an old house.'

'Was it successful?'

Groot shook his head. 'It was demolished.'

'When?'

'Yesterday morning.'

Challis nodded. The house that Pam Murphy had told him about. 'Demolished before the protection order could come into effect?'

'Yes.'

'Was Mrs Wishart upset?'

'I expect so.'

161

'Were the residents upset?'

'I expect they were,' Groot said.

He sounded more sullen than professionally outraged or disappointed. 'And Shoreham?'

Groot brightened. 'A rather arrogant young man chopped down trees he shouldn't have. He was fined and obliged to replant.'

'Mr Jamie Furneaux?'

'Well, yes.'

'Was he angry with Mrs Wishart?'

'I really couldn't say,' Groot said, making it sound as though he had nothing to do with the grubby end of the business.

They walked back along the corridor, Groot pausing to duck into the photocopy room. Challis, waiting outside the door, saw the set of Groot's body as he stood close to the weeping secretary and murmured in her ear. The woman went rigid, gathered her pages together and hurried out, brushing past Challis. 'We have pressing deadlines,' muttered Groot, rejoining him.

Challis questioned the department's other planners and office staff, learning only that Ludmilla Wishart was well liked but in a stressful job, the stress coming from abusive calls, which the office staff attempted to divert, and from Adrian Wishart, her husband.

'Did you ever see him abuse her in any way?'

None of them had.

'Threaten her?'

No. But he was obsessive, forever keeping tabs on her.

'This is in confidence,' Challis said, 'but could she have been involved with someone else, in a romantic sense?'

Not that they knew of. 'I don't think she'd dare,' someone said, relating the observation to the husband's obsessiveness.

Challis decided to be direct. 'What about her relationship with Mr Groot?'

That earned him hunted looks, as if the walls had ears. One of them said, 'Let's just say he likes being the boss.'

Challis and Smith and Jones returned to CIU for the remainder of the morning. Ellen arrived at lunchtime, poking her head around Challis's door and saying, 'Grab a sandwich?'

They walked down High Street to Café Laconic, where they ate little goats' cheese pizzas in the sun. Ellen filled him in on her meeting with Carmen Gandolfo. 'She suspects the husband.'

'She's not the only one,' Challis said. 'Her boss and workmates didn't have a good word to say about the guy.'

'Who's checking his alibi?'

'Scobie.'

'Wishart could have hired someone.'

'True.'

'Did your famous antenna tell you anything about the planning department?'

Challis shrugged. 'Nothing I could take to the bank. She might have made enemies, but we knew that. Her boss is unpopular, but so is ours.'

Ellen grinned. A little red Subaru Impreza throbbed past, wreathing them in toxins. She waved to clear the air. 'According to Gandolfo, Mrs Wishart suspected Groot, or someone at Planning East, of leaking departmental decisions and deliberations to the wrong people.'

Challis looked past her and into the far distance, his way of thinking through the next stages and anticipating cockups. Eventually he took out his mobile phone and called CIU. 'Pam? Doing anything?'

She sounded faintly harassed. 'Lot of schoolie stuff, sir.'

'Okay, tell Smith and Jones that I want them to run checks on everyone who worked with Ludmilla Wishart. Mainly financial.'

'Sir.'

Challis and Destry wandered back to the police station, signed out the CIU Camry and headed a short distance south around the coast. Penzance Beach was a ribbon of sandy soil around a small bay, with humble holiday shacks and more modern architect-designed houses screened by ti-trees, wattles and gums. City people holidayed there, but most of the residents were retirees and people who worked locally. Challis steered slowly along the main access street, which followed the line of the beach, behind the beachfront houses. An uncomfortable feeling settled in the car: Ellen Destry had lived here until recently, before her marriage ended and her daughter went away to university and the house was sold. Challis had been a mealtime guest now and then, back when he'd been mildly attracted to her without it crossing his mind that they'd end up together.

Then the road turned inland and immediately climbed to a bluff above the town. Here all consistency had fled, as houses, egos, vantage points and monetary worth battled it out. And at the very top was a raw gap in the mix of expensive trees, gardens, fences and walls. Challis pointed. 'An old house was demolished there yesterday morning. Our victim tried to stop it from happening.'

Challis had called ahead and Carl Vernon was waiting for them. The amateur historian took them into the cluttered sitting room of his cottage, the kind of room that in a tiny house is lived and worked in. A cracked and faded green leather sofa faced a small, dusty television set and a wall of shelves crammed with books, vinyl records, cassettes, CDs and a small sound system. Two glass cabinets contained sharks' eggs, shells and driftwood, and a huge table with ornate legs supported a laptop computer, a printer and piles of manila folders and typed manuscript pages.

'Excuse the mess.'

It was a mess, but comfortable and focussed. Challis looked at the man who'd made it. Carl Vernon was about sixty, with salt-and-pepper hair, sinewy legs inside loose, faded shorts, and broad tanned hands that had presumably created the typescript on the table but looked chopped about and grimy, as if he spent most of his time tackling weeds, chopping firewood or tinkering with engines. His face was lean and seamed, steered by a blade-like nose. An intelligent face.

Challis looked closer and saw grief there. No tears or histrionics, just quiet sorrow and disbelief. Of course the world was full of actors.

'Perhaps you could tell us about your relationship with Mrs Wishart.'

'Relationship? We all had a relationship with her.'

'Meaning?'

'The residents' committee. You know about the house that was demolished?'

'Yes.'

'Ludmilla was helping us to gain a protection order.'

'I understand that it failed.'

'It didn't fail. We were too late, that's all. There is a distinction—moral if not legal. I'm confident that we'd have been successful, except the new owners were tipped off by someone.'

'Strong words.'

'It's true. Everyone knew it.'

'Who tipped them off?'

'I'm afraid I don't know.'

'Did Mrs Wishart know?'

'She had her suspicions.'

'She didn't confide these to you?'

'Not specifically.'

Challis said, 'Could *she* have tipped off the new owners?'

'Mill? No!'

'You sound very sure.'

'I've never seen anyone so upset as she was yesterday.'

'What time was that?'

'Twice. First thing in the morning, and again around four o'clock in the afternoon.'

'Why twice?'

'As soon as the bulldozing started, I called her. Of course it was too late by the time she got here. She said she'd look into the legalities and get back to us.'

'What did she tell you on her second visit?'

'That she intended to hold an inquiry, and block or delay any building work on the site.'

'That wouldn't make the new owners happy.'

'The Ebelings can get fucked, as far as I'm concerned—pardon my French. They're new-money people. Vulgar. More money than sense or taste.'

Challis's mind clicked on Pam Murphy's unauthorised LED inquiry. The subjects had been Hugh and Mia Ebeling. 'One of our detectives lives near here.'

'Pam? Lovely girl. She had a word with the hard-hat guys, but it was all too little, too late.'

'So, there were some very heated people here yesterday.'

'Yes.'

'Could others on your committee have suspected Mrs Wishart of being a spy for the Ebelings?'

Vernon looked doubtful. 'She was terrific. No nonsense. Honest. Tireless. Everyone liked her.'

'Mr Vernon,' said Challis, 'what if I said that she was sleeping with someone other than her husband?'

The question was one way of provoking a guilty flicker. Instead, Vernon exploded. 'You must be joking.'

'It's been known to happen.'

'Not to that poor lass. Not the way her husband followed her around everywhere.'

29

Adrian Wishart had offered his uncle Terry as an alibi, and Scobie Sutton tracked the man down to a tiny electronics repair shop on the Nepean Highway in Cheltenham, part of the southeastern sprawl of Melbourne. The Nepean was long and depressing, stretching between the Peninsula and the city, where commerce ruled and the traffic moved in choked-off surges from one set of lights to the next. Wishart TV and VCR Repairs and Service sat opposite Cheltenham Toyota and between Blockbuster Video and a bicycle shop. Scobie parked and checked his watch. Challis had asked him to time the journey from Waterloo: fifty minutes. The air reeked of carcinogenic toxins. He entered the shop.

He found himself in a tiny reception alcove fitted with a grimy counter. Beyond an open doorway behind it were benches crammed with the guts, wiring looms and motherboards of TVs, VCRs and DVD players, together with coils of insulated wire, pliers, soldering irons and small electrical components of silvery metal or grey plastic.

A bell pinged and a man came through from the workshop, saying, 'Sorry, pal, I'm about to close—family emergency.'

'Are you Mr Terrence Wishart?'

'Yeah, but whatever it is you're selling, I don't want it.'

Scobie had seen Adrian Wishart's photograph in Ludmilla's wallet;

now he made a mental comparison between that image and the man before him. Terry, in his early sixties, was a balding knocked-about version of Adrian. Where Adrian was neat, refined, almost ascetic in appearance, Terry had the look of a man who liked a few beers after work and shopped at K-Mart. He'd probably struggled at school, was divorced and didn't expect to marry again. In some ways, he'd given up. But not in all ways. There were things he was proud of. Several photographs hung on the walls of the alcove: Terry in the dress uniform of an Army lieutenant, caught by a flashbulb as he shook hands with an elderly colonel; Terry with his arms around two similar men in the bar of a Returned Services League club; Terry at a wall of remembrance; Terry at the War Memorial in Canberra, patting the flank of an armoured personnel carrier.

He caught Scobie's gaze and said, 'Vietnam.' He shook his head at the wonder and horror of his experiences. 'That was a doozy.'

'I bet it was.'

Wishart seemed to collect himself again. 'Like I said, I need to close. Sorry.'

His face was tense, bewildered, behind whiskers, pouchy fat and broken capillaries, as though bad things were happening and he wasn't ready for them.

'I'm a police officer,' Scobie said gently. 'I take it you've heard about your nephew's wife?'

The wind went out of Wishart's sails. He placed both hands on the counter as though to brace his heavy torso and said, 'It's terrible. I can hardly believe it. It was her birthday yesterday.'

'You had a present for her.'

'That's right. Nothing special. A DVD/VCR combo, repair job that someone failed to pick up. Good as new.'

'Adrian drove up to collect it yesterday afternoon?'

'That's right.'

'What time was that?'

Wishart froze, then straightened indignantly. 'Hang on, what's this in aid of? Are you checking up on him?'

'Standard procedure, Terry.'

'The poor guy's all cut up about it and you're checking on him? Jesus.'

'If you could confirm the time, I'll be on my way.'

Wishart, disgusted now, stared off into space. 'Got here about one o'clock. I closed the shop and we went down the club for a counter lunch.'

'The club?'

'My local RSL. They do you a good meal.'

Scobie was hoping the servicemen's club had installed bar and carpark cameras. And if necessary he'd check every speed and intersection camera on the Nepean Highway. It was what he was good at. Challis knew it and usually gave him the task of tracking the movements of suspects via surveillance cameras and credit card and mobile phone use.

'How long did you spend there?'

'Got back to the shop about three. I had some repairs to complete, so Ade sat with me for a couple of hours while I worked. We don't see each other that often.'

Wishart swiped at his eyes suddenly. 'Poor bastard. Poor Mill.'

'You were fond of her?'

'She was great. Lucky man, my nephew. Poor bastard.'

'So he left here about five yesterday afternoon?'

Terry Wishart screwed up his face in thought. His expression cleared. 'Yep.'

'Did he tell you his plans for the evening?'

'It was Mill's thirtieth, they were going out to dinner.'

'Did he say what time?'

'Nup. But he likes to eat early.'

'He left here at five, an hour to get home, then shower, change and drive to the restaurant...'

'So?'

'He expected to find Mrs Wishart waiting at home for him?'

Terry shifted about uncomfortably. 'Ade could be a bit, you know, uptight about things like lateness. Mill wouldn't want to piss him off.'

'Except she wasn't there, and she didn't return.'

'No.'

'Did he tell you that? Call you last night and tell you?'

Wishart shook his head. 'This morning. He was so cut up he could hardly get the words out.'

'Can anyone verify that he was here all that time? Customers? People who work for you?'

Wishart looked doubtful. 'I work alone. A couple of customers came in, but Ade was out the back, reading the paper while I tinkered. Look, he really loved Mill, we both did. Really loved her. If I find the bastard that done this…'

'Where do you live?'

'Above the shop. Why?'

'What time did you close yesterday?'

'You prick. Five-thirty, then I was upstairs. Stayed in all night.'

'When I arrived just now you said you're closing for the day. Are you driving down to be with your nephew?'

Wishart shook his head. 'He's coming here. Says he can't stay in his place a minute longer. Too many memories.'

Then Scobie drove to Terry Wishart's RSL club, which didn't have any working CCTV cameras. The young staff knew Terry, however. He ate lunch there almost every day, and often stayed on rather than return to his shop. Nice bloke. Friendly. Liked his beer. A bit sad. Yeah, there could have been another bloke with him yesterday, hard to remember, so many faces in and out. But it was pretty likely. Old Terry didn't like to eat or drink alone. He had plenty of mates, army buddies. Full of war stories. Vietnam. He'd be much too young for World War Two.

Scobie went away thinking about lonely, isolated men. That led him to other thoughts, as he headed southeast to Waterloo. It led him to his daughter's school concert last night, and how proud he was, how he'd had tears in his eyes to see Ros up there on the stage, singing her little heart out.

It had been the loneliest moment of his life. Beth was there, but not there. He'd tried to jolly her along. He'd kept peering at her face for a reaction to match his, but neither the music nor her daughter had moved her. He thought of the word 'automaton'.

30

Two of the schoolies had had their bicycles stolen, so Pam Murphy spent part of the afternoon investigating that. Then she was called to a dispute on the foreshore, a motel manager claiming that a schoolie had let all of his tyres down, the kid claiming the manager had put his grubby hands inside her singlet top. Then up High Street to investigate a shoplifting incident blamed on a gang of schoolies but probably committed by the proprietor, who had a history of suspected insurance rip-offs.

All of this wasted time and shoe leather, and so Pam didn't reach HangTen until five o'clock, as businesses were closing for the day. 'A word, Caz?'

'I have to balance the registers and lock up.'

'It's important.'

Caz Moon had very white hair and black eyebrows today, a bruised look around her eyes, purple lips. She'd ditched her jeans and wore a torn skirt over an unravelling petticoat over holed tights. It shouldn't have looked attractive but it did. Pam tried to figure out why. It was Caz herself, she decided, Caz's air of containment and intelligence.

'Sit,' said Caz, indicating a stool behind one of the counters. 'We'll talk as I work.'

She was deft and focused, closing one cash register after the other, setting the lights, locking display cabinets, alarming the rear doors. Pam's questioning was no distraction to her; she answered without missing a beat.

'Where were you last night?'

'Out clubbing—or what passes for clubbing in dear old Waterloo. You saw me, remember?'

'The schoolies bring you a lot of extra business?'

'Some.'

'But they attract toolies, right? Locals who try to take advantage of them? Mostly we think of a toolie as a guy.'

'Is that a question?'

'But there are female toolies. Yesterday I warned off a thirty-five-year-old woman.'

'Huh,' said Caz without interest.

'You're not a toolie, are you, Caz? You don't fraternise with the schoolies?'

'Unavoidable. Turn a corner, and there they are.'

'But you don't seek them out? Don't try to pick up the guys, have a drink with them?'

'Babies,' Caz said. She was adding figures in her head.

'Where were you last night?'

'You already asked me that.'

'I mean later, around midnight. The early hours.'

'Home.'

'Can you prove that?'

'Do I need to?'

'What do you know about GHB and Rohypnol?'

'Date rape drugs,' said Caz without hesitation.

Pam nodded and said, 'Dropped into the victim's drink in a bar or club or at a party. She feels woozy, a "concerned" male friend takes her home, rapes her when she passes out, and she wakes up the next day feeling sore and confused and can't remember anything.'

'Your point?'

'Has it ever happened to *you*, Caz? Or a friend of yours?'

Caz shook her head as she briskly wiped a phone handset. 'This is Waterloo. I don't think GHB and roofies have reached past the suburbs yet.'

'Very droll,' Pam said. She paused. 'If you could get your hands on that sort of gear, would you go so far as to use it on anyone?'

'I'm not into girls,' Caz said. 'I know it's chic in some circles, but I'm not into that. No offence.'

Pam wasn't a lesbian. Caz was stirring. She wasn't doing it out of spite or bigotry, but she was being combative, and Pam had to wonder why. 'Did I say girl? You might want to give it to a boy. A particular boy.'

Caz stopped what she was doing and gazed into space as though she found the prospect intellectually absorbing. 'But wouldn't the drug cause "erectile dysfunction"?' she asked, hooking her fingers around the term. 'And wouldn't that defeat the purpose of the exercise?'

Pam grinned. 'Depends on the purpose.'

Caz didn't grin but gave the ghost of a smile. 'I guess so.'

'Like, you might want to strip off all his clothes, lipstick his genitals and leave him out in the open for all to see.'

'Interesting. What would you call that—making a statement?'

'I'd call it revenge,' Pam said.

'Really,' said Caz evenly. She began to bundle the day's takings together, according to denomination. She filled out a deposit slip and packed everything into a canvas sack with ANZ Bank logoed on it.

'Night safe?'

'Uh huh.'

'There are thieves about, Caz. I hope you take precautions.'

'Precautions? Like birth control or the morning-after pill in case I'm doped and raped?'

It was said with the tiniest increase in heat. 'Please tell me what happened to you,' Pam said.

'Nothing happened.'

'Was it last year? Last weekend? A girl was sexually assaulted in the early hours of Sunday morning.'

Caz sighed. 'These things happen when people congregate and booze and drugs are involved.'

'Was it Josh Brownlee?'

'Who?'

'The boy you called out to last night.'

'Is that his name?'

'Cut the crap. I heard you. I heard you say, "Raped anyone lately, Josh?"'

'Me? You probably misheard. The music was pretty loud.'

'Caz, was it Josh Brownlee who drugged and raped you?'

'Me? Of course not.'

Caz had barely faltered. Pam wondered how long the girl would be able to keep it up—wondered how long *she* would be able to keep it up, for that matter. 'The more people who come forward, the better our chances of gaining a conviction.'

'Has Josh been a naughty boy?'

'Cut it out, Caz. Help me, please?'

'What's it like, being a copper?'

Pam blinked. Caz seemed genuinely interested. 'There are moments of boredom, there are disappointments, but there's also exhilaration and satisfaction when you get it right.'

'Exactly,' said Caz elliptically. She said, 'What's it like for *women* in the police?'

'Getting better.'

'I've seen you with those two uniformed guys, the fat one and the good-looking one. What's that like?'

'We're just colleagues, pitching in together.'

'I doubt it,' Caz said promptly. She paused. 'They both like you.'

It came out of nowhere and Pam blushed. 'Getting back to—'

'Steer clear of both of them,' Caz said.

Pam scowled. 'I'm afraid I'm not here to—'

But her mobile phone rang and Challis said, 'Where are you?'

Pam walked out of the shop to take the call and heard Caz lock the door behind her and knew she couldn't do a thing about it. 'Just down the street from the station.'

'Briefing room, ten minutes.'

'But sir…'

'Briefing room. Murder takes priority.'

31

Ellen Destry should have been at the end-of-day briefing, but she was breaking into Adrian Wishart's house. A familiar roaring set up in her ears. It had nothing to do with the noises she made, for she was whisper quiet, but with the heightened flow of her blood. With excitement, apprehension and a sense of entitlement, in other words.

Now she stood perfectly still in Adrian Wishart's sitting room until her blood eased and she could hear the external world again.

Nothing.

She was alone.

No sirens, next-door voices or unexpected occupants to undo her.

She flexed her hands in their latex gloves and began to move. This was not the first time she'd broken into someone's house and it wouldn't be the last. It was part of her secret life. It was also part of her detecting life. She didn't know if other police officers did it or not. Some surely did, but did not admit it. Perhaps Challis did it, too, but if he were like her he'd never admit it.

Ellen moved swiftly through the house, checking for unwelcome surprises or obstacles, mapping the layout of each room and locating the escape routes. Then she went through again, identifying areas of interest for a more concentrated sweep. She didn't know what she expected to discover about Adrian Wishart, only that she'd formed a loathing for him and expected to find something that proved his role in the murder of his wife—a phone number, photographs or other evidence of a lover or a hired killer. The house had been formally searched already, but only to learn if there were hidden aspects of Ludmilla's life. Her computer had been removed. Correspondence. Financial papers. The warrant hadn't extended to the husband, not without hard evidence.

She felt alive when she made these covert forays into other people's private worlds. The sense of elation was never far away. She was powerful at these times. Victorious. She had a hold over Adrian Wishart today and he didn't know it.

Not that she'd be able to use anything she discovered, or not in any formal or legal sense. The search was illegal and anything she found would be ruled inadmissible by a judge. But she might find something that guided the direction of the investigation.

As she moved from room to room, Ellen tried to see the furnishings and decorations as if she were Ludmilla Wishart making a home, a nest, and failed. It wasn't a failure of the imagination; rather, it seemed to Ellen as if Ludmilla had played only a small role in designing and decorating the house. It was as if she'd been negated or sidelined by her husband. Ellen didn't believe that women were necessarily fussy and decorative, and men harsh and utilitarian, but she was convinced that Adrian Wishart was responsible for the almost mathematical precision with which the rooms, furniture and paintings had been arranged, and she itched to soften the effect. If she lived here she'd be afraid to bump a chair out of alignment, smudge a glass surface, leave a crumb behind or shed a cotton thread. Order and control ruled this house. Unchallengeable principles governed it.

Ellen began her fine-detail search in the bathroom. First she took digital photographs of the contents of the cabinets, then examined labels and shook bottles and tubes, before replacing everything exactly where it had been, according to the images stored in her camera. Ludmilla had been prescribed a birth-control pill, Adrian an anti-inflammatory.

She repeated her search technique in the other rooms, hunting through all the obvious places: hollow cavities behind skirting boards, under the cistern lid in the en-suite bathroom, behind paintings, inside freezer and pantry containers. No drugs, and only a little alcohol. No pornography, no sex aids, no secret stash of love letters.

Then, tucked under bills, junk mail and what were probably unopened birthday cards in a bowl on a hallstand, Ellen found an envelope containing $250 in cash. With it was an invoice in the sum of $250 made out to Ludmilla Wishart by Grant's Gardening, the words 'cash payment appreciated' at the bottom. Ellen pocketed the envelope and its contents without thinking and moved on to Adrian Wishart's studio, the only room she'd not yet searched.

She checked the time: 5 p.m. She'd be late to Hal's briefing, and Wishart might be back at any time. She'd seen him leave, confirming Scobie's report that the uncle was expecting him, but what if Wishart changed his mind about the drive to the city? She picked over the files, desk diary and drawers desultorily, made a quick search of the man's laptop, and rummaged through the scraps in his wastepaper bin. On the surface, his life was clinical and hardhearted. She needed to find where that would tip over into committing murder.

A car passed by the house. Ellen darted to the window and saw a taxi winding its way along the street and out of sight. As a reflex, she grabbed the curtain edge and heard the rings rattle on the rod above her head. She looked up. A hollow metal rod, with decorative knobs on each end. Quite a thick rod. Roomy. She remembered her favourite lover's-revenge story about breaking into the cheating boyfriend's home and stuffing his curtain rod with rotting fish. Taken him days, weeks, to isolate the source of the awful smell.

Ellen dragged a chair over. One of the decorative ends was dusty. She unscrewed the clean one and there, nestling inside it, was a USB memory stick.

32

Early evening in the briefing room, Challis, Sutton, Murphy and the Mornington detectives, Smith and Jones, arranged around the long table, a table now as comfortably part of their lives as their kitchen tables and just as battered. Challis thought how useful CIU's table could be to the forensic lecturers at the police academy, its surfaces imprinted with DNA traces, prints, stains and ballpoint pen impressions.

'Where's Ellen?'

'Don't know, boss.'

Challis unfolded from the wall. The evening was mild, the air heated by the west-facing glass, and so he'd provided bottles of juice and mineral water, potato crisps and salted peanuts. 'First things first,' he said, tossing back a peanut and perusing a fax from the lab. 'The mucus found on Lachlan Roe's sleeve came from the attacker, not Roe. They've extracted DNA, but it doesn't match anyone in the system.'

No one responded. It was a familiar disappointment. Even Pam Murphy seemed to gesture philosophically without actually shrugging her shoulders. Smith and Jones looked bored; it wasn't their case.

'But Roe goes on the back burner,' Challis continued. 'Our priority is finding who murdered Ludmilla Wishart. Here's what we know about her last movements.'

Just then, Ellen entered, fast and lithe in her long cotton skirt and sleeveless top but somehow not cool and collected. She'd hurried to the briefing from somewhere, and that had flustered her, but Challis saw other disturbances in her mood and demeanour, too. Regret, perhaps. A hint of waspishness or even guilt. In the four or five seconds it took for her to enter, apologise and claim a chair, Challis cast his mind back over his day, wondering if by action or omission he'd pissed her off in some way. He gave her a full-wattage smile that she tried and failed to return.

'We were outlining Ludmilla Wishart's movements yesterday,' he told her, before turning to the whiteboard, which had ceased over the years to be truly white. Pointing with a ruler he said:

'Lunch from twelve-thirty to two o'clock with a female friend. Then rather than return to the office she drove to three separate properties. These movements have since been confirmed—the last because her body was found at the scene and according to the pathologist she was killed where we found her, not killed elsewhere and transported there.'

He paused. 'We have to consider the fact that her murder was work related. She started as a planner for the shire, then a year ago became Planning East's infringements officer, a job that took her all over the place, looking into complaints and non-compliance with planning restrictions, issuing notices and bans, checking on court- or tribunal-ordered restoration and regeneration work.'

'A job that pissed people off,' said Smith. Like Jones, he'd settled into a faintly untidy middle age, as if waiting for retirement and unwilling to over-achieve, or even achieve.

'Yes.'

'Enough to kill her, though?' said Jones.

'People have killed for a lot less,' Ellen said. She looked calmer now, focused on the proceedings.

'True.'

Ellen turned to Challis. 'What did you learn about the Shoreham site?'

Challis explained that the wealthy Premier's even wealthier cousin owned it. 'Name of Jamie Furneaux, but he's been overseas for four months, so he's more or less out of the frame.'

'Overseas. That's handy.'

'He was being hounded by the press for chopping down trees without a permit. They were blocking his sea views, needless to say. He made huge bonfires of the timber, and that involved the local fire brigade—to whom he made a generous "donation". All in all, the press had a field day. He was fined $20,000 and ordered to replant the whole area with indigenous trees and grasses. We think the victim was there to check that he'd carried out the work.'

'Had he?' said Sutton.

'Yes.'

Challis had been resting his hands on the back of a chair. Now he straightened. 'These places and times are her broad movements for the afternoon. We need to know which routes she took, where she might have stopped, who she might have encountered or visited *between* appointments. Scobie?'

Scobie Sutton was an arrangement of skinny bones inside his old suit. He rarely looked happy; today he looked to be at his wits' end with life. He stirred and said, 'I checked her mobile phone records. She made no calls yesterday.'

'None?'

'Several from her office phone yesterday morning,' Sutton amended. 'It should be mentioned that her mobile phone was not on or near her body or her car, and it's not in her office or in her home.'

'Handbag and wallet are also missing,' Challis said. 'If the phone's switched on, maybe the service provider can locate it?'

'There should also be an MP3 player,' said Ellen. 'A birthday present from her friend at lunch yesterday.'

'Assuming this isn't a mugging but staged as one, the killer will have dumped everything somewhere,' Sutton said. 'Meanwhile her credit card use shows one purchase yesterday afternoon at three-forty: she bought forty-seven litres of unleaded petrol at the Caltex on the way in to Waterloo.'

'If they have CCTV,' Challis said, 'check to see who else was there at the same time—buying petrol, using the shop, lurking.'

'You think she was followed?'

'It's possible.'

'Her husband followed her on Tuesday, according to one witness,' Ellen said. 'And according to her best friend, he'd call or e-mail her several times a day, hang around outside, visit her office.'

'Did he have reason to?' asked Smith.

'Do you mean, did he suspect she was having an affair? There's no indication she was. Her husband's a pathetic loser, that's all. A stalker.'

Sutton cut in: 'But the husband's alibi is sound. He was with his uncle. The guy confirms it.'

Challis tapped the whiteboard again. 'Next we come to this man, Carl Vernon. Vernon heads a residents' action group in Penzance Beach. When the group got wind that an old house in the area was about to be bulldozed and a new one erected in its place, they contacted Ludmilla Wishart.' With an uneasy glance at Ellen, he went on: 'Ludmilla's husband said he feared she was having an affair with Vernon.'

'So he *did* have a reason to follow her,' said Smith.

'Vernon denies it,' Challis said, 'and I tend to believe him. In fact, he said that when he was meeting with Ludmilla on Tuesday afternoon, the husband showed up.'

'It confirms what Ludmilla's friend told me,' Ellen said. 'Adrian Wishart always seemed to know exactly where and when his wife had been during the day.'

Challis nodded. 'We have another angle via Carl Vernon and Carmen Gandolfo. Apparently Ludmilla suspected that someone in

Planning East is on the take, receiving payment in exchange for sensitive information that gives an unfair advantage to people who want to avoid or evade planning restrictions.'

He turned to Smith and Jones. 'What did you guys find out about Groot and the other planners?'

Jones had half-moon glasses suspended on the tip of his nose. He read from a foolscap pad, holding it at arm's length: 'No one has a criminal record or known criminal associates. A couple of speeding fines. Groot blew over .05 on the Frankston Freeway a couple of years ago, but no other traffic infringements.'

'Financial history?' said Challis.

'That's where it gets a little more interesting. The planners aren't highly paid and all of them have hefty mortgages, but so do I and most of the people I know. But Groot and his wife have had extensive work done on their house: swimming pool, landscaping, sundeck…'

Challis mused on it for a while. It seemed to him that there was a lot of money around, despite talk of recession. Sure, people were suffering, but the middle class seemed to be doing extraordinarily well. They didn't buy dull, sensible, locally-made cars any more but exotic European models, and they changed cars every year or two. Challis's father had held on to his car for twenty years, but people of Challis's generation didn't do that. They bought flash cars, owned holiday houses and sent their kids to private schools. The money had to come from somewhere. Mostly loans, he suspected. Mostly honestly, in other words. It was money that could be traced.

'Dig a little deeper,' he told Smith and Jones. 'See who paid for the work on his house.'

'Boss,' they said.

Scobie Sutton cleared his throat. 'Anything on her laptop?'

Challis searched through the faxes, reports and e-mail printouts that were the bane of his existence. Finding the one he wanted, he said, 'The laptop is fairly new, according to the technicians. There's very little on it apart from drafts of her reports.'

He turned to Pam Murphy. 'Murph, you met Carl Vernon yesterday morning.'

She'd been slumped in her chair, alert but apparently bored, playing with a plastic cup. Now she went pink and sat upright, as if aware that he knew she'd made her unauthorised LED search as a result of talking to Vernon. Clearing her throat, she summarised how she'd met Vernon during the demolition of the house known as Somerland, and said fervently, 'It was heartbreaking to watch. People were angry, in tears. That's when I heard whispers that a corrupt shire employee had tipped off the owner of the property so he could demolish it before it a protection order could be granted.'

Ellen had been doodling in her notebook. She said, 'There are three ways of looking at that. One, Ludmilla herself was corrupt, and the property owner killed her to protect himself. Two, Ludmilla was about to reveal the identity of the corrupt employee—and it has to be pointed out that this person might *not* be a Planning East employee or even a shire employee—and he or she stopped her. Three, Ludmilla approached the demolition guy or the developer, saying she intended to take action against them—'

'—and it got her killed,' Challis said.

33

At the conclusion of the briefing, Ellen scurried away, saying she had a headache. Challis followed her out, wanting to commiserate, wanting to find out what lay behind it, but she brushed him off, saying, 'Don't fuss, I'll be okay,' so he shrugged and let it go. He'd learn what the matter was eventually. Or he wouldn't.

He worked for an hour after the briefing, trying to clear the backlog of forms and correspondence. Then the phone rang and Ollie Hindmarsh said, sounding like shovelled gravel, 'You lousy cow.'

Challis considered his reply. 'Who's this?'

'Don't get smart. I've had reporters after me all day.'

Challis wasn't in the mood. 'Yeah?'

'That little prick and his blog,' Hindmarsh said. 'Thanks to you, the whole world knows.'

Challis burned slowly and surely. 'Are you saying I leaked it to the press?'

'I am.'

The words dripped from Challis: 'I'm not interested in you or your hurt feelings. I'm only interested in whether or not Dirk Roe attacked his brother or said or did something that encouraged someone else to do it. If you can't control your staff, that's not my concern.'

Hindmarsh's voice shifted, growing phlegmy and strident. 'He took the blog off-line two days ago, as soon as he realised the police knew about it! So how come the media are quoting extracts at me?'

'It was a blog, Mr Hindmarsh. It's probably still floating around out there in cyberspace for all to see.'

'Do your job, inspector. You can't even catch the person who beat up a harmless man of the cloth, and now I see you've got a murder to investigate. God knows how you're going to manage that.'

The evening traffic was muted outside Challis's window and the corridors were almost silent. A line of cars idled along the McDonald's drive-through lane, headlights burning, toxins rising. Challis said, 'Let me reiterate: your harmless man of the cloth contributed racist observations to his brother's blog. He likes to call himself an "elect vessel", meaning he believes he has the ear of God. He thinks that modern technology is bad—except in that it may be used to influence an election—not that he ever votes. A woman's role is to cook, clean and reproduce. And at your behest, he was appointed chaplain of Landseer School, where he didn't counsel troubled adolescents but told them to get down on their knees and pray.'

Hindmarsh said nothing and the night deepened until finally there was a click in Challis's ear.

Time to go home.

Something had happened to Ellen Destry that afternoon. She'd been hurrying to the briefing, conscious that she'd spent too long in Adrian Wishart's house, when her good opinion of herself began to fracture.

It had nothing to do with breaking into a scumbag's house and picking over his secret life, for that was exciting, even desirable. Pocketing the money had been exciting, too. It was something she did, something she'd done from time to time over the years.

But always, always, the thieving would come back to haunt her afterwards. It would eat at her. It never went away. And it had kicked in on the way to the briefing. She'd tried telling herself that she didn't have a psychological problem, and it was okay to steal from scumbags, and even that ordinary rules didn't apply to her. She tried telling herself that Adrian Wishart was the kind of guy to keep the gardener's hard-earned money and say he knew nothing about it. She imagined some big guy coming around and roughing Adrian up.

Then she thought: What if the gardener is too tactful to ask for his money? She thought: It's not my money. She thought: I need help.

She might have made it to the briefing on time, but just as the police station came into view, she'd turned around and driven back to the house where Ludmilla Wishart had lived, feeling sick at heart. She tried telling herself that she had good professional reasons for returning the envelope of cash—if Adrian Wishart suspected that someone had been sneaking around in his house he might get rid of crucial evidence, or even accuse the police of theft—but she couldn't sustain it. Quite simply, a part of her was bad. It needed fixing. She wanted to be loved, desired, admired. She knew that if Hal ever learned about this side of her, she'd die.

But she'd left it too late to return the gardener's $250. Adrian Wishart's little red Citroën was parked in the driveway. She turned around, raced back to Waterloo, arrived late at the briefing.

Knowing she couldn't face Challis afterwards, she'd driven straight home, poured herself a stiff drink and climbed into a bath brimming with hot water and fragrant salts.

Now, as the evening light drew in, she was still in the bath, occasionally letting out the tepid water and adding hot, her skin wrinkling like a prune.

Not that it worked to cure her. She still felt estranged from her old self, the competent, dignified self. It wasn't that she'd broken into Wishart's house—he was as guilty as sin; she'd do it again in a heartbeat—but that she wanted or needed to pocket the money she'd found there. She was no better than she'd ever been. This was no way to lead her life.

Hal would be home soon. She pulled the plug, dried herself with a thick clean towel, opened the wardrobe to grab her dressing gown. It was a small wardrobe, stuff crammed onto a shelf above the clothes rail and on the floor, and when she hauled out her dressing gown the tails of it dislodged the lid on one of Hal's shoeboxes. She crouched to replace it.

She paused. He'd scrawled 'Bushfire Keepsakes' on a label pasted to the lid. She should put it back. Instead, she pulled the gown around her and sat on the floor and sifted through the contents. Passport. Bank and insurance statements. His will, inside an envelope. A bundle of letters. Ellen glanced at the sender: his wife, the address of the prison where she'd killed herself. Feeling ratshit, she sorted through the photographs. A studio shot of his wife. Hal and wife on their wedding day. Holiday snaps. His late parents. His sister. His niece. Two graduation photographs.

And, finally, photographs of herself: at that Christmas party last year, a candid shot at her desk, shaking hands with the super, receiving an award from the assistant commissioner. Ellen wept a little as she visualised her lover deciding what he held dear, what he wanted to remember, what he'd save if a bushfire threatened to burn his house down.

'As for me,' she muttered, 'even my dressing gown is stolen.'

Her resistance was so low that Telstra could call now and she'd sign up for the most expensive phone plan they offered.

Ellen replaced the shoebox and headed for the sitting room, seeking distractions. She didn't want to call anyone. She couldn't be bothered with music. She switched on the TV idly and flicked through the channels, and there was Ollie Hindmarsh, feigning outrage, greasily explaining to a battery of microphones that he'd sacked Dirk Roe as soon as he'd been informed about the fellow's blog.

'Yeah, right,' said Ellen. Talking back to the TV always made her feel better.

'Furthermore,' said Hindmarsh, 'Dirk Roe was merely my electoral office manager, essentially a clerical role, not an aide or advisor.'

But did Hindmarsh endorse Roe's views?

Of course not, don't be absurd.

Ellen, her depression forgotten temporarily, sensed an implication in the denial. Hindmarsh seemed to be saying, in his bluff, strong-chinned way, that he scarcely knew what a blog was, that to a true Australian like himself—male, older generation, ex-armed services—a blog was somehow unsavoury and effeminate.

'But the Roe Report endorses *you*,' a reporter pointed out.

'I'm not responsible for anything Mr Roe says or does.'

'You employed him.'

'And I sacked him,' Hindmarsh said. 'Look, I have a sizeable staff. It's a responsible job. Mr Roe was merely a paper pusher in my electoral office, which is scarcely the seat of power. I spend most of my time in the city, as you well know.'

'Arsehole,' said Ellen. Like most Liberal Party supporters and politicians, Hindmarsh was the kind of man who'd endorse white supremacists, anti-Semites and crackpot fundamentalists if the sum effect were just one more vote won than lost.

Buoyed a little, she called her daughter's mobile phone.

'Just seeing how you are.'

'Fine, Mum,' Larrayne said.

She sounded bright and happy and there were no background noises of the kind that might make a mother tense up—no partying flatmates, pub music or barrelling traffic. 'What are you up to?'

'Nothing much.'

Larrayne had always been like this, even as a little kid at school. Ellen would discover weeks later, usually by chance, that her daughter had been appointed captain of the netball team, chosen to recite a poem at assembly or awarded a distinction for a maths test. Larrayne's world was subterranean. She offered glimpses into it only rarely.

'How's work?'

'Fine.'

Her university exams over for the year, Larrayne was working in a bookshop called Paydirt, a dingy warren of crime paperbacks beneath street level in the heart of downtown Melbourne, within spitting distance of the town hall, the cathedral and the shopping arcades. It was entirely possible that she'd got the job by telling the proprietor her mother was a cop.

'Want to come down for the weekend?'

'Have to work. Sorry.'

Larrayne didn't altogether approve of Ellen's living with Challis. She didn't approve of her father having a girlfriend, either. The separation and divorce were still raw, she wanted a return to how things had been, even though she herself had left home and lived in the city now. She'd thaw eventually. Maybe.

'You at home?'

'Yes.'

With or without a guy? There were things that Ellen wanted to ask and know, but then Hal's old car came creeping up the driveway, headlights dipping and levelling as he negotiated the potholes.

'Speak to you soon,' Ellen said.

Josh was watching the adult channel, $15.95 worth of fake moans and silicon tits, alone for the first time this Schoolies Week and too scared to go out. He jacked off desultorily and thought about his miserable day.

Miserable because he'd accomplished nothing, despite his fine intentions. He was going to report that female cop to the cops who investigate other cops, what were they called, Internal Affairs, Ethical Standards? Hell, he was the victim here. But then he had second thoughts. Cops protected each other, right? You only had to read the paper. Plus, if that bitch explained *how* she'd found him—naked, his balls painted with red lipstick—he'd be a laughing stock.

And so he'd spent the day doing nothing.

At that moment he spotted a rectangular white shape at the corner of his eye. At first he didn't want to turn his head and look. Images and great surges of strange energy came to him sometimes, and he feared this was one of those times. Then he did look and saw that somebody had slipped an envelope under his motel room door. Feeling a kind of creeping dread, he opened it.

A poorly lit photo of him on the sand, naked, balls all red.

At the start of the evening news, Scobie Sutton opened to a knock on his front door.

'May I help you?'

The man standing under the porch light shot out his hand. 'Hello, you must be Beth's husband, Scobie, correct?'

Scobie's good manners were automatic. He shook the proffered hand. 'May I help you?'

'I'm Pastor Jeffreys of the First Ascensionists Church.'

He was also Pete Jeffreys and he owned the local HomeWare franchise. He sold mattresses, rugs, linoleum and cheap sweatshop furniture. You saw his fleshy, trying-too-hard face everywhere: the local paper, a hoarding outside his shop, flyers in your letterbox several times a year. He was always announcing clearance sales.

Scobie got a creepy feeling, as if forces were aligned against him. He opened his mouth but the shopkeeper got in first:

'If I could just have a quick word with Beth. Won't take a moment.'

'I don't think…'

With what might have been genuine emotion, Jeffreys said, 'Your wife was very close to Mr Roe. What happened to him hit her hard. She needs support in this trying time. We're devoted to her, as she is to us. I know she'd like to see me.'

'She's lying down,' said Scobie truthfully, wondering why he hadn't said she was out, or wouldn't want to see the man.

Jeffreys watched him keenly for a moment, then nodded. 'Tell her

I called, will you?'

'Yes,' said Scobie, wondering why he'd said that, too.

So much for the new ruling that police officers should never patrol solo after dark: five Waterloo constables, including Andy Cree, were off work with some gastric bug, so Tank was on his lonesome in a divisional van, prowling the little towns and back roads around Waterloo.

One domestic, one pub brawl, one road rage incident. He wouldn't get off work until midnight, then he was expected to go on duty again tomorrow morning, 8 a.m. to 4 p.m. The timetabling at Waterloo was completely fucked up as far as he was concerned.

At 10 p.m. the dispatcher directed him to the Penzance Beach area, reports of a drag race. The culprits were long gone. Tank turned the car around, heading back, and just happened to drive past Pam Murphy's house on his way out. There was a candle flickering behind a curtain in a side window.

Which probably explained Andrew Cree's Mazda coupe parked in her driveway.

34

Friday morning.

Challis checked the overnight incident log as soon as he arrived at work, and buried in Thursday night's litany of burglaries, car theft and assault were two items of immediate interest to him: Ludmilla Wishart's handbag had been handed in at the front desk, and there'd been a break-in at Planning East.

He clattered down the stairs. It was 7.45 and a handful of the keener 8 a.m. starters were drifting into work, cluttering up the corridors and yarning with the duty sergeant. Challis edged through them and asked for the handbag. 'Why wasn't I told?'

'Sorry, sir. One of the probationers handled it, logged it as missing property handed in by a member of the public.'

Challis checked the log. The handbag had been spotted by an elderly woman walking her dog on the beach below the cliffs at Shoreham at six o'clock on Thursday morning. She had handed it in at Waterloo that evening, after a Probus class. Challis sighed. Someone from the police would have to talk to her, a necessary part of covering all the bases, but it didn't seem likely that she had anything to do with the killing. He signed for the handbag, hooked a ballpoint pen under the strap and carried it upstairs, where he spread the contents out on the incident room table. He peered at it with the others, separating the items with the same ballpoint pen.

'On the surface,' Ellen said, 'it looks like a simple mugging.'

Challis nodded. Wallet, hairbrush, a packet of tissues, lipstick, Lifesavers, a diary and an address book—both small, bound with thin black leather—ballpoint pens, lint, tampons and crumpled parking receipts. He flipped open the wallet. 'No cash or cards,' he said. 'Medicare card, library card, that's it.'

'What about her mobile phone?' asked Sutton, staring gloomily at the bag and contents.

'There should be an MP3 player too,' Ellen said.

'If she was murdered, they'd both have been tossed into the sea,' said Challis. 'If she was mugged, they've been sold or kept. I tried phoning her mobile and got a recorded message, saying it's switched off or out of range.'

He placed everything into individual brown paper evidence bags. 'These can go to the lab. Meanwhile, Scobie, I want you with me.' He glanced at Ellen, unwilling to give her a direct order. 'Ellen?'

She gave him an unreadable look. 'Pam and I will speak to the demolition contractor.'

'That leaves Hugh Ebeling, who ordered the demolition,' Challis told her. 'Later this morning, you and I will drive up to the city and see what he has to say for himself.'

'Yes.'

When he got to the yard with Sutton five minutes later, Challis saw that both CIU cars had been signed out. 'We'll take your car,' he muttered to Sutton, hoping the man didn't want to talk. He wanted time to think about Ellen: Ellen distant last night and this morning, sometimes watching him with great apprehension and intensity. 'Nothing,' she'd said, when he'd asked what was eating her.

But Sutton, driving the elderly Volvo inexpertly and inattentively, did talk, prattling on about his daughter, the way she was always altering the ring tone on his mobile phone or altering the desktop display on the family computer. 'Kids and their gadgets,' he said.

'Huh,' grunted Challis.

There was a pause, then Sutton rattled out the words, 'Boss, I think I've done something stupid.'

Challis grunted again. Sutton, approaching a school crossing, braked erratically, jerking Challis out of his reverie. 'What stupid thing?'

'Sorry, boss. I have to get it off my chest.'

Challis waited, Sutton waited, as the children crossed the road, the crossing guard returned to the footpath and the world turned over. Someone tooted and Sutton trundled on again. Challis was irritated with the man's abject proprieties. 'I'm not getting any younger, Scobie.'

'Sorry. It's this business with the wife.'

'Her involvement with that crackpot church?' prompted Challis.

'Uh huh,' Sutton said, and closed his mouth with a click. His Volvo swerved to avoid a double-parked car, found its lane again and a moment later gave every indication of passing a school bus on a blind corner. If Challis hadn't been so lost in thought since last night, he'd not have let Sutton drive. Ellen had warned him often enough. The side street for the planning office came into view and at the last minute Sutton steered into it.

'They were at my place last night,' he said.

'Who were?'

'On my doorstep. I think they want to lure her away from me. What if they go after Ros? Kids are so impressionable.'

There was a police car outside the planning office, John Tankard taking a statement from Athol Groot. Tank looked sour about something. His partner, Andrew Cree, was photographing a glass-panelled door at the side of the building. A couple of schoolkids stood nearby, bored rather than curious. A glazier waited to measure and replace the broken glass. Challis noted all of these things as Sutton glided toward the kerb and executed a perfect park.

'Speak now or forever hold your peace,' he said.

In a rush, Sutton said, 'Yesterday I leaked the Roe Report to Channel Seven.'

Challis stiffened. He turned to Sutton. Then he began to laugh.

'I thought you'd be angry.'

'You've done us a good turn, Scobie.'

They got out and crossed the road to the planning office. 'I hope you showed the blog to your wife,' Challis said.

Sutton shook his head unequivocally. 'Oh no, unpleasant things upset her.'

'Fuck that,' snarled Challis. 'She needs to know what these people are like. Morning,' he said to Tankard, Cree and the chief planner.

'Sir, Scobie,' Tankard said.

'What have we got?'

Cree jumped in, all bushytailed. 'The side door was jimmied open sometime last night. Discovered by a cleaner at five this morning.'

'Yeah, thanks, Andy,' Tankard said.

Whatever their beef was, Challis couldn't be bothered with it. 'Anything taken?'

'They stole a laptop and a printer,' said Groot agitatedly. The early morning air was cool, but he looked plumply flushed and moist inside his suit coat.

'That all?' Challis asked, stepping through the breached door. The forensic team had been and gone, leaving the frame powder-brushed for prints. More powder on interior doorjambs, desks and filing cabinets.

'Don't think so. Haven't had a close look yet,' the planner said.

'Whose computer?'

'Mine.'

'The only laptop in the building?'

'Yes. As you can see, the other members of staff have PCs.'

With state-of-the-art widescreen LCD monitors, noted Challis. Why hadn't the thieves taken those? 'Where was the printer?'

'Here,' Groot said, pointing to a desk against one wall.

'Networked?'

'Yes.'

Challis gazed around at the wall charts, cabinets, blueprints, folders and desk clutter. Why not the slimline cordless phones? The portable hard drive on one of the desks? The wireless router?

Maybe the thieves had been in a hurry.

'Is there a box for petty cash?'

'Yes.'

'Where?'

'My bottom drawer.'

'Let's see.'

The cashbox was there and intact. The drawer would have been easier to jimmy open than the outside door. Trailed by Groot and Sutton, Challis went from one filing cabinet, work station and office cubicle to the next, running his gaze along each cabinet and desk drawer. Only one desk drawer showed signs of damage—very faint.

He pointed to it. 'Mrs Wishart's desk, correct?'

'Yes.'

'It's been tampered with.'

'Oh.'

'When did that happen? Before last night?'

Groot blinked. 'Don't really know.'

'Perhaps she lost her key one day? Needed to force it open?'

'Don't know.'

'Or her husband came around to collect her things after the murder and needed to force the lock?'

'It's possible,' said the planner doubtfully, staring back down the weeks and months. 'It's possible her husband came to collect her things.' He warmed to this theory, saying, 'He was always hanging around, you know.'

'Or whoever broke into the office last night also broke into her desk.'

'I really couldn't say.'

Then one of the office staff arrived and he seemed to swell and go rigid. He ducked away from Challis and hissed at the woman, 'You're late.'

She paled. 'Sorry, sorry, my kids are sick.'

'Even so,' Groot said.

35

Meanwhile Destry and Murphy were driving to interview the demolition guy, Ellen at the wheel, trying to concentrate on how she'd approach the questioning. But her thoughts kept sliding back to the break-in and her awful mood last night and this morning, so that at first she didn't take in what Pam Murphy was telling her.

Then one word registered. 'Revenge?' she said, struggling to pay attention.

'Uh huh. He doped her with GHB at last year's Schoolies Week, raped her, and forgot all about it. *She* didn't forget all about it. She recognised him. I even heard her accuse him: "Raped anyone lately, Josh?" He probably wondered what she was talking about.'

'Sorry, who are we talking about?'

Irritation from Murphy, very faint. 'Caz Moon, Sarge. Manages the surf shop in High Street.'

'Got you.'

Ellen couldn't afford to zone out. She gripped the steering wheel as if that might help her to concentrate. 'You're saying she got him back by doping him and leaving him naked on the beach with lipsticked balls?' The image struck her properly then, and she laughed.

Pam laughed.

'Did he name her?'

'No.'

'So you can't prove any of this. You haven't got enough to question her, let alone arrest her.'

'Not her, Sarge, *him*. I want to put him away. That sexual assault last Saturday night—I'm betting it was down to him.'

They sat quietly as the road unwound through farmland and then between an industrial park and a new housing estate on the outskirts of Frankston. Ellen slowed: a list of the park's tenants listed 'Delaney Demolition, Patrick Delaney, prop.' A minute later they'd parked outside a nondescript building: prefabricated cement walls, aluminium windows, shrubs struggling to survive in sunbaked bark chip garden beds. There was a chain link fence behind the building, crammed with heavy trucks and dozers, dump bins, and individual piles of recyclable doors, window frames, bricks, baths, stoves, tiles, corrugated iron roofing sheets and fireplace surrounds.

There was no receptionist, only Delaney peering over half-lens spectacles at a keyboard, poking a key, checking the monitor, and cursing. He looked up with relief. 'What can I do you for, ladies?'

He was solid, his rolled back sleeves revealing decades of sun damage and a glimpse of skin as white as ivory. He wore a check shirt and jeans, grey hair showing at his throat. His job was to break things, and he looked competent to do it, but he also looked genial and grandfatherly. The pages torn from calendars and stuck to the walls were of fishing boats and racing cars. Ellen showed her ID and introduced Pam Murphy.

'Planning East's infringement officer was murdered late on Wednesday afternoon. We believe you encountered her earlier that day.'

'Whoa,' said Delaney, putting up his hands. Then he frowned in concentration, casting his mind back. His face cleared. 'That old joint down in Penzance Beach?'

'Yes.'

'She arrived just as we were finishing. Spitting chips, but what could I do? I was hired to do a job. The permit to demolish was valid.'

'Was she angry with you, specifically?'

'I guess so. Because I was there, if you know what I mean. But like I told her, I was hired to do a job, it was a legitimate job, just as hers was a legitimate job. You're saying she's dead?'

'Murdered.'

'The same day I saw her?'

'Yes, so I do have to ask you, Mr Delaney, did you see her again?'

'Nup. We had another job to go to, fibro farmhouse near Baxter. My boys are there now.'

Pam spoke. She said, 'Fibro? So there's asbestos in it?'

Delaney regarded her calmly, a half smile creasing the edge of his mouth. 'All legit. I have a permit to handle asbestos and my guys are all suited up in bio-hazard gear, all right?'

Ellen recognised Pam's tactic, but also recognised that it hadn't got them anywhere. 'Who hired you to demolish the house in Penzance Beach?'

Delaney cocked his head at her. 'The guy who bought the site.'

'Name?'

'Hugh Ebeling.'

'How much notice did he give you?'

'He rang me the night before.'

'So a rush job.'

'Yes. He tried calling several demolition firms, but no one could do the job there and then, there's so much work on at the moment. Then he called me and got lucky. I had a spare crew and a spare few hours between jobs.'

'Why the urgency, did he say?'

Delaney shifted his massive form uncomfortably. 'Said he had builders lined up to put in a cement slab before Christmas.'

'You believed him?'

'Sure.'

'But?'

Delaney coughed delicately. 'But the planning lady, the one who got murdered, told me an application had been made to preserve the existing building. I swear I didn't know that. As far as I knew, the guy had a permit to demolish and there was no preservation order.'

Ellen nodded. 'No one's blaming you,' she said.

'It feels like it. I don't want no one taking me to court.'

'There was no preservation order,' Ellen said. 'There was an application, that's all. You're in the clear.'

'*Legally*, in the clear,' Pam butted in. 'Not morally. That was a lovely old house.'

'Pam,' Ellen said.

'He doesn't even recognise me, Sarge,' Pam said. She fronted up to him. 'Do you, eh?'

Delaney peered at her uncertainly. His face cleared. 'You were there.'

Ellen cut in. 'Do you think the man who hired you knew that a protection order might be issued?'

'Wouldn't know,' said Delaney. He looked uncomfortable again. 'But the planning lady reckoned someone had tipped him off.'

'She told you that?'

'Yes. She was that mad about it.'

'Did she say who?'

Delaney shrugged. 'None of my business. But it would have to be someone in the know, right?'

'Someone in the planning department?'

'No idea.'

'I need to see the job order,' Ellen said.

Delaney fished it out of a tray on his desk. Ellen copied down Hugh Ebeling's address and telephone numbers, and returned to the car with Pam Murphy. She didn't say anything to Pam. What right did she have to rebuke her? Pam had justice and a high moral sense on her side. Pam wasn't a sneak thief.

Settling behind the wheel, Ellen called Challis with an update. 'Next stop, Ebeling and his wife?'

'Yes. Collect me at the station and we'll drive up together. Tell Pam to check on Carl Vernon and the residents' committee.'

'Will do.'

She started the engine and eased the lever into Drive. At that moment, Pam's mobile phone rang. Ellen drove slowly back to the freeway, half listening in on the conversation. 'You're kidding,' Pam was saying. 'Uh huh…uh huh…But not the sexual assault? Damn… okay, thanks.'

She pocketed the phone and settled a complicated gaze on Ellen. 'That was the lab.'

'And?'

'I'd asked them to run Josh Brownlee's DNA, thinking I'd get him on sexual assault…'

Ellen gave her a crooked grin, acknowledging the initiative. 'And?'

'No luck. But—and I guess you're going to like this—he did leave that mucus trace on Lachlan Roe's elbow.'

Ellen felt lighter, some of the badness leaking away. 'Then let's go and pick him up,' she said, stopping the car to call Challis with the change of plan.

36

But at the Sea Breeze Apartments they were told that Josh Brownlee had checked out.

'After breakfast,' the manager said, desultorily watering a row of rosebushes at the rear of the building. He wore a wife-beater singlet, tight shorts and a beer gut.

'Damn,' said Ellen.

'Paid through till Sunday, too,' the manager said.

Pam, feeling nasty, said, 'If you'd care to give me the refund, I'll be sure he gets it.'

The manager backed away agitatedly, cigarette bobbing amid the bristles around his mouth. 'Can't do it. Regulations.'

Ellen fixed him with the lenses of her dark glasses. 'Did he say where he was going?'

'Dunno. Home?'

The motel building and grounds were better tended than the manager. It was quiet here at the rear, cool, leafy, the air smelling of freshly watered garden beds. Seagulls called out, and on the foreshore road at the front of the building a pair of joggers chuffed by but, otherwise, this corner of the world was asleep. Ellen glanced at all the curtained windows: schoolies inside, unlikely to stir before noon.

'I have his home address,' Pam said as they returned to the car.

Here on the street the sun was beating on glass and metal, softening the tarry road.

'Where?'

'Oliver's Hill.'

They drove off in the hot car, Ellen steering along the foreshore and out onto the Frankston road while Pam searched the street directory. Although Oliver's Hill was part of the depressed bayside suburb of Frankston, it was above it literally and sociologically, with big houses that looked out over the bay and down on the struggle below. There was no underemployment on Oliver's Hill, no fast-food obesity or here-today-and-gone-tomorrow kinds of commerce.

'Should we call first?'

Ellen shook her head. 'We don't want him to run again. We also don't want the parents thinking about a lawyer before we get there.'

At Somerville she headed down Eramosa Road to the freeway and then up and over a spine of hills to the Nepean Highway, which skirted Oliver's Hill. Pam directed her to an exit before the road began its plummet into the main part of Frankston. As Ellen wound through the hillside streets she found herself gazing keenly at the houses on either side. Where had it come from, this sudden interest in where and how other people lived?

Their destination was a 1960s brick house on three levels to account for the steepness of the block. Nothing redeemed it apart from its size and the vast blue haze or the bay's curving waters, which could be glimpsed between a pair of ghost gums. 'I don't see his car,' Pam said as they got out.

There was only a white Holden, parked in a carport attached to the upper level of the house. No sign of Josh's little boulevard racer in the driveway or on the street. They stepped through a small gate and along a flagstone path to a solid wooden door with a small triangle of gold glass set in it. Ellen couldn't work the place out. This was the main entrance, but did it lead to the main living areas? In any other house, this would be the back door. She rang the bell.

A woman dressed in paint-flecked sleeveless overalls and a singlet top opened the door. She took one look at them and seemed to know. 'Is this about Josh?'

There was paint over her hands, fine dots of it on her face and in her hair. 'Yes.'

She sagged briefly against the door. 'I'm Sue Brownlee. You'd better come in. My husband's here.'

She took them along a corridor of partly-open bedroom doors to a kind of landing arranged with sofas and a flat screen TV, then down a flight of steps to a sitting room, which Ellen guessed made up the middle level of the house. The air was dense and heavy with paint odours. The man standing there was dressed in a fine suit, crisp white shirt, a blue and gold tie. He looked as wretched and tense as his wife but came forward decisively and stuck out his hand. 'Clive Brownlee. Sue called me at work. I just got here.'

All four of them were posed on a nondescript carpet. Ellen looked inquiringly at the man's wife, who said, 'I asked Clive to come home because Josh burst in all upset and then went out again. I wasn't expecting him till Sunday.' She paused. 'I was painting the laundry. It's my day off.'

'Did he say where he was going?'

'He acted so upset,' Sue Brownlee said.

They were frozen there, the parents apparently unable or unwilling to think clearly. 'Perhaps if we all had a cup of tea?' said Ellen gently.

Relieved, the Brownlees led Pam and Ellen to the kitchen, which was like an annexe to the middle floor of the house. They sat on stools on either side of a high bench. Clive Brownlee filled the kettle, his wife rummaged for cups. The kitchen, like the other parts of the house that Ellen had walked through, was faintly worn and out of date, and she chided herself for assuming that Josh Brownlee came from a background like Zara Selkirk's. All they had in common was the Landseer School. Zara Selkirk came from real money, the kind that was offhand, almost unthinking, while the Brownlees, it seemed, spent most of theirs on school fees and the mortgage. Theirs was the anxious, struggling face of the middle-class.

'Did Josh say what he was upset about?' Pam said.

Sue Brownlee's hand went to her neck, her long, paint-flecked fingers stroking it. 'I asked what was wrong and he grabbed my neck and shook me. He said: "No one's paid enough." He scared me.'

'Did he say who hasn't paid, or what they haven't paid for?'

The parents exchanged a glance. 'He takes drugs,' Clive Brownlee said finally. 'They affect his mood. He imagines things. He can get quite violent sometimes.'

His wife said tensely, 'Please, what's he done?'

Ellen ignored the question. 'Did your son stay here long before going out again? Did he unpack, for example, or repack?'

'*What's he done?*'

Ellen said evenly, 'We wish to question him in connection with an assault.'

'Oh, God. Who?'

'A man named Lachlan Roe. It's been in the news, but does the name mean anything to you other than that?'

The Brownlees stared at each other, making connections. 'The Landseer chaplain.'

'Yes,' Pam said. 'Josh was a Landseer student?'

'He finished last year. A day kid, not a boarder. He caught the school bus at the end of the street.'

Clive Brownlee passed around cups of tea. Ellen had no intention of drinking hers but was merely marking time. 'What was Josh's involvement with Mr Roe?'

Something deep and desolate lies behind this, she thought, watching the Brownlees. And perhaps not recently, given that Josh no longer attended the school.

The father choked the words out. 'Our other son, Michael, was also at Landseer. He committed suicide halfway through last year.'

'I'm so sorry,' Ellen said.

'It hit Josh hard. He feels responsible, you know, the older brother.'

'Is that when he started taking drugs?' Pam asked gently.

Brownlee's hands were resting palm up, empty and vulnerable on the table. He leaned toward her. 'It's as if he feels he should have made a better job of looking after Mike.'

Pam glanced at Ellen. They got to their feet. 'Was the chaplain involved in some way?'

The parents, raw and baffled, failed to reply.

'Do you know where Josh might have gone when he left here?'

The parents exchanged a look. 'When he's cross with us he goes to his Uncle Ray's.'

'And where's that?'

'Ray trains horses. He's got a place in Skye.'

Farmland, northeast of Frankston. 'Perhaps you could call him,' Ellen suggested.

There was a kitchen phone, but Josh's father left the room, knocking into a chair and the doorjamb as his body began to let him down. Soon they could hear his voice in another part of the house. There was an exclamation, then silence, and then he was in the doorway, looking shocked.

'He was there, but he left. He's got Ray's shotgun.'

Pam said authoritatively to Ellen, 'Let me drive, Sarge.'

37

'It could be argued,' said Challis carefully, as though he didn't fully agree himself, 'that you have a motive for murder.'

That roused them out of their sleepy disdain, Hugh Ebeling, Mia Ebeling, their lawyer, Marcus Delarue.

'Inspector,' drawled Delarue. 'Watch your mouth.'

He wore a charcoal grey suit, white shirt, silvery blue tie and highly polished shoes. He was the kind of lawyer who always looks clean and precise, as though groomed by valets before every appointment. He was also bloodless—pale hair, pale skin. He wasn't the kind of lawyer who sails in the Whitsundays and stands around a racetrack. But his eyes were lawyers' eyes, sharp and focused.

'You tell him, Marcus,' Hugh Ebeling said.

They were in the developer's Italianate house in Brighton, Ebeling choosing his home over his downtown Melbourne office for this meeting with Challis. Perhaps he's afraid that tongues will wag, Challis thought. Perhaps he wants to impress or intimidate me. Fat chance: in Challis's view, seafront Brighton was for drug lords seeking respectability and judges and business tycoons who were losing it. Their wives liked to shop. Their children, abandoned at exclusive boarding schools, rose to take their places.

'Perhaps you could both start by telling me your movements on

Wednesday afternoon and evening,' Challis said.

He looked at them; he didn't look at the lawyer. Hugh Ebeling wore casual trousers and a polo shirt, a tall, boyish-looking man with the confidence of a bullying prefect. He'd be a man for sailing and watching the horses run. Mia Ebeling was a leggy blonde, the blondness a little desiccated now that she was in her early forties. She wore tailored jeans, a scoop-necked shirt and an air of regal outrage, as though Challis had neglected to use the tradesmen's entrance.

'My clients were here in the city,' Delarue said.

Challis ignored him. 'Mr Ebeling?'

'In my office. Arrived as usual at seven-thirty and left at six.'

'Did you go straight home after work?'

'No, I met a client for drinks at the Windsor.'

'I'll need to confirm that.'

There was a huge walnut coffee table on the vast Afghan rug between Challis and the others. Delarue plucked a sheet of paper from his briefcase and slid it across the table to Challis. 'Names and phone numbers.'

Challis nodded his thanks and said, 'Mrs Ebeling?'

Bored now, she said, 'I was with my personal trainer all morning.'

Of course you were, thought Challis. He caught a gleam in Delarue's eyes. The guy knows what I'm thinking, Challis thought, wanting to share a grin with him.

'And then?'

She said, in a kind of fury, 'I had lunch with a friend—' here Delarue slid another name and phone number to Challis '—and we spent the afternoon in this very room, preparing for a charity auction on Saturday.'

Her husband leaned his gangly trunk forward, ropy tanned forearms on his knees. 'And after that my wife took a taxi to my office and we had dinner at a restaurant in Flinders Lane.'

Challis nodded, jotting the details in his notebook.

The lawyer said precisely, 'In other words, inspector, my clients were not down on the Mornington Peninsula at the time of the murder.'

Yeah, but they could have hired somebody, Challis wanted to say, knowing that Delarue wanted him to say it. He glanced at the husband and said, 'Who tipped you off?'

'I beg your pardon?'

'Inspector, please.'

'You had a demolition permit for a house called Somerland in Penzance Beach, but—'

'A perfectly valid permit!'

'—but the National Trust, the local residents and Mrs—'

'Morons,' muttered Ebeling. 'Anti-progress, the lot of them.'

'Pathetic little people with pathetic little lives,' said Mia.

Their lawyer was looking on in interest. Challis said, 'These same pathetic little people were pursuing an emergency application for heritage protection from the State Government. You knew that. You knew you had to act fast. Apparently you were lucky to find a demolition firm that could do the job on short notice.'

'Rubbish.'

'You were tipped off by someone,' Challis said. 'You had a day at most in which to act.'

'Bullshit,' Ebeling said, glancing irritably at his lawyer.

'The National Trust classified the house on Tuesday,' Challis said, 'and it was flattened in just a few minutes on Wednesday.'

Delarue said, 'Let us be clear on this. Mr and Mrs Ebeling had a valid permit to demolish the existing structure?'

'Yes.'

'And there was no overriding order in place stopping them from doing that? No interim heritage amendment from the planning minister?'

'No.'

'Then my clients acted lawfully.'

The clients beamed at Challis. It chilled him a little, the shared emptiness. He decided to needle them. 'They acted unethically,' he said. 'They don't care about preserving the heritage of Penzance Beach, or forging good relations with the people who live there. They're not even interested in replacing the house they demolished with a building that might sit harmoniously with the surroundings. All they want is to erect a monstrosity that stands as a monument to their egos.'

The outrage was almost comical. Ebeling's jaw dropped and he said, 'Marcus, do we have to listen to this?' and his wife said, 'Awful little man,' spitting the words out.

There was tiny gleam of enjoyment in Delarue's eyes, but he said, 'You're editorialising, Inspector. Tut tut.'

Challis shook his head. 'The fact is, Mrs Wishart was an impediment to your clients in three ways. One, she was trying to stop the demolition from going ahead. Two, she knew the identity of the shire employee who was bribed by your clients—'

'Bullshit,' shouted Ebeling, his veneer slipping, a man who'd turn nasty when crossed.

'—and three, as a kind of fallback position in case the existing house *was* demolished, she'd implemented delays to the planning process for the house your clients wish to erect on the site,' continued Challis. He referred to his notes: 'A five-bedroom house on three levels, with extensive decking and a reflection pool. Like I said, a monument.'

'You want to think about your tone, you miserable little pen-pusher,' said Mia Ebeling. 'I intend to lodge an official complaint.'

'That's your prerogative,' said Challis.

They all sat and looked at each other. Challis realised that the Ebelings and their lawyer didn't think his accusation required an answer. He decided to keep pushing. 'Owing to Mrs Wishart's actions, you're not allowed to start building until you meet with the objectors and settle your differences with them. You might find yourselves returning to the Development Assessments Committee for months, even years. You must have been very angry with her.'

'Meddlesome bitch,' said Mia Ebeling.

'Mia, please,' the lawyer said.

'Well she was.'

Call him old fashioned, but Challis tended to believe that women were by nature warm, nurturing and conciliatory. If mean, vicious and sly, it was to cope in a man's world. But Mia Ebeling was probably mean, vicious and sly all on her own. 'So, good riddance?' he suggested.

'My clients have solid alibis,' said the lawyer hastily. 'They are very distressed about the death of Mrs Wishart, but were not in any way involved and will vigorously challenge any further attempts to implicate them in this awful crime.'

'Well put,' said Challis.

38

Then Challis drove from the Ebelings' house in bayside Brighton to the centre of the city, where he prowled around for thirty minutes before finding a public carpark with a vacancy. Five minutes later he was in the foyer of the state's planning appeals tribunal, where the marble, the steel, the glass and the attitudes were cool, verging on cold—like the judge's aide standing before him.

'The judge is overseas,' she said.

'When will he be back?'

The aide was about twenty-five, dressed in a slimline black dress, stockings and heels. A recent law graduate, guessed Challis. She gazed at him unblinkingly over the rim of chic half-lenses. 'Justice Marlowe is giving a paper at a conference in San Francisco.'

'When will he be back?' said Challis again.

She cocked an eyebrow faintly as if to say that while police officers were as much on the side of law and order as lawyers and judges, their job was grubbier, and it showed in their manner and breeding. 'He's staying on for a couple of weeks.'

'Skiing at Aspen?' said Challis idly, but saw to his surprise that he'd scored a hit. The aide flushed and said, 'May I ask what this is about?'

He outlined the matter swiftly: the Ebelings, the demolition of

Somerland, the development of the site and how it involved Ludmilla Wishart.

The aide swallowed. Challis intuited that behind the severe grooming she was young and insecure and probably adored the judge. Raising doubts about the judge's bias wasn't going to get him very far, so he said, 'As I'm sure you're aware, a group of Penzance Beach residents—old-timers and preservationists and historical society people—have lodged an objection to the development.'

'I cannot comment on cases before they've been heard. Not even then.'

'I was wondering, did the victim correspond with the judge at all? Have the Ebelings?'

'Justice Marlowe will be back in a fortnight,' the aide said, turning on her gleaming high heels.

'An off-the-record confirmation is all—'

'Put it in writing,' she said over her shoulder, heading for the lifts with a scrape of fabric and a trim clatter.

Challis headed out of the city again, taking the Monash Freeway and striking heavy traffic. Melbourne was a city that preferred motor vehicles and roads to trains and trams, even though the road system didn't work because there were too many cars because the public transport system didn't work because…

He exited at Blackburn Road and wound his way behind Monash University to the Westall Extension, which bypassed Springvale and put him on the Frankston Freeway. It wasn't much of a freeway: road works had limited the speed to 80 km/h for years now.

After Frankston he headed across to Somerville and a house on several hectares of cleared land abutting French's Reserve. The owners had cleared the land without first lodging an application. According to Ludmilla Wishart's files, Planning East had threatened to take the owner and the clearing contractor to the magistrates' court, where they'd be liable for fines of up to $120,000 and a requirement to undertake replacement planting.

He pulled to the side of the road and re-read the file. The air outside his open window was mild, full of cut-grass odours and something heavier, marshier. That made sense: the nearby paddocks had been slashed for hay, and French's Reserve was, according to a report in the file written by a Melbourne University ecologist who'd studied it for ten years, 'a regionally significant wetland'. Challis read on: 'Any clearing of the land adjacent to the reserve will have a detrimental impact on a rare orchid, "Astral ladies' tresses", and on the growling grass frogs, the southern toadlets, the swamp skinks, the dwarf galaxias and the southern brown bandicoots.'

Challis glanced out at the denuded land, which lay torn and sunbaked between his car and the Reserve. He thought that $120,000 plus an appearance in court and other reparations was a pretty fair motive for murdering the person who'd brought it all upon you. Then he saw the For Sale sign, and when he drove in to the farmhouse, he saw that it had been cleared of all furniture and all desire for a future there.

He made a note of the real estate agent's phone number, and headed further southeast to Bittern, where a husband and wife named Read had removed indigenous trees from a house block in a residential zone without a permit. When warned by Ludmilla Wishart to cease, they went on to remove understorey vegetation. They were fined $16,000 in the magistrates' court in Waterloo, and from the dock had hurled abuse at Wishart.

He found the Reads on their property, directing as two teenage boys planted trees and grasses on the area that had been illegally cleared. The Reads were elderly and grossly overweight, Tom Read wheezing in a wheelchair and Bev Read in a walking frame.

'We paid the fine,' said the husband, gasping the words out.

His wife was smoking. 'We're putting in new trees and that.'

'So leave us alone.'

Challis said firmly, 'After sentencing, you were heard shouting "You'll get yours, bitch" at Mrs Wishart.'

'I been drinking,' wheezed Tom Read.

'He was that upset,' his wife said, the cigarette bobbing in her mouth, grey smoke wreathing her grey face and hair.

They were unlikely murderers. They'd probably cheated, thieved and lied for all of their lives, but they weren't killers. They were the kind to sulk and blame others when they got caught, not get violent.

Challis's last call was to the environment protection manager for the eastern zone. 'I've just been to French's Reserve,' he said.

Jessie Heinz looked like a Girl Guide leader: tanned, energetic, comfortable in a khaki shirt and shorts, probably never owned a dress in her life. 'That one's a nightmare,' she said. 'The owners put the place on the market a month ago and skipped to Queensland.'

'Do you know if they threatened Mrs Wishart in any way?'

'They threatened *me*. Set their dogs on me.'

'But Mrs Wishart?'

'Her role in this one was behind the scenes,' Heinz said. She paused. 'They'd have a greater motive to murder me. I made an issue out of the threat to the ecology of the reserve. They couldn't seem to get it into their heads that it was serious. They kept saying, "We can clear our own land if we want to" and "What ecology?" and "The reserve's on the other side of the farm and a breeding ground for mosquitoes." They called me a tree-hugger.'

It was said with a grin and Challis grinned back. 'Are there any other sensitive ecological issues that you and Mrs Wishart were investigating? We're aware of the tree clearing at the property where her body was found,' he said, 'but what else was she working on? Particularly issues that hadn't made it as far as a written report.'

'Trees,' said Heinz. 'It's always trees.' She crossed her office to a wall map. 'About a hundred trees have been vandalised along this part of the bay in the past year.' She indicated the coastline between Waterloo and Flinders. 'It's the same on the other side of the Peninsula. People drill holes in the trees and fill them with poison. The trees die, we have to cut them down. Or they skip the poisoning and come along after dark with a chainsaw.'

'People with homes overlooking the sea?'

'And property developers. There's been a flurry of apartment developments all along both coastlines in the past decade.'

Heinz paused and grinned again. 'We've had to get quite creative. Sure, we plant five trees for every one killed, but we've also been wrapping the poisoned trees in bright orange plastic, and we're seeking council approval to erect view-blocking screens like they have along the Surf and Bass coasts.' She paused again. 'Ludmilla's ideas.'

'That would have made her very unpopular.'

'But who would have known it was her?' Heinz demanded.

Deciding that he could trust her, Challis said, 'Tell me about Mr Groot.'

She looked at him steadily. 'Pro-development.'

'For example?'

'He doesn't appreciate the village atmosphere of the coastal towns. Twice now he's approved the commercial development of a general store, one dating back to the 1920s, another to 1935. Sweet little buildings, kind of the village hub. Sure, they needed some tender loving care, but he was allowing Melbourne developers to put up six-storey shop and apartment blocks in their place. The other planners hate his guts, but he always knows the fine print and can be pretty insistent and persuasive.'

'A slash-and-burn kind of guy.'

'An over-development kind of guy.'

39

There was no point in mobilising an armed response team to protect Caz Moon. By the time a team had geared up, found its way from the city to this corner of rural Victoria and been briefed, Josh Brownlee would be long gone.

And so, as Pam raced them down and across the Peninsula to Waterloo, Ellen put contingency plans into motion. First she ordered a chopper from Frankston and then ordered the police station at Waterloo to send a couple of cars down High Street to HangTen.

'Our person of interest is driving a red Impreza and should be considered armed and dangerous. Received?'

'Sarge.'

'If you can, evacuate the nearby shops and divert traffic at each end of the block.'

'Sarge.'

Then she called HangTen, Caz Moon grasping the situation swiftly, not asking Ellen to repeat who she was or her connection to Pam Murphy.

'I'm using the cordless phone,' she told Ellen, sounding breathless. 'I'm at the back door now, locking it…done. I'm moving to the front door…done. Are you sure he has a gun?'

'Highly likely. Are you alone?'

'No customers. Chloe's with me, the other sales assistant.' There was a pause. 'Are you sure he's coming after me?'

'Pretty sure.'

'If we stay here in plain view, he could shoot through the glass.'

'Yes.'

'If we leave the shop, he could ambush us.'

'Yes.'

Ellen had a sense of wheels turning, and asked, 'Is there a secure room you can hide in? A storeroom, maybe?'

'Storeroom. It has a steel door and no windows.'

'Hide there now,' Ellen said.

Something then, a sixth sense, a shift in the quality of the connection, an intake of breath, told Ellen that they were too late. 'Caz?' she said, trying not to convey the panic she felt. Paddocks sped past her window, trees, a dam, a horse with a couple of birds upon its back. They were still several kilometres short of the town. Traffic was sparse. 'Caz?'

Caz's voice came then, sounding steady enough. 'He's here. Outside, two wheels up on the footpath. Nearly hit someone. He's getting out. Yep, a gun.'

'Caz, for God's sake, take Chloe and run to the storeroom.'

Ellen heard scrapes, breathlessness and whimpering, as though the two women were duck waddling to the rear of the shop behind the only available cover, glass-topped counters and racks of clothing. 'Are you nearly there?'

'Nearly. He just rattled the door.'

'Are the lights on or off?'

'Off. First thing I did.'

'So he might think you've closed the shop and gone home?'

'No. I didn't have time to wheel the sales racks in from the footpath.'

'Please, Caz, hide in the storeroom.'

More sounds and then Caz said, 'He's pounding on the window and yelling.'

'Caz—'

'I know, I know, hide.'

A radio transmission cut in. It was John Tankard. 'Suspect sighted. I can confirm that he's armed. A shottie. He looks agitated.'

'John,' said Ellen, as Pam Murphy floored the throttle and expertly flicked past a delivery van, never once glancing at her passenger, 'be very careful. Did you evacuate the area?'

'Didn't have time, but people started evacuating themselves when they saw the gun.'

'No shooting, John, not if there are people about. Not unless it's absolutely necessary. We'll try to talk him into surrendering. Received?'

'Sarge.'

'Are you alone?'

'Andy Cree's with me. We've got a second car at the roundabout.'

Ellen put a face to the name: the good-looking rookie, Pam Murphy possibly sweet on him. 'Impress on Constable Cree and the others, no shooting. I don't want any headlines.'

'Sarge.'

'What's our person of interest doing?'

'Pounding on the window of the surf shop.'

'Where are you?'

'Other side of the street, waving people to get out of the way.'

'Get them *well* out of the way.'

'Sarge.'

'Check his car—any other head on board?'

'He's alone, Sarge.'

Switching back to her mobile phone, Ellen said, 'You there, Caz?'

The reception was scratchy suddenly, the young shopkeeper's voice fading in and out. 'In…locked…'

She's in the storeroom and the walls and steel door are interfering with the reception, Ellen guessed. Then John Tankard cut in again: 'He's spotted us.'

'Keep your heads down.'

'Don't worry.'

'What's he doing?'

'Getting back into his car.'

'Be prepared to follow, but don't panic him. I've called for a chopper.'

'He's already in a panic, Sarge.'

'Don't aggravate it, John, okay?'

'Okay, Sarge.'

'*You* drive, not your partner.'

'Sarge.'

She knew that Tankard had done an advanced-driving course; she didn't know about Cree and didn't have the time to find out. But when Pam Murphy gave the briefest recriminatory flicker just then, she guessed she'd trodden on toes. Couldn't worry about that now: 'All we do is track him, okay?'

'Received.'

'Where is he now?'

'Heading for the roundabout.'

'Tell them to let him through.'

'Sarge.'

Pam and Ellen were no more than two minutes away from Waterloo now. If Josh Brownlee headed for home, he'd pass them going the other way. But there were other possible exits from the town: further south toward Penzance Beach, or directly across the Peninsula to Mornington, on Port Phillip Bay. Pam said, 'All we need to do is get him on a straight stretch of road, Sarge. Take him when there are no cars around.'

'But how?'

'Mobile take-out.'

'You know how to do that?'

'Yes.'

Ellen knew that the younger woman had received pursuit car

training. 'Does Tank know?'

'Yes.'

Ellen switched to the radio, saying, 'John?'

'Sarge.'

'Where is he?'

'Heading for Jamieson's Road.'

Pam and Ellen were on Jamieson's Road. It was quiet and straight for long stretches. Pam braked immediately and did a U-turn. Ellen looked back over her shoulder. 'We're on Jamieson's now.'

'Facing which way?'

'We turned around so he should be coming up behind us any minute. Where are you?'

'Just behind him.'

'Are both Waterloo cars on his tail?'

'Affirmative.'

'We do a mobile take-out. You up for that?'

'Am I?' Tank said. 'Just say the word.'

Ellen visualised the gleam in the eyes of the beefy young cop. 'By the book, John. This isn't the Grand Prix.'

'Sarge.'

The voices were quieter after that, calmer but more tense, as Pam Murphy mapped out the strategy and Ellen relayed instructions to the pursuit cars. 'He'll come up behind us. Pam will keep her speed down. Before he pulls out to overtake, your two cars need to come up fast behind him, one on his rear bumper, the other beside him. He'll be boxed in and have nowhere to go.'

'Sarge.'

'John, *you* need to be the one to come alongside him.'

'Sarge.'

'If we meet oncoming traffic, drop back and let it through.'

'Sarge.'

'I'm hoping the chopper will give us plenty of warning if there is other traffic ahead.'

Then there was silence, only the rush of their passage through the air and the muted howl of their tyres. Pam Murphy was driving at 110 km/h. She dropped back to 90, then 80, her eyes on the rear-view mirror, finally murmuring, 'There he is.'

Ellen had made radio connection to the helicopter by now, a spotter advising, 'You have a clear stretch ahead.'

'Start taking your positions, John.'

'Sarge.'

They said nothing. Pam dropped speed, then accelerated a little, keeping Josh Brownlee on their tail while the other cars came into position. The little Subaru was close behind the CIU car now, itching to pass. Then John Tankard's voice crackled, 'Permission to draw alongside.'

'Permission granted.'

Ellen, head craned to watch through the back window, saw the police car swing out from behind the Subaru and draw abreast of it. Brownlee glanced at it wildly, then at her, and then into his rear view mirror, for the second police car was now riding his rear bumper.

She sensed his panic and shrieking fury. He had nowhere to go. Pam began to brake, slowing to 70, 60, forcing Brownlee to brake. He was firmly boxed in now, cars on three sides, a grassy bank on the fourth, and Ellen saw him thump the steering wheel with his fist. Still the tight knot of cars continued to decelerate, and then Josh Brownlee flicked the wheel and bounced the Subaru against John Tankard's car. The Subaru yawed, overcorrected, and shot off the road, slamming into the bank. It bounced back onto the road, side-on, and metal crumpled as the trailing car smacked into Brownlee's door.

It was one way of concluding the pursuit. There was damage done, cuts and bruises, but no one was seriously hurt. No one died. The police cars could be put together again. Ellen and Pam tumbled out of the CIU car, feeling exhilarated. They joined Tankard and Cree, Cree calling tow trucks and an ambulance using his mobile phone, Tank securing the shotgun.

'Everybody okay?'

'Sarge.'

Ellen, still exhilarated, put the issue of the paperwork out of her mind. She put her actions in Adrian Wishart's house out of her mind. Instead, she hugged Pam Murphy, and then she proceeded to arrest poor, pathetic Josh Brownlee, who was sitting there in the grass, weeping and holding his bleeding scalp.

40

By now it was early afternoon. Scobie Sutton had spent the morning obtaining CCTV and speed camera coverage of the Nepean Highway. Assuming that Adrian Wishart had joined the Nepean as far south as Frankston on Wednesday afternoon, that was a lot of ground to cover, but all he needed were time-stamped images revealing the guy had driven to and from his uncle's place at the times claimed in his formal statement.

Meanwhile he was still waiting for Ludmilla Wishart's phone and credit card records, and he was trying to locate Peninsula-based CCTV and speed cameras. So far all he'd got were frowns and scratched heads. It was as if the local bureaucrats had never been asked to provide that kind of information or cooperation before—and perhaps they hadn't.

An hour passed. His eyes hurt. The grainy images jerked and flickered until one vehicle began to look like another and the locations merged. A second hour, a third. He was due to collect Ros from school and take her to netball soon. He couldn't rely on Beth to do that kind of thing any more. But Challis was breathing down his neck, wanting to know where Ludmilla Wishart had been, wanting to know where her husband had been.

He almost missed it, the beetly little Citroën zipping through a

Nepean Highway intersection. He checked the time: 12.17. That matched the uncle's account. According to Terry Wishart, Adrian had arrived at his shop after twelve-thirty but before one o'clock. Then they'd gone to lunch at Terry's local RSL.

Scobie rubbed his eyes. Now he had to track the Citroën's return journey. Ludmilla had been seen alive at around four or four-thirty, and according to the post-mortem report, murdered late afternoon or early evening. Adrian had reported her missing at 8 p.m., claiming he'd left the city to drive back to the Peninsula at around 5 p.m. Scobie decided to map movements and times as though Wishart had lied. How long would it take him to return to the Peninsula, track down his wife, then murder her? More than an hour—maybe as much as ninety minutes, or even two hours. So he might have left his brother as early as three o'clock, three-thirty.

Scobie's window was suddenly very wide.

Time passed and his eyes felt scratchy, as if he'd been in a sandstorm. He knuckled them. That didn't help, only aggravated the problem. He made several trips to the men's bathroom to splash water on them. He even went to the sick bay and searched futilely for eye drops, until a civilian collator took pity on him. She belonged to their church. Of course, she asked about Beth.

'I haven't seen her for ages, Scobie. Is everything all right?'

'Everything's fine,' Scobie said.

'I heard she'd joined another denomination,' the woman said carefully.

If Scobie had been a different kind of man he'd have said, 'Fuck you.' He thanked the woman and returned to the monitor and the tapes.

Eventually he was convinced: Adrian Wishart had not driven back along the Nepean between 3 p.m. and 7 p.m. In the hands of a good lawyer, that might seem like compelling evidence, but Scobie knew there were other routes back to the Peninsula, and other means of transport.

He'd have to start all over again.

41

A doctor came to the police station, examined Josh Brownlee—cleaned a small cut and gave him some painkillers—and cleared him for interrogation. Now they were in one of the interview rooms in the corridors behind the reception desk, Josh and a solicitor hired by his parents on one side of the plastic table, Pam Murphy and Andrew Cree on the other. John Tankard was holding up the wall behind them. There were only four chairs in the room and Cree, the slippery little prick, had got in first. Tank watched and listened, his back and legs aching. At times like this he felt his excess weight in every bone. Ellen Destry might have been there too, but she'd left it up to Murph, saying she intended to go back and search Josh Brownlee's bedroom and computer.

Tank listened to Murph run through the preliminaries for the benefit of the tape, and then watched her tap her folders and reports into alignment, taking several silent seconds over it, both to give herself time, he presumed, and to unnerve Brownlee.

'Josh,' she began.

If Brownlee were older, or looked less pathetic—a cut on his forehead, nose swollen and traces of caked blood in his nostrils—she might have called him 'Mr Brownlee'. Right now, to everyone in the room, he was just a sad kid named Josh.

'Josh, let's start at the beginning,' Murph went on. Tank could see from her posture how tense she was, and it was excitement, not the fear of failure. 'You attended Landseer as a day student, not a boarder?'

'Yes,' mumbled the boy.

'You did Year 12 *last* year, not this year?'

'Yes.'

Josh stared at the table top, pouring his misery into the layers of it already there, expressed in scratches and stains over the long years.

'Yet you attended Schoolies Week this year, as though you were still in Year 12?'

'Yeah.'

Tank wondered if the solicitor, a middle-aged woman, had seen her own kids go through all kinds of adolescent shit. Maybe she believed in owning up and atonement; she was making no attempt to halt Murph's flow.

'We'll go into the question of why you did that later. As a Year 12 student last year, did you have any dealings with the chaplain at your school, Mr Lachlan Roe?'

'Not much.'

'But you knew him, knew who he was?'

'Yes.'

'Have you had any dealings with Mr Roe *since* that time? This year, I mean?'

'No.'

'None?'

Josh showed a glimmer of spirit and looked up at her and down again. 'You said it yourself, I'm not at school any more.'

'Let's go back to Monday evening of this week.'

Josh shrugged sulkily.

'Can you account for your movements, Josh?'

He shrugged again. These kids are great shruggers, thought Tank.

'Just, you know, hanging around.'

'Alone?'

'You know, with other kids.'

'Other kids,' said Murph heavily. 'Kids *younger* than you? Kids who were in Year 12 *this* year? Or do you mean kids like yourself who had a ball last year and wanted to do it all again? Kids who didn't want to grow up? Or maybe you were hanging out with the toolies this year?'

Josh flushed dangerously and the solicitor laid a gnarled, be-ringed hand on his forearm to caution him. 'Really, Constable Murphy,' she said, 'where are you leading us? What crime are you investigating here? My client has been charged with traffic and firearms offences, and as you know, there are mitigating circumstances, such as the attack on him Wednesday night…'

Pam smiled sweetly and gathered her thoughts. 'Josh, did you or did you not encounter Mr Roe at or near his house on Monday evening?'

Josh swallowed. 'Don't think so.'

'It's only a few days ago.'

'I think I said hello.'

'It is alleged, Josh, that you had an altercation with him. What do you have to say to that?'

'No.'

'It's even possible that he provoked you in some way.'

She's trying to give him an out, Tank thought.

'I put it to you that there was a scuffle, Josh, and Mr Roe was accidentally knocked unconscious. Isn't that right?'

Tank watched as the kid struggled with this version of the truth, which put a gloss on the incident so that he wouldn't feel so bad about beating the crap out of the chaplain. Seeing a kind of relief suddenly flood Josh's face, Tank realised he was nearly there. Wanting to amp up the pressure on the kid, Tank stepped away from the wall and, with a quick, complicit, flirty smile at Murph, said, 'You gay, Josh? Did you try to pick him up? Vice versa?'

The fallout was extreme, the solicitor hard and protective, Murph furiously throwing down her pen and Josh shrieking, 'No! No!' and throwing himself at Tank. Tank wrestled the kid into his chair again, saying, 'Looks like I touched a nerve, eh, Josh?'

The solicitor said furiously, 'Constable Tankard, you're provoking my client needlessly. He's been in a car accident—'

'Cleared by the doctor,' flashed Tank.

'—and so I suggest we stop this charade immediately.'

Tank opened his mouth to reply. Murph snarled, 'Shut it, Tank, okay?'

No one saw the slow smile that Andy Cree gave him. Tank felt hot and explosive, but subsided against the wall, not meeting anyone's gaze.

Meanwhile Murph was saying, 'Josh? Do you want to have a break?'

The solicitor said, 'Yes, he does.'

Josh said, 'No, I don't.'

The solicitor threw up her hands theatrically but sat back as if to say that if her client was set on acting against his best interests, what could she do about it?

'All right, Josh; let's go back to Monday evening. You admit to meeting Mr Roe?'

'Yes.'

Tank wondered what game Murph was playing. There were too many undercurrents for him. The whisper around the station was that Josh Brownlee's DNA had been found on Roe's clothing, so why wasn't she blindsiding him with that, asking him to account for it? Maybe—it came to him suddenly—the DNA sample she'd obtained from him hadn't been authorised, and so she couldn't use it legally. She wanted an admission. But how did it fit in with all the other stuff, the rape on Saturday night, the whispers of sexual assault at last year's Schoolies Week, Josh found naked on the beach Wednesday night, and all that shit with the shotgun?

'Did you talk to Mr Roe?'

'Yep.'

'What about?'

Josh scratched abstractedly at the top of the table as if looking back through days, months and years of misery. The solicitor said, 'What does this have to do with the misdemeanours with which my client has been charged?'

Pam ignored her. 'Josh?'

'Stuff.'

'Your brother Michael went to Landseer, correct?'

Josh trembled and his face spasmed in grief. 'Yes.'

'Did he have contact with Mr Roe?'

Josh exploded. '*Mister* Roe! Why do you keep calling him that? Why do you give him that kind of respect?'

'He's lying in a hospital bed, Josh, beaten so badly he could die.'

Tank knew that wasn't true. The doctors had confirmed that Lachlan Roe would live. He'd be a vegetable, but he wasn't going to die.

'Good! He deserves it!'

Pam asked what they all genuinely wanted to ask: 'Why, Josh?'

'For what he did to Mike.'

'Your brother?'

'Yes.'

'Michael went to him for advice last year? At school?'

'*Yes*,' cried Josh. 'The bastard had just been appointed chaplain. All this crap at assembly, all these politicians were there, how great the school chaplaincy program was, how great Roe was, how he'd offer guidance and support.'

Murph said gently, 'But he didn't, did he, Josh?'

'He killed my brother!' Josh said shrilly, face distended, spittle flecking the table.

'Something he said to Michael? Something he did?'

Josh wrenched his head from left to right, not meeting their gaze, his neck tendons standing out like rods under his skin. 'Mike was gay.'

He didn't say anything after that, and Tank tried to put it together. Murph said, 'Michael was upset or confused about his sexuality?'

'Yes,' whispered Josh.

'Did your parents know?'

'Fuck no! You don't know what they're like.'

'Did he confide in you?'

'Not much,' said Josh miserably.

'But you knew.'

'He left me a note! He fucking wrote me a letter, then took an overdose and killed himself.'

Pam reached across the table and held his hand. 'Do you still have the letter?' she asked presently.

'No,' Josh said, eyes sliding away, returning his hand to his lap, so that Tank knew he was lying. Maybe Sergeant Destry would find it.

'What did it say?'

Josh leaned forward tensely. 'He'd gone to Roe for help. He wanted to know how to tell Mum and Dad and me he was gay, how to broach it.'

Josh stopped. Murph said, 'What advice did Roe give your brother?'

The tears spilled down Josh's face. He said, very distinctly, 'The bastard told Mike that being gay was an abomination in the eyes of God and all right-thinking people. He said Mike should be ashamed and beg forgiveness and change his ways. He said Mike was sick, a sick person, with sick thoughts. He said Mike made his skin crawl.'

Even Cree seemed affected. Pam said, 'And your poor brother had nowhere to turn?'

'He could have come to *me*,' Josh said, pleading. 'Why didn't he come to me? I'd have understood.'

'It's not your fault, Josh.'

'It *is* my fault. I would have understood. I know kids who are gay. I'm not anti-gay.'

Murph said gently, 'Michael was too distraught to think clearly,

Josh. He felt he had nowhere to turn, and took his own life.'

'Shouldn't have happened!' Josh said.

'You were so angry with Mr Roe that you argued with him,' suggested Pam, 'and it escalated.'

Tank was watching Josh. He saw the kid almost say something like, 'No, I tried to kill the bastard,' but then a glimmer of intelligence replaced the heat, and his face closed down again. He cocked his head at Murph. 'Something like that.'

Pam said, 'Josh, for the benefit of the tape, are you admitting to the assault on Lachlan Roe at or near his home on the evening of Monday, the sixteenth of November?'

'Yes.'

'You will be charged with assault, Josh. Do you wish to add anything in relation to this matter?'

Some of the tension had lifted. Josh muttered, 'Nup.'

'What about today, Josh? The shotgun. Why did you need it?'

A kind of shiftiness came into the kid. 'I was still upset over last Monday.'

Tank found himself stepping away from the wall, saying, 'Why go after that chick in the surf shop, Josh? What did she have to do with your brother and all that other stuff?'

Murph shot him a frown. He gave her one of his old looks, from back when they were partners in a patrol car, a look that said, 'Bite me.'

Irritated, she returned her attention to Brownlee. 'Did Ms Moon drug you and take away your clothes one night this week, Josh?'

The lawyer gaped and looked at her client, who shook his head carelessly. He'd recovered some of his cockiness. 'Nah,' he said coarsely. 'Got drunk, that's all, decided to have a swim in the nuddie and forgot where I put my clothes.'

'Traces of the date-rape drug GHB were found in your system.'

That's how she got his DNA, Tank thought.

'I was partying. Must have taken it by mistake.'

'It's not shameful to admit you were taken advantage of, Josh.'

'Wasn't taken advantage of.'

'I put it to you, Josh, that you intended to accost or even shoot Ms Moon, that you wanted to pay her back. What do you have to say to that?'

'Bullshit.'

Josh had folded his arms stubbornly, the powerful emotions long gone. He seemed to have some control over this new issue being raised. The other matter, his brother, he'd had no control over.

'The question is, Josh, why did she take advantage of you?'

'She didn't.'

'Was it revenge? Revenge for something that happened to her?'

The solicitor said, 'Where is this leading?'

'It is alleged that Josh and his little pals raped one or more of the young townswomen last year. They considered these women to be an easy target—working class, uneducated, therefore of loose morals and no account. Except that Caz Moon surprised you, didn't she, Josh?'

'Constable, please,' the lawyer said.

Josh said, 'Where's the evidence?'

'So you're not denying it?' Pam demanded.

'Where's your evidence?'

That was a good question, and there it ended, with Josh Brownlee charged and bailed and likely to plead to mitigating circumstances for his rampage that morning.

'You okay, Murph?' said Tank later. He'd tracked her down to the canteen, where she was drinking fucking peppermint tea with Cree. 'Good job in there,' he added, conscious that Cree was watching him.

She said, very distinctly, 'Tank, when I am conducting an interview, kindly butt out, okay?'

Cree smiled then, nothing and everything in it, and edged his chair closer to Murph. Tank couldn't bear to watch it. He couldn't think of anything clever to say. Finally he asked, 'Does his DNA tie him to any of the sex stuff?'

She sighed and pushed her mug of tea away. 'Afraid not. But he was involved, I know he was.'

'But you got him on the assault,' Cree said. 'It was brilliant, Pam, absolutely brilliant.'

Tank wanted to thump him. More so when Murph bumped shoulders with the prick and said, 'Win some, lose some.'

42

They thought she'd gone to search Josh Brownlee's bedroom but Ellen Destry was knocking on the door of a house on the Seaview Estate in Waterloo, a small sign on the fence behind her, 'Grant's Gardening Services'.

'Mr Grant?'

He was a generic blue-collar guy, with a shaven skull, face ruddy from beer and the sun's rays, still dressed in his work wear of shorts and a T-shirt. The voice was metallic: 'You got him.'

'My name is Sergeant Destry, Waterloo police station.'

He looked alarmed. 'Is it Tina?'

She smiled. 'Nothing to be alarmed about, sir. I understand that you did gardening work for Mrs Ludmilla Wishart?'

The voice was less metallic as emotion gripped it. 'Christ that was awful.'

Ellen fished inside her jacket. 'This was found during a search of Mrs Wishart's possessions.'

He took the envelope from her, opened it, peered at the invoice and the cash. 'Well, I'll be buggered.'

'Sir?'

'Didn't think I'd ever get paid. The husband's a prick, no offence, but his wife's also been killed, so no way was I going to hassle him.'

Ellen nodded, sizing him up. A woman with a child on her cocked hip appeared behind Grant, smiled pleasantly, disappeared again, cooing to the child. The yard and garden beds were tidy, the work van clean. But appearances weren't everything. 'Who's Tina?'

'My oldest daughter. She's at netball practice.'

Ellen nodded. 'Sorry about this, Mr Grant, but may I ask your movements on Wednesday afternoon? It's routine, we're questioning everyone who came into contact with Mrs Wishart.'

'No worries.' He jerked his head. 'Our youngest needs a cochlear implant. We were up in the city, five o'clock appointment.' He gave her the details.

Ellen beamed. 'Thank you, sir.'

'Hey, no, thank *you*,' Grant said.

Feeling marginally better, Ellen drove to Oliver's Hill and searched Josh Brownlee's bedroom fruitlessly in the waning light of late afternoon.

As evening settled, Scobie Sutton took his daughter to the Jubilee Park netball courts in Frankston. The indoor courts this time, the stored-up air still and sweltering, the huge building having baked in the sun all day.

Ros played for the Tyabb Allstars, their uniform a shapeless, pale blue sleeveless top over an unflattering dark blue skirt. It seemed to Scobie that the very dowdiness of the uniform affected their ability to play well. They plodded around the court and fumbled the ball. Meanwhile their opponents, the Somerville Silhouettes, who wore close-fitting scarlet outfits with pert short skirts, were swift and decisive. They were also coquettish preeners.

Not an observation I can share with the netball mothers, Scobie thought. They'll think I'm a dirty old man.

Not a reflection he could share with Beth, either; she wasn't there.

'Please come,' he'd said.

'Next time,' she told him.

That had been at four o'clock, two hours ago. To his dismay, she'd still been in bed. He saw the future, Beth spending her life replacing one faith with another, continuing her drift away from husband and daughter. What the hell was he going to do? Who could he talk to? Her mother and sister? What would they think? Would they help?

'Where's Beth this evening?' said one of the netball mothers.

They were all sitting on the tiered wooden seats, surrounded by schoolbags, bits and pieces of clothing, older and younger sisters, grandparents, sole parents, both parents, bottles of water from which the netballers took gasping swigs between quarters. What could he say in reply? The netball mothers were at the same time school mothers and town mothers, and knew everyone's business. 'I think she's coming down with something,' he said.

'There's a bug going around.'

Heart bug, thought Scobie. Soul bug. At that moment Ros threw a goal, surprising herself, surprising everyone, and the little dance she gave, of unalloyed joy on her skinny legs, made everything better for Scobie, just for a little while.

By now it was fully dark. With a Mediterranean and a margarita from Westernport Pizza, the latest Batman DVD from Blockbuster, and a red wine from the drive-through bottle shop, Pam Murphy and Andrew Cree were chilling out in Pam's sitting room, Andy temporarily back in his boxer shorts, Pam in a thigh-length T-shirt. The pizzas had got cold; they'd lost interest in the film. Already the bed was beckoning again; or the sofa or the carpet. Andy yawned. His head was in Pam's lap, his bare neck and shoulders against her bare thigh, a major distraction and a reminder that your senses matter. It seemed to Pam that for months, years, all she'd done was apply her brain to catching a crim or solving a crime. Yeah, she tested her body every day, but only in the sense that it was a machine, a police machine. Her sense of herself as a *sensory being* had atrophied. All those moist smells, textures and elasticities that she'd denied herself for too long.

When the film credits came up, she pressed the eject button on the remote. She had her wine glass in her other hand. She wished that she had a third hand. She wanted to stroke the lock of fine hair away from Andy's forehead or feel around inside his boxers. 'Switch off? Watch some TV?'

'You choose.'

He turned his head and kissed her stomach just as she switched over to the TV. It was the late news and Josh Brownlee's arrest.

'I wish I could get him on rape as well.'

'Who?' Andy murmured, nuzzling her, raising goosebumps. He glanced at the TV. 'Oh, that guy. You got him for bashing Roe. Forget the rape.'

'You can't forget a rape.'

They were silent, lost in separate thoughts. Andy said, 'I bet he was trying to prove himself.'

'What do you mean?'

'His brother's a poofter, right? He's scared he's a poofter, too, so he tries it on with this Caz chick.'

Pam said mildly, 'I think it was a bit more than that, Andy.'

'Whatever.'

Pam chewed on the inside of her mouth, thinking about Josh Brownlee. She wanted someone to pay for the rapes. Caz Moon's act of revenge wasn't enough. At the same time, she wanted to hate Josh Brownlee more comprehensively, but Lachlan Roe, with his evil and harmful ideas, kept getting in the way of that. She wished that she could be more like Andy Cree and not care.

She switched off the TV, drained her wine glass and, with her free hand, started fooling around again, making up for lost time.

John Tankard was manning the front desk that evening, and he was clock watching. 'At dead on eight o'clock I'm out of here,' he told a couple of the uniformed guys, who were hanging around, shooting the breeze. They were about to go on duty, which mostly meant ensuring that the schoolies didn't drown in their own vomit.

'You could come and ride with us, Tank.'

'Yeah, right.'

'We know you're up for it, Tank. When those schoolie chicks get on the piss they're gasping for a screw.'

Not the ones Tank had encountered during the week—or not gasping to do it with *him*, anyway. 'I need some shuteye,' he said.

'Mate, it's Friday night.'

Eventually Tank was alone. The night looked smeared and half lit outside the glass entry doors. Shadows flickered past; he heard a hotted-up car lay down some rubber at the roundabout; someone whistled somewhere in the dim reaches of the building. He didn't think he'd ever felt as lonely as he did right now, and he knew that a lot of it had to do with Andrew Cree and Pam Murphy. He flicked through *Police Life* tormentedly and then a guy came barging in, young, with pudgy hands and face, cropped hair, a soul patch under soft, moist lips. You looked at him and knew his voice would have a whine running through it.

'Help you, sir?'

Then Tank recognised him. Dirk Roe. 'Help you, Mr Roe?'

Roe said, 'Check this out.'

He was the kind of guy who owns the latest electronic gizmo. He thrust a Blackberry at Tank, the screen showing that it was logged on to the Internet.

'I'm going to do you cunts for this.'

Tank, peered, wondering—not for the first time—whether or not he needed glasses. Eventually he realised that he was looking at an image of Lachlan Roe, lying in a pool of blood.

'That's my brother,' Dirk said. 'That is a crime scene photo, splashed all over the Web.'

'Not by us, sir,' said Tank stoutly. 'Not by the police.'

'Bullshit! Who else could it be?'

'A pedestrian walking by…' Tank said, going on to list some other plausible but unlikely culprits, all the time knowing *exactly* who.

Bronte-Mae McBride was like, so wasted. She'd gone to Point Leo with a gang of other schoolies, partly because Waterloo was the pits, partly to try twilight surfing. So they'd got there, they'd staggered over the dunes, losing half their gear along the way, it felt like, but now all they wanted to do was chill out, swig bourbon and coke from a can, snuggle under blankets, pass a joint around. Bronte-Mae had to go home tomorrow. Her parents had lined up a summer job for her, starting Sunday, helping out at Rebel Sport in Frankston. If her Year 12 results were okay, she'd start at RMIT next year, Occupational Health. So this was her last night and she wanted it to be memorable, she wanted it to mean something.

She found herself kissing that guy Matt from Landseer. Given that she was perhaps the last eighteen-year-old virgin in the history of humankind, and this was her last night, and he was so nice and such a good kisser, and the moon was shining on the water, she shifted her body so that his hand could slip inside her pants. It felt so good. Then her hand was inside his pants and before she could properly explore what a cock felt like, and mark this milestone, he was breathing funnily and her hand was sticky. He gasped, 'Sorry!' and she hugged him for all she was worth.

The others might or might not have noticed. Either way, did she want an audience if this was going to go any further? 'Let's find a quieter spot,' she whispered.

So they headed along the beach toward Shoreham, to a dark hollow, where he made love to her properly this time, and it was magical, not clinical, despite the condom business, there under the moon and stars.

'What's this?' said Matt at one point.

'Matt, it's a breast.'

'No, this.'

A small cloth bag half hidden by driftwood.

43

Hal Challis hadn't yet seen Ellen Destry in all of her phases. Their situation was too new for that. The things he did know about her he'd learned over the years and they were constant: she was beautiful; she was an efficient and creative work colleague; she was fearless, loyal, smart, quick and proud. And more recently he'd discovered the shifting contours of her bare skin, the little cries she uttered, and the swiftly changing moods and expressions when she was at her most intense and intimate: a kind of surrender, bawdiness, a delight in taking charge, selflessness…

But when he'd called her from his car late that Friday afternoon to suggest they eat at the Thai restaurant in Waterloo, she said no curtly, saying she had dinner under control, and when he arrived home she barely inclined her cheek for a kiss but continued to hack at chicken breasts and add them to a bowl of marinade. He'd scarcely seen her all day. He'd missed her. But the tension was palpable. 'What's wrong?'

'Nothing.'

'Tell me.'

Instead she washed her hands and began to slice cloves of garlic, and within seconds her thumb was bleeding and she was shouting, 'Fuck. *Fuck*, fuck, fuck, fuck.'

'Wash it under the tap.'

She scowled furiously but complied.

'What's wrong, Ellen?'

'Nothing.' Then: 'I never know where anything is in this place.'

Hovering in the doorway, he decided to take the reply at face value. 'What are you looking for?'

She turned to him with a ragged expression. 'What am I looking for?'

'Yes.'

Whatever it was had nothing to do with where he kept his garlic crusher. He waited. She examined her thumb and said, 'Forget it. Sorry I snapped.'

'Did something happen today?'

'Hal, forget it, okay?'

His heart said to cross the room and wrap his arms around her. His head told him to wait. He left the kitchen and found a bandaid in the medicine cabinet. While he pasted it over her thumb she stood stiff and mute, then returned to her chopping board. He sighed unconsciously, poured her a glass of Merricks Creek pinot and left it at her elbow. She glanced at the wine, sniffled, said nothing, but some tiny realignment of her body seemed to signal appreciation, and so Challis wandered through to the sitting room and tried to think his way into his CD collection. What would match her mood just then, her present needs? He settled on *Eric Clapton Unplugged*.

Anyhow, *he* needed it.

No protests from the kitchen.

He spread his Wishart case notes over the coffee table and flipped through them half-heartedly. It was no good, his mood was shot.

He wondered if she felt trapped. They hadn't been together for long but she'd had some months of freedom between her divorce and setting up house with him. And she hadn't actually *chosen* to set up house with him: she'd been minding his place while he tended to his dying father in South Australia last month, and had simply stayed on when he returned.

An arrangement, an understanding, sealed by one sudden, glorious fuck just one hour after he'd pulled up in his car.

But this was his house, not hers. She'd not made her mark on it yet and maybe was hesitant to. Maybe she hated the house but liked—loved?—him. Maybe if she hated the house, she'd grow to hate him.

Or the other way around. She knew him now and didn't like what she knew, and couldn't wait to get out.

She was waiting for the right time to tell him and it was driving her crazy.

Challis felt a kind of surliness settle inside him. He'd always been too solitary to have much of a love life and the two main relationships of his recent years—recent meaning the past ten years—had ended disastrously. First, the wife who'd tried to kill him, then the editor of Waterloo's weekly newspaper, shot dead by a killer he was hunting.

So he must have been mad to fall in love with Ellen Destry. Not only did he work with her, she was also under his formal command. Did those kinds of relationships ever work? Were they as valid as relationships that resulted from meeting someone by chance, like at a party? Wasn't it true that couples who met through work later found that work was all they had in common? Don't you need more than that? Did he and Ellen have more than that?

A little bit of him fractured inside. He took a swig of the wine in an effort to shake off the blues and began flicking through the Wishart case notes, looking for anomalies, looking for connections. His hammering heart eased, and after a while he realised that he'd left the autopsy report back at the office. He heaved a sigh. He should have scanned everything and stored it on his laptop or portable hard drive but he was a hands-on kind of cop. He needed to hold a file in his hand, not read a screen. He didn't want to become one of those wankers who walks around wearing a memory stick on a lanyard around his neck.

But Ellen always stored her files electronically. She'd probably have the autopsy report on her memory stick—not that she was a wanker.

He cocked his head: judging by the sounds and smells, she'd fired up the wok and begun adding onions, garlic, ginger, the chicken and strips of capsicum, so instead of bothering her he went searching for her work gear. Sometimes she dumped everything in the hallway, sometimes the bedroom, sometimes the floor of the walk-in robe. Mornings were occasionally a little tense, Ellen storming up and down, demanding to know where her keys were. Or her bag. Or her wallet, her memory stick, her sunglasses.

Maybe his life was too orderly for her? She needed chaos?

He located her briefcase in the hall, her bag in the bedroom. The briefcase merely yielded files. The bag was a bag of many zips and compartments, and he found pens, mints, receipts, address book, note book, tampons, tissues, business cards, lint and three memory sticks.

For some reason he selected the memory stick that was slightly different from the others. It was called a TrackStick, and when he plugged it into his laptop, he found himself looking at local maps and a record of coordinates, dates and times. In wonderment he carried the laptop through to the kitchen, saying, 'What's this weird stuff on your memory stick?'

Her gaze, at first faintly impatient, grew alarmed, then mortified. To his astonishment, her body went into an imploring or self-protective spasm, as if she'd witnessed a shocking accident, he were about to attack her, or her child had been torn from her breast. She balled her fists, her face crumpled and she began to cry gustily, shaking her head.

He was appalled and went to her immediately, first placing the laptop on the table. 'Ells, sweetheart, what's the matter, what is it?' he said, folding her against him.

And she froze, her body resisting him. Only her face surrendered, pressed into his chest, tears wetting his shirt.

'Ells?'

She stepped back, raw with emotions, turned jerkily to the wok and switched off the gas. 'You're going to hate me.'

'Hate you? Why?'

'You don't know me.'

'Tell me what's wrong.'

She gestured at the door through to the sitting room. 'Can we turn that crap off first?'

'Crap? That's Eric Clapton crap.'

She didn't smile at the old joke. He followed her through to the sitting room, where she snapped off the CD player. The silence and her mood—cool, almost cold—frightened Challis.

'Please tell me.'

She sat on the sofa. She said, 'No, you sit over there.'

So he sat opposite her, in the armchair.

'I've got something to tell you and it will change how you see me.'

Challis wanted to say: Don't be so dramatic. He reckoned that he'd seen and learned everything about human nature, and didn't figure he'd be surprised by what she had to reveal. What mattered was that Ellen thought it mattered. 'Okay.'

'I steal things.'

He waited.

'I've always stolen things, ever since I was a kid.'

He nodded. He almost told her he'd been nabbed for lifting chewing gum from the corner store when he was eight years old, but thought better of it.

'I feel the urge when we search people's houses,' she went on. 'Suspects, victims, it doesn't matter, if there's cash lying about, trinkets, I feel the urge to take it.'

Challis waited. What was he supposed to say? *How much? How often?*

'I mean,' said Ellen, 'I almost *never* steal; it's been years, in fact. I've been fighting it. The last time I did it I put the money into a church charity box.'

'Okay.'

'*Not* okay. The desire is there all the time.'

He nodded.

'I told you you'd hate me, think less of me.'

In fact, Challis had no thoughts about the matter and knew his face hadn't betrayed any. He felt desperately sad that she was so upset, that's all. He said simply, 'I love you.'

Tears pricked her eyes. 'No you don't. How could you?'

'I love you.'

She wailed, 'It's over.'

'No it isn't.'

'I'm a police officer and I steal. Don't you get it?'

'Counselling. Therapy. Hypnotism.'

'It's not that simple.'

'Yes it is.'

'I feel grubby.'

'So get clean.'

'I'm a police officer.'

'You still catch the bad guys, right? You don't take bribes, you don't look the other way?'

'I'm a hypocrite.'

'Who isn't?'

She was shaking her head in frustration. It was as if she wanted him to hate her. 'And the job,' she continued. 'They're not going to let us work together now that we're living together. Even if they did, the dynamics have changed. Even if we stop seeing each other and live apart, we can't go back to the way things were. Would we take on separate cases? What if we weakened and fell into bed together, or had a quarrel, how could that not affect how we related to each other? If I disagreed with you professionally about something, or vice versa, would we be able to keep our feelings, our shared history, out of it? What if you subconsciously favoured me sometimes: how do you think Pam and Scobie would feel about that? What if you subconsciously punished me?'

Challis said immediately, 'I'm not supposed to tell you this, but

McQuarrie knows about us.'

'Oh, shit.'

'It's okay,' Challis said, holding up a placating hand, 'he's not going to transfer one of us to the bush or take disciplinary action. He has a high opinion of you.'

He went on to outline McQuarrie's proposal for three new units on the Peninsula, saying, 'I'm not supposed to tell you yet. He wants me to think on it and let him know which one I think he should offer you. You'd be promoted to senior sergeant.'

To his astonishment, her face fell. 'Oh Hal, how can I even go on doing this job, let alone head a new unit? Listen to what I've just said about myself. How can you even support such a move? It's out of the question.'

'You'd be mad not to accept,' he growled.

She flinched and looked away.

He pushed on. 'First things first. Right now, we've got a job to do. A killer to catch.'

She breathed in and out. She seemed to struggle mightily with herself. 'Okay. All right. And speaking of killers... That memory stick—I found it hidden in Adrian Wishart's place.'

He stared at her.

'I broke in,' she said.

'Another thing you do.'

'It's not funny,' she flashed at him, her chin jutting.

'I'm not laughing.'

'Yes, it *is* another thing I do. Not often, and always case related.'

She was daring him to hate her. He said, 'You don't do it to steal. You do it to get a feel for the person living there and maybe find something the police can use.'

She gaped at him.

'Ells,' he said, 'you're not the first copper to do it and you won't be the last.'

She swallowed, the motion distinct in her throat. 'You, too?'

'It's been known to happen.'

She looked momentarily confused, and waved both hands jerkily as if to wipe away the distractions.

'You've seen what's on the device?' said Challis. 'The maps and co-ordinates? What's that all about, I wonder.'

Ellen shifted uncomfortably. 'You know more than I do. I was kind of trying to forget I had it.' Then she looked at him intently and said, 'Hal, I almost took some money as well.'

Challis went very still. 'Hidden? A lot?'

'No,' she said, and explained the circumstances, staring miserably at the floor.

'Come with me,' Challis said, grabbing her hand and dragging her back to the kitchen. When they reached the laptop he said, 'Okay, forget the past ten minutes, think like a cop.'

They stood together, staring at the screen. Presently he sensed Ellen grow calmer, her focus clearer. He waited, and after a while she pointed and said, 'I know what this is.'

'What?'

'GPS locations. Adrian was mapping his wife's movements.'

'How does it work?'

She took out the memory stick and examined it. 'This is the locator. He sticks it in his wife's car or bag, and retrieves it at the end of the day to see where she's been.'

Challis's mouth was dry. 'We need to see if it shows her movements on Wednesday. If so, he was at the murder scene. He retrieved it.'

'Killed her, you mean,' Ellen said.

'Yes.'

Challis let Ellen sift through the data. Eventually she looked around at him. 'Tuesday, and the days prior to Tuesday, but nothing for Wednesday.'

'Damn.'

'But it shows intent.'

'Ells, we can't use it in court. It's not logged on as evidence. It was stolen from the guy's house.'

She winced, chagrined. 'Sorry.'

'Not to worry. We'll think of a way.'

That was a pact, and a renewal, and the strain evaporated until the next time.

44

And so first thing on Saturday morning they examined the list of items that had been removed from Adrian Wishart's house: the home computer, shared by Wishart and his wife, letters, photograph albums, household files...

And four items grouped together as: *Four (4) USB flash drives/ memory sticks.*

'I can't risk adding a fifth to the list,' said Challis. 'Or crossing out the 4 and substituting a 5, without alerting the guy's lawyer further down the track. It's part of the formal log now.'

'Sorry, Hal,' Ellen said again.

'We'll work it out.'

They were in the CIU incident room, the first floor quiet. But not quiet downstairs: the station was always busy on Saturday mornings, with a steady stream of people reporting incidents from the previous night or needing a police officer to witness a statutory declaration. There was also Adrian Wishart, cooling his heels in an interview room—and not a happy boy.

'Has anyone examined the flash drives yet?'

'Scobie's had a quick look. One contains digital images of houses and other buildings, including the house that was demolished, another job applications and different versions of Wishart's CV, the third some articles on domestic architecture written by Wishart for architectural magazines. The fourth is new, still in its packaging.'

Ellen felt a tingle. 'The paperwork doesn't stipulate that it's new, still in its packaging.'

'True.'

'So we do a switch.'

Challis raised an eyebrow at her. 'Could work…'

'Did Scobie report to you verbally about the details of the memory sticks? Or did he add a formal written note to the murder book?'

'Verbally.'

'Then we're okay.'

Challis had brewed coffee in the tearoom. Grabbing Tim Tams from someone's private stash, they headed downstairs to Interview Room 2, where Adrian Wishart was stewing with his lawyer. Challis had seen the lawyer around town. Her name was Hoyt and she operated from an office suite above a pharmacy on High Street, specialising in wills and property conveyancing. That didn't make her ineffectual in criminal matters however, and she exploded when Challis and Ellen entered the room:

'It's unconscionable, keeping my client waiting like this. I should also point out that he's already been interviewed and provided a full and open account of his movements the day his wife was murdered. He's grieving, and treating him like this is prolonging the pain.'

She had to say all of that, while Challis and Ellen nodded pleasantly, and Challis followed up with an apology. 'We're terribly sorry, but some important new information has come to light and it needed processing.'

'What information?' demanded Hoyt.

She was a thin, raddled-looking smoker, the skin of her face pinched and grey, no nourishment on her bones. She also looked uncomfortably hot: the room was warm from too many bodies overnight and noxious smells lingered. It was partly why Challis had chosen it.

He turned to Wishart, who was wilting, his hair damp, face drawn, moist patches showing on his shirt. 'You were tracking your wife's movements.'

Wishart frowned. 'Don't know what you mean.'

Challis revealed the TrackStick in a clear plastic evidence bag and stated the evidence number and a description for the tape. 'This was found in your home and subsequently logged into evidence.'

Wishart looked hunted; his eyes darted; he swallowed. He'd hidden it in a secret place. If he challenged them on that, he'd also have to explain the hiding place and the reason for it. 'So?'

'A flash drive,' said the lawyer. 'So what? Is there blood on it?'

A weak crack and it annoyed Challis. 'It's a GPS device. Suspicious people like your client hide these devices in their spouse's handbag or briefcase or glovebox, or in their teenage kid's backpack, and it records the various locations visited during the day or night, and how much time was spent at each location. You simply plug it into your computer afterwards and up comes the information.'

'So what?' said Hoyt dismissively. 'You can't blame people for wanting peace of mind, especially parents of autistic or Down Syndrome children, or husbands whose wives spend a lot of time visiting remote locations and angry clients.'

Wishart gazed at her in appreciation, then swung his gaze to Challis. 'That's what I was doing,' he said. 'I was worried about my wife.'

Challis had expected this. 'Did you track her movements on the day she was murdered?'

'No, I was at my uncle Terry's shop in the city. I told you that.'

Challis picked up the TrackStick. 'You've been tracking your wife for weeks.'

Wishart shrugged. 'So?'

'Why didn't you track her on Wednesday? Was it because you knew where she'd be and had already intended to kill her?'

'I didn't kill her.'

'I think you were insanely jealous and protective of your wife. You needed to control and monitor everything she did.'

'No.'

'That's why you used a tracking device. It wasn't to protect her—after all, you could only read the findings *after* the event—but to know her every move, so that you could stalk her, anticipate her, challenge her, ambush her.'

'No!'

Ellen had broken her Tim Tam into nibble-sized portions. She wet a finger, transferred a flake of chocolate to her mouth. 'Did she really have a lover, as you suggested the other day? Carl Vernon denies emphatically that he was her lover.'

'I was mistaken. On reflection, all of her movements were innocent. Work related. But I was worried about her. People would threaten her.'

'Tracking your own wife,' said Ellen flatly. 'A pretty sleazy thing to do, Ade, don't you think?'

He flushed and Hoyt said, 'It's not a crime. That tracking device is not hard evidence. You're fishing. You're badgering my client. We're finished here.'

They had to let him go.

Only Smith and Jones were in the incident room, hunched over a computer screen, plenty of nudge nudge, wink wink in their body language. Porn, thought Ellen. They made her feel immensely weary. They each gave a little jump, then Smith joggled the mouse, Jones returned to his desk.

Hal, at her side, seemed equally fed up. 'Seen Scobie?'

Smith and Jones pantomimed bafflement and helpfulness. 'Haven't seen him all morning.'

'We need his analysis of Ludmilla's bank statements. We need to know if she shows up on CCTV cameras.'

This time it was a slow-dawning appreciation for the urgency and seriousness of the work. 'We'll let him know, boss.'

'Pam?'

'Haven't seen her, boss,' Smith and Jones said, some undercurrents in the way they said it.

The room was oppressive. Ellen tugged on Challis's sleeve. 'Let's grab a bite to eat.'

They clattered down the stairs. In the canteen Challis said, 'The TrackStick helps confirm our instincts about Adrian, but it doesn't prove he killed his wife.'

Suddenly Ellen couldn't look at him. Ever since last night a vague, unwelcome anxiety had been settling in her, and now it took shape. It wasn't so much that she felt bad about stealing the TrackStick, or being found out, as that she thought less of her confessor. Not by much, hardly at all, but in a tiny corner of herself she was disappointed in Challis. Why didn't he hate her? Why wasn't he admonishing her, punishing her?

Maybe helping him nail Wishart would cure that. Her mouth very dry, her face probably revealing her wretchedness, she placed a hand on his slender forearm. 'It comes down to his alibi. I vote we have another crack at the uncle.'

Challis was doing his long stare across vast distances. He blinked, recovered, and said, 'You're right. Could you do that? Deep background first. Really check him out.'

45

Ellen's first step was to phone Scobie Sutton. 'Where are you? We badly need everything you've got on Ludmilla's movements, especially CCTV.'

He sounded fretful. 'Look, I'm in the car, okay? Taking Ros to a party. My wife isn't well, so some things will just have to wait. I'll be in before lunch.'

Ellen closed and opened her eyes. She knew about the wife. But what if Scobie were giving vent to other grievances? Maybe he thinks I'm Hal's favourite, she thought. Maybe he thinks we don't respect his work, thinks we're ganging up on him.

If so, what she asked him next was going to make him crankier. 'Scobie,' she began carefully, 'about Terry Wishart.'

'What about him?'

'He's Adrian's alibi. No reflection on your initial interview, but I'm going to go have another crack at him.'

'No skin off my nose.'

Relieved, she said, 'What's he like?'

She could picture Scobie at the wheel of his car, frowning in his wondering way as he mused on her question—and driving badly, his little girl there in the car with him. She said, 'Would he lie to protect Adrian? Are they close? Is there any love lost between them?'

'They're opposites, apart from being different generations,' Scobie said finally. 'He's blue collar. Adrian's smooth, educated. Terry mends electrical gear, lives alone, stuck in the past.'

'The past?'

'His army days,' Scobie said. 'He's a bit sad, spends all his free time down at his local RSL club.'

'Thanks, Scobie.'

Army. Who could she call on a Saturday?

With reluctance she kept returning to just one person, her ex-husband. She stared at her desk phone for a while, biting the inside of her cheek. It hadn't been an easy marriage, not toward the end and not even for many years before that. They might have drifted apart anyway, but when Ellen's career in the police force took off and Alan's didn't, the split came hard and fast. Alan Destry resented not only the fact that his wife belonged to CIU—'The elite,' he'd say disparagingly—but also that she'd been fast-tracked through the ranks. 'Because you're a woman,' he'd sneer, somehow overlooking the fact that he'd twice failed the exams she'd passed with ease.

Then he'd looked around for other ways to fault her. She was never at home but always out on some case, and so she was not a good wife to him, or a good mother to their daughter. And she'd been sleeping with Challis all that time. Or probably sleeping with Challis. Or *wanted* to sleep with Challis.

He, on the other hand, had kept more regular hours, which entitled him to call himself a good father. His job wasn't glamorous—he was a traffic cop, wrote up tickets, manned booze buses, aimed speed cameras, did a bit of accident investigation work—but it was honourable and important. He kept repeating it, like a mantra, as if Ellen disparaged what he did.

Then there were all of the little things she did wrong. Her habit of never switching lights off when she left a room, for example. Or leaving a heater burning with a window open in winter. Forgetting to pass on phone messages or fill the car with petrol. And he hated it that she'd kept herself trim while his body grew slack from beer and the hours he spent behind the wheel of a car.

As desire and love leaked away, Ellen had grown to hate that body. Its bulk, emissions, and hairiness. The way he chewed his food. The way he sniffed instead of blowing his nose. The way his mouth sometimes hung open.

Ultimately, desire and love gave way to disgust, and she moved out as soon as Larrayne had left home to study in the city.

Thinking of all these things now, Ellen saw a connection between herself and Ludmilla Wishart. Had Ludmilla wanted to leave her husband? There were no children to keep her at home, but had she feared what her husband might do if she did leave? Had she been waiting for the best time to leave him?

What exactly would *be* the best time for someone in Ludmilla Wishart's position? Finding the courage to leave? Finally suffering some kind of unconscionable mistreatment?

Well, her husband had done something unconscionable, and it had been pretty final.

Then Ellen compared her husband with Ludmilla Wishart's. Both men liked to control. They had tempers. They were jealous.

But she couldn't, in good conscience, take it further than that. Alan hadn't stalked her. He hadn't tried to kill her, or play mind games with her. He hadn't wanted her to leave, certainly, but he hadn't tried to stop her, either, beyond a bit of pleading and the expected kinds of emotional blackmail. In fact, he'd found the separation and divorce liberating, in the end. He soon found a place to live. He found a girlfriend. He was having another shot at the sergeant's exam and felt pretty confident this time.

'Been studying like a bastard,' he told her, later that Saturday morning.

'Good luck,' she said, meaning it, touching his wrist briefly.

They'd arranged to meet in the little coffee shop within the Bunnings Warehouse in Frankston. The place was crammed, like it always was on

261

weekends, men and women in a do-it-yourself mood, shopping for paintbrushes, power tools, seedlings from the garden centre. A Bunnings store was Ellen's idea of hell, but Alan said he could give her a few minutes between chores, otherwise he wouldn't be free until next Tuesday.

'Thanks for seeing me,' she said.

'No worries,' he said shyly. He paused. 'You look good.'

In fact, *he* was looking good. He'd lost weight. He was taking care of his appearance. But he was still a big, hairy man. She didn't love him any more.

Didn't want him.

Then he had to go and spoil it. 'How's Hal baby?'

'Cut it out, Alan.'

'I can be a bit jealous of your boyfriend, can't I?'

He wants me to be jealous of his girlfriend, she realised.

'You found yourself someone before I did,' she countered.

He grinned. 'Fair enough.'

He'd bought a file with him. It lay between them on the little table, a glass-topped table with metal legs of slightly varying lengths, so that you wouldn't want to lean your elbow on it or trust your watery coffee not to spill. Or even buy it, Ellen thought. They hadn't talked about or looked at the file, but now, ostentatiously, Alan opened it.

'My mate did that digging you asked for. E-mailed the results.'

His mate in the Army Records Office. Alan had been a military policeman before joining Victoria Police, based near Seymour when he met Ellen. Six weeks after he was posted to Townsville, she had written to say: 'Guess what—I'm pregnant.' So long ago. Now their baby was a young woman.

She shook off the memories. What mattered was the fact that one of Alan's service mates had stayed on in the Army and was willing and able to help him.

'What did he find?'

'This,' Alan Destry said with a flourish and a smirk, pulling out a

262

sheet of paper.

Ellen froze. 'Not funny, Al.'

The page was blank.

'I'm not being funny, Ells, honest.'

'Terry Wishart's records are sealed, I take it?'

'Nup. They don't exist.'

Ellen frowned. 'Removed?'

'Sweetheart,' said her ex-husband in his heavy way, 'Terry Wishart doesn't exist. Or he does, but he was never in the Army, never in the Navy, never in the Air Force, never in the reserves.'

'But he belongs to the RSL. Scobie Sutton checked him out. There are pictures of the guy with his Army mates.'

'Pictures of him with his RSL drinking buddies *now*,' Alan said. 'Bet there are no pictures of him in uniform or with his mates in 1970.'

'So he's a fake.'

'Got it in one,' Alan said. He leaned over the table confidingly, a familiar gesture to Ellen, a signal that he was about to instruct her in something. 'He fabricated the whole thing, and he's not the only one. My mate says he's looked into a dozen cases so far this year. Genuine veterans like cooks and drivers saying they saw active service, when all they did was sit around on some base back home, and wannabes like this Wishart joker, who were never in the armed services to begin with. They march on Anzac Day, wearing medals they bought off eBay, join the RSL so they can hear and swap yarns…Makes them feel good, I guess. Fucking losers.'

'But don't they get found out?'

'Eventually. Meanwhile they glean enough detail by just standing around shooting the breeze with genuine vets. If you press them for extra detail, they say their service records are sealed or don't exist because their work was so secret.' He shook his head. 'Pathetic.'

It was pathetic. It was also a lever. 'Thanks, Al,' Ellen said, and she planted a big, surprising, appreciative and sisterly kiss on his Saturday morning stubble.

46

There is a point in a journey when the varying landscape seems unvarying and the motions and sounds of your passage lull you into a dreaming state. That happened to Challis somewhere behind Chelsea, on the Frankston Freeway. He was driving, Ellen was his passenger, and this journey up to the city they'd made many times before, separately and together. The temperatures inside and outside the car were mild, thin cloud had reduced the glare, and the traffic was sparse. He should have been concentrating furiously on the immediate concerns of his life. In no particular order, these were the need to break Adrian Wishart's alibi, help Ellen feel better about herself and decide what should happen between them. But Challis's mind strayed and drifted and he couldn't hold on to any of his serious thoughts for more than a few seconds.

Except one: that as far as he was concerned, nothing much had changed. He felt comfortable driving along with Ellen Destry beside him. He felt comfortable living with her. He felt comfortable being her lover. Did it matter that she had itchy fingers? Was he so perfect?

But her silence and demeanour suggested that she was judging herself, and he tried to hang on to that thought and work through it.

*

Ellen Destry wondered what he was thinking. He was silent and preoccupied, but then, that was his natural state. She wasn't someone who had a desperate need to fill all silences, but what was *this* silence about? She'd confessed something momentous to him last night: was he weighing it all up? Was he going to say it was over and kick her out? She half wanted him to, for that would save her from taking the first step. The silence grew and she thought her head would burst and she put her hand on his thigh.

A faint spasm transmitted itself through his clothing to her fingers. She snatched her hand away.

He said hoarsely, 'Put it back. Please.'

She did. 'Hal,' she said, and felt like crying.

'We'll work it out,' he said, and he sounded pretty definite about it.

They decided to hit the uncle hard. They barged into Wishart Electronics, Ellen badging a customer and telling him to leave, Challis shutting the street door and turning the sign from OPEN to CLOSED. 'Hey!' Terry Wishart said, from behind the counter.

And, just as abruptly, they turned good-cop, all smiles, friendliness and good humour. After announcing that this was merely a follow-up visit, double-checking some matters left over from Constable Sutton's visit earlier in the week, Challis gazed about with frank admiration. 'Nice little business you've got here. Doing well?'

'Okay,' said Wishart warily.

'I should clone you and install you at my place or in the cop shop. The equipment's always breaking down.'

Wishart laughed a little desperately.

'Hey,' said Ellen, gazing at one of Wishart's photographs, Wishart leaning nonchalantly against the tracks of an army tank, 'were you in Vietnam by any chance? So was my dad. I don't know what he did there: he'll never talk about it.'

This was the right approach, Challis realised, watching Terry Wishart closely. It would reassure the guy and enable him to maintain his lie without having to elaborate on it. He saw Wishart's soft chest swell, and heard him say authoritatively, 'Some of what we did there was hush-hush. We're not allowed to talk about it.'

'Sort of like secret missions and stuff?' said Ellen.

Wishart's face grew enigmatic. 'That's correct.'

'You must have been scared. You must have been *brave*,' Ellen said. She clasped herself as if she felt cold. 'I know *I* could never do it.'

'Well,' Terry Wishart said modestly.

Then Challis and Ellen both turned and looked at him, and waited, and beamed big smiles at him. Presently Challis said, 'It's all bullshit, isn't it, Terry?'

'Pardon?'

'You're no more an Army veteran than I am,' Ellen said.

Wishart spluttered, 'Don't know what you mean.'

'You were no closer to South-East Asia than your TV set,' Challis said.

'We checked,' said Ellen.

'You've been telling lies,' Challis said.

'All those guys at the RSL club, all those *genuine* vets...'

'What are they going to think when they find out?'

'You'll be a laughing stock.'

'You'll have to sell up and move to Outer Woop Woop.'

'After they come around here and beat the shit out of you.'

'After the *Herald-Sun* and "Today Tonight" demolish you in public.'

Wishart's gaze flicked from one to the other. He grew sweaty, greasy with it, and seemed smaller suddenly. He collapsed onto the stool behind the counter. 'Please. Leave me alone.'

'Who should we inform first, Sergeant Destry?' said Challis. 'The newspapers? His mates?'

'I think we should tell everyone,' said Ellen, but she was swallowing a little, her heart no longer in it. Who didn't have pathetic little secrets?

In his delicate way, Challis seemed to read her. He said, in a gravely courteous voice, 'Mr Wishart, you provided the police with an alibi for your nephew's movements on Wednesday, the eighteenth of November. Would you care to revise that statement?'

'All right!' screeched Wishart. Then, subsiding, he muttered it: 'All right.'

'Adrian was here, yes?'

'Yes.'

'You had lunch together?'

'Yes.'

'But he didn't stay with you for the whole afternoon, did he?'

'No.'

'Where did he go?'

'Back to check on Mill.'

'In his car?'

Terry shook his head. 'Too distinctive. He took my car.'

'What time was this?'

'He left around two-thirty.'

'Half past two on the afternoon of Wednesday the eighteenth of November?'

'Yes.'

'What car do you drive?'

'Falcon station wagon.'

And there were millions of them on the road, thought Challis. 'What time did he return?'

'Almost seven o'clock.'

'Early evening, not seven the next morning?'

'Correct.'

'Did he say why he wanted to check on his wife?'

'She was having an affair.'

'He wanted to catch her meeting her lover?'

'Yeah. He knew he'd be spotted if he drove the Citroën.'

'What was his state when he returned?'

'What do you mean?'

'Dress, manner. Was he dirty? Any blood on his clothes? Was he excited, depressed, tearful, agitated?'

'Why?'

'Well, he'd just murdered his wife.'

'No way. Uh, uh, no way,' said Wishart emphatically.

'He'd cleaned off the blood?'

'There was no blood!'

'Did he ask you to get rid of his clothing? The tyre lever? Did you provide him with a change of clothing? Have you checked to see if he replaced the tyre lever from your car?'

The questions were coming thick and fast, and Terry Wishart backed away, saying, 'He didn't kill her! He'd never do that! He followed her, that's all.'

'We have to arrest you for providing a false statement to the police, providing a false alibi for a suspect,' said Ellen gently. Mainly she didn't want Terry to warn his nephew.

'No, please.'

'It's all right,' said Challis smoothly, 'you'll be out in no time.'

'Just,' said Terry Wishart helplessly, 'just don't tell anyone about the Army stuff. Please?'

47

The murdered woman's husband was returned to the interview room and his lawyer recalled. Adrian Wishart looked tense and wary, but more contained than afraid—as if he were expecting tedium, another session explaining his side of the story to a couple of slow thinkers. Sitting upright, a long-suffering expression on his face, he demanded, 'What now?'

His lawyer, Hoyt, followed with, 'Either charge my client or let him go.'

Challis gazed levelly at each of them, turned his attention to Wishart, and said, 'We've just come from a long talk with your Uncle Terry.'

The hesitation was no longer than a millisecond, but it was there. 'So?'

'Fought in Vietnam...'

Wishart eyed him. 'So?'

'He must have seen some pretty terrible things.'

The lawyer leaned forward. 'Inspector Challis, I hope you're not about to suggest that Terry Wishart isn't a reliable or a credible alibi witness for my client, owing to his war experiences. He's telling the truth.'

'Truth,' said Ellen. She looked tired, wilting in the stifling air, but still tense and focused. 'I don't think we've heard much truth from the Wishart boys. And they *are* boys.'

The lawyer ignored her, addressed Challis. 'Terry Wishart was formally interviewed?'

'Yes.'

'*Re*-interviewed.'

'Yes.'

'And?'

'There are some anomalies,' Challis said.

A nerve twitched at the corner of Adrian's left eye. His veins stood out. He was tightly wound but otherwise inclined to be impatient and contemptuous. 'What anomalies?'

'We need to go back several years,' Challis said.

Wishart blanched, but Hoyt frowned, looking for a trap. 'Are you suggesting a family tiff? A falling out?'

'No.'

The lawyer stared intently at her client. 'Adrian, is your uncle competitive with you? Jealous? Envious?'

Ellen could see where this was going. Before Wishart could open his mouth to reply, she cut in: 'Ade,' she said, with a big, blokey smile, elbows on the table, 'remember all those photos on Terry's wall? His Army mates, excursions to the War Memorial, stuff like that?'

'What about it?'

'He served in Vietnam, didn't he?'

'Where's this going?'

'Your parents ever talk about that time, Terry going off to war?'

'No, not really.'

'No stories of waving him off, greeting him on his return?'

'No.'

'And what about Terry? Any tall tales from the trenches?'

'It was pretty hush-hush, his Army work,' Wishart said desperately. 'He can't talk about it.'

'I wonder why.'

Faint alarm showed in the lawyer's eyes, as though she sensed hidden shoals ahead. 'Getting back to the matter at hand—'

Challis ignored her. 'What your uncle can't talk about,' he said, 'is the fact that he didn't serve in Vietnam.'

Wishart's mouth was dry. 'Rubbish. He—'

'He wasn't even a soldier. He made it all up.'

'He's a sad, pathetic little man,' said Ellen. 'With emphasis on the words "sad", "pathetic" and "little".' She paused. 'A bit like you, really.'

Wishart glanced wildly at his lawyer, who'd thrown down her pen tiredly and apparently lost some of the will that had got her out of bed that morning. She examined a spot on the lapel of her blouse, ignoring him.

'Your Uncle Terry has a desperate need to be loved and admired,' said Challis, with a kind of gentleness that only a fool would underestimate, and Wishart was no fool.

'A need to belong,' Ellen said.

Still Wishart wouldn't fold. 'He has medals…'

'Oh, cut the crap, Ade. He bought them on eBay, and you know it.'

'I need time to be alone with my client,' Hoyt said.

Challis continued to watch Wishart. 'You knew the shame of being found out would kill him. You were counting on it.'

'Of course, we haven't told anyone his secret,' Ellen said.

'We're not cruel.'

'But he has agreed to stop the charade and tell the truth.'

'The thing he fears more than anything is his mates finding out.'

'He'd do anything to avoid that.'

'All right!' said Wishart, slamming his hand onto the table between them. His head slumped. 'So he lied for me. So what.'

'Emotional blackmail,' Ellen said. 'Families, eh?'

'I want time with my client,' Hoyt said.

Wishart turned to her. 'Forget it, I need to say what happened.'

Hoyt made a broad gesture with her arms as if to say it was his funeral. Wishart nodded at her, turned to Challis and Ellen and said,

'I admit I followed my wife.'

'On Wednesday afternoon?'

'Yes.'

'In whose car?'

'Terry's.'

'Because yours is too conspicuous?'

'Yes.'

'Why did you follow her?'

Wishart bowed his head. 'The tracking device had showed her regularly going to Bluff Road in Penzance Beach. Sometimes twice a day. I couldn't stand it any longer, I had to know, so on Tuesday I followed her in my car. I've never done that before, I swear.'

'And?'

Wishart said woodenly, 'And I saw Mill with that fellow from the residents' committee. I thought they were having an affair. But they spotted me, so on Wednesday I followed her in Terry's car.'

'And what did you see?'

'Nothing. I mean, nothing suspicious. All they did was look at the site where that old house was.' Wishart twisted his mouth. 'I now accept they weren't having an affair.'

'Did anyone see you? Did your wife or Mr Vernon see you?'

'No. I was careful about that.'

'And then?'

'I thought I'd attract attention if I waited too long in the vicinity, so I drove back to the city.'

'You didn't follow your wife to the murder site?'

'On my honour, no.'

'You weren't in the habit of following her but you were in the habit of tracking her movements with the GPS device?'

'Yes.'

Challis folded his arms, sat back comfortably and said, 'I put it to you that you followed your wife to the house near Shoreham and murdered her.'

'No!'

'What, then? Are you saying she was murdered by someone else?'

'Yes!'

'Who?'

'I don't know. I'd tell you if I knew.'

'What time did you leave the area?'

Wishart frowned, making a production of it. 'Between four-thirty and five, I guess.'

Challis supposed that it could be true. A good defence barrister would add some definition to the hazy outline and make it seem probable. We need hard evidence, he thought.

'Why didn't you tell us this before? Didn't you want us to find your wife's killer? You know how crucial the early stages of an investigation are.'

'I was *ashamed*,' said Wishart with a burst of feeling. He turned to Ellen, eyes damp, and seemed to shrink before her. 'You said I was pathetic. Well, it's true, I am.'

'How awful for you,' said Ellen.

48

All Pam Murphy had wanted to do that Saturday was spend it in bed with Andy Cree, but tomorrow was the end of Schoolies Week and she was expected to be around until then. So, late morning, she kissed Andy goodbye, drove to Waterloo and tackled the paperwork on Josh Brownlee for the Director of Public Prosecutions. Josh had been remanded in the lockup and would appear before a magistrate on Monday. He might not get bail, owing to the serious nature of the attack on Lachlan Roe. Or maybe his parents would fork out for a good lawyer, one who'd air the damage that Roe had caused. She almost felt sorry for Josh, but recalled that the little shit was also a rapist—probably a rapist—and for that she hoped they'd throw away the key.

The only cure for her sour mood was to think about Andy, his body and smile and the way he made her feel. She glowed, a tingling low in her abdomen.

The hours wore on. The paperwork mounted. Eventually she grew aware of sniggering in the corridor outside CIU. What the hell was going on? There were fewer people around, as usual on a Saturday, but all morning she'd sensed an unmistakeable undercurrent of cloaked conversations and sudden, red-faced silences. And now the sniggering.

She looked up, catching Smith and Jones staring at her from across the office.

John Tankard had spent the last few hours watching Pam Murphy's rented house in Penzance Beach. He saw Murph leave for work, but Andy Cree had remained, the shit.

What made it worse, he was starving. He'd also been obliged to take a slash against a ti-tree, hoping the people in the fibro holiday shack behind him weren't watching. That would be great, a patrol car comes out from Waterloo and says, 'What the fuck are you doing, Tank? We got a report of some guy waving his donger around.'

Then, at noon, Cree emerged, to stand beside his car yawning, scratching his balls, hair a sex-tossed mess. Tank got ready, hand hovering at the ignition key, but Cree went back inside again. An hour passed before Cree drove away, Tank following him through the blind dirt lanes of Penzance Beach and out across farmland to Frankston-Flinders Road, and all the way to Somerville.

Cree lived in a block of flats behind the supermarket. There was some heat in the air now, forecast top of 34 degrees today, one of those very still days, cicadas buzzing crazily, the world a little heat-stunned and waiting for a thunderstorm.

'Oi,' Tank said.

Cree had his key in the lock. He saw Tank coming up the path and grew tense, casting his gaze behind and to either side of Tank. 'To what do I owe the pleasure?'

Tank had printed out the Web photos of Lachlan Roe. 'You took these shots. You posted them on the Internet.'

Cree glanced at them, then up at Tank, searching Tank's face. 'Mate,' he said mildly, 'what are you on about?'

'You took these,' Tank said, experiencing a flicker of doubt.

'Now, why would I do that?'

'Used your mobile phone.'

'I'm going inside, John.'

'If you fuck with Pam, I'll—'

'So that's it,' said Cree, turning the key in his lock. 'Not amused, okay?'

Then he was inside, beginning to close the door. 'I don't know what your beef is, Tank. *Your* problem, not mine. As for those photos, check with the crime scene techs before you go accusing me.'

Dirk Roe was at his brother's bedside, talking and talking, willing his voice into Lachlan's ear and consciousness. 'Pictures of you all over the Web. I couldn't believe it. It's not right.'

He peered at the slack face. 'Can you hear me? It's me—Dirk.'

He lost interest and gazed at the pale walls, a kind of beige, not a colour you could name. One of the nurses came in and he watched her covertly, tight uniform, the seams of her underwear showing through. Dirk began to hum madly before he caught himself. He swallowed. More than anything he was trying to stave off utter ruination, for he had nothing left. Sacked and bereaved and no one left in his life to love him. 'Irreparable brain damage,' the doctor had said. But the doctor was a foreigner, what did he know?

'I can talk to my brother, right?' Dirk had demanded. 'He'll be able to hear me? It'll bring him back?'

'No,' the doctor said. 'I'm sorry.'

Dirk leaned over Lachlan and said, 'Someone's got to pay.'

49

After delivering his daughter to a church hall behind the shops in Somerville, where her ballet, jazz and tap teachers had set up stow-away tables groaning with cupcakes, doughnuts and lime cordial for the end-of-term party, Scobie Sutton did the shopping, determined not to be rushed just because Challis and Destry wanted it that way. And so it was lunchtime before he arrived at work that Saturday.

He began by examining tapes and speed camera photographs from four locations: Planning East's carpark, the traffic lights in Tyabb, the Caltex service station in Waterloo and a stretch of Frankston-Flinders Road between Penzance Beach and Flinders. Mapping Ludmilla Wishart's movements had so far involved a mixture of guesswork, her desk diary entries and tiny amounts of actual evidence. If only Wishart had planted his tracking device on his wife on Wednesday: all Scobie had to go on so far was a single credit card transaction—at 3.42 on Wednesday afternoon, Ludmilla Wishart had purchased 47 litres of unleaded petrol from the Caltex service station. The timing and location indicated that she'd been on her way to meet Carl Vernon in Penzance Beach; according to Vernon, she'd been on time.

Backtracking through her diary, Scobie guessed that she'd been coming from Tyabb, where she'd investigated an unauthorised bed-and-breakfast development. She'd stopped for petrol, made her way to see Carl Vernon, where she stayed for about thirty minutes, then driven to the big house on the headland near Shoreham, where she'd been murdered.

With a ham and gherkin sandwich under his belt, washed down by dense black tea, Scobie began fast-forwarding through the videotapes from the Caltex service station. The quality was poor and the camera had been badly angled. It was also possible that the time and date notations were inaccurate, so he started running the tape at the normal speed well before 3.42, the time at which Wishart's credit card had registered the petrol purchase.

He spotted Ludmilla at 3.37, her silver Golf edging cautiously into the top segment of the screen and stopping at pump 5, the pump obscuring the woman and her car a little. He saw her head emerge, saw her arm take down the nozzle and disappear with it. Then the arm reappeared and he saw her pass through another quadrant of the screen, presumably to pay for the petrol. She re-emerged, got into the Golf, drove away.

But given that the camera had been poorly installed or knocked out of alignment at some point, only the two pumps closest to the road were visible. They formed the foreground of the image. The greater part of the screen was focused on the stretch of main road in and out of Waterloo, showing clearly the access ramp into the service station, a bus stop and an Australia Post box.

And a late 1980s Mercedes. Twenty seconds after Ludmilla Wishart's Golf appeared at the pumps via the access ramp, a Mercedes sedan had pulled to the side of the road and idled there, a faint puff of exhaust smoke showing. Twenty seconds after Wishart drove out again, it followed.

Scobie put his head in his hands and closed his eyes, thinking hard. He'd seen that car before. He wasn't a petrol head or a car nut, and an older-style Mercedes isn't a car you'd normally remember, but his brother-in-law had offered to sell him one earlier in the year. He was trading up to a new car but had been offered only $1,000 as a trade-in price when the car was worth at least $7,000. 'Diesel,' he told Scobie, 'low mileage, full service history.' Scobie had been mildly tempted, but he didn't have $7,000 to spare and Beth had insisted that if they were going to buy another car, it needed to have airbags. In the end, Scobie's brother-in-law had sold the Mercedes for $5,000 on eBay, and Scobie had been kicking himself ever since.

So who owned this one and where had he seen one like it recently? If he hadn't been so miserable in the head about his wife, he'd have been paying more attention to the life around him.

Then he remembered: the break-in at the planning office. The Mercedes had been parked at the rear. The only staff member in attendance at the time was the chief planner, Groot.

He replayed the tape. The Mercedes outside the service station was in profile, so he couldn't get the plate number. The windows were heavily tinted. No side window stickers, no fox tails hanging from the radio antenna. But there was a towbar, and one hubcap was missing.

He ejected the tape and walked through to the incident room and the photo arrays on the whiteboard: Ludmilla Wishart, Adrian Wishart, Ludmilla's car, the broader crime scene, the clump of mud that had formed and dried inside a wheel arch before falling out near the crime scene.

He went to one of the plastic tubs on the long table, knowing there'd be more photos of the mud. He found them, together with a preliminary report from the laboratory. Wading through terms like 'locus', 'diatoms', 'vegetable matter' and 'moisture gradient' he understood that the mud had originated near a marsh or a wetland.

And probably from a local marsh or wetland, Scobie thought, telling himself that mud collected inside a wheel arch from further afield would have shaken loose long before the driver reached the Peninsula—or more specifically, the murder scene. He bundled the photos together and called Challis.

Challis listened, said, 'I'm at the hospital. Coming back now.'

While he waited, Scobie phoned his house, a kind of trepidation settling in him. He half wanted Beth not to be home. It would confirm one of his greatest fears, that she'd run off with the Ascensionists. He could see his wife in some remote compound, wearing a drab and shapeless cotton dress, her hair to her shoulders and tied in a scarf, chanting ecstatically and doing a cold man's bidding.

But she answered in the dull tones that had become her habit and to his questions and nervy patter she gave monosyllabic replies that were, if anything, worse than all of his imaginings.

50

The call from Scobie Sutton came as a relief. Challis, in the canteen, said, 'I'll be right up,' and pocketed his phone.

The canteen was a depressing place on Saturdays and Sundays, understaffed, the food stale. He looked despairingly at yesterday's congealed lasagne and Irish stew and settled for a ham-and-salad roll, biting into it as he trudged up to CIU. The bread was crusty on the outside, almost wet on the inside.

He found Sutton in his office, the detective standing four-square before the desk when another officer would have taken a seat to wait. 'Sit,' Challis said.

Instead of doing that, Sutton laid out a number of photographs. 'I think I know who our killer is.'

Intrigued, Challis stood beside him, looking down at the array. Close-ups of the mud deposit, taken from various angles; a Golf at the pumps of a service station; a detail of the same scene, only enlarged to reveal an older-style Mercedes sedan parked on the road outside the service station.

'This car,' Sutton said, poking the Golf, 'is Ludmilla Wishart's. *This* car'—the Mercedes—'pulled in a few seconds later.'

'Following her?'

'I think so. It pulled out again soon after she did.'

'There are plenty of these old Mercs around, Scobie, and we can't see the plates.'

'True, but I know who owns a car exactly like this one.'

Sutton was spinning it out. Challis guessed that he was trying to regain lost ground in some way. 'Good work.'

Sutton flushed. 'Thanks.'

'So, whose car is it?'

'Mrs Wishart's boss, Groot.'

'How sure are you?'

'I've just been around to Groot's house. His Mercedes was parked out in the street. I took these pictures.'

Sutton was holding a digital camera. The little LCD screen glowed and then he was scrolling through a dozen images. It was as if he'd set out to create abstract representations of the mechanical era: Challis saw axles, springs, shock absorbers, brake lines, panels and under-body insulation, taken at unnatural angles and harshly lit.

'See the mud traces clinging here, and here? I scraped off a small sample.'

'Excellent,' Challis said.

'I sent it to the lab.'

Challis picked up one of the photographs. 'This is enough to bring him in for questioning.'

'I agree.'

'But Groot can argue that his job entailed travelling from site to site. If the mud at the murder scene came from his car, it's not proof of *when* he was there, and a long way from proving he murdered Ludmilla Wishart.'

'I checked the phone records of everyone in the planning office,' Sutton said. 'There were calls to the Ebelings from his office phone the day before the house at Penzance Beach was demolished.'

'But did Groot also call the Ebelings at other times?'

'Well, yeah,' Sutton admitted.

'And did our victim also call the Ebelings?'

'Yes,' Sutton conceded.

'Any calls to the Ebelings from anyone in the planning office can be explained away as work related, not a tip-off,' said Challis. 'The Ebelings applied for, and were granted, a demolition permit. They also applied for planning permission to build a new house. You'd expect calls back and forth over a long period.'

'But why was Groot following Ludmilla?'

'*That*,' said Challis, 'won't be so easy for the guy to explain away. You collect his financial records. I'll bring him in for questioning.'

They both questioned Groot. Before the planner could muster outrage, Challis came in hard and fast.

'Here's you, in your car, following Ludmilla Wishart on the afternoon she was murdered. We have photographs from other CCTV cameras backing it up, and they're being enhanced to show the numberplate and your face in more detail.'

A lie, but feasible. Groot crumpled a little. He'd been gardening and wore a long-sleeved khaki shirt, jeans and a heat flush that might have been from the sun or exertion but was probably his unravelling nerves. 'I wasn't...I mean...'

'You followed Mrs Wishart to the house above the beach between Shoreham and Flinders, and you killed her.'

'No! I was out checking on planning applications and I happened to spot her on the road! That's all, I swear.'

'You followed her. Stalked her. Was it obsession? You wanted to have sex with her but she wouldn't be in it?'

'No! I'm happily married.'

'Your wife didn't look too pleased just now.'

'Leave her out of this.'

Challis said thoughtfully, 'Of course, a more sinister explanation suggests itself. You tipped off the Ebelings that the old house they'd purchased in Penzance Beach was about to come under a heritage protection order, so they'd better move fast if they wanted to demolish. Ludmilla found out about it and threatened to ruin you. Or was it blackmail?'

'I don't know what you're talking about.'

'How much did the Ebelings pay you?'

'I have a passionate commitment to protecting the Peninsula's heritage,' spluttered Groot. 'Flora, fauna, heritage buildings...'

There was a pause while he wiped his forehead and temples and under his soft jaw. 'I'm a conservative planner.'

'We have your financial records going back five years,' Challis said. He didn't elaborate.

Groot looked lost and bewildered.

Challis poked the photographs again. 'You followed her.'

'I didn't! I mean, I did, but only because I'd spotted her on the road by chance and was wondering what she was doing in that neck of the woods. We at Planning East are aware of accusations that we take bribes. Where there's smoke, there's fire. Ludmilla's job placed her in a very sensitive position.'

Challis was disgusted and let it show. 'Blame the victim, right?'

Groot shifted his bulk. His shirt collar had darkened as his body, his guilt and the rising heat of the interview room betrayed him. 'It's my responsibility as department head to—'

'You followed her, you murdered her to protect yourself from being outed as corrupt.'

'No! I saw her turn off the main road and realised she was going in to check on that house where all the trees had been cut down. It was a legitimate detour for her, so I just kept going. Went back to the office.'

Challis switched tack again. 'You've had some work done on your house.'

Groot flushed. 'So?'

'A developer like Hugh Ebeling would have plenty of tradespeople in his pocket. His bribe payments don't go directly into your account but into theirs: that's how he pays you.'

'Certainly not.'

Challis displayed more photographs. 'These clumps of mud were found at the murder scene. They're unique. First, they can be matched to a marshy area on the Peninsula. Second, they can be matched to the wheel arch of a Mercedes 190 E—*your* car, in fact.'

Groot looked aghast. His mouth was as dry as his big, fleshy trunk was soaked through. 'There are plenty of these old cars around.'

'But not plenty that still have traces of mud clinging to them, traces that can be shown by chemical analysis, computer enhancement and 3D digitalisation to match exactly the clumps that had once adhered to the passenger side rear wheel arch and later fallen off at the murder scene, traces that can be shown to come from a marshy area that you'd visited as part of your duties.' More bullshit, but it sounded good.

'I think I need a lawyer.'

'I think you do,' Challis said.

Scobie Sutton hadn't said a word but was as happy as a habitually gloomy man can be, Challis thought, glancing at the man beside him.

The lawyer arrived an hour later, a property lawyer from Mornington, a slender, quick-moving man with a clipped manner and a sharp, off-centre nose. He conferred with Groot, and emerged after five minutes saying, 'My client wishes to make a statement.'

By now Ellen had joined them and the interview room was stifling, so Challis moved the interrogation to a conference room that had taping facilities. When the equipment was ready, he announced their names and the place and date and said, 'Please go ahead, Mr Groot.'

'It's true that I followed Mrs Wishart last Wednesday,' Groot said, and stopped.

Challis said, 'For the record, this was on the afternoon of Wednesday the eighteenth of November?'

'Yes.' Another pause.

'Please make your statement, Mr Groot,' Ellen said.

'I followed Ludmilla because I wanted to talk to her, alone, out of the office.'

Pause. Challis, Ellen and Sutton merely stared at Groot this time.

Groot swallowed. 'I believed that Mrs Wishart possessed potentially damaging information about me and I wanted to clear the matter up with her. I have a wife and two kids and a huge mortgage to worry about. If she made this information public, I faced losing my job, being fined, maybe even going to jail. Plus people adversely affected by the planning decisions made by my department would begin suing us for millions of dollars. I couldn't allow that to happen.'

Challis noted the word 'allow'. He watched and waited.

'I followed her to where her body was later found but I *swear* I didn't kill her. She was alive when I left her.'

He was begging to be understood, begging to be believed. Challis waited.

'I asked her not to ruin my career. I said we could work something out. Sure, the Ebelings had demolished that old house, but maybe I could swing it so the shire blocked their new one. She didn't say anything. I don't know what was going through her head. I got really upset and yelled at her but I didn't kill her. She was alive when I left. I swear it.'

The planner folded his short arms; the arms seemed to pop out again. Challis said, 'The break-in at the office. You staged that?'

'Yes.'

'You were looking for any evidence that Mrs Wishart might have against you?'

'Yes.'

'Did you find it?'

'She'd followed me! She had photos of my car parked at the Ebelings' house in Brighton!'

He sounded outraged. Challis said coldly, 'Just for the record, the wetlands mud inside your wheel arch came from French's Reserve?'

'Yes.'

Challis was relieved to have established that. 'Your conversation with Mrs Wishart got heated?'

'She wouldn't even look at me!'

Ellen leaned forward. 'What did you hit her with? A tyre iron, was it?'

'I didn't hit her.'

The lawyer had been scribbling notes and listening without interruption. Glancing mildly at Challis, Ellen and Sutton, he said, 'You have your statement, people. There is no admission of murder.'

Challis ignored him. 'Athol Groot, I'm placing you under arrest on suspicion of the murder of Ludmilla Wishart on...' he began, going on to recite the familiar formula, thinking that all the guy'd had to do was maintain his story that it wasn't unusual for him to be driving around the Peninsula, and claim that he'd visited the Shoreham site on a separate, earlier occasion. But he hadn't and now he was sunk.

51

Pam Murphy was collecting a file from her car when they released Adrian Wishart. She wasn't supposed to park in the little slip road adjacent to the police station—it annoyed the local residents and visitors to the station—but everyone grabbed a spot there if one was available, especially on weekends, and so she had a clear view of the main entrance as Wishart stepped out with his lawyer. He looked pleased, if bewildered, and shook his lawyer's hand effusively, pausing, shaking again, holding on, not wanting to let go.

She'd known something was going on in CIU, but after lunch had moved downstairs to a small office behind the lockup. It was her way of avoiding the sniggering and getting her work done. She was snowed under today and didn't want Challis or Destry grabbing her for some trivial and time-consuming CIU matter. She'd yet to complete the paperwork on Josh Brownlee, and had been asked to write an informal 'from-the-point-of-view-of-a-cop-on-the-beat' contribution to the Schoolies Week reports that Sergeant Destry was compiling for Superintendent McQuarrie and the town council. The schoolies report promised to be a major pain in the bum. Pam didn't quite trust her own impressions and decided to spend the afternoon reading the daily logs kept by the uniformed officers and drawing up a questionnaire she'd later distribute to the town's shopkeepers, hoteliers and landlords.

Using an electrician's van and a gum tree to screen her from the windows along the front of the station, she slipped across the road, heading for the side door. A voice said, 'Excuse me? Pam? Excuse me.'

She turned in agitation. A teenage girl, a schoolie by the look of her: miniskirt, a short, tight T-shirt, sandals, a bouncy blonde ponytail, a pretty, untroubled face, confirming Pam's opinion that a kind of natural selection was operating. If you were granted a private school education and a week beside the sea after your exams, you were also granted healthy blonde good looks. If you were poor, went to the local high school and dropped out before Year 12, you looked like crap.

And sometimes the blondes knew they were born to rule, but not always. This girl was one of the nice ones. 'Bronte-Mae,' said Pam with a smile.

It had been last Monday night, Bronte-Mae somehow misplacing her wallet, keys, friends, sobriety and dignity. Pam had saved her. Saving distressed kids was as much helping them see that their circumstances weren't hopeless as it was lending them twenty bucks and putting them to bed.

And now here was Bronte-Mae again, bubbling over, saying, 'I found this on the beach.'

A small woven bag, the kind they had in Oxfam catalogues. 'I'm in the middle of something right now,' Pam said. 'Can you take it to the front desk?'

'Oh,' said Bronte-Mae, her face falling. 'Okay.'

She was glowing but full of teenage hesitations and helplessness. Finally she said, 'It's just that I think it's that lady's, the one who got murdered.'

For a moment then, Pam grew very still. Then she motioned with her hand.

Greatly relieved, sparkling with it, Bronte-Mae released the bag. 'I found it last night, near Shoreham. I forgot about it till this morning'—she blushed—'when I woke up.' She looked stricken suddenly. 'Was it okay to search it? I only wanted to know whose it was. I didn't take anything.'

Pam worked her fingers over the surface of the little cloth bag, feeling something small, hard and rectangular within. If you were the kind of woman who bought Third World craft items, you'd keep your mobile phone, glasses or tampons in a bag like this. She couldn't see a name anywhere. 'What makes you think the bag is Mrs Wishart's?'

'There's a little birthday card inside.'

Pam eased open the drawstring top. An iRiver MP3 player, with earphones, a USB cable, an instruction booklet and a tiny card. Reluctant to touch anything, she said warmly, 'This is fantastic.'

'Really?' beamed Bronte-Mae.

'Really,' said Pam. She lowered her voice confidingly. 'This is off the record, but we've been looking for this. I have your contact details from last Monday. We may need a statement from you later.'

Glowing, Bronte-Mae began to retreat. 'Okay, cool. Well, see ya! Thanks for everything! I've had the best week of my life!'

A sexual glow, thought Pam. I can relate to that.

She waved to Bronte-Mae, then hurried in through the front door of the station. There was no straightforward route to CIU from there. First she was obliged to use the security keypad beside the reception desk, and then enter the warren of corridors behind it, passing open office doors, the sergeants' mess and half-a-dozen guys crowding around the noticeboards, before finally climbing the narrow stairs, swerving to avoid a couple of officers clattering down them. And, all the while, there was that continued sense of whispers and subterranean nastiness in the atmosphere of the building. Twice she out-stared a couple of guys who were gaping at her. 'What?' she demanded. 'Nothing,' they muttered, hot in the face.

She poked her head around the door of the incident room. Ellen Destry was there, gathering files together. 'Sarge, I—'

'Sorry, Pam, can it wait? We've just charged the chief planner with the Wishart murder and I—'

'Ludmilla Wishart's MP3 player, Sarge. Just been handed in.'

The CIU sergeant went tense. 'You sure?'

'Yes.'

'Where and when?'

Pam told her. The sergeant pulled out her mobile phone and dialled. 'Hal? We've got Ludmilla's MP3 player...Murph...the lab for prints...'

Pam began to edge away, knowing Ellen would find a dozen tasks for her to do. She needed to write those reports first. She reached the corridor, the head of the stairs, the bottom of the stairs, feigning deafness when Destry called, 'Pam?'

Her bolthole behind the lockup consisted of filing cabinets, shelves of reports, manuals and handbooks, and two computers. A constable from Community Liaison had been pecking away at one of the computers, but he'd been called away to an emergency, and so the room was hers for now. She settled herself at the other computer and began to write her initial impressions of Schoolies Week. Thirty minutes later, she completed the first draft, saved it to her memory stick, pressed 'print'.

Nothing happened. A message came up to say that the computer was not connected to a network printer. Frustrated, she removed her memory stick, slotted it into the second computer and called up her document. Again she pressed 'print'. The command went through.

Her gaze wandered to the bottom of the screen. Apparently the guy from Community Liaison still had a window open. Tucked away among the icons were a short banner and an abbreviated Web address. In an idle mood, she clicked on it.

And saw herself spread naked and pale on top of her bed.

Or rather, she didn't know who it was until her eyes strayed from the groin and breasts to the face. The Web address was *www.inandoutofuniform.com*. Sure enough, there she was *in* uniform, too, a copy of that academy graduation shot she kept in the pewter frame on her dressing table.

Then her mobile phone rang and it was Inspector Challis, saying she was needed to help review the evidence against the planner, Groot.

52

By now it was mid-afternoon, the station quieter, the CIU briefing room very quiet. Smith and Jones had gone home to mow their lawns or whatever it was the two men did on their weekends. Ellen Destry and Scobie Sutton were itemising and logging into evidence the contents of Ludmilla Wishart's little woven bag before it was all sent to the lab. Challis was drumming his fingers, waiting for Pam Murphy to arrive.

She drifted in finally, looking stiff and tight to Challis's eyes, as if holding powerful emotions in check. He raised his eyebrows at her. She shook her head and took her seat.

He started the briefing. 'As you know, we've arrested the head planner, Groot. The thing is, both he and the husband had motive, both were in the vicinity, both acted strangely. So let's compare them. Ellen?'

She stirred. 'The husband had a history of following his wife around. On Wednesday afternoon he was acting true to form—mad and obsessive though it might seem to us. And he knew how weird it would seem to an outsider, so he covered it up. It was a "normal" day, so to speak. When we pinpoint what *wasn't* normal about that day, we find Groot.'

Challis nodded. He turned to Pam Murphy, who was chewing the inside of her cheek, staring fixedly at the surface of the table, barely in the room. Was she thinking he'd made a terrible mistake in arresting Groot? 'Pam? You don't think Groot did it?'

She blinked. 'What? I mean, sorry, I was trying to see it from his point of view.'

It was a quick recovery—and a lie. Her mind had been miles away. He couldn't waste time on her. Crossing to the whiteboard, he scrawled Groot's name at the top. 'What do we know about this guy?'

'He was at the scene,' Ellen said. 'He lied about it, but later admitted it.'

'There's also physical evidence showing he was there,' Sutton said. 'CCTV footage of him following her the day she was murdered.'

'I'm thinking what he might argue in court,' Challis said, grabbing the back of a chair in his habitual way. 'He was railroaded by us. He was confused. He got his times and dates wrong. Yes, he was at the site of the murder—but at another time and for work-related reasons. He didn't confront Ludmilla Wishart about anything. The police bullied him and he was confused.'

'He was taking bribes,' Sutton said. 'Ludmilla Wishart found out and was going to expose him. He had motive.'

'Do we have proof that he was taking bribes? The Ebelings will deny paying him. He can claim it was a beat-up, that Ludmilla was mistaken, or acting maliciously. As for the money, he won it on the horses.'

'So we make sure he can't argue these things in court,' Ellen said. 'We dig deeper into his past: financial records, friends, family and acquaintances, his work history, phone records, witnesses who can place him with the Ebelings or with other people who might have benefited from council tip-offs over the past few years.'

'A huge job,' muttered Sutton.

They sat in thoughtful gloom for a while. 'Is this guy clever?' Challis asked. 'He makes a partial admission, a plausible admission, one that reflects badly on him, thinking we'll see it as the truth, that he couldn't be guilty of the greater crime?'

'Much like the husband,' Ellen pointed out.

'Or they're both telling the truth,' Sutton said.

'But what do we think?'

'Groot did it,' Ellen said. 'We know he's a bit of a bully, and finally he went that one step further.'

'I agree,' Sutton said.

Pam Murphy was miles away again.

Then there was a snap like a muted pistol shot and Murphy was looking in dismay at the two halves of her pencil. She swallowed, went red, said 'Sorry,' and slammed out of the room. Challis cocked an eyebrow at Ellen, who shrugged.

'We need hard evidence that Groot was taking bribes and that Ludmilla knew about it,' Challis continued. 'Otherwise Groot's barrister will attack the victim in court: Ludmilla Wishart was given to making crazy claims about her workmates, she was the one taking bribes to finance her lazy husband's lifestyle, she had a secret lover, and so on. Or he'll claim she was mugged—and how do we know that *didn't* happen?'

He walked around the long table to peer down at the murdered woman's MP3 player and woven bag. 'But would a mugger toss this away?'

'Unlikely,' Sutton said, unfolding his long legs in a rearrangement of bony angles.

'I'm trying to see it through Groot's eyes,' Challis said. 'He kills her, then, to make it look like a mugging gone wrong, he pockets her cash and her phone and dumps the rest of her stuff down on the beach. But why not take her MP3 player as well? Wouldn't that reinforce the notion that she was mugged?'

Ellen shrugged. 'He was in a hurry. He took the obvious things. He didn't bother to open that little bag, probably thought it had her sunglasses in it.'

'Feasible,' said Challis doubtfully.

He pulled latex gloves from his pocket, said 'Glove up, Ells,' and held the MP3 player before his nose. 'How do you work one of these?'

'You obviously don't have a teenage daughter,' Ellen said, with a snap of her glove.

They sat side by side; Challis felt a jolt of desire when their shoulders touched. She was subtly scented: not only her shampoo and soap but also an underlay of skin and hair. But she was all business, murmuring, 'Let's see,' headphones plugged into her ears. He felt a twinge of disappointment; then, marvellously, she leaned against him, and he thought: *To hell with what Sutton thinks.*

They watched the glow of the little screen, the menus flickering from category to sub-category, category to sub-category, as Ellen worked her way through the contents. Suddenly she froze and removed the headphones: 'She used it to record notes to herself.'

'What kind of notes?'

'Listen,' she said, plugging him in.

53

Testing, testing, one two three, the quick brown fox did a pee by the apple tree, etcetera, etcetera...

Then a faint click, Ellen guessing that Ludmilla Wishart had replayed the test run. The MP3 player was new, a birthday gift, so she'd have been playing with it, trying out the various functions.

The time is now...2.45 and I'm at lot number five, Harcourt Drive, in Tyabb, where the owners have laid the foundations for an unauthorised bed-and-breakfast establishment.

That had been listed on her desk diary. They heard Wishart announce her intentions and then there was a faint, atmospheric hiss, an interruption, before the voice returned, announcing the results of the meeting. Amicable results, apparently.

A pleasant voice, Ellen thought. Calm, unhurried, educated and a little self-conscious but pleased with her new toy.

The time is now 3.20 and my next destination is Bluff Road in Penzance Beach. I will need to buy petrol along the way.

Pause, and then her voice came back wryly: *Not that this little gizmo needs to know that.*

Ellen pictured Ludmilla Wishart's journey from the Tyabb address to the site of the demolished house in Penzance Beach, with a stop for petrol along the way, Groot tailing her in his old Mercedes, Adrian tailing her in his uncle's station wagon. Why hadn't the two men spotted each other? And it all would have consumed forty minutes in real time, if Ludmilla had wanted to leave her gizmo recording while she narrated the conditions and events of her journey:

Taking this bend at eighty kilometres an hour…passing a school bus… just hit a bump…have finished putting 47 litres of unleaded petrol into the tank of my car…

But of course Ludmilla Wishart said none of these things but quickly stopped mucking around with her new toy and recorded only those observations that she would need later when writing up her notes.

There was a pause, a soft electronic interruption, and she returned:

Bluff Road, Penzance Beach. It is now 4.25 in the afternoon. Met with Carl Vernon as arranged. Discussed the demolition of the house known as Somerland. Local residents very upset, as noted this morning. I advised that I'd applied to the planning minister for an interim heritage amendment that would protect Somerland, but, unfortunately, Hugh and Mia Ebeling had exercised their right to demolish before it could be considered or granted. What I didn't tell Mr Vernon was that my boss had almost certainly tipped off the Ebelings, and that I shall report him to the authorities.

And Groot had known that, Ellen thought. He followed her, intending to talk her out of it, and killed her when that failed.

In the meantime I advised Mr Vernon that the residents' association should take steps to block the Ebelings' intended development of the site or at least press for a drastic modification of the excesses of the planned building, which at present is a structure on three levels. My advice was that the association should attend any and all Development Assessments Committee meetings and present transparencies that show what impact the proposed structure would have on their views not only across the water but also in other directions. Pause. *Leaving Penzance at 4.35 to drive to Shoreham.*

Another pause, and when Wishart's voice started again it was electric with suppressed emotions:

I need to get this down immediately, in case anything happens. I'm outside the property known as Westering, at 450 Frankston-Flinders Road, which is accessed from Frankston-Flinders Road via a very long driveway down to a headland overlooking the beach. The owner, Jamie Furneaux, who is presently overseas, was charged and fined for removing 52 pine and other trees, and ordered to plant indigenous trees to compensate. I can confirm that Mr Furneaux has abided by the conditions of the ruling made against him. But Mr Groot, the chief planner, arrived soon after I did. He actually followed me! I am annoyed. I am also, I must admit, a little afraid. I've seen Groot angry and emotional before, but not like this. He kept going on and on about how I would ruin his career, he had a wife and children to support, he could go to jail, and anyway, what did he do wrong, all he did was keep the Ebelings apprised of the progress of their applications to demolish an old house and erect a new one. I said, how much did they pay you? He got angry and said they hadn't paid him anything, but I didn't believe him. Then he got a bit physical with me, grabbing my arms and shoving me against the car. God, he's repulsive. He scares me, too. He went away in tears but that doesn't mean he won't try to hurt me in some way. Physically? Professionally? I wish I knew what was going through his head. Anyway, this record is in case something bad happens to me.

There was a sense of time passing, even though only a second had elapsed on the recording, and Ludmilla's voice returned, sounding altered in unnameable ways but suggesting puzzlement and faint annoyance:

Ade? What are you doing here?

Ellen heard a man's voice, a low undertone, none of the words distinguishable, and Ludmilla Wishart's response:

You were parked behind that shed the whole time? Whose car is that?

More deep growling, then Ludmilla again, admonition and tension in her voice:

Ade, you mustn't follow me like this—I was so embarrassed when you showed up yesterday, I don't know what Mr Vernon thought... Of course he's not... I'm not seeing anyone on the sly... Who? That was my boss, Mr Groot... No, Ade, I'm telling you... He didn't hug me, he was a bit cross about a work matter and grabbed my arms for emphasis, that's all... No, Ade... I do not... I do love you... There's no one else... No... Of course I don't want to leave you... But she's my friend, I can't stop seeing her... I've never slept with anyone but you... I think he's disgusting...

Adrian Wishart's voice came clearly now, asking her about the MP3 player. Ludmilla made no mention that she was taping:

Just listening to music... Carmen gave it to me at lunchtime... No, she loaded some songs on it for me... Honest, I didn't spend any of our money on this, it was a gift...

Ellen Destry and Hal Challis hunched over the little device, frozen, listening to the fear, the pleading and the barely controlled hysteria in Ludmilla Wishart's voice. Adrian Wishart sounded angry, almost shrieking at his wife as he first accused her and then dragged her out of the car and beat her with the meaty sounds of death blows, all the time talking and shouting. There were other sounds then, muffled ones as he cleaned up, and finally his voice, sobbing the words:

See what you made me do? Don't you know I love you?

54

Pam Murphy tried to keep a cool head. First she made a mental list of the options open to her. She could report Andrew Cree to the new senior sergeant in charge of the station's uniformed officers. Or to Ellen Destry. Or to Ethical Standards, at Force Command headquarters. Cree would be formally investigated, possibly charged with several offences and probably kicked off the force.

But his nastiness would emerge again, wherever he was, whatever he did for a living, and other women—maybe women with fewer resources than she had—would suffer.

Also, Cree had been a very busy networker since arriving at Waterloo. If he didn't exactly have close friends among the uniforms, the probationers and the clerical staff, he did have cronies. He had influence. In a culture that valued the simple bonds between men—beer, football, hatred of women—he had influence. This was Australia, after all. These things mattered and always had.

So if she took formal action against him she'd be the one to suffer most. Bullets delivered to her mailbox, dog shit in her locker, car tyres slashed open. A whispering campaign: she was a lesbian, or frigid, or sleeping her way to the top.

And she couldn't count on the young female cops to help her, either. Some of them were blokier than the blokes. Better, more vicious haters.

Should she tackle Cree head on? That was her instinctive inclination. He was not such a big guy, or particularly fit or brave. She could beat the shit out of him so that he and his mates got the message loud and clear.

But would he? Would they?

And what if she lost, or won but they all scoffed at her anyway, called her a sore loser, couldn't take a joke? And what if he lodged an official complaint that saw her charged with assault? She could be busted back to uniform or even drummed out of the force.

What could a female member of Victoria Police do? Not much. To Pam Murphy's knowledge, women who complained were ostracised and bullied until they quit the job they loved and had been expensively trained to do. Or they quit meekly and carried their stress-related illnesses for years.

Even though she was supposed to be on duty, and tonight was the last night of Schoolies Week, Pam Murphy drove home to Penzance Beach, thinking, thinking, and seeing Cree's declarations of love for what they really were. At home she walked from room to room, still thinking, renewing contact with the gritty core of selfhood that had always been there, deep inside her. She stared at the crumpled bedclothes. Her little shack was blighted now. She could almost smell Cree in the air. She bundled together the bedding and the towel he'd used—it was lying on the bathroom floor—into the washing machine and turned it on, extra detergent. She took up the Police Academy graduation photograph and wiped away his greasy paws.

Then she called him, as light and innocent as a girl in love.

Then she called Caz Moon.

There was nothing for Scobie Sutton to do now. Challis told him to go home, the paperwork could wait, Adrian Wishart wasn't going anywhere. 'See you Monday, Scobie. Spend some time with your wife and daughter.'

So Scobie went home and there was Ros, giddy after her party, dancing around the house, an antidote right then to all of his gloomy thoughts. 'Where's Mum?'

'Lying down.'

Scobie thought about the long walk down the hallway to the bedroom, but there was a knock on the door. The crackpot pastor stood there, proffering his hand, which Scobie shook, even though he knew it was a mistake. 'I'm afraid Beth's indisposed,' he said, to gain control and shut the visitor down. To reinforce it he backed up a step and made to shut the door.

The guy actually shoved his foot in it.

Scobie looked past Jeffreys to a station wagon parked at the kerb, two kids inside. To show he's a family man, Scobie thought. The sour feelings, the sharpened perceptions, the ability to see how things truly are, were new to Scobie, and coming in fast. 'No,' he said.

But suddenly Jeffreys was looking past Scobie's shoulder, his damp face wreathed in smiles. 'Beth, how lovely.'

Scobie did a little dance of frustration, one hand blocking ineffectually as Beth ducked around him and stood before the pastor. He tried to jostle her aside, saying, 'She doesn't want to see you. Tell him you don't want to see him, love, please. She's finished with you crackpots.'

'I think we should let her decide that, don't you?' Jeffreys said, reverting to his hard-nosed mercantile voice.

Before any of them could move, Ros was inserting herself in the doorway, her little body toned by netball and the recently acquired knowledge that her mother needed more help than her father could provide. 'Go away,' she said sternly. 'Mum, come inside this instant.'

Jeffreys stepped back, astonished, then revealed a flash of something nasty before he put his hands up placatingly. Scobie beamed at him, feeling small and huge at once.

*

Meanwhile John Tankard's shift had finished at 4 p.m. but he'd stayed behind for a quick aerobics workout in the station's little gym which left him fatly hot, pink and sweating even after a shower. Then he prowled the corridors, canteen, carpark and storerooms, looking for Cree. He'd seen those pictures of Pam; he intended to make the prick remove every image he'd ever posted on the Web.

Pam's shining admiration, not disregard, would be his reward.

She wasn't inside the station. Nor was Cree.

He looked out into the yard, finding one of the probationers who'd been watching porn in the basement on Wednesday.

'Seen Andy Cree?'

The probationer, washing and waxing one of the patrol cars, straightened his back and looked blank, mouth open. Finally he woke up, wrung soapy water out of his chamois and said with a frown, '*Andy* Cree?'

Christ Almighty, thought Tank. 'No, Aloysius Cree. *Yes*, Andy Cree. Have you seen him? Did he leave the station? If so, did he say where he was going?'

'Where he was going?'

Tank closed and opened his eyes. 'Yes.'

'He didn't say.'

With barely controlled fury, Tank turned to go.

'But he reckoned he was on to a good thing,' the probationer said.

Tank turned back. 'What do you mean?'

'Said he was going to dip his wick.'

'But he's on duty,' said Tank foolishly.

'You know Andy,' laughed the probationer.

'Yeah, I know him,' said Tank. Then he had a thought: 'That DVD you were watching the other day.'

The guy blushed. 'What about it?'

'Cree set that up?'

The probationer looked hunted. Finally he nodded.

Tank pointed at the driver's door. 'Missed a spot.'

His own car was baking in the sun. He cranked up the air-con and drove out of the carpark, flipping open his mobile phone. 'Murph?'

'What?'

'Look, I need to talk to you. It's a bit delicate.'

'If it's Cree's Internet bullshit, I already know about it.'

'Oh.'

'Anything else?'

Tank shook himself into good order. 'Let me deal with it. I'll get the bastard to take the site down.'

She said in a hands-off voice, 'Butt out, Tank.'

Tank couldn't believe it. 'A bit of gratitude wouldn't go astray.'

'Yeah, thanks,' she said and hung up.

55

At the close of that long day, Challis said, 'Uh oh, a flaw.'

'Not funny.'

'I don't mean the kleptomania, I mean I've found another split end.'

Too late, he saw that Ellen didn't appreciate the joke. She punched him, hard, saying '*Not funny,*' and sat upright, everything about her fierce and clenched, the post-coital flush across her breasts now signifying fury, not release or languor.

He pulled her down. 'Sorry. I'm truly sorry.'

'Not funny,' she mumbled.

Evening light was closing in around the house, the air from the open window carrying dwindling hints of the day's heat, roadside dust and freshly mown hay. Adrian Wishart was in the lockup and all was right in the world.

Or not. Ellen propped herself on one elbow and said, 'We have to talk.'

'Uh oh.'

Her voice low and dangerous, she said, 'I want you to be serious.'

In fact, he was deadly serious, but he was also afraid. Suddenly big, hot tears started in Ellen's eyes. They splashed down her cheeks and neck to spot her breasts and the sheet. She made a fist, bumped it against his upper arm and said, 'It's not working.'

He waited. At one level, her words failed to land and register. He was also thinking that this had been the shortest relationship in his patchy history.

'I don't mean the sex—' she ran her hand over his chest '—the lovemaking. I don't mean that.'

He found his voice. 'What, then?'

She swung upright again and sat with her legs crossed, looking down at him. 'Living together.'

He didn't trust himself to speak. She tilted back her head and gazed seriously into the distance in a mannerism he knew well. She was looking for the key, and it needed to be concise and accurate. He'd seen her do it in briefings and interrogations.

'The thing is, I didn't choose to live with you. I was looking after your house while you were away, you came back, we fell into bed together immediately. Fell in love, too, I guess. Finally, after years of unresolved whatever.'

She glanced at him to see that she was on track. Reassured, she went on: 'It seemed like an easy solution for me to go on living here. But this isn't my house. I didn't create it with you. Even with some of my things here, it's not my place. It's a storage unit. I feel that I'm storing *myself* here as much as my fridge. Which is a better fridge than that piece of crap you have, incidentally.'

She grinned, if a little sadly. He returned it. 'Little things bother both of us,' she continued. 'Like my rearranging the pantry. My way makes more sense, but I know it annoyed you. And it still isn't my pantry, despite the makeover. Do you know what I'm saying?'

'Yes.'

She glanced at him swiftly, sharply. 'Yes,' he repeated.

'These may seem like small matters, but in some ways they're huge.'

'Meaning?'

'I need to find my own place. I'm not ready to live with you and I don't *need* to live with you. Everything's been too soon after my divorce. I need to spend time…running my life without struggling with anyone. Or having to take them into account.'

'Oh.'

'Don't say "oh". Haven't you been listening? What I'm saying is, I love you but I don't need to live with you to prove it.'

Challis was very still. There seemed to be a roaring in his ears. He adored watching her breasts in their various configurations. Right now, with Ellen cross-legged, shoulders bowed, hands clasped in her lap, they were tucked pertly between her upper arms.

'So a makeover on two levels: I find somewhere else to live, and I set up a new unit based in Mornington. The only thing that doesn't change is that I keep on loving you. And quit staring at my boobs.'

'Gorgeous nipples,' he said.

He stroked her thigh absently, the skin tight over the long bone, dimpled with tiny fair hairs, a couple of moles, a faint crease from the sheets. He heard a duck call softly outside. There were up to twenty of them sometimes, the young ones fully grown now, and as the light failed each day they would forage quickly, almost desperately, over a wide area of the surrounding grass.

Ellen arrested his hand with hers fiercely and said, '*Talk* to me. What do you want? What do you think about what I've been saying?'

He said carefully, 'I don't want us to stop seeing each other.'

'I don't either!' she said exasperatedly. 'Haven't you been listening?'

'We have a modern arrangement, separate houses, and see what happens?'

'Yes.' She looked at him and the tears threatened to spill again. 'It could be good, Hal.'

'You'd make a terrific head of any new unit,' he said.

'Tell McQuarrie I want sex crimes.'

'Okay.'

They stared at each other and he reached up and pulled her down to him. She struggled away and said, 'I'm not finished.'

He knew she wasn't. He searched for the words: 'Your…problem.'

She flushed. Outside the ducks and the lone ibis honked a warning and flapped crazily into the air. This was the time when the foxes began to prowl.

'I promise I'll get help.'

'Ells, it's no big deal. It's not the end of the world. I'm not judging you. It's just a darkish little current running through you. It doesn't stop you being a good cop.'

'Yeah? How can you understand about living together and everything else and not understand how affected I am about this? *I'm going to get counselling.*'

'Fair enough.'

'Until I do,' Ellen said, 'I won't feel right about anything, about having my own place and heading a new unit.'

Challis saw her inward look, her fierce concentration, as she seemed to run through her mental checklist. Then, apparently satisfied, she slid down. Slithered beside him, long, warm, elastic, everything humming with potential.

Then she propped herself on one elbow and reached across to the bedside radio, accidentally biffing him on the jaw. 'Sorry.'

They both wanted to hear the 7 p.m. news. According to an earlier bulletin, a Waterloo police constable had been found passed out at the base of a flagpole in the grounds of a primary school, naked. Ellen had called the duty sergeant, who gave her the name of the constable and a couple of details that hadn't made it over the airwaves. Apparently Andy Cree's dick had been glued to the mouth of a blow-up doll. The doll was faintly suggestive of a schoolgirl; put that together with the location, and you had a whiff of paedophilia.

Now the 7 p.m. bulletin was saying that certain items had been removed from Cree's flat.

'Porn?' guessed Challis.

'Probably.'

'Was he set up?'

'Probably.'

'But deserved?'

'Probably,' Ellen said.

She switched the radio off and nuzzled him. He responded. His on-switch was faster than any radio's.

Afterwards, they lay there. Suddenly Challis said, 'I'm starving,' and swung off the bed. And there was enough illumination left in the sky, and he passed close enough to the window on his way out of the room, for the rifleman on the slope outside to take a pretty accurate shot at him.

56

Dirk Roe, with a nice amphetamine and vodka buzz on, fired another shot. That Challis cunt had vanished but his woman was right there, also fucking naked. Dirk felt an old, desperate yearning to see her like that: dirty thoughts, *you naughty, naughty boy*, his mother slapping him for peeping on her in the bath, his father thrashing him later with a broom handle. So many thrashings: broom handle, belt, whatever came to hand. He sobbed and swallowed and fired off a couple of wild shots to make himself feel better, the rifle recoiling hard, comforting smacks against his shoulder.

Dirk was pretty sure he'd been born out of time and place. He belonged to an earlier era, would have been a bushranger maybe. Protecting his family's honour, avenging dishonour. Crouching in the tricky shadows, he levered another cartridge into the chamber, sighted on the shattered window and realised, *shit*, he'd been shooting not at the people who'd fucked him over but their reflections in a mirror.

But did he panic? Did he, fuck. Dirk slithered from shadow to shadow to get a better slant on the room, to where a mirror couldn't fool him.

Nothing. They'd hit the floor, the cunts. Dirk giggled. See how *you* like it, scared, knowing that bad things were coming, no one to help you. *Gentle Jesus, meek and mild, look upon a little child*, whispered Dirk, biting the inside of his mouth. His mother and his father, looking down from heaven and finding fault. Dirk snivelled a little bit.

'A society gets the police force it deserves,' he muttered—then yelled it for good measure, so those cunts in there, pissing themselves under the bed, could hear him. You had Drug Squad detectives dealing drugs, assistant commissioners interfering in corruption investigations to protect their mates, whole stations moving stolen goods, sacked officers corrupting serving officers, women motorists forced to give blowjobs so they wouldn't lose their licence…

So you'd expect cops like that to leak to the media. Now his name was blackened, his brother's name was blackened. Dirk thought of Lachlan in the hospital, his bloodless skin, the bandages…

'Someone has to pay!' shrieked Dirk and he fired another shot.

Then the bedroom door moved and he sensed one shadow, and another, slip through the gap. He grinned. He felt very alive. It wasn't such a big house, and the garden wasn't so full of obstacles, that he couldn't cover all of the exits.

He ran in a half crouch to the other side of the house, holding the rifle across his chest. In an earlier era a wronged man made his own justice. People respected that. No red tape, no tangling web of bureaucratic crap.

Hindmarsh calling him a moron. Dirk had run the Roe Report in his *own* time, right? Plus, the Report had actively *promoted* the guy, so a bit of gratitude, please. Racist? Sexist? *Realistic*. Telling it like it is.

'*I'm not a moron!*' shrieked Dirk. His mother's frown, just like his father's sneer.

'I'm not stupid! I'm not!' Dirk said, tears mingling with the snot on his face.

He made another circuit of the house. He fired the last round, replaced the clip with a fresh one. Good old Dad—'No government's going to interfere with my right to defend myself'—the rifle never registered, never declared, never relinquished during the amnesty. His father had been born out of time, too. Fire and brimstone. Purity of thought and action. *Thou shalt not release thy seed unless for procreation*, the words measured out with his belt.

'You bastard!' he yelled at the house. 'You ruined me!'

Then, carrying through the still night air, one of those nights when the whole world is breathless, expectant and sweet smelling, Dirk heard a distant siren. Otherwise everything was reduced to this little patch of fear and retribution under the moonlight. Dirk, tall and true, ready to die—but not before he'd avenged Lachlan, and not before he'd avenged himself.

Another part of him was asking: if I get out of this, what the fuck am I going to do for a job? Who'd hire me?

Change his name? Move interstate, maybe overseas? That would work. Go somewhere he wouldn't be hampered by rules and regulations. But where? Nowhere left on the planet for a man of his outlook, talent and inclinations.

A mercenary.

French foreign legion.

Born out of time, Dirk was. He ran around the house again, doubled over, rifle at the ready…

And jumped in fright: the sliding glass door to the deck at the rear of the house was open.

The gap dark and gaping like a cruel mouth.

Dirk trembled. '*Cry baby*,' his father would shout. '*Bloody great calf of a boy. Snivelling little wretch.*' The belt buckle biting. Blelt bluckle bliting…bell bluttle…

Something narrow, hard and coldly metallic pressed against the hinge of his jaw, and the cop behind him murmured, 'Put it down or I'll blow your head off.'

Dirk's insides curled up. He badly wanted to piss. A mosquito whined around his ear, and he realised his bare forearms were itchy from brushing against some bush, and there was a spider web in his hair. He hated spiders and insects. He dropped the rifle and windmilled his arms around his head, convinced that creepy-crawlies were marching up his body, stirring the fine hairs on his arms and legs. '*You great sook,*' his mother said.

'*Dirk!*' shouted the cop. '*Pay attention.*'

And the guy actually slapped him. 'Pay. Attention.'

Shocked, astonished, Dirk said, 'You hit me.'

'Dirk, look at me. *Look at me.*'

Dirk looked. The inspector had the rifle now, a fireplace poker in his other hand. Dirk looked around wildly. 'Where's your gun?'

'What gun?'

'The gun you stuck in my jaw.'

'For Christ's sake, Dirk,' the cop said wearily, 'this isn't television. I don't own a gun.'

The woman was in the shadows, wearing a T-shirt now, tousled, beautiful. Calmly watching.

'Gentle Jesus, meek and mild,' cried Dirk, over and over again.